Penny

Penny Ingham has a degree i
archaeology; she is often to be f
with a trowel in her hand. She pi
and at the BBC, but now lives in Hampshire and writes full time.

Follow Penny:
Website: pennyingham.wordpress.com
Facebook: @PennyInghamAuthor
Instagram: @penny.ingham

Praise for Penny's novels

'A pacy, engaging, enlightening and hugely enjoyable novel.'
The Historical Novel Society

'An exciting best seller bringing history alive,
featuring forbidden love, jealousy and betrayal
and based, to a large extent, on fact.'
The Basingstoke Gazette

'For history and archaeology buffs, this novel is a treat.'
Book Bag

'Fast moving, exciting…superb historical fiction.'
Hair Past a Freckle

'I couldn't put it down.'
Swift Coffee blog

'Historical fiction at its finest.'
BeckieWrites.com

er lowly apprentice. The redoubtable Agnes Bisset
r have allowed such disorder to go unchecked.
 from lips to fingers to fabric with practised ease,
wore she would try harder to maintain some
 order, for her grandmother's sake.

se this afternoon,' Richard Burbage announced
rbage owned the Theatre, and the company bowed
ity in all things. He was not a handsome man, his
 big and his lips too thin, but his dignified bearing
n took a noble role. In costume as Duke Orsino,
t cloak slung jauntily over his shoulder, its fur trim
t gleamed.

 of the audience was beginning to drown out the
 'tiring house and Magdalen felt a familiar pang
and panic combined. They had but twelve players,
ntices. It was not enough to stage *Twelfth Night*
ther play for that matter, but the company had
opened after a year of plague, and the coffers
d so the players were doubling up, taking two,
oles per play; a dizzying amount of costume
to oversee.

praisingly, she decided not to add a ruff about
head 'tire. The audience expected magnificent
en they might wonder why a noblewoman's
ved a shipwreck perfectly intact. Magdalen had
wn second-hand at a time when the coffers

ations here and there, she took something old
hing new. She replaced the sleeves of a gown.
blet to create a fashionable peasecod paunch.
inked. She sewed ribbon and lace, and beads
dded buttons, and the players strutted about

2

In fond memory of Marija Currell
1950-2020

'Thus the whirligi

(T

March 1592
The Theatre, London

John Wood looked ver
face paint, and his han
blond wig. Magdalen w
her lips were clamped a
She shook her head, a
attached the sleeves t

A cacophony of fra
'Where are my yell
'Help me fasten m
'I can't find the cu
She glanced arour
of the perform;
uncomfortably hot
chests, and prop;
crowns and sea c;
she shrugged her
The 'tiring house

Magdalen h
would nev
Moving pin
Magdalen s
semblance o
'A full ho
jubilantly. Bu
to his author
nose being to
meant he oft
he wore a sho
brushed until
The clamou
mayhem of th
of exhilaration
and two appre
easily, or any o
only recently r
were empty. Ar
three or four r
changes for her
Eyeing John a
his neck, nor a
costumes, but e
apparel had survi
bought John's ge
were full.
With a few alter
and created some
She padded a dou
She slashed and p
and feathers. She a

the stage as proudly as the peacocks at Greenwich Palace.

She had paid over the odds for John's costume but no matter, for he looked beautiful - at least, his apparel did. He was sweating profusely now, and she frowned with concern. She thought of him as a brother, and she fancied she could read him like a book. He had walked the boards since he was twelve years old, so it was unlikely he was succumbing to stage fright now. She prayed this was an excess of beer and not the ague or the sweating sickness or, Christ forbid, the plague.

The door opened and Christopher Beeston charged into the 'tiring house. A big, strong man with an untidy thatch of straw-blond hair, he was often given the soldierly role.

'We need more fruit! Is there any more fruit?' he cried.

Flinging an empty wicker basket onto Magdalen's work bench, he raced frantically about the small room, his unruly hair falling into his eyes. In his haste he tripped over a prop box and a cascade of goblets, daggers, books and gaudy jewels spewed out.

'Heavens, that hurt!' he swore, hopping on one foot. 'Are you listening to me, Maggie?'

Magdalen spat the pins into the palm of her hand. 'What did you say?' she queried absently.

'We need more fruit! And more bags of nuts!'

'You've sold it a'

'Well, I suppo   at's for the best.' Christopher was backing out the way he   u come. 'They'll throw it all straight back at us if they don't ¹ e the play. I'll try and sell a few more cushions.'

'You're n _ in costume yet,' she called after him, but he was gone. Ma dalen glanced about the 'tiring house again. Will Kempe was in costume for Feste the clown. Older than the rest, Kempe was bald save for tufts of wiry, grey hair sprouting over his ears. He had wicked, twinkling eyes, a bulbous nose, pock-marked cheeks and a mouth built for bawdy.

3

She had enjoyed making his 'tire; a gaudy creation in proud, cockerel red. He had been dressed for some time and was evidently bored for necklaces hung from his huge, over-exaggerated cod-piece. 'Who will taste my wares?' he demanded, thrusting his groin suggestively at anyone who crossed his path but no-one was paying him any heed.

Magdalen returned her attention to John. His eyes looked unfocussed. May God protect them all, perhaps it *was* the plague. Instinctively, she took a step backwards, increasing the distance between them.

'You must tell Burbage you are sick. We cannot risk -' she broke off in mid-sentence as Peter and Slinko, the young apprentices, burst in with an explosion of high spirits. Peter was twelve years old, small for his age and never stopped talking. Slinko was thirteen, quieter, shooting up, as skinny and rangy as a bean pole.

'We've been playing football with some 'prentices,' Peter decried to no-one in particular. 'There must have been at least twenty on our side. It was the best sport. The game lasted all the way down Shoreditch, all the way past the screaming loons at Bedlam and it only ended when a Frenchie fell into Houndsditch. Do you know why it's so difficult to tell the difference between a Frenchie and a pig? Because they both sound the same, *awee! awee!*'

Magdalen shook her head disapprovingly. 'Did you help the poor boy?'

'Yes, we fished him out,' Peter replied, unperturbed. 'He was covered in filth. Stank like a fresh turd. We told him he'd probably die, what with all those foul miasmas. The 'prentices told us to leave him there, so we did. We couldn't bear the sight of him, or the smell of him.'

'You should be ashamed of yourself, boy,' Richard Burbage

bellowed across the room. 'You will sweep the stage for a week.'

Peter looked close to tears. 'Yes, sir. I'm sorry, sir.'

Magdalen gently ruffled the boy's hair. 'Get your costume on, lad. Quick about it.' Glancing at John Wood again, she noticed his exposed Adam's apple. Perhaps he should wear a ruff after all.

'Five minutes!' Burbage announced, instantly bringing the 'tiring house to order. Magdalen hastily grabbed the ancient Prussian pitcher and poured Malmsey wine into a wooden cup and then, as was the players' custom, they passed the cup around and drank to the Muses. And when the gods were appeased, they began.

Slinko opened the stage door and the odour of a thousand bodies, some rank, some richly perfumed, drifted across the boards. Carried in its wake came exotic wafts of tobacco smoke; the sharp, fresh scent of sawdust beneath the groundlings' feet; the stale tang of spilled beer; the bruised sweetness of apples; the tartness of oranges, and the mouth-watering aroma of freshly-baked gingerbread.

Richard Burbage walked slowly across the stage, followed by his courtiers. His stately, majestic presence immediately quieted the audience. A thousand pairs of eyes, alight with expectation, were now fixed upon the stage. Over the players' shoulders Magdalen caught a glimpse of the one-penny groundlings in the yard, closely packed like herrings in a barrel. Beyond, in the crowded seating galleries, a brightly-coloured menagerie of finery, come to see and be seen. She realised she was holding her breath, for there was something magical in the air. The actors were taking their places, an everyday metamorphosis from humble players to kings and queens, courtiers and clowns. It was a kind of alchemy, and it never failed to enthral her.

The sweet, melancholy notes of a lute floated across the stage.

5

Sick with unrequited love for fair Olivia, Burbage sank to the floor, reclining upon the heaped cushions, his manner one of hopeless dejection:

'If music be the food of love, play on;
Give me excess of it, that, surfeiting,
The appetite may sicken, and so die...'

Slinko quietly closed the door. One day, Magdalen hoped to watch an entire play rather than snatched vignettes. But now, there were more pressing matters, for John Wood was sitting on the stool at her workbench, his head in his hands.

'My mind has gone blank. I can't remember my lines,' he mumbled.

'Where is your cue script?' she whispered, her fears somewhat allayed. Perhaps he was merely suffering from stage fright after all.

In response to her question, he shrugged dejectedly. Magdalen couldn't weigh him up. Perhaps a drink would restore his wits. A scream of high-pitched laughter pierced the hush of the 'tiring house and she turned sharply. Peter and Slinko were wearing empty fruit baskets as helmets and attempting to joust with wooden stage-swords.

'Boys!' she hissed sternly. 'The performance has begun! Stop that, or Burbage will know of it!'

The boys removed the baskets from their heads. Slinko looked suitably penitent, but Peter's doleful expression quickly dissolved into a fit of giggles. Magdalen shook her head at him. Refilling the wooden cup with Malmsey, she placed it in John's hand. He took a small sip then returned to staring vacantly at the floor. In desperation, she grabbed the prompt sheets from the hook on the back of the stage door and waved them under his nose. They were a confusion of scribbled notes and crossings out, but perhaps they were better than nothing.

With a show of great reluctance, John took the pages from her. Beneath a smudged mess of sweat and white paint, his complexion was as grey as a corpse, and he looked as if he was about to be sick. Magdalen's heart faltered. Everyone knew sweating, delirium and vomiting were the first signs of the plague, along with a burning, all-consuming fever. Tentatively, she touched his forehead. To her immense relief, his skin felt clammy and cold.

John shook her off irritably. 'Go away, Magdalen.'

There was a distinct edge to his voice now.

The first scene was over. Burbage and the rest were back in the 'tiring house. It was time for John, as the noblewoman Viola, to land upon the shore of Illyria. His face paint hastily repaired, John stood up, swaying slightly as he walked on stage.

With a mounting sense of unease, Magdalen gestured to Slinko to leave the door slightly ajar. She could see John gazing about the Theatre, his manner one of consternation and wonder, as might be expected from someone shipwrecked on a foreign shore:

'What country, friends, is this?'

'This is Illyria, lady.'

'And what should I do in Illyria when my brother is in Elysium…'

There was more to his speech, but John had fallen silent. There was confusion in his eyes, quickly rendering to pain and then he groaned and clutched his belly. His knees gave way and he crashed to the boards. The audience froze like a courtly tableau. The groundlings and the bum-cushions fell silent, not a single nut was cracked, nor an orange loudly sucked. Even the furtive fumblings and pleasurable moans on the back row ended abruptly. All eyes were on John's collapsed form.

Suddenly, everything was in motion again. The players were

converging on John, arms outstretched as if their touch might somehow heal him. Magdalen was moving too, running from the 'tiring house to the stage, pushing her way through the players to fall to her knees at John's side. He was having difficulty breathing, gulping for air. And then he vomited on the boards, a putrid broth of half-digested meat.

His lips were swelling and tinged with blue. Horror-struck, Magdalen realised she had seen this before. This was not stage fright, nor sweating sickness, nor plague. This was poison, most likely aconite, although they had called it wolfsbane on the farm.

The players closed up, a brightly coloured fortress of doublets and cloaks, kirtles and gowns, protecting John from a thousand pairs of morbidly curious eyes. Through the players' legs Magdalen could see the groundlings pressing forward for a closer look and heard those at the front cry out, afraid they might be crushed. In the galleries, the audience was on its feet, the hum of voices growing louder. They sounded shocked but at the same time exhilarated, and at that moment she hated them all.

John continued to heave until his stomach was empty, and then he coughed up bile, and finally he coughed up blood. Sapped of strength, he curled into a ball, clutching his belly. Magdalen lifted his head onto her lap and removed his wig. His cropped, black hair was clamped to his scalp with sweat, but his skin felt cold.

'They've done me in.' His tongue was swollen, too big for his mouth, and his words were difficult to decipher.

'Who?' Magdalen asked urgently. 'Who did this to you?'

'I should have listened…' His hand searched for hers and his fingers unfurled. There was a piece of paper in his palm, folded repeatedly until it was no larger than a sovereign. 'Take it.'

She did as he asked. The paper was damp with his sweat.

'This is… your fault…' he gasped, fighting for air.

What on earth did he mean by that? Had she heard him correctly? 'John, why is it my fault?'

But he didn't speak again. Magdalen held him for what seemed an eternity, her arms growing numb from bearing his weight, unchecked tears running down her cheeks. London had seen so much death these last few years, but she had never grown accustomed to it. It still had the power to fracture her heart. But it was not the plague that had taken John to God. It was poison.

She looked up at the throng of players. For all their rivalries, they were a tightly-knit family, a band of brothers. She had known these men since she was a child, and it was impossible to believe any of them were capable of murdering John.

Perhaps she was in some way responsible for his death. She thought back over the last twenty-four hours. If she had paid more attention, could she have prevented this?

Would John still be alive?

TWO

'Journey's end in lovers meeting, every wise man's son doth know'

Nine hours previously

Magdalen awoke with the nightmare still clinging. Over the years, she had learnt to bury her worst memories in the darkest recesses of her mind, but they had a tendency to worm their way to the surface whilst she slept. Behind her bed curtains all was in darkness, but vivid images were lingering in her head:

Her parents are lying on the bed, and her eight-year-old self is curled up between them. They are both cold, reeking and bloody, taken by the plague two days since. She lies there, eyes tight shut, waiting to die. If God has taken her parents, surely He will take her too. She wants Him to take her because she doesn't want to be alone. But as the days pass, and she doesn't die, she grows more afraid than ever. What is she to do? Where is she to go?

No, don't think of it. Don't dwell, Magdalen scolded herself.

She slipped out of bed, opened the shutters and felt the cool morning air slide over her skin. On the rooftops, pigeons took to the air, a flurry of wings in a cold, grey sky. She turned around and surveyed her bedchamber.

Ancient, uneven floorboards sloping towards the river, leaning further with every passing year. Bare plaster walls, soft rose-red, the colour of clay baked in the sun. A small table neatly stacked with work baskets; a treasure trove of buttons and bodkins, needles and thread, thimbles and lace. The few clothes she possessed hung on a hook on the back of the door. Sheets of paper strewn across her bed.

Through the lathe and plaster wall, Magdalen could hear her grandmother snoring in the next room. From below, came the sound of even deeper snores, reverberating through the floorboards like distant thunder. If Magdalen hadn't disliked Christopher Mountjoy's wife so much, she might have pitied her for having to endure such a monstrous din.

The Mountjoys' third lodger, Will Shakespeare, slept at the top of the house in a room infused with the bitter, glutinous smell of rag paper; the sooty, metallic tang of gall-oak ink, and the exotic scent of Castille soap.

Magdalen thought back to their conversation of the previous evening. Will at his writing table, facing away from her; a tidy heap of goose-quill shavings beside his right elbow. Twenty-nine years old, he was neither particularly tall nor particularly handsome and he rarely stood out in a crowd. In company, he tended to let others do the talking whilst his deep, chestnut-brown eyes quietly observed the world.

'What will you read tonight?' he had asked, not bothering to turn around.

Magdalen had moved slowly around his room, eyeing the piles of books, folios and pamphlets. Her grandmother had taught her to read when she had first come to London and since then she had devoured almost every book Will acquired. Juvenal, Martial, Plutarch, Machiavelli's *The Prince,* Ovid's *Metamorphoses.* She had even ploughed her way through all three volumes of Raphael Holinshed's history *Chronicles.* A pamphlet she had not seen before caught her eye. It was hand written and entitled, *A Choice of Valentines by Thomas Nashe.* She picked it up.

'Not that one.'

Magdalen looked up, startled. Did Will have eyes in the back of his head? 'Why not?' she asked.

Will hesitated. 'It's not suitable. But I have finally finished *Venus and Adonis*. It runs to one thousand, one hundred and ninety-four lines. I can only hope they are not all rotten to the core. Here. Take a few pages.'

Her eyes lit up. Ovid had written of Venus and Adonis in his *Metamorphoses*, the goddess of love's tragic infatuation with a beautiful human youth. What little Magdalen knew of carnal relations between a man and woman, she had learnt from listening to the players' lewd banter and from the muffled grunts emanating from the Mountjoys' bedchamber. She welcomed any opportunity to learn more.

'Thank you, Will.'

Magdalen was half way to the door when her gaze settled on the pamphlet that had originally caught her eye. Above the title, *A Choice of Valentines,* Will had scrawled in his distinctive hand, *Nashe's Dildo*.

She stared at Will's note, intrigued, and then she surreptitiously picked up the pamphlet and slid it beneath the pages of *Venus and Adonis*.

'You've just taken Nashe, haven't you?'

Magdalen jumped guiltily. Will still had his back to her. How could he possibly know?

'Yes,' she whispered, mortified.

Will sat back in his chair and laughed, his shoulders heaving. The gold ring he wore in his left ear lobe glinted in the candlelight. 'Be gone with you.'

She was relieved he hadn't turned around or he would have seen her flush the colour of pickled beetroot. Back in her bed chamber, she had sat up half the night, drawn in by Thomas

Nashe's tale of a young man's visit to a brothel. The watchman had called three o'clock before her eyelids had finally begun to droop and she had fallen into a fractured, heated sleep.

Two pigeons swooped past the window, startling her from her reverie and her gaze focussed on the papers scattered across her bed. Perhaps there was time to read a little more. Slipping beneath the blankets again, she pushed the loose pages of *Venus and Adonis* aside, and picked up Nashe's pamphlet:

'...And then he flew on her as he were wood,
And on her breech did thack, and foyne a-good;
He rubbed, and pricked, and pierced her to the bones,
Digging as far as earth he might for stones.
Now high, now low, now striking short and thick;
Now diving deep he touched her to the quick.'

Magdalen was beginning to feel strangely hot, even though the air in her bedchamber was biting cold. She read on, page after page, until she heard the floorboards creaking above her head, soon followed by the sound of Will pissing into his chamber pot. She sighed. Her precious moments of solitude were over. It was time to face the day. That afternoon, John Wood, who wasn't afraid of heights, would climb the ladder to the Theatre's thatched roof, raise the flag and sound the fanfare for *Twelfth Night*.

Climbing out of bed, Magdalen felt a sudden pang of guilt. What would Agnes say if she discovered her granddaughter was reading lewd poetry instead of the Holy Bible? And how would God judge her for such wickedness? Ashamed, she carefully hid *Nashe's Dildo* and *Venus and Adonis* at the bottom of her largest work basket, away from prying eyes. She pulled a comb through her long, unruly curls, rubbed her teeth and washed her hands and face, the water in the ewer so cold it made her gasp. She chose her undergarments for warmth; woollen stockings and thick holland linen. Her outer garments, she chose for comfort; an unstiffened bodice of soft mock velvet, for how was she supposed to hurry about the 'tiring house with an unforgiving slab of wood laced tightly about her frame? Next, a dark green kirtle, tied at the waist with no cumbersome hooped farthingale beneath, her skirts falling in soft folds to the floor. And finally, her long sleeved, madder-root red waistcoat, for what was life without a splash of colour? Fastening her thick leather belt about her waist, she pulled on her boots and hurried downstairs.

In the kitchen, Tom and Rich, the Mountjoys' apprentices, were enthusiastically devouring slice after slice of bread and butter. Mistress Marie Mountjoy was butchering a plucked chicken, a kitchen knife in her hand. Strands of silver ran through her thick black hair but she was still an attractive woman with a tiny waist, pert bosom and dark, sultry eyes. She looked Magdalen up and down and her expression soured.

'Child, you are not seemly,' she scolded. That waistcoat and belt! What are you? A Barbary pirate? What will people think? I cannot allow you in my workshop in such wanton attire. You will scare away my customers. And where is your ruff?'

Magdalen bowed her head. She didn't deliberately dress to annoy Marie Mountjoy. Her belt had once belonged to Will Shakespeare, and it was strong enough to carry her purses crammed with pins, combs, ribbons and laces. And she hated ruffs. No matter they were fashionable, she found them suffocating, like a starched noose tightening about her neck.

'Today is Saturday. I do not work for you on a -'

'*Oui, oui, je sais, je sais,*' Marie interrupted testily.

Magdalen had noticed her landlady often reverted to her native French when angry. Magdalen had also noticed that Marie tended to reserve her coquettish Gallic charm for her wealthy customers. Marie was in full flow now:

'And as for your hair! I've seen gypsy girls with more decorum! And where is your coif?'

Magdalen feigned deference, but her mind was elsewhere. She had much to do at the Theatre today. Ripped seams to mend, a gilded throne to repaint, and Burbage had promised her six pennies for each cue sheet she copied for Will's new play, *Romeo and Juliet*.

Marie's fury was showing no sign of abating. 'I truly regret my decision to offer lodgings to theatre folk. You bring shame to our house.'

Magdalen knew her place in the world. She knew better than to answer her landlady back. Nevertheless, she seethed in silent indignation as the tirade continued.

'I am an honest God-fearing woman, but you -' Marie broke off to glower at Magdalen's grandmother who had wandered into the kitchen, bringing with her the sharp tang of urine.

Marie's nose wrinkled in distaste. 'This cannot go on. You know as well as I that she belongs in Bedlam.'

Magdalen paled. 'No! Do not speak of it, I beg you!'

When Magdalen had first come to London, ten years since, her grandmother had been a fine, big boned woman, but of late Agnes Bisset had shrunk. She had become as desiccated as the roasted songbirds they sold on Three Needle Street. In the early days, Agnes had ruled the 'tiring house with a rod of iron but now she rarely left the Mountjoys' house on Silver Street.

'Who belongs in Bedlam?' Agnes queried.

Sadness crept over Magdalen as she bent to kiss her grandmother's cheek. Her skin was as dry and musty as ancient parchment. 'Good morning, Grand-Aggie,' she said brightly.

Agnes shrugged her granddaughter aside and began her morning ritual of setting the table with a useless assemblage of empty chafing dishes, pipkins, frying pans and cauldrons. Tom and Rich paid her no heed. Marie tutted disapprovingly and returned to the plucked chicken on the chopping board. Magdalen tried not to look at its naked body, its blue-grey, glistening flesh. It looked so small, so pitiful. Without warning, her empty stomach heaved.

Will came downstairs, his hair neatly combed, his beard neatly trimmed. Magdalen noticed he smelled pleasantly of freshly starched linen and his expensive Castile soap.

'Pierre!' Agnes said warmly and handed him a pewter plate with a bobbin of red thread upon it. 'Will that suffice?'

Will did not miss a beat. 'Yes, indeed, thank you,' he replied courteously.

Magdalen grabbed some cheese from the pantry, and snatched the bread board from the apprentices. Her eyes held an unspoken apology as she gave Will his breakfast. Pierre was Agnes's late husband; the grandfather Magdalen had never known.

'I'll eat as I walk,' Will said in his soft Warwickshire burr, wrapping his bread and cheese in a linen cloth. 'There's much to be done today. You'll be with us shortly?'

He was addressing Magdalen, but it was Agnes who replied, '*Oui, oui, bien sur, mon cher*, when I have tided the kitchen. The boys make such a mess.'

'Yes, indeed,' Will replied solicitously. 'Anon, anon.'

Will left for the Theatre; Agnes sat down and stared into space, and Magdalen set about clearing away all the empty dishes and cooking pots. Soon after, Margaret arrived. She was a plump, pretty girl with buttercup-blonde hair and pale blue eyes. She was to be married in a matter of days but in the meantime, she continued to cook and clean and shop for the Mountjoys.

'Good mornin', Mistress Mountjoy,' she said, bobbing a curtsey.

'You are late again, girl,' Marie said accusingly. 'I had to begin preparing the dinner myself.'

'My 'pologies. The 'prentices are out on the streets today, noisy and vexing as the Devil himself they are. Came the long way round, I did, to keep out of their way.'

Marie brought her cleaving knife down on the chopping board with such venom the chicken carcass took to the air and landed with a thud. 'I am too busy to listen to your excuses, Margaret. The bed linens need changing today. Get to work!'

'Yes, mistress.' Margaret curtseyed again.

'Boys!' Marie glared at the apprentices. 'In the workshop! Now! I want the floor swept and the benches tidied. Cleanliness is Godliness, remember that. If you play the fools, you will forfeit your half day.'

The boys' faces fell. Marie turned next to Magdalen. 'And you, girl, go and change your apparel.'

Magdalen nodded obligingly, although she had no intention of obeying Marie's command.

'A busy day ahead! Much to be done. Quickly now!' Marie blustered, wiping her hands on her apron, and storming from the kitchen.

For several moments no one spoke and no one moved, stunned by the tempest that was Marie Mountjoy. Gradually, the dust settled and the kitchen came to life again. Tom and Rich dived for the bread board. Margaret helped Magdalen clear the table, all the while maintaining a high-speed monologue.

'Would you believe they've put a loaf up to three pennies? Daylight robbery, that's what it is. An' those 'prentices, standing on the street corners, bawlin' how them Frenchies are takin' our jobs...ooh, I shouldn't have said that.'

She glanced anxiously down the corridor, but Marie Mountjoy had already disappeared into the workshop.

Agnes was eyeing Margaret suspiciously. 'Who are you? What are you doing in my kitchen?'

'This is Margaret. She works for the Mountjoys,' Magdalen reassured her, just as she did every morning.

Agnes gave Margaret a filthy look and sank into silence again. Magdalen took half a yard of London russet wool from the basket by the hearth. Kneeling before her grandmother, she placed the fabric in her lap. 'The costume you're working on,' she said gently.

In the past, Agnes would have decorated a gown with exquisite *mille-fleur* in tiny stitches. Nowadays, she went over and over the same spot, until the accumulated thread was raised like a black tumour. She glanced at the fabric and then at her granddaughter, a look of puzzled bewilderment in her eyes.

Magdalen took her hand and squeezed it gently. 'I'm going to the Theatre now, but Margaret is here.'

'That girl is the spawn of the Devil,' Agnes said viciously.

'You don't mean that, Grand-Aggie. I'll be back soon. I love you.'

Agnes pulled her hand away irritably. 'Be gone with you, girl.'

Magdalen's throat tightened with suppressed emotion. Not so long ago, her grandmother would have showered her with fond hugs and affectionate kisses. But lately, Grand-Aggie often seemed bewildered or angry by any show of tenderness. At times such as this, Magdalen felt her world was teetering on a cliff edge and might slip away from her at any moment, no matter how tightly she held on.

Magdalen took the shortest route to the Theatre, out through Moorgate and across Moor Fields. They were often a patchwork of laundry, pegged out on the grass to dry, but it had rained for days and the muddy fields were quiet. Avoiding a heap of rotting turnips, she took the track towards Shoreditch. Her grandmother swore it had once been a sweet-smelling place of hedgerows, elm trees and bridges over babbling streams, but now the reek of overflowing cess pits and boiling bones from the gluemakers' workshops hung like a cloying fog over its narrow, overcrowded streets.

Magdalen was so preoccupied she barely noticed the stench. Her grandmother's wits were unravelling like a piece of badly woven cloth. In desperation, she had bought rosemary from the sweetly scented herb market by St Bennet's Church, and made Agnes infusions 'for remembrance'. When these proved useless, she had bought evil smelling remedies from the apothecary, which Agnes refused to drink. Finally, she had visited Simon Foreman for potions 'to heal a troubled mind'. Each potion cost more than a week's wages, but their only obvious effect on her grandmother had been terrible bouts of gut-rot.

Magdalen was now heavily in debt to both men. If either called in a reckoning, she would find herself in Bridewell prison with all the other pitiful debtors, thieves and whores. A splash of water landed on her head and she looked up, eyeing the overhanging jetties for an open window and an upended chamber pot. But it was only rain, falling from a heavy, grey sky to join the stream of filth flooding down the middle of Hog Lane. Her boots soaked through to her stockings, she hitched up her kirtle and hurried on. Like Simon Foreman, Marie Mountjoy had been quick to take advantage of Agnes Bisset's fragile state of mind. She had raised Magdalen's rent repeatedly, knowing full well she had nowhere else to go, for who would be willing to offer lodgings to an unmarried girl who worked in a den of vice, and her lunatic, incontinent grandmother?

To keep a roof over their heads, Magdalen now worked five mornings a week in the Mountjoys' dingy, oppressive workshop.

She began at first light and finished as Saint Olave's bells rang ten o'clock, before running across Moor Fields to start her day at the Theatre.

Magdalen turned into Curtain Road. Even at this early hour Shoreditch was full of the clamour of carpenters' hammers; mean cottages and overcrowded tenements springing up on every spare inch of land. Scores of blue-coated apprentices were milling about; young men, angry with the world. In an effort to give them a wide berth, Magdalen didn't notice the amputee until she almost tripped over him. Sitting with his back against the wall, his one remaining leg entrenched in the mud, he raised a hand beseechingly.

'Now then, lass, you're a pretty one and no mistake.' He was missing a great many teeth and he whistled as he spoke. 'Lost m' leg in France, dog hole of the world, have pity, pretty lass.'

Magdalen stared at him, remembering her late father. He had fought for the Queen in France long before she was born. He had survived the war and come home with all his limbs intact, but her mother often whispered he was never the same. A big, strong, tenant farmer had left for war, but a shrunken man with a haunted look in his eyes had returned in his place.

'What's wrong with you, lass? Are you moon-mad?'
Magdalen could ill afford it, but she placed a ha'penny into the old soldier's outstretched palm and hurried on. Outside the dilapidated Curtain Theatre, a patch of celandines bloomed on the roadside, a splash of yellow in a sea of mud, and she felt her spirits lift. Spring was near. On the farm, the changing seasons were the rhythm of life. Days had turned to their tune. But in the city the seasons crept by, barely noticed save for the promise of fresh vegetables, milk and eggs on the market stalls.

The gates to Burbage's Theatre were open. The building stood on Giles Allen's land, but Allen had built a great stone wall to separate his fine residence from the stink of Shoreditch. The Theatre's multi-sided, lime-washed walls towered over the hurly burly of stews and ale houses, tanneries and slaughter yards. For Magdalen, it was a shining beacon rising above the squalor of its grim surroundings. A sanctuary from the troubles of her life. A world within a world, where great kings fought on bloody battlefields, where star crossed lovers met tragic ends, where foolish Falstaff, hiding in a basket of dirty laundry, was unceremoniously cast into the river.

The players were on stage, gathered around Burbage. Magdalen hid at the back, hoping her lateness would go unnoticed. The players all looked half frozen, their noses red, their breath misting the air. The apprentices, Peter and Slinko, were yawning behind their hands. Will Shakespeare was covertly eating his bread and cheese. Richard Cowley was glaring at John Wood, who in turn was studiously ignoring him.

Will had once called Richard Cowley 'ill-faced and worse bodied' and, in truth, he was not a pretty youth; rotund, with lank brown hair and the complexion of a tallow candle. Cowley caught Magdalen's gaze, his malicious expression at odds with his chubby, child-like features.

'Harlot,' he mouthed. She ignored him, turning away so he would not see the hurt in her eyes.

Burbage was addressing a lengthy rant at Christopher Beeston. 'Such behaviour will not be tolerated. I am disappointed I need to remind you of the fierce competition we face from Henslowe's players over the river. Just as I am disappointed I need to remind you of the terms of your contract. Two shillings will be deducted from your wages for tardiness of any kind. In the same way, two shillings will be deducted for any display of drunkenness within the Theatre -'

He stopped in mid-sentence and rounded on Magdalen.

'There you are. Better late than never. I want you to collect the weeks' playbills. I would send Peter or Slinko, but they have run wild quite enough of late.'

Magdalen's heart sank. Richard Field's printing press was in Paternoster Row, the booksellers' quarter behind Saint Paul's. Almost two miles away. She would be gone most of the morning. She was about to protest, but decided against it. She could not afford to complain.

'Yes, Master Burbage,' she replied dutifully.

Grabbing a shilling and six pence from the 'tiring house coin purse, she drew her cloak about her shoulders, and went out again. She was so lost in her thoughts she barely noticed the drizzle falling from a sky of unrelenting grey. On Friday, Burbage would be staging a revival of Will's play *Richard the Third*. Once again, Burbage was to play the crookback king. At yesterday's rehearsal, his hump-back had slipped and settled around his arse. Everyone had found it amusing, apart from Burbage himself. She needed to fashion some stronger straps. *Richard the Third* was a history play, not a comedy.

Half way along Bishopsgate Without, where the mud and pot-holes gave way to paving stones, a well-dressed lady stepped out from the gateway of the old Priory of Saint Mary Spital, now a pretty enclave of fine houses and lodgings. As the lady climbed into her waiting carriage, Magdalen saw a flash of a silk rose embellishing a dainty shoe. John Wood needed courtly apparel for his role as Richard the Third's wife, Lady Anne Neville. Perhaps she could fashion silk roses for *his* shoes…

Magdalen was passing Bedlam now. Marie Mountjoy was pressing for her to place her grandmother there. It was, after all, an institution for people distraught in their wits. Beyond the imposing gates, poor wretches wandered aimlessly about the forecourt, their heads shaved to cool their troubled minds.

Magdalen shuddered, and swore to herself she would never abandon her grandmother to such a God-forsaken place.

Once the log jam of carriages, carts and drays had cleared the gate, she headed south into the hurly-burly of the city. A gentleman's coach charged past, narrowly avoiding a collision with a black-cloaked lawyer on horseback. Sullen-faced apprentices, goodwives, flower-sellers and water carriers scattered like cockroaches before the coach righted itself and hurtled on, spraying mud in its wake.

Her stomach was rumbling loudly, so Magdalen bought a hot pie from a street seller at the top of Three Needle Street. Lured by the charms of the Royal Exchange, she allowed herself a few minutes to wander its crowded colonnades, admiring the extravagant displays of lace, sleeves and ruffs, silks and furs and ribbons. Exquisitely adorned ladies and gentlemen strolled by.

The ladies sniggered with ill-concealed derision at Magdalen's unusual attire. The gentlemen's gazes, however, were far more appreciative, their eyes lingering over her flowing auburn hair and tight-fitting waistcoat. Magdalen took no pleasure in their blatant appraisal. Acutely uncomfortable, she hurried on past milliners, furriers, tobacconists and sugar shops, their delicate confections spun into fantastical shapes, each strand as fine as the silver wire in the Mountjoys' workshop. Stopping outside an apothecary shop, she read the labels of the curios on display.

'The shell of a tortoise from Virginia'

'A crocodile from the Amazon River'

What wonders must Sir Francis Drake have seen? How extraordinary it would be to sail around the world. Would she be brave enough to do it? Could she cross the vast oceans, losing sight of land and everyone and everything she had ever cared about? She had heard stories of women who disguised themselves as sailors and pirates…

A hand landed on her shoulder, startling her. She turned around, her mouth full of pie.

'Thought I'd find you here, Magdalen.' Richard Field's apprentice gave her a toothy grin.

Magdalen returned his smile, and took the playbills from him. 'Good day to you, Philip. I trust you are well?'

'Aye, well enough. I see bills for *Titus Andronicus*.' Philip's eyes gleamed. 'Isn't that the play where the barbarian queen eats her sons in a pie? The one where a lady has her hands cut off and her tongue cut out?'

'Yes, that's right.' Burbage used sheep's blood and entrails from the butcher in Hog Lane, and gave him a seat on the front row in return.

'I want to see that again!' Philip said enthusiastically.

Magdalen had never understood why *Titus Andronicus* was so popular. In truth, she found its violence and cruelty hard to bear. Smiling ruefully, she handed Philip a shilling and sixpence, and bade him farewell. Light rain was falling as she set to work along Cheapside, tearing down old, sodden bills and thrusting notices for *Twelfth Night* onto rusty nails. Returning to Corn Hill, she felt the hairs on the back of her neck start to prickle. She looked over her shoulder apprehensively. A man clad all in grey save for a startlingly white ruff, was ripping down the playbill she had posted by the Stocks Market. In his other hand he held a pile of crumpled bills by finger and thumb, as if they were the living embodiment of the plague. To her dismay, she realised he must have been following her for some time.

She looked closer. It was Adam Cooper. A fanatical, outspoken Puritan clergyman who enjoyed the sound of his own voice, renowned for preaching from a pulpit or a street corner, or wherever else he could find an audience. As far as Magdalen understood it, Puritans dreamed of a simplified church, where man could communicate with God without the need of intermediaries swathed in gold brocade. The Puritans also believed in frugality and denial. They did not appear to believe in gaiety, feasting, drinking, plays, music or indeed anything that made life bearable.

Adam Cooper's long face was pallid, scabrous and framed by lank, thinning hair. Holding her playbills before him, he addressed the growing crowd:

'The theatres teem with nips and whores! They are vile pits of corruption. It is written in twenty-two of Deuteronomy that when a man wears women's apparel he is accursed, and when a woman wears man's apparel, she is accursed also. The players are Godless creatures, and their souls will be damned for all eternity. And you also will be damned if you visit such a place.'

Magdalen felt a shiver of apprehension. Was her soul truly damned for all eternity? Surely the Church no longer sanctioned Purgatory? Or did it? There had been so many changes it was hard to fathom what she was supposed to believe. Not that her grandmother had ever wavered. She had stubbornly held fast to her Catholic faith. Unfortunately, it was not the faith Her Majesty Queen Elizabeth had chosen to endorse but, as the years passed, Agnes had become oblivious to the potentially fatal consequences of following the old religion. In truth, she had become oblivious to everything but the confines of the house on Silver Street.

Adam Cooper had a flair for oratory, his voice a crescendo of righteous indignation. 'And when these foul pageants are ended, the players meet in their secret concaves to play sodomites or worse. I beseech you, in the name of the Father, the Son and the Holy Ghost, do not visit such a place, for they reek of sin and debauchery.'

Magdalen could think of nothing in the Bible to suggest Christ would have considered Will's plays 'foul pageants'. Besides, the Queen commissioned them, so how could they reek of 'sin and debauchery'?

Cooper tore a playbill into tiny pieces with a theatrical flourish. He let the fragments of paper drift to the ground and stamped them into the mud. Then he took another and did the same.

Magdalen frowned. The playbills were the company's only means of announcing a performance. Without them, they would most likely play to an empty house. She couldn't stand idly by while he ripped down all the bills she had so diligently posted. She had to try and stop him. And yet, it was an unforgiveable sin to challenge a man of God. She could hear her grandmother's voice inside her head, '*remember your place*'.

Magdalen's frown deepened. Within the walls of the Theatre, she enjoyed a modicum of respect as Burbage's wardrobe mistress. However, outside the Theatre she was, at best, an unmarried woman without means, a voiceless nobody. At worst, she was the 'players' whore'. Constantly moving between two markedly different worlds was like walking a tightrope. One false move and she would fall to her ruin.

Cooper held out another playbill.

May God forgive me, she thought. Stepping forward, she called out, 'Sir, may I request you return the bills to their nails.'

'Who speaks? Who denies the word of God?' Cooper's eyes darted this way then that, searching the crowd.

'And you are mistaken, sir,' she added. 'The Holy Bible does not condemn players.'

People were turning to look at her, and she felt her resolve begin to crumble. She was sorely tempted to turn tail and run, but her loyalty to Burbage's players held her fast.

'Our plays are not sinful,' she went on, 'they are officially licensed by Her Majesty's Master of the Revels.'

26

'Then he is a licentious fool!' Cooper retorted.

She wondered if he was making a pun. If he was, Will would have been impressed. But when she saw the look on the clergyman's face, she realised he was in earnest.

'I cannot see your face beneath your hood, girl, and you do well to hide your shame, for you are a fallen woman. Behold this whore of Satan who services the players in their theatres of sin and vice and lasciviousness!'

A flare of hot anger shot through Magdalen. She was a virgin, chaste and untouched. How dare he brand her Satan's whore? How dare he publicly humiliate her? Besides, he was a hypocrite. She had often glimpsed him in the back row of the Theatre, hiding his gaunt features beneath an overly large hat, watching Will's plays in rapt admiration.

She glanced about. It was obvious the crowd were beginning to turn against her. The women were whispering behind their hands and she caught snippets of their disapproval:

'Brazen hussy…'

'Throwing away her virtue…'

'Shameful…'

An elderly man muttered 'whore', and spat at her feet. A younger man eyed her slyly, appraisingly.

Magdalen's cheeks were burning. 'How dare you insult me so, sir? The Lord Chamberlain is our patron. Richard Burbage's players are reputable and renowned, and I am their wardrobe mistress not their whore!'

Adam Cooper's expression shifted from righteous fury to wide-eyed surprise. His mouth began to move wordlessly like a floundering fish, and suddenly he was on the move, ramming into her shoulder with such force as he fled that the remaining bills flew from her hand and fluttered to the ground. Magdalen watched the clergyman until he disappeared into the crowds on

Three Needle Street. What had caused him to flee so hastily? Was it something she had said? Why was she always so rash? Why did she always utter the first thing that came into her head? If the Puritan chose to report her to the constable, she would be whipped through the streets as a scold.

Without Adam Cooper to incite their disapproval, the crowd was beginning to drift away. No-one offered to help her pick up the playbills, even though she knew many of them would be in the audience for *Twelfth Night* that afternoon. Damn them. They were all as hypocritical as Adam Cooper.

'Madam? Can I be of assistance?'

Magdalen felt a hand at her elbow and turned sharply. She didn't recognise the man at her side. On her guard, she retreated a pace and looked him up and down. His deep blue doublet gleamed with the distinctive sheen of satin. His thigh boots were crafted from soft, luxurious, cordwain leather, turned over to the knee. Fine apparel, and a rapier at his belt. He was high born, a gentleman. And strikingly handsome too, with jet black hair framing a long straight nose and strong, angular jawline. Almost six feet tall, he had a soldier's build; broad shoulders tapering to a slim waist, and strong muscular legs. His mouth was curving into a hint of a smile, and she wondered what amused him. A thought struck her. Had he watched her humiliation and found entertainment in it?

'No thank you, sir,' she replied curtly, and bent down to retrieve the bills.

'Here, let me.'

To her astonishment, the stranger crouched down beside her and began to help, carefully wiping each bill on his cloak. It smeared the filth and made the damage worse, but she could not deny it was a thoughtful gesture. They gathered the bills, then stood up in unison.

'Thank you.' She held out her hand to take his share, but he kept hold of them.

'Would you do me the honour of telling me your name?'

Their eyes met and, unexpectedly, she felt her breathing quicken. 'My name is Mistress Magdalen Bisset.'

'I am honoured to make your acquaintance, Mistress Bisset.'

Magdalen couldn't understand the effect he was having upon her. She spent her days surrounded by handsome players, and he was no fairer of face.

Unnerved, her tone was sharper than she had intended.

'And might I ask who you are, sir?'

He doffed his hat and bowed, a flamboyant, courtly gesture, all sweeping hands and swinging cloak. 'Matthew Hilliard, at your service.'

Magdalen's outward composure gave no hint of her inner confusion. She tried to tell herself she was not impressed by his gallantry. Will's plays often portrayed the world of courts and kings. She saw displays of chivalry upon Burbage's stage every day. She tried to tell herself she had met the likes of Matthew Hilliard before, over-confident young bucks at the 'tiring house door who wrongly assumed she was the players' whore. She had given those men short-shrift, sending them on their way with a look cold enough to freeze Hell twice over. Surely Matthew Hilliard was no different from the rest? But none of them had ever made her heart race or her skin burn as if she was standing too close to the fire.

Flustered, she said, 'Thank you for your assistance, sir, but I must take my leave.'

'Wait!'

She turned back warily. 'Yes?'

'Do you truly work at the Theatre?'

So, he *had* been in the crowd. He had witnessed her

humiliation, and done nothing to bring it to an end. Like the rest, he had enjoyed the spectacle.

She squared her shoulders. 'Yes, I work at Burbage's Theatre in Shoreditch but I am their wardrobe mistress, not their whore.' The words were out before she could stop them and she groaned inwardly. What did it matter if this man thought her a doxy or a nun?

'I assure you, such a notion never crossed my mind. I wish I had arrived sooner. I would have sent that objectionable wretch on his way, by force if necessary.'

His voice was deep, unhurried, mesmerising, and a sudden image of a galleon sailed across Magdalen's mind, its hapless sailors drawn inexorably towards a siren's song. Would he truly have stood up to Adam Cooper? Perhaps he would, for when all the others had drifted away, he alone had stayed to help.

When she did not reply, he went on, 'If you are intending to post the rest of the bills, please allow me accompany you. Let me protect you from ranting Puritans.'

An alarm bell was tolling inside Magdalen's head, growing louder by the heartbeat. He was high born. She was a lowly nobody. His intentions were dishonourable. There could be no other explanation but the realisation hurt, like salt in an open wound. 'Is there nowhere else you should be, sir?'

'Nowhere else I care to be. Tell me, what does the Puritan find so offensive about your play?'

'They hate all our plays,' she replied. It was common knowledge the Puritans wished to close down the theatres. How could he not know such a thing?

Seemingly reading her mind, he replied, 'Forgive my ignorance, I am late come from Oxford.'

'Oxford?' Magdalen repeated, only half listening now. She wanted to be away from this confusing, maddening man. She wanted to go home. Not to Silver Street but to the Theatre, where everything made sense. Where order sprang from chaos, where far-away kingdoms blossomed from the bare branches of tattered props and ancient lutes and Will's sugared poetry. She felt safe there, a world away from the poverty and the prejudice and the casual cruelties of the city. There she could try and forget her humiliating encounter with Adam Cooper. There she could try and forget Matthew Hilliard and the kindness in his eyes.

Dropping a curtsey, she said, 'I must take my leave. Good day to you, sir.'

She walked away, but she did not get far before she realised he was following her. 'Where are you going?' she asked nervously.

'I have lodgings in Norton Folgate. It seems we are headed in the same direction.'

Magdalen didn't believe him and her sense of unease intensified. If the rumours in the Mermaid were true, London was on the brink of another invasion, a city teeming with Catholic spies, afraid of its own shadow, and especially afraid of strangers.

She maintained a brisk pace through the Stocks Market, posting bills as she went. She hoped he might lose interest but he doggedly remained at her heels, his right hand resting firmly on the hilt of his rapier. A small part of her wanted him gone; the sensible, logical part that knew no good could ever come of their acquaintance. But at the same time, she revelled in his closeness, the look of him, the fresh, clean scent of him.

'Do you make all the costumes yourself?' he asked, taking a bill from her hand and ramming it forcefully onto a hook outside the Black Swan inn.

'Some, not all,' she replied sparingly.

'And the props?'

'Some -'

'But not all?' He finished her sentence, one eyebrow raised, a hint of a smile on his lips.

Despite her best intentions, she found herself smiling back.

He knows I am wary of him, she thought.

They walked on, through the crowded colonnades of the Royal Exchange and then up Corn Hill.

'There is talk of Will Shakespeare in Oxford. How his plays are performed before the Queen,' Matthew said.

Magdalen nodded, remembering Greenwich palace at Christmas. The lanterns in the gardens, twinkling like stars fallen to earth. The vast candlelit dining chamber pooled with golden light. Pillars wreathed in holly, ivy, Lenten roses. Huge silver censers, their fragrant smoke as sweet as a summer's day.

'The Oxford fellows mock him,' Matthew went on. 'They call him a country bumpkin. I think they are jealous of his success.'

'It is the same for him in London,' she replied. 'It is true he did not go up to university, but he is not an un-educated man. He has read more books than I have had hot dinners.'

'Are you partial to a hot dinner?' There was a hint of a smile again, and she knew he was teasing her.

'Some,' she said.

'But not all?' he replied.

Their eyes met and held and she felt suddenly, strangely, weightless. Magdalen looked away first, her grip tightening about the remaining playbills as if they might anchor her to the earth. The rain had stopped. She could not say when the last drop had fallen, just as she could not say when her wariness of Matthew Hilliard had trickled away. Like the rain, it had eased slowly, imperceptibly. She realised she was enjoying his company and happiness welled inside her, rare and unexpected.

They had reached Leadenhall market. It was crammed with meat and poultry stalls, the smell similar to a performance of

Titus Andronicus, but with added chicken shit. Matthew skewered a playbill on the hook beside the well.

'*Twelfth Night*,' he mused, studying the bill. 'Is there mischief?'

Magdalen thought of the character of sanctimonious Malvolio, fooled into believing Olivia was in love with him, fooled into wearing the crossed yellow garters Olivia despised. She had long suspected Will had written the role with Adam Cooper in mind.

'There's a great deal of mischief, and no-one is as they seem,' she replied lightly.

When he didn't reply, she cast him a quick, sideways glance. Something had changed. He was staring out over the lead roof of the old mansion, his eyes narrowed, and Magdalen could not decide if he was angry or merely lost in thought. When he finally turned to face her again, his expression was resolute.

'I find myself short of funds,' he said bluntly, all trace of good humour gone. 'I have some skill with a blade, so I am fencing at the Curtain but it pays badly, the audiences are cut-purses, and the rapiers are sharp. I need safer employment before I lose my limbs. I have often fancied the life of a player,' he went on, as if he were stating his liking for pears.

Magdalen's eyes widened in amazement. Burbage's players were, without exception, from humble backgrounds, yet Matthew Hilliard's manners and dress spoke of privilege and wealth, so why would he seek out such a lowly profession? It didn't make sense. Unless his family had been struck by some misfortune? Wealth was hard won but easily lost. Perhaps his father was a merchant adventurer, a precarious state of affairs by all accounts. Perhaps his ships had been lost to the treacherous Goodwin Sands?

'You? A player? I'd wager your family have other plans for you.'

'They did, once. But no longer.' His eyes slid from hers, but not before she saw a suggestion of anguish, quickly suppressed.

The clock on Leadenhall's tall tower began to strike eleven. Only three hours before the performance. She could not delay or Burbage would have her scrubbing the boards for a week.

'I must leave you now. I have much to do.'

'Wait! Do you have need of another player? If I came to the Theatre, would Burbage hear me read?'

Magdalen hesitated before answering. Burbage was sorely in need of another player, but she knew he could not afford to hire an experienced actor, let alone an apprentice.

'I doubt Burbage would be interested in hiring a novice,' she began apologetically.

His face fell and she regretted her candour. He alone had come to her aid. He alone had stooped to pick the playbills from the mud. And now he was asking for her assistance, it was surely her Christian duty to help him in return.

'Come to *Twelfth Night*,' she repented. 'You'll find us easily enough, just follow the crowds from Bishopsgate. And if you like what you see, then come to the 'tiring house afterwards.'

'Thank you. Truly.'

His manner was warm and sincere and Magdalen found herself staring at him, utterly confounded. He was as changeable as the tidelands beyond her parents' farm; neither land nor sea, a constantly shifting in-between place, unpredictable, fickle, re-shaped with every tide.

'I can't promise you anything,' she said honestly.

It would all depend of Richard Burbage's mood, which was more often choleric than sanguine.

'I understand. I am most grateful. I will not take up any more of your time. Good day to you, Mistress Bisset.'

His smile softened his piercingly blue eyes and without warning, Thomas Nashe's poem darted into her head:

'Now high, now low, now striking short and thick;
Now diving deep he touched her to the quick...'

She felt her cheeks begin to burn. What was the matter with her? Perhaps Marie was right. Perhaps she *was* a wanton. Swamped with shame, she bobbed a curtsey and hurried away. At the crossroads with Grace Church Street some instinct made her stop and look over her shoulder. Matthew Hilliard was standing where she had left him. He raised a hand in farewell, then turned and walked away.

The realisation he had been watching her all the way down Aldgate Street made her believe summer had arrived, bringing sunshine after months of endless grey. Aware of the lateness of the hour, she ran the mile or more back to Shoreditch, where she found a youth in vivid blue livery loitering outside the Theatre.

'Can I be of assistance?' she asked breathlessly.

'I have a message for the tailor of the Lord Chamberlain's Men.'

'Yes?' she said, instantly on her guard.

The Theatre's coffers were too depleted to allow for the extravagance of a tailor. Occasionally their patron, the Lord Chamberlain, donated some of his own apparel. But more often than not Magdalen resorted to rummaging through the second-hand clothing market on Long Lane by Houndsditch. She unpicked and altered, ever mindful of the audience's hunger for a window onto the rarefied world of the Queen's court. She salvaged and improvised, ever mindful of their thirst for originality, spectacle and enchantment. But she was far too proud to admit Burbage's penury to this brightly plumaged young peacock.

'Tell me, and he will hear, it,' she said.

'My orders are to give the message in person.'

'Not possible. Master Bisset is at Westminster today.'

'Very well,' the youth demurred. 'My Lord, the Earl of Southampton requests the tailor of The Lord Chamberlain's Men attend him at five o'clock tomorrow afternoon at Lincoln Place on Chancery Lane. My Lord wishes to reward him with a commission.'

'I have it. Good day to you.'

'Good day.'

Magdalen watched the youth walk away, inwardly cursing her own stupidity. What had she done? And how could she possibly undo it? She was so distracted it took her a moment to realise John Wood and Richard Cowley were by the old horse pond, wielding rapiers from the prop box and prowling around each other like mastiffs at a bear-baiting.

'You arse-swiving sodomite!' Richard snarled, his rapier slashing through the air and narrowly missing John's chest.

John darted backwards and almost lost his balance, his boots slipping through the putrid green mud at the edge of the pond. Managing to right himself, he yelled, 'Crawl back to your mother's tit, you snivelling, back-stabbing, yellow-livered -'

In response, Richard roared something incomprehensible and charged headlong at John, knocking him flat on his back in the fetid shallows. Two ducks took to the air, squawking loudly. John's rapier flew from his hand and landed in the stagnant water, sinking without trace. He tried to get up, but Richard moved fast. Standing astride him, he lowered his rapier until the tip rested on John's doublet, directly over his heart.

'Why does Burbage give you all the best female roles, eh?' Richard's eyes were wild, his features warped with hatred. 'Is it because you suck his cock, you stinking turd.'

Richard was applying pressure to the blade now. The Theatre's rapiers were notoriously sharp. Burbage said it added a certain piquancy to the fight scenes. Magdalen watched in horror as the tip of the blade pierced John's fustian doublet.

'Richard, no!' she cried. The noxious water lapped against her boots as she grabbed Richard by the arm and dragged him away. John struggled to his feet, drenched in stagnant water.

'You know Burbage's rules,' Magdalen rounded on them furiously. 'No fighting! He'll dock you two shillings if he hears of this.'

Richard raised his arms in mock surrender.

'But you won't tell him, will you, Maggie-kins?' he purred, an ugly smirk contorting his pale, moon-like face. 'It was all done in jest, wasn't it, John?'

But John pushed past them without a word and stormed into the 'tiring house. It was only then Magdalen noticed the words, 'Sinners & Sodomites' daubed upon the door. For one dreadful moment she thought they were written in blood but on closer inspection she realised it was red paint, still wet.

Two hours later, John was dead in her arms. If she had but known it, that was the moment, the precise moment, when her life began to unravel. All over again.

THREE

'I am sure care's an enemy to life'

The audience was in uproar; men shouting, women screaming, but Magdalen barely heard them. The players clustered around her seemed ghost-like, unreal. The only thing of any substance was John's body, heavy and limp in her arms. She closed his eyelids and used her handkerchief to wipe the paint from his face and the vomit from his swollen lips. Tears streamed down her cheeks as she gently stroked his hair. In her heart, she knew he was gone, but a small part of her refused to accept it. A small part of her hoped he would open his eyes and laugh mockingly at her despair.

She was still cradling him when the constable and his deputies arrived to clear the Theatre. It took some time because many of the groundlings were reluctant to miss the spectacle of a real death on stage and had to be forcibly removed. In the chaos, the cut-purses were no doubt having a field day.

Magdalen resisted Burbage's attempt to extricate John from her arms. She shook her head and held him tighter still. And then the searcher came. Goodwife Colet was a tiny woman with a thin, pinched face. Wisps of grey hair strayed from her coif and her hands were gnarled and liver spotted. Over her plain woollen kirtle, she wore an ancient leather apron. It was moulded to her scrawny frame and stained with the blood and gore of her trade. Despite her diminutive stature, she was a surprisingly strong woman. Briskly removing John from Magdalen's grasp, she laid him out on the boards.

Magdalen stood up shakily and went to join the players. The searcher began her ritual, looking for signs of life, for any obvious wounds. The old woman made no comment about John's unusual apparel, but Magdalen sincerely wished he wasn't wearing women's clothing. She longed to give him some dignity in death, but it was too late now. Goodwife Colet finished her examination and clicked her fingers at the constable's men. They lifted John onto the stretcher and covered him with a blanket. It was stained and frayed, and Magdalen's heart twisted as they carried him down the steps and across the yard.

'What say you, Goodwife Colet?' the constable enquired.

Edmund Stow was as large as the searcher was small. His bald head resembled a bantam's egg balanced atop his bloated frame; his eyes squashed by puffy, swollen cheeks.

'Poison, Master Stow.' The searcher bustled past him without stopping. Presumably there was another corpse awaiting her judgement. 'I'll send him to the coroner.'

'Poison?' Edmund Stow called after her. 'Are you certain? Not a surfeit of pickled herrings or some such?'

'Poison, sir. I would stake my reputation on it,' the old woman pronounced as she hurried after Stow's men.

A heavy silence fell upon the stage.

Surreptitiously, Magdalen examined the note John had thrust into her hand.

It was addressed, '*For the attention of John Wood*'.

Unfolding it, she found just three words, '*leave it be*'.

Leave *what* be? Magdalen wondered.

What had John said? *'I should have listened.'* Listened to whom?

Edmund Stow was eyeing each of the players in turn.

'This is a sorry turn of events,' he said, although he did not sound sorry at all. 'I will start at the beginning. Who had reason to poison John Wood?'

Magdalen glanced about the stage. Peter and Slinko appeared close to tears. The rest of the players looked stunned. No-one replied.

'No? Not even an inkling? Tell me this then. Did anything out of the ordinary happen today?'

Peter and Slinko began to whisper furiously. At length, Slinko pushed Peter forward.

'I saw a man, sir,' Peter stammered. 'Just before the play began. He was running down the corridor by the banqueting chamber.'

'Go on, boy,' Stow urged.

'He was running so fast he crashed into me, sent me flying, sir. He didn't stop. It was odd 'cos we don't allow the audience back stage before a performance.'

'Can you describe him?'

Peter thought for a moment. 'He had clean boots.'

'Clean boots?' the constable repeated.

'Yes. It was strange 'cos who has clean boots?'

A flash of irritation crossed the constable's face. 'Was he a large man, or small? Did you see his face? What was he wearing?'

Peter's eyes lit up. 'He was wearing a dark grey doublet. And I saw a ruff, he wore a ruff.'

'Do you take me for a sponge, boy? You're describing half the citizens of London,' Stow said angrily.

Magdalen remembered Adam Cooper's grey doublet and his neatly starched ruff. Was the clergyman's hatred of players so fervent that he would commit murder to cleanse their souls?

'Poison,' Stow mused. 'A woman's weapon, is it not?' He turned, fixing his piggy-eyes upon Magdalen.

'I know you. You are Mistress Bisset's granddaughter.'

'Yes, sir,' she replied, her heart thumping with alarm.

'So, tell me, why did you poison John Wood?'

Magdalen felt suddenly ice-cold, as if she had plunged into the Thames in January, as if every last gasp of air had been driven from her lungs. All around her, the players erupted in cries of outraged indignation.

'I will have silence!' Stow bellowed, but no-one was listening to him.

'I - I did not poison John!' Magdalen stammered. 'He is - he *was*, like a brother to me.'

'You knew him well?'

'Well enough, sir.'

'You were intimately acquainted?'

'No! I swear on my life!'

But the constable had the bit between his teeth. 'Was it a lover's quarrel? Did he spurn you for another? What do they say? Hell hath no fury like a woman scorned.'

Magdalen was sinking deeper into the icy water, the glimmers of daylight above her head becoming fainter as she drifted down into the darkness. The players' protests were growing louder and angrier by the minute but they sounded very far away. The constable banged the tip of his staff upon the boards, once, twice, three times, dragging her back to the surface of her unfolding nightmare.

'I will have silence!' Edmund Stow bellowed. 'Tell me, Mistress Bisset, as his *sister* then, who were his enemies? Who bore him a grudge?'

Magdalen thought of Richard Cowley's brawl with John earlier that day, the hatred in his eyes. Did he hate John enough to kill him? But she had no proof, and she knew she would never forgive herself if she falsely accused him.

'Everyone liked John, sir. He didn't have any enemies.'

'Everyone has enemies,' Stow replied. 'You came to London from Hampshire, did you not?' he added, eyeing her appraisingly. 'You were raised on a farm. You understand plants, which will heal, and which will harm?'

Magdalen dug her fingernails into her palms, focussing on the pain rather than the panic threatening to overwhelm her.

'I left Hampshire when I was eight years old. I have no knowledge of such things, sir.'

'Don't lie to me.'

Cold fear washed over her, and she could feel tears threatening. *Don't you dare cry,* she told herself.

'I loved John like a brother. I swear I am innocent, sir.'

'Believe me, girl, the truth will out.' Edmund Stow glared at her for a long moment, perhaps hoping he might see into her very soul. She found herself staring back at him, held fast by his malevolent spell. When at last he released her from his gaze, her legs felt as wobbly as marrow jelly.

Stow's eyes were sweeping across the stage, seeking a new target. They settled on Burbage and narrowed, taking aim.

'It seems most likely John Wood was poisoned here at the Theatre.'

'That is an outrageous accusation!' Burbage shot back indignantly. 'You cannot seriously believe one of us killed John?'

'I believe whatever the evidence suggests, Master Burbage,' Stow replied haughtily. 'Tell me, what refreshments do you provide for the players?'

'We have a pitcher of Malmsey in the 'tiring house, and one cup.' Burbage was visibly fighting to remain calm. 'Before every performance, we share the cup and raise a toast. If someone had poisoned the wine, we would all be dead.'

'Bring me the pitcher and the cup.'

Burbage glanced at Magdalen, but Stow shook his head.

'No. She stays here. Send the boy.'

Peter soon returned with the pitcher and cup. Stow sniffed them both cautiously. 'You have all drunk from this cup?'

The players nodded.

'But you gave John a second drink, after the play had begun, didn't you, Magdalen,' Peter said brightly.

Stow's beady eyes fixed upon Magdalen again. 'Is this true?'

Magdalen opened her mouth but no words formed. Peter was right. She *had* offered John another drink, but only because he had looked so unwell. Will Kempe glared at Peter and rolled his eyes in disgust. Several other players shook their heads despairingly. Peter, suddenly comprehending the gravity of his careless words, fought back tears.

'So, you do not deny giving the player another drink, Mistress Bisset?' There was a gleam of triumph in the constable's eye.

'He was ill. I was trying to help him.'

'I don't believe you. He was your lover. He cast you aside. He scorned you. He humiliated you. And you hated him for it. You hated him so much that you killed him.'

'No!'

Her anguished denial was drowned out by the players' furious protestations. Stow banged his staff on the boards with such force that they reverberated beneath Magdalen's feet.

'I will have silence!' A bead of sweat ran down his forehead, dripped off the end of his nose and splashed on the boards.

'What have you there, girl?' He nodded at her left hand.

Slowly, she unfurled her fingers. 'It was in John's hand when he died.'

'Why were you trying to hide it from me?'

'I wasn't hiding it. I -'

'Give it to me.' He snatched the note from her hand.

'*Leave it be,*' he read aloud. His head snapped up. 'He was telling you to leave him alone wasn't he!'

'The note is addressed to John, not me.'

Stow turned it over and instantly looked put out. 'Does anyone know what this means?'

As one, the players shook their heads.

'I want paper, an ink pot and a quill,' the constable demanded. 'I want each of you to write *leave it be.*'

Burbage sent Peter to the 'tiring house again and the players and the apprentices each took their turn with the quill. Magdalen went last, casting a quick glance at the thirteen different hands. The spelling ranging from '*leef it be*' and '*layve it bee*' to '*lif it by*'. All were acceptable, for London was a melting pot of England's different dialects and its citizens wrote as they spoke, with wondrous variety. She had seen Will sign his surname three different ways in a single week, depending on his choler. She put down the quill and passed the paper to the constable.

'You can write, Mistress Bisset. In truth, I did not expect you to have any learning.' Stow looked more closely. 'I see you alone used the same spelling as the note found in John's hand. Why is that?'

Magdalen couldn't believe she had been so foolish. Stow had not expected her to read or write, so why had she picked up the quill? 'No one else saw the note apart from me. I remembered the spelling,' she replied, her voice very small.

'I grow weary of listening to your excuses and your lies.' Edmund Stow raised his staff and pointed it at her midriff. 'I believe you murdered John Wood. When the coroner hears my testimony, he will believe it too.' Like a player in a tragedy, he paused for dramatic effect before continuing with grave solemnity. 'You will be taken from here and held in Newgate until such time as an inquest is convened -'

A tempest had engulfed the theatre in a whirlwind of noise and fury, and yet Magdalen was in the eye of the storm, in a place of eerie stillness.

'This will not stand, Stow!' Burbage roared. 'We are the Lord Chamberlain's Men. He is the Queen's cousin, and we are under his protection. Magdalen is one of us. Therefore, she is also under his protection. Do you truly wish to suffer the wrath of the Queen by bringing false accusations against us?'

Stow's eyes darted warily from Burbage to Magdalen and back again. Seizing the advantage, Burbage pressed on. 'We have been honoured to perform before the Queen three times this year. Her Majesty favours us. If you dishonour us, you dishonour the Queen and such treachery would not go unpunished.'

'How dare you defy my authority? How dare you be so presumptuous as to speak of dishonouring her Gracious Majesty? I could have you arrested for treason,' the constable blustered, but Magdalen could see the uncertainty and the fear in his eyes.

'I have said nothing to dishonour Her Majesty. And nor do I defy your authority. I merely speak the truth,' Burbage replied levelly.

Stow's engorged face was the colour of a ripe turnip, his vast shoulders heaving with impotent fury. 'In deference to the Lord Chamberlain, I will allow Mistress Bisset her liberty until the inquest. At which time, mark my words, I will secure a murder charge. In the meantime, I will take my leave.' Breathing heavily, he stomped down the stairs, hazelnut shells crunching beneath his feet as he marched across the yard. 'This is not over, Burbage,' he bellowed and slammed the door behind him.

For several moments all was silent within Burbage's Theatre. And then, quite suddenly, Magdalen's legs gave way and she collapsed onto the boards. Like a shoal of fish moving as one, the players converged upon her, but no-one seemed to know what to do or say.

'For God's sake,' Will Shakespeare exclaimed. 'You're all looking at her as if she were a piteous dog run over by a coach. Get her something to drink.'

Magdalen drew herself into a ball. She rested her head on her knees and closed her eyes, but she could still see the terror in John's eyes, still feel the weight of him in her arms. The Theatre was her sanctuary, her safe haven from the troubles of the world, so how had death sneaked inside?

If Burbage had not spoken for her, she would be on her way to Newgate now; a place of hopelessness, disease and death. There were metal grilles in the walls and she had seen the starving prisoners, arms outstretched through the bars, begging for alms. Without her income from the Theatre and the workshop, she would be entirely without means. She would be one of those skeletal wretches pleading for a scrap of bread from a charitable passer-by.

'Do not fret, Magdalen,' Burbage said briskly. 'We all know you would never harm John.'

But his words offered little comfort when Stow seemed hell-bent on proving her guilt.

Will Shakespeare patted her shoulder reassuringly. 'Stow is a sanguine coward. A huge, dull-eyed, hill of flesh. Mark my words, this will come to nothing. All will be well.'

She looked up at him, her face as pale as whey. 'It wasn't my handwriting on the note. I don't understand why Stow -'

'All will be well,' Will repeated.

'But how can it be? If I am sent to trial and I am convicted, they will hang me, and then what will become of my grandmother? The Mountjoys will throw her out and she'll die alone, in some foul back alley.'

'That will not -' Will stopped in mid-sentence. The doors to the courtyard had opened, and Henry Carey, the first Baron Hunsdon, blazed into their midst, closely followed by two liveried attendants and his beautiful young lover, Amelia Bassano. It seemed bad news travelled fast, even reaching the rarefied air of Greenwich Palace.

Burbage hurried down the steps to greet their patron whilst Magdalen got to her feet. As one, and with theatrical precision, the players bowed in deference to their Lord. Magdalen gave a wobbly curtsey.

An aura of wealth and power and privilege shimmered about the baron and his entourage. First cousin to the Queen, Lord Chamberlain, Knight of the Garter and Privy Councillor, Lord Hunsdon was approaching his seventieth year but he was still handsome and impeccably groomed. His speckled grey beard was neatly trimmed, his ankle length cloak bordered by leopard fur.

Despite having a wife of almost fifty years at home, he was notoriously besotted with the young woman at his side. Allegedly, the Queen turned a blind eye to his moral laxity, on condition Amelia Bassano never appeared at court. With black hair and dark eyes, Amelia was beautiful, although not in a conventional sense, the preference at court being for pale-skinned blondes.

Out of long-ingrained habit, Magdalen surreptitiously assessed her attire. Amelia was dressed in the height of fashion, her waist and hips dramatically accentuated by a wide, wheel-shaped farthingale. A tall, wide-brimmed black hat perched atop her lustrous hair, and an open, pearl-trimmed ruff framed her olive-skinned face. Her white, tinselled-satin gown was embellished with more tiny pearls, her sleeves thickly padded. The Sumptuary Laws might have permitted such magnificent attire for a baron's wife but certainly not for his mistress, although who would dare question the authority of the Queen's cousin?

'A bad business, Burbage. A damned bad business,' Lord Hunsdon blustered, strangling his vowels with the affectation shared by all royal courtiers.

'Yes indeed, Your Lordship,' Burbage replied soberly. 'We are all shaken, and saddened. He was a talented -'

But the baron was talking over him. 'Yes, yes, a grievous tragedy indeed.'

Whilst his expression was suitably grave, Magdalen sensed an absence of sentiment in his tone. She had long suspected he saw his lowly players as little more than performing monkeys, proud of them in the same way the Queen was proud of the exotic animals in her menagerie at the Tower.

'The constable says your wardrobe mistress will hang for it?' Lord Hunsdon surveyed the stage, and spied Magdalen. 'I presume this is the girl? Why is she not in Newgate?'

Magdalen stared at him, chilled by his callous tone, before swiftly remembering her place and lowering her gaze to the boards.

'Mistress Bisset has been sorely slandered by the constable's accusation,' Burbage replied. 'She is chaste, and above reproach.'

'Mmm.' The baron sounded sceptical. 'Either way, this incident looks badly on you all. You theatrical fellows have a sore reputation for violence. That scoundrel Marlowe has only just been released from Newgate, has he not? And now this? The assize court will likely use it as an excuse to finish you.' He was eyeing the players, evidently trying to work out who was missing.

'John Wood, Your Lordship,' Burbage said, through gritted teeth.

'God rest his soul,' Lord Hunsdon muttered perfunctorily.

Amelia Bassano's long, delicate hands fluttered towards her

face. She gave the smallest gasp, and crumpled in a faint. The Lord Chamberlain caught her before she fell.

'Mary, Mother of God!' he exclaimed. 'Some help here!'

His liverymen hurried to his side. Assisting Amelia to a seat in the lower gallery, they began fanning her with their caps. The baron patted her shoulder ineffectually, all the while making strange cooing sounds, like the pigeons on the Mountjoys' roof. With her intricately decorated pomander raised to her nose, Amelia quickly regained her composure. Lord Hunsdon leant closer, and Magdalen distinctly heard him whisper, 'my darling, my precious sunbeam'. Amelia remained suitably decorous; her back straight, her head held high, but a hint of amusement played on her full, sensuous lips. Patting her shoulder again, Lord Hunsdon returned to the yard to resume his conversation with Burbage.

Magdalen noticed that whilst courtly convention decreed Amelia's hands should be clasped lightly in her lap, instead they rested protectively over her belly. It was not yet common knowledge that Amelia was with child, but Magdalen overheard a great deal of whispered gossip as she moved about the banqueting chamber after a performance, serving wine and sweetmeats to London's elite. For most unmarried mothers without means there were few choices beyond starvation or prostitution, but it seemed money could buy anything, even respectability. Lord Hunsdon had arranged for Amelia to marry her first cousin, Alfonso Lanier, a court musician. Rumour had it Lanier was a sodomite, and was being paid handsomely for his discretion.

'This matter must be resolved quickly, for all our sakes. If it is not, I will have no choice but to withdraw my patronage,' Lord Hunsdon proclaimed carelessly.

The players glanced at one another in alarm. Without

aristocratic patronage the troupe would be reduced to little more than strolling players, officially classed as rogues and vagabonds. Their future would be uncertain indeed.

Lord Hunsdon was bidding Burbage farewell. Amelia must have been listening to his conversation because she immediately stood up and straightened her gown. She was evidently fully recovered, for her hips swayed seductively as she walked the short distance to his side. Without exception, the players' eyes followed her progress, mesmerised by her powerful, exotic beauty.

Magdalen watched Amelia too, marvelling at her boldness. It would never have crossed her mind to draw attention to herself in such a deliberately provocative display. If, on occasion, she felt a man's eyes upon her, she would wish the ground might open up and swallow her whole, whereas Amelia appeared to be relishing holding the players in her thrall.

It seemed the Lord Chamberlain also enjoyed the spell Amelia had woven for he proudly took her arm as he led her from the Theatre. His liverymen closed the doors behind them, and a hushed stillness fell over the stage. Perhaps it was fanciful, but Magdalen sensed a lingering aura of wealth and power; the air somehow gilded with faint echoes of Lord Hunsdon's gleaming jewels and sparkling cloth-of-gold.

Burbage turned slowly to face the players on the stage. His face was pale and drawn.

'If the Lord Chamberlain withdraws his patronage, we will be finished.'

Henry Condell stepped forward. One of the older players, a mop of soft dandelion-clock hair framed his kind and gentle face. 'Worry not. We are popular at court. There is every chance another nobleman would look favourably upon us.'

'Don't be naïve, Henry! A player has been murdered and our

wardrobe mistress stands accused. We are tainted. No one at court will dare look favourably on us now,' Burbage snapped.

'Maybe not at court, but the groundlings and the bum-cushions will flock to us in their thousands. They adore a scandal,' Will Kempe sniggered. 'Even now they will be wagering which of us will die next, and in what manner.'

Magdalen hung her head in shame. John's final words had been true. It *was* her fault. She had known he was sick. She should never have allowed him to go on stage. If she had insisted he took a purge, perhaps she could have saved his life. But instead, John was dead and she had brought ignominy upon Burbage and his men. She looked around at the players. Her grandmother had called them 'my boys'. She had nurtured them, kept them safe.

I didn't keep John safe, Magdalen thought bitterly.

'Perhaps the constable is right, Magdalen,' Richard Cowley said slyly. 'After all, we only have your word for your innocence.'

The atmosphere, already severely strained, soured like five-day-old milk. 'That's enough, Richard,' Burbage growled.

Richard shrugged his shoulders. 'I'm only saying what you're all thinking. As Stow said, poison is a woman's weapon.'

'You beef-witted bastard! No-one is thinking that apart from you!' Will Shakespeare rounded on him.

'I am no bastard, but you are the son and heir of a mongrel bitch!' Cowley raised his fists and adopted a pugilistic stance.

'Enough, Richard,' Burbage warned. 'Anyone would think you were still full of your mother's milk.'

Christopher Beeston clapped his hands. 'Aye, enough. I'm going to the Mermaid to raise a cup to John. Who'll be with me?'

'Is that fitting? After everything that has happened today?' Burbage sounded weary.

'I believe so,' Christopher replied. 'When John wasn't at the Theatre, he was at the Mermaid. It was his second home.'

Burbage raised his hands in a gesture of resigned acceptance. The players returned to the 'tiring house, their mood subdued and sombre, in stark contrast to the usual mayhem. Magdalen loosened laces and unpinned wigs. She dropped cushions into the prop box, and linens into the laundry basket. She folded breeches, doublets, cloaks, but all the while her hands continued to tremble.

If a murder was committed by poison, it was generally accepted a woman was the culprit. It wouldn't matter there was no evidence. She was going to be convicted. She was going to be taken in a cart to the gallows on Tyburn Hill. Nausea rose within her. Spinning on her heel, she flung open the back door and vomited into the mud. Straightening up shakily, she wiped her mouth with the back of her hand.

'Magdalen? Are you unwell?'

She turned around.

Will Shakespeare was eyeing her solicitously.

'I am quite well,' she lied.

He raised an eyebrow. He didn't believe her.

'Then come to the Mermaid with us.'

She shook her head. 'Not today, Will. I would rather go home.' She wanted nothing more than to curl up in her bed and surrender to the oblivion of sleep.

'If you go back to Silver Street now, Marie will set you to work. Is that truly what you want?'

Magdalen thought of the Mountjoys' dingy workshop. Christopher Mountjoy standing too close, his eyes lingering over her breasts. 'No, I don't want that,' she agreed dully. 'Wait while I fetch my cloak.'

The Mermaid was quiet. It was unusually early to start drinking, even for Burbage's men. The inn had a low ceiling, stained brown with tobacco smoke, and an uneven wooden floor. It was furnished with mismatched tables, benches, stools, and a few padded chairs that were so comfortable men had been known to draw weapons over them. The walls were covered in old, peeling bills of plays and bear-baiting, and penny-pamphlets recounting the lurid scandals of the city. There would be pamphlets recounting John's death on sale by tomorrow morning. There was always money to be made from the misfortunes of others.

The players pulled two tables together and sat down. The fire was unlit, so too were the candles and the gloom of the place suited their mood. Magdalen half expected to see John at the table. She couldn't believe he was gone; couldn't believe she would never again see his impudent grin. Death was commonplace in London, whether from plague or sickness, or opportunist, back-street robbery or tavern brawl. But John's death was different. John had been murdered.

When she was a child, a neighbour had poisoned her husband with blue, cowl-shaped aconite flowers. Magdalen remembered seeing him lying in the road, his eyes bulging, his swollen tongue lolling from his blue lips. His wife had been hung from the gallows in the Bury. Magdalen closed her eyes against the memory but the image stubbornly remained, vivid and tormenting.

Burbage raised his cup of Mad Dog. 'To John Wood, an outstanding player, an exceptional fellow and a faithful friend.'

Magdalen's eyes shot open. They were fine words but spectacularly wide of the mark. Burbage may have given John the best female roles, but he had railed relentlessly against his tardiness, drinking and brawling. Nevertheless, the players raised their cups and drank deep.

'It's the Sabbath tomorrow,' Burbage went on, 'so, let's take a rest day to remember John as each of us sees fit.'

'Is it possible the Puritans poisoned John?' Christopher Beeston asked, stretching a huge, ham-like arm across the table for the beer jug.

'It's a big leap from daubing obscenities on the 'tiring house door to murder,' Henry Condell replied.

'But have you heard them preach? They're vitriolic in their hatred of the playhouses.' Beeston turned to his brother in arms and fellow player, William Sly. Beeston was fair skinned and blond, whereas Sly was tall, dark and devastatingly handsome. Exact opposites with regard to appearance, they were alike in every other way, their chief pastimes being women, dicing and drinking to excess.

'We drank with John a while last night, didn't we, Sly,' Beeston said. 'He was in good humour. Could someone have slipped a draught in his beer after we left him?'

Sly shrugged. 'I don't know. Can a man drink poison and still be alive the following day?'

'It would depend on how much poison he drank,' Magdalen replied, without thinking.

To a man, the players turned to look at her.

'So I've been told,' she added hastily, aware of Richard Cowley's suspicious gaze. In truth, Edmund Stow had not been far off the mark. As a child she had tended the herb garden with her mother and she knew full well the healing and the harming properties of the plants that grew there.

'I can't afford not to work, not now Elizabeth is with child again. What will we do if they use John's death as an excuse to close us down?' Henry Condell asked grimly.

'We could tour the provinces,' Will said, staring into his beer. 'As we did last year when the plague took hold.'

'God help us. There are only so many flea-infested mattresses a man can endure,' Christopher Beeston groaned.

'You had maids-a-plenty sharing those infested beds, Chris,' Sly grinned. 'I cannot weep for you.'

'Weep for the fleas, then!' Fourteen-year-old Alex Cooke laughed, too loudly. Slight of figure, sweet of face and fresh out of apprenticeship, he was always chosen for the lesser female roles. 'I had such fair company in my bed, night after night, that the fleas had no peace, what with all the sighing, and the bouncing and the thrusting -'

Sly rolled his eyes and spoke over him. 'Spare us your bragging, Cooke. The only stuffing you came close to was the mouldy wadding of your mattress.'

Alex's face fell. He idolised Sly and Beeston and yearned to share their adventures, but they treated him as a beardless child.

'Plague has come to Petty France by Houndsditch again,' young Peter chirped up for no apparent reason.

'There's *always* plague by Houndsditch,' Will Shakespeare replied dourly.

'Don't you have something to say to Magdalen, Peter?' Henry Condell asked pointedly.

'I'm sorry, Maggie,' Peter said. 'I didn't mean to get you into trouble.'

'Trouble?' William Kempe spluttered incredulously. 'You've damned near put the noose about her neck, boy!'

The apprentice looked close to tears again.

'Pay no heed, Peter,' Magdalen said. 'You were merely speaking the truth.'

'He did not speak a friend's truth!' Kempe snarled. 'If I were you, Maggie, I would seek to be better strangers with him.'

Magdalen wished Kempe would hold his tongue. Peter was just a child. Nevertheless, she had to admit the boy was reckless, and often spoke without thinking. She glanced about the table. Will was still staring into his cup. Christopher Beeston and

William Sly were casting dice, and coins were changing hands. Judging from Sly's smug expression, he was winning. Only Henry Condell showed any outward sign of compassion for Peter, his brow furrowing with concern. The two young apprentices lodged with him, and Magdalen felt certain if anyone could keep the boys in check, it would be sensible Henry and his sweet, level-headed wife.

'The coroner will not earn his fee unless he records a verdict of murder, *and* a suspect is convicted at the assizes. The odds are not in Magdalen's favour,' Richard Cowley said blithely.

'Your tact is without equal,' Will Shakespeare growled.

Magdalen's head hurt. She pressed her fingers to her temples, trying to loosen the knot of pain. Richard Cowley was right. It *was* in the coroner's best interests to strive for a conviction.

'Every one of us will swear an oath in defence of your good name,' Burbage said, his tone resolute. The players nodded in agreement, apart from Richard Cowley, who was studiously examining some ancient initials carved into the table top.

Magdalen was beginning to wish she had crept back to Silver Street. Her world had turned upside down and she had no idea how to set it right again. She put her head in her hands, and her obvious distress cast an even greater pall over the gathering. At length, William Kempe's bulbous eyes slid to the landlord.

'Perhaps Francis murdered John? He's best placed to slip something in his beer.'

They all turned to look at Francis Johnson. He was dunking dirty cups into a bucket of equally dirty water before slamming them back onto the board.

'It's possible,' Burbage replied. 'But I've never taken Johnson for a murderer. And what motive could he have?'

'None that I can think of,' Kempe admitted.

Magdalen remembered Richard Cowley's rapier piercing

John's doublet. Could it have nicked John's skin? If the tip was poisoned, could it have been enough to kill him?

She looked up, into Richard's eyes.

'Poison is a woman's weapon,' he repeated, seeming to have read her mind. 'A coward's game. There's no honour in it.'

'When is there ever honour in murder?' she shot back but Richard had already turned away, gesturing to a serving girl for more Mad Dog.

The shadows lengthened. The landlord lit the fire, the serving girls laid out soggy saffron cakes, and the players' spirits began to lift, warmed by the crackling fire, and by wine and cakes and ale. And with every cup of Rhenish she drank, Magdalen's spirits lifted a little too. The tavern was starting to fill up. Word spread fast through Shoreditch, and now all the poets and playwrights who had ever felt envious of Burbage's lauded band of brothers were crawling out of the woodwork to gloat over their misfortune. Robert Greene was first to arrive, his distinctive quiff of long, red hair waxed upright like a cockerel's comb. He made straight for their table, and addressed Burbage.

'I see you're still paying that country-bumpkin to write speeches stuffed with far-fetched metaphors.' Turning to Will Shakespeare, he announced mockingly, 'If it isn't the upstart crow, beautified by my feathers.'

Magdalen winced. Will had borrowed the plot of Greene's *Pandosto* for *The Winter's Tale*. In truth, the playwrights and poets all stole from each other, but Will took their ideas and made them a thousand times better, filling the Theatre and its coffers day after day, whilst Greene lived in back-street poverty.

'The pot is calling the kettle black, or Greene, in your case,' Will replied lightly, but Magdalen could see tension in his eyes.

Greene spat something brown and glistening onto the floor. Magdalen hoped it was tobacco. Sitting down on the bench beside her, he attempted to manhandle her onto his knee. 'Weep not, darling, smile upon my knee, when thou art old, there's grief enough for thee,' he crooned.

Magdalen recognised the song. It was Greene's own. Extricating herself from his arms, she shoved him hard. He fell off the bench and landed on his back, legs in the air like a deceased fly. Everyone cheered loudly and raised their glasses. Greene mumbled something. It sounded like 'misshapen dick'.

Christopher Marlowe arrived next, and the tavern lit up as if the stars had fallen through the thatch. He greeted them all in turn, embracing some, kissing others on the lips. But he offered no kiss to Will. Instead, they simply shook hands like two fencers before a bout. It seemed fitting, for they were presently engaged in an increasingly spectacular play-writing dual, lobbing masterpieces at each other across the Thames. When Marlowe attacked with the gore-fest *Tamburlaine*, Will struck back with blood-soaked *Titus Andronicus*. Marlowe lunged with his study of a weak king, *Edward the Second*, so Will parried with *Richard the Second*. All of London was waiting to see how Will would respond to Marlowe's *The Jew of Malta*.

'William.' Marlowe released Will's hand, and moved on.

'Christopher,' Will replied and turned back to his beer.

Magdalen found their relationship hard to fathom, but hidden beneath the jealousy and rivalry, she often suspected a lurking mutual respect.

Stepping over Robert Greene, who had fallen asleep on the floor, Marlowe sat down beside her. 'How now, Magdalen?'

She nodded absently. She had drunk a great deal of Rhenish, but she would never admit her inebriation, not even to Marlowe because it was not seemly. But he must have noticed her glazed expression because that familiar, half-smile was playing on his lips, as if he was enjoying his own private joke at the world's expense. Although he was fast approaching thirty years of age, there was still a boyish charm to his features; the soft doe-eyes, the beard-less cheeks, the wisps of a moustache above full, generous lips.

'I think you've had enough of this.' He picked up her cup of Rhenish, and proceeded to drain it.

'Hey!' she exclaimed but it was a half-hearted protest, for her head was pounding like cannon fire.

'You will have heard about the constable?' she said quietly.

'Edmund Stow is highly fed and lowly taught. Pay no heed to him,' Marlowe replied airily.

'But what if the Puritans bribe the coroner to convict me? We all know they are looking for an excuse to close us down.'

He shook his head. 'I won't let that happen.'

She wished she could believe him, but Marlowe was the most unreliable man on earth. He had recently fought in a brawl which had resulted in an inn-keeper's death. Although it was his friend, Thomas Watson, who had struck the fatal blow, they were both hauled off to Newgate prison to await trial. Marlowe had been released a month later, miraculously without charge. Perhaps he really did believe he was invincible now. In the history books in Will's room the ancient Greeks had called it *hubris*, and no good had ever come of it.

'You look like Christmas, Magdalen.'

'Christmas?' she repeated, bemused.

'Yes, your green kirtle, your red jacket.' Marlowe broke into song, 'the holly and the ivy, when they are both full grown.' He had a beautiful baritone voice.

'And *you* look -' she eyed his tawny-orange doublet slashed to reveal yellow satin beneath; the wafer-soft, wide collar falling across his shoulders; the row of shiny buttons marching down his chest and belly. He had come into money recently, of that there was no doubt. 'You look like a pageant, as always, Marlowe.'

'Tawny is the colour of mourning, is it not?' he asked with feigned innocence.

Magdalen laughed, but it made her head hurt.

'You remind me of my sister,' he said, suddenly serious.

'I didn't know you had a sister,' she said, taken aback.

'Her laugh sounded just like yours. There was something so joyous about it.'

Magdalen noticed he was using the past tense. 'Is she -' she began cautiously, but Marlowe spoke over her.

'She was married at twelve years old, and she died in childbirth at the age of thirteen.'

Magdalen's heart lurched with pity. 'Oh! I am so sorry…'

He was staring into the distance now, his eyes full of bitterness and remembered grief. Marlowe was a man of bluster and bravado; his every word designed to shock or offend. She had known him for ten years and in all that time, she had never seen his defences down. But now, the window to his soul was open wide and the view was so unexpected and so intimate, she felt obliged to hastily avert her eyes.

When Marlowe spoke again, he no longer sounded sad but angry. 'Answer me this. How can you have faith in God when he allowed my sister to die in agony?'

Magdalen glanced about anxiously. Queen Elizabeth was Supreme Governor of the Church of England. To deny God was to deny the Queen. Marlowe's words were blasphemous and heretical and he was risking a great deal by uttering them in a public place. But, if she was honest, she often asked herself the same question. Why had God allowed her parents to die? And why was He allowing her grandmother's mind to unravel?

Keen to stop Marlowe's dangerous tongue, she replied, 'God

works in mysterious ways. It is not for us to question Him.' It was the phrase Reverend Judd, the vicar of Saint Olave's, often used to comfort the bereaved, the sick, the dying.

Marlowe gave her a strange look, as if she had disappointed him in some way and then he turned to Will Shakespeare.

'So, what's this I hear about a revival of *Richard the Third*?'

'Aye, the crookback king,' Will replied. He was never a noisy drunk. He tended to grow increasingly maudlin, unlike the rest of Burbage's players who were now shouting at the top of their voices and laughing uproariously at nothing in particular.

'That reminds me of the time you and Burbage went to that whorehouse by Bishopsgate. The one by the sign of the Black Boar.'

Will shook his head. 'Not that old chestnut again, I beg you.'

Eager, expectant faces were turning in Marlowe's direction, perhaps sensing Will Shakespeare's imminent humiliation.

Marlowe cleared his throat and flung a languid arm over the back of his chair. 'As I was saying, William Shakespeare and the esteemed Richard Burbage had enjoyed a merry night in the cups. Make no mistake about it, their livers were burning hot.' Roars of approval rang around the table and Marlowe smiled, clearly revelling in the attention. 'William and Richard had their eye on the same whore, a pretty lass by the name of Dusky Sal. They were so inflamed, neither was willing to wait their turn.' His eyes were glinting wickedly now. 'And then William turned to Richard and said, I should be first, because William the Conqueror came before Richard the Third!'

Everyone laughed and banged the table with their cups. Will rolled his eyes and raised one hand above his head in mock acknowledgement. Marlowe was grinning but Magdalen wasn't. Will was a married man with a wife and three children at home in Warwickshire. As far as she was concerned, he was the perfect husband, the perfect playwright, the perfect lodger. She didn't want to believe this tale.

Perhaps Marlowe misunderstood her long face because he lowered his voice and said, 'you shouldn't waste your woe on John. He wasn't worth it.'

'What do you mean?'

'He was a wastrel.'

Magdalen bridled. 'Surely no more than the rest of us?'

'You think you knew him, but you didn't.'

'Then enlighten me.'

'For a start, he had gambling debts he could never hope to repay, and so he took up with any nobleman, or woman, stupid enough to loan him a sovereign. He was sharing Rizzley's bed until last week.'

Magdalen didn't believe him. Admittedly John drank too much and enjoyed throwing the dice, but he would never sell his body to pay off debts. And besides, although she often saw the Earl of Southampton, or Rizzley as Marlowe called him, ensconced in a private box at the Theatre, he never visited the banqueting chamber to mingle with the players.

'I am sure you are mistaken.'

'I am not mistaken. I am acquainted with Rizzley, and trust me, he is *not* discreet. He and John were lovers.'

'But surely the Earl of Southampton would not...' Her words trailed away. She put her head in her hands and let out a loud groan. 'Oh God, I've done something very foolish.'

'That's what comes of drinking a whole barrel of Rhenish.'

'No, listen,' she said impatiently. 'The earl sent a liveryman, requesting the tailor of the Lord Chamberlain's Men attend him at five o'clock tomorrow, for a commission. I told the liveryman it would be so.'

'What of it?'

'Burbage has no tailor.'

Marlowe smiled. 'Well then, *you* should take the commission. I warrant you have doublet and breeches a plenty in the 'tiring house. Don a cap, and you'll make a fetching youth.'

Magdalen laughed. Will's plays often featured players portraying women disguised as men. They tapped a rich vein of comedy, but it was pure frivolity. In reality, such deceit would never work.

'Kit, be serious for once. Tell me, what am I to do?'

'Do you need the money?'

'Yes, I do. You know I do.'

Marlowe's deep brown eyes were no longer playful. 'You can fashion Rizzley a cloak with your eyes closed. *The Jew of Malta* is playing at the Rose tomorrow. Come with me, as my guest. Afterwards, we'll raid Henslowe's 'tiring house and fit you out in apparel suitable for an esteemed tailor. I'll accompany you to Rizzley's, if you wish. He is always best pleased to see me.'

Magdalen was momentarily speechless.

'Lost for words? I think that must be a first,' Marlowe teased.

'You know the law forbids women to take an apprenticeship, or join a guild. Women cannot be tailors. I cannot feign to be someone I am not!'

'Then you will never be a player.' Marlowe's eyes had begun to dart about the tavern.

He never stayed in one place for long and she knew he was growing restless. She had to make a decision, and quickly, but how could she agree to such an outrageous scheme? The penalty for taking costumes from Burbage's Theatre was twenty shillings. For all she knew, Philip Henslowe, the owner of the Rose, might demand twice that much. And God alone knew how the Earl of Southampton would react if he discovered he had been played for a fool.

On the other hand, Edmund Stow was convinced she was

guilty of John's murder. If she attended the appointment with the earl, there was a slim chance she might learn if there was any truth in Marlowe's scurrilous gossip. And an even slimmer chance she might inch closer to the truth about John's death. Marlowe was making to leave. She grabbed his arm.

'Very well. I will indulge you in this madness, on condition you ask the earl about his relationship with John. I am certain you are mistaken.'

Marlowe sat down again, grinning. 'You always see the best in everyone. That is one of the many reasons why I love you.'

She smiled tolerantly at him. He didn't love her. As far as she knew, he didn't love anyone. 'Please, Kit. This is important. I have to find out who murdered John. I don't want to hang for something I didn't do.'

'Neptune's arse, Magdalen! I won't let you hang!'

'How can you say that when Edmund Stow is convinced I am guilty?' she asked, exasperated.

'Then we must find someone else for him to hang, mustn't we,' Marlowe said lightly. 'Someone nobody will miss.'

'Tell me you jest?'

He shrugged his shoulders. 'I must warn you, if you want me to speak to every nobleman who's ever swived John, we'll be grey before we're done. And that's before we start on the women. There were scores of them.'

'Killed anyone lately, Marlowe?' William Kempe yelled. He was sitting cross-legged on the table top, beer cup in hand, grinning malevolently.

'Fuck you, Kempe!' Marlowe replied evenly.

'Yes, please!' Kempe's blood-shot eyes brightened.

Attempting to stand up, he slipped on a spillage of beer and landed heavily on his arse. The assembly erupted into loud applause. Never one to miss an opportunity to entertain, Kempe managed to struggle to his feet, and began an impromptu jig along the table. Henry Condell took up the fiddle, and there was no stopping Kempe now.

Will Shakespeare yawned. 'That's my cue. I'm for home.'

'Of course you are!' Richard Cowley jeered. 'You… you…' He was so drunk he was having difficulty articulating.

'Cowley is winding up the watch of his wit,' Will said drily. 'By and by, it will strike.'

Cowley's fury miraculously restored his eloquence.

'See how the tight-fisted, clod-hopping bumpkin leaves before he has to buy a round!'

'You have a tongue that could sour even the ripest grape, Cowley,' Will retorted. Turning to Magdalen, he asked pleasantly, 'Shall we walk back together?'

She nodded, for it was not wise to walk the streets alone at dusk. As she followed Will to the door, Marlowe caught her eye, raised his cup and shouted, 'until tomorrow, Magdalen. To mischief and misadventure!'

She could not bring herself to return his smile.

They took the shortest route to Silver Street, over Finsbury Fields. A mist was rising from the cold earth, giving the fields a spectral air, and Magdalen was glad to have Will at her side.

'The inquest will be held soon, won't it?' she asked, hurrying to keep up with his long strides.

'It is usually the case, yes.'

'What am I to do, Will?' she asked plaintively.

'Do not concern yourself. The Lord Chamberlain is a man of the greatest influence. He will not allow the wardrobe mistress of his troupe of players to be accused of murder.'

'No, Will, you are mistaken. Didn't you hear him? He wants me in prison.'

'Enough. Think no more on it. All will be well. On a different matter, I want you to take a copy of *Venus and Adonis* to the Earl of Southampton tomorrow.'

'You were listening to my conversation with Marlowe?'

'Yes, I was listening. I am a magpie by trade. A thief of wit and words. Surely you know that by now?' Without waiting for her reply, he went on urgently, 'You must ask the earl to do me the honour of reading my poem. I need his patronage. It rankles that we players are considered base and lowly. And it rankles that I am mocked for my accent, scorned for my lack of university education. I am as well read as any nobleman. You know it to be true. You have seen the books in my chamber.'

'It's true,' Magdalen agreed patiently. She had heard all this before; it was his stock refrain. There was a chip on Will's shoulder that all the books on Paternoster Row could not dislodge.

'My father applied for a coat of arms, but he was turned down on the grounds our lineage is not worthy. Those heralds have no more brains than I have in my elbows. My father was dishonoured by their rejection. It has played a part in the ill-health that continues to plague him.'

Magdalen remained silent as Will gave vent to his bitterness and frustration. She knew from past experience he was not seeking her advice, merely her ear, and so she confined herself to the occasional sympathetic nod.

Will was still fulminating when they arrived on Silver Street and Magdalen was beginning to lose patience. She had lost someone today. Someone she cared for deeply. And, as if that was not enough, she now stood accused of his murder, whilst Will bemoaned his lack of heraldry, at great length.

'It is my dearest wish to re-apply to the College of Arms on my father's behalf, but the fees are more than twenty pounds.

Where am I to find such an amount when Burbage pays no more than two pounds per play?'

'From what I have read so far, *Venus and Adonis* will sell like hot cakes, just you wait and see,' Magdalen said, stifling a yawn.

'Maybe.' Will did not sound convinced. 'It is not easy for me. I have no influential parents to make introductions, no university friends to open doors.'

'You have more talent than all those reprobates in the Mermaid put together. You don't need anyone to make introductions for you.'

'How naïve you are, Magdalen. Everyone needs a helping hand, a greased palm.'

Stung by his sharpness, she cast him a wary glance. In the moonlight she could see the determined set of his chin, the intense emotion in his eyes. Because he was not as loud or as outrageous, or as dangerous as Marlowe, it was sometimes easy to over-look his fierce, burning ambition.

They had reached the Mountjoys' door and Will was turning the key. 'I need Southampton's patronage,' he whispered fervently. 'You must not return without giving him *Venus and Adonis*, do you hear me?'

A sense of melancholy was settling on Magdalen's heart. As they tiptoed up the stairs and wished each other a hushed 'good night', the truth crept up on her, as cold and clinging as river-mist: she could rely on no-one but herself to clear her name.

Burbage had professed his willingness to help, but if it came down to a choice between saving her or saving his precious Theatre, he would choose the Theatre every time. Marlowe had pronounced he would not let her hang, but he was as unreliable as the weather, not least because he had a tendency to disappear without trace, often for months on end.

And Will cared for little but his own ambition. He had always appeared faultless to her, a gloriously idealised father-figure. But tonight, for the first time in her life, she had begun to realise that he was not perfect, but just as flawed as the next person. Was this what it meant to grow up? This profound, aching sense of loss?

Feeling her way in the darkness, she undressed and climbed into bed. She was exhausted, but sleep took a long time to find her. She knew Walter Wiseman, the coroner, was notorious for recording verdicts based wholly on gossip and hear-say. Just as she also knew that many people regarded her as the players' whore; a woman without morals or decency and therefore entirely capable of cold-blooded murder. Her name was blackened before the inquest even began.

As she drifted towards fractured sleep her thoughts returned to Christopher Marlowe. The idea of disguising herself as the tailor to the Lord Chamberlain's Men was immoral, dangerous and bordering on lunacy. But if it meant discovering the truth about John, if it brought her closer to finding his killer, then what choice did she have?

FOUR

'Disguise, I see thou art a wickedness'

Sunday 29th March

Magdalen awoke the next morning with a splitting headache and a deep sense of foreboding. Memories tumbled like butter in a churn: John dying in her arms; the frayed blanket covering his corpse; Edmund Stow raising his staff and declaring her a murderer.

She had thought of John as a brother, but she realised she knew next to nothing about his life outside the Theatre. She didn't even know where he had lodged.

And what did the note mean? Leave it be. Leave *what* be? Something so dangerous it had cost John his life?

Why had she agreed to visit the Earl of Southampton wearing apparel from Philip Henslowe's costume chests? The Bible brooked no argument. Thou shalt not steal. And what had Adam Cooper said? It is written in Deuteronomy that when a woman wears man's apparel she is accursed.

When would the coroner set a date for the inquest? How long did she have to prove her innocence?

Hot pin-pricks of dizzying panic flared across her skin and, quite suddenly, she couldn't breathe. Stumbling out of bed, she flung open the wooden shutters. The sky was a wash of pale grey, the world balanced on the cusp of a new day. Entranced, she listened as birdsong pierced the stillness. The cold morning air weaved around her limbs and whispered across her feverish skin, as soothing as a camomile balm, and gradually her heart stopped racing, and her laboured breathing eased. Turning around, she lifted the lid of her work basket and retrieved the pages of *Venus and Adonis*. Padding back to bed, she slipped beneath the coverlet again.

The greenwood was sunlit, full of birdsong. In its dappled glades, the goddess of love was enamoured with Adonis, a beautiful human youth, sweet above compare.

'*A thousand honey secrets shalt thou know,*' Venus promised, but all in vain, for Adonis lived only to hunt wild boar and did not return her love:

'She red and hot as coals of glowing fire,
He red for shame, but frosty in desire.
Backwards she pushed him, as she would be thrust,
And governed him in strength, though not in lust.
So soon was she along as he was down,
Each leaning on their elbows and their hips,
Now does she stroke his cheek, now does he frown,
And gins to chide, but soon she stops his lips...'

Magdalen found it hard to believe Will had penned these lines. Even in his cups, he tended towards melancholy rather than sanguine. She could not imagine him in the act of carnal love. In truth, she did not *want* to imagine him in such a way. And yet, his description of Venus's desire was so ardent, so frenzied. Was he remembering someone in particular when he penned those lines? Was he thinking of his wife in Stratford, the woman he never spoke of?

Magdalen ran her fingers over Will's handwriting, the slanted hand, the bold loops, the copious deletions neatly scored through. Was *Venus and Adonis* a poem about love, or was it about lust? She barely knew Matthew Hilliard but her pulse had raced in his presence. Was that lust? The sin Reverend Judd preached against so fervently?

The floorboards creaked above her head. Will was awake. Instinctively she listened for her grandmother's snores in the next room but all was silent. With a mounting sense of alarm, Magdalen leapt from the bed. Pulling on the clothes she had abandoned the previous night, she ran to her grandmother's chamber. As she had suspected, it was empty, the bed in disarray. She ran downstairs. The kitchen was empty too, the fire unlit. The Mountjoys were still abed.

Unlocking the back door, she stepped out into the small courtyard. Pear trees were trained along its high walls, their branches embroidered with sprigs of delicate white blossom. Raised herb beds stood either side of the central cobbled pathway. The rosemary bushes were in flower, a haze of soft blue, and fresh green shoots of mint and parsley were pushing through the black soil. A flurry of sparrows took flight as Magdalen ran down the path and unbolted the gate to the back lane. Her hood pulled up to hide her face, she peered cautiously left and right. All was quiet. Closing the gate behind her, she hurried along the lane, keeping close to the high walls of the neighbouring gardens.

She knew exactly where her grandmother had gone. Anthony Bonvince was a butcher by trade. He had grown wealthy from supplying meat to the livery companies' halls, and had purchased a fine property in Noble Street, barely fifty yards from the Mountjoys' home. Magdalen turned right into the narrow alley that ran behind the row of grand houses. Opening the gate that led into Anthony Bonvince's back garden, she was immediately confronted by Bonvince's son, barring the way. A strapping youth in his early twenties, his hostile demeanour softened as recognition dawned.

'Oh, it's you,' he said quietly and stood aside.

Inside the house, the kitchen smelled enticingly of freshly baked bread, but as Magdalen descended the stone steps to the cellar, the welcoming aroma was quickly replaced by the foul stench of sewage. Anthony Bonvince's neighbours were notorious for failing to empty their cesspit and consequently it regularly overflowed and seeped through the adjoining walls.

There were more than a dozen people crowded inside the cellar including Anthony Bonvince and his wife, Cecily; Father Dawbeney, and Magdalen's grandmother. Cecily Bonvince had covered her old pantry table with an embroidered cloth. The makeshift altar was adorned with two gold candlesticks bearing beeswax candles; an exquisitely decorated gold chalice, and a large gold plate which held the remains of a bread loaf. A wooden crucifix hung on a peg on the wall and a censer was breathing clouds of incense into the ice-cold, putrid air.

The Mass was evidently over because the congregation was milling about and conversing in hushed tones. Father Dawbeney had removed his pale orange vestments to reveal a grey doublet beneath. The old priest smelled of musty linen, his skin was mottled and his few remaining strands of hair floated about his bald pate like steam rising from a boiled egg.

Fighting to control her anger, Magdalen approached him and said quietly, 'Father, I have begged you time and again not to allow my grandmother to hear Mass. You put her in danger. You put us all in danger.'

Father Dawbeney gave her a look of utter disdain.

'Magdalen, you will refrain from addressing me so brazenly. You forget your place.'

Magdalen lowered her voice still further. 'Forgive me, Father, but you know my grandmother is confused of late. Some would say you are taking advantage of her.'

'How dare you speak to me with such insolence?' the old priest spluttered, his pale, fleshy lips flecked with spittle. 'You have a wicked tongue, child. It has need of a scold's bridle to hold it in check. I blame your grandmother for your waywardness, for allowing you to associate with lewd and lecherous players. These good Catholics,' he waved a hand around the cellar, 'wish to celebrate the Mass and it is my duty before God to oblige.'

Magdalen followed his gaze. Her grandmother was helping Cecily Bonvince clear the 'altar', reverently packing the candlesticks and gold plate into a large oak chest. Magdalen shook her head despairingly. If the house was searched, it would be the first place the watchers would look. 'Will you at least take the gold plate with you, Father?' she pleaded.

'They are not mine to take, child. Just as the Lord suffered for our sake upon the cross, so must we all be prepared to suffer for our faith. I am ready to die for my faith, as are all those gathered here.'

Agnes Bisset had finally become aware of her granddaughter's presence. 'What are you pestering the good Father about, Magdalen?' she enquired.

Magdalen noticed her grandmother was holding a set of rosary beads, yet another banned Catholic frippery which, if discovered, could lead them all to Tyburn.

'Nothing,' she replied wearily. 'All is well.'

'I hope you are showing respect to your elders, Magdalen,' Agnes went on briskly. 'Father Dawbeney does me a great kindness by performing the Mass here. My legs are so bad these days, it is difficult for me to walk to church.'

Magdalen turned to face the priest again. 'The rest of your

congregation may be prepared to die for their faith, but my grandmother has no comprehension how dangerous this is. She believes Mary Tudor still sits on the throne. Does that not concern you?' she whispered furiously.

'What concerns me is that the Queen is a bastard and a heretic. She has turned away from the Pope and from the true faith.' Fresh globules of spittle glistened about Father Dawbeney's mouth.

'You should not say such things out loud,' Magdalen began, but he cut her off.

'I must say such things, my conscience demands it. And you will learn to hold your tongue, or I shall report you to the constable for lewd behaviour. He shares my disgust for the playhouses. He would strip you naked and whip you through the streets until your back ran red with blood.'

The old priest had begun to breathe heavily, and the twisted smile that formed on his pale, wet lips turned Magdalen's stomach. She took her grandmother's arm.

'Come. The day draws on. We must be away from here.'

Outside in the cold morning air, Agnes began to wheeze like a pair of leaky bellows. She stopped to rest a moment outside Windsor House, one of the grandest stone-built properties on Noble Street.

'It wasn't always Windsor House,' Agnes said breathlessly. 'In the old days it was called Neville's Inn, because the Neville family, the Earls of Westmorland, owned it.'

'A noble family indeed,' Magdalen agreed, wondering how her grandmother could not remember an event of half an hour since, and yet could vividly recollect the distant past. 'We should walk on a little farther, Grand-Aggie,' she coaxed.

She dreaded running into a watcher. What possible excuse could she give for being abroad at such at early hour? All was quiet until they reached the corner of Silver Street, and then something disturbed the rooks roosting in the yew trees in Saint Olave's churchyard. They took to the air, swirling frantically and filling the sky with their harsh, jarring shrieks. Magdalen thought she could see someone standing in the shadows beneath the yews, or was she merely imagining things? She looked harder and suddenly the figure was in motion, darting beneath the overhanging branches, a silhouette of a dark cloak, too far away to see a face. She watched the figure weave between the gravestones, jump over the low churchyard wall in an athletic bound, and disappear into the gloom of Maiden Lane.

A man's gait. Who was he? How long had he been watching them? 'Come, Grand-Aggie,' she urged. 'We must make haste.'

When at last they reached the Mountjoys' house, Agnes was grey-faced and shaking with exhaustion. Magdalen boiled some water, made her a fennel infusion and put her to bed. As she watched her grandmother slip towards sleep, she tried to reassure herself the man in the churchyard had merely been taking an early morning stroll. And yet, why had he run away if he had nothing to hide? One thing was certain: by whatever means, she had to keep Grand-Aggie away from Anthony Bonvince's cellar.

Her grandmother let out a loud, rumbling snore. Magdalen patted her hand affectionately, her mind drawn back to the day she had left Hampshire on the miller's cart, to live in the big city with a grandmother she had never met. At first, she had been wary of Agnes Bisset's huge wobbling bosom, her no-nonsense demeanour and her ready, full-throated laugh. But she had quickly discovered that beneath Agnes's bluster, there lurked a generous heart. Her presence had loomed large over the 'tiring house. She was the players' mother hen, a font of common sense, her bark far worse than her bite.

Stricken with grief at the loss of her parents, Magdalen had clung to Grand-Aggie's side, and learnt how to create a pattern, to cut cloth, to sew. How to embroider and panel and pink and braid. How to tell the difference between fine lawn linen, woven with gossamer-fine thread, and middle of the range holland. How to recognise high quality, scarlet broadcloth wool, dyed a rich red using wildly expensive kermes, and humble, madder-root-red stammel, a staple for petticoats. And finally, Agnes had taught her about silk; from the rich, glossy sheen of satin twill to the distinctive, luxurious pile of velvet.

Magdalen sighed. She was losing her grandmother, slowly, agonisingly, bit by bit, and she had no idea how to turn back the tide. She wondered if she should buy another of Simon Foreman's potions. He had spoken in hushed tones of the miraculous properties of ground unicorn horn. She knew it was madness to sink ever deeper into his debt, but if there was the slightest chance the potion might work…

Across the street, the bells of Saint Olave's were calling the good citizens of Cripplegate to church. Kissing her grandmother's forehead, she hurried down the stairs.

Saint Olave's was an unremarkable church, with a tower and a porch and two ancient, ill-kept, alms-houses clinging like ivy to its north facing wall. Its small pest house stood a stone's throw from a row of freshly dug graves. Magdalen shivered. The plague was never far away, a constant threat, impossible to ignore.

Inside the church, Christopher and Marie Mountjoy were sitting with their fifteen-year-old daughter Mary. Will was several rows behind them, the jaunty gold ring hanging from his left ear lobe setting him apart from the congregation's more soberly dressed tradesmen. Magdalen squeezed into a pew at the back, painfully aware that people were turning to look at her. Gossip travelled faster than the plague, and she suspected everyone knew Edmund Stow had openly accused her of John Wood's murder. She stared at the floorboards, consumed by a confusing mix of anger, shame and fear.

The service began and, with a palpable sense of reluctance, the congregation turned away from Magdalen and towards Reverend Judd. His sermons, inspired by the Book of Homilies, were renowned for lasting upwards of two hours. Magdalen listened dutifully for a while, but she soon found herself thinking about John, the note in his hand, the constable, the inquest, Newgate, the gallows…

Grasping the edge of the pew, she fought hard to regain her composure. Sunlight was streaming through the plain window glass and dancing across the unadorned walls. Beneath the whitewash, she could see ghostly traces of a painting of the Last Supper.

In truth, Magdalen understood the appeal of the old religion. Reverend Judd's church had been stripped back to the bare essentials, entirely devoid of visual awe and wonder.

The vicar had progressed to the Creed. 'We acknowledge one baptism for the forgiveness of sins...'

However much she sympathised with Catholics, Magdalen knew with absolute certainty she wasn't prepared to die for them. She had to stop Grand-Aggie hearing Mass, and she had to persuade her to come to church. The penalty for non-attendance had recently increased to an exorbitant twenty pounds a month. If Reverend Judd ever decided to impose the fine on her grandmother, she would have no hope of paying it.

'And we look for the resurrection of the dead, and the life of the world to come...'

Magdalen often prayed she would be reunited with her parents in the world to come, but what if Adam Cooper was right? What if God *did* disapprove of the playhouses? Perhaps all that awaited her in the afterlife was the eternal fires of Hell. Who would care for her grandmother if she was convicted of John's murder? She had to keep Grand-Aggie safe; she had to keep a roof over her head. And in order to do that, she had to prove her innocence, for all other roads led to the noose.

She became aware that Mark the builder's son was nudging her impatiently. The service was over and she was blocking his exit from the pew. Hurriedly, she got to her feet. Reverend Judd was waiting in the porch to bid farewell to his parishioners. She averted her gaze and tried to slip past him, but he tapped her on the shoulder.

'May I offer you my condolences for the player's death. And I presume your grandmother is still too ill to attend church? I will pray for her speedy recovery.'

'Thank you, Reverend.' Magdalen suspected he knew full well why her grandmother did not attend church, but she sensed he was a kind man, a true Christian soul.

The congregation was gathering in the churchyard, the younger generation courting under the watchful eyes of their parents, the older generation sharing news and gossip. Today, judging by the furtive glances they were casting in her direction, Magdalen was certain they were gossiping about her. She looked about, hoping she might spy a friendly face, but Will Shakespeare had already slipped away.

As was his wont, Christopher Mountjoy was making no attempt to mingle with the crowd. He stood to one side, a sullen and solitary figure. Magdalen noticed his daughter, Mary, was exchanging shy smiles with the Mountjoys' senior apprentice, Stephen Bellott. Mary never smiled at Magdalen. Taking a leaf from her mother's book, she either resolutely ignored their lodger, or spitefully blamed her for anything that went wrong.

Mary's mother, Marie, was attempting to infiltrate a tightly knit group of merchants' wives. Dressed in their Sunday best, they had formed an impenetrable circle of cold shoulders and false laughter. Marie was laughing along with them, trying to catch their eye, but for the most part the women ignored her. Occasionally, one or other of them glanced scornfully in her direction before quickly looking away again.

At first, Magdalen had found it hard understand why her landlady endured such calculated snubs week after week. But she had soon realised that Christopher was responsible for his wife's predicament. Surly and hostile, he had withdrawn from the world, leaving Marie no choice but to fight for the business they had worked so hard to establish, and to fight for the place in society she so desperately craved.

Magdalen returned briefly to Silver Street and found her grandmother still asleep. In her own room, she noticed Will had placed a copy of *Venus and Adonis* on her bed. Written in his neatest hand, the loose pages were held together with a length of braid taken from her workbasket. She shook her head at his gall. Nevertheless, she slid the pages into her leather satchel alongside her workbook and measuring parchments, and hurried out again.

In the city, the church services were over and people were spilling out into the streets. There was a tangible air of anticipation and excitement. Freshly posted bills told of a free concert at the Royal Exchange, of bear and bullbaiting on Bankside and '*the most lamentable tragedy of the Jew of Malta at the Rose Theatre at 2 o'clock*'. Magdalen bought a pie from a street seller on Cheapside then turned down Bread Street, passing richly decorated merchants' houses and well-kept inns.

There was a long queue for a wherry boat at Queen's Hithe but she had expected as much, for a great many people were crossing to Bankside. She joined the throng as it slowly edged towards the stairs but she barely noticed the jostling mob. All she could hear were the jurymen, their cries resounding inside her skull: *'Guilty! Guilty! Guilty!'*

Someone bumped into her, causing her to stumble into the man in front. He turned around, his irritated expression quickly shifting to a smile as he registered her pretty face. Two wherry boats arrived and the crowd surged forward, carrying her along the narrow street. Mindful of thieves, she kept her hand firmly over the purse at her belt. Reaching the jetty, she stepped into the nearest wherry, paid her penny and sat down. She found herself wedged between a young apprentice who was picking his nose and merrily flicking his snot at his friend, and a plump woman eating a pork pie from a basket on her lap, her ample bosom catching the crumbs.

The waterman used an oar to push away from the quay, and was soon regaling his captive audience with news of a pod of giant whales sighted beyond Greenwich. Half the poor beasts had beached and would most likely die. Some folk suspected Catholic spies from Rheims were hiding in their bellies, waiting for nightfall to cut themselves out. At this point in the story, Magdalen stopped listening and gazed at the bridge instead. Weighted down with towering houses and shops, their overhanging jetties bulging out over the river, she often wondered why it did not simply sink without trace.

At last, the wherry reached Bankside. The snot-flicking apprentice and his friend disembarked, closely followed by the plump lady who showered her with pork pie crumbs. Magdalen stepped ashore and looked about. The south bank was in a festive mood. People dressed in their Sunday best, dogs barking and street sellers yelling. Children were throwing bread into the pike ponds; screaming at the slick, gaping mouths that rose from the murky waters. Men were gathered around a cock fight. Flags were flying from both the bear baiting and the bull baiting arenas, and from Philip Henslowe's theatre, the Rose. Before John's death, Magdalen would have revelled in the festive atmosphere, but today she was too preoccupied with her own pressing concerns. Buying a cup of small beer from a stall, she sat down beneath a sycamore tree, its tight green buds bearing the promise of longer, warmer days. She could only pray she would still be alive to enjoy them. She took a sip of beer, and then another, but the warm, watery brew did nothing to alleviate her anxiety.

'Mistress Bisset!' Marlowe was walking towards her, waving two cushions above his head. 'You look radiant, as ever!'

'Good day to you, Master Marlowe. I'm looking forward to your play,' she replied, instantly brightening.

'It's a trifle, Magdalen, a meaningless trifle.'

'I doubt that very much.'

He pulled a face, and brushed her words aside with a dismissive wave of his hand. 'I am glad you're here,' he said, sitting down beside her. 'Henslowe is in a foul mood. One of his whores has disappeared, run off with the takings from his brothel by the sign of the Red Fox.'

'How many brothels does Henslowe own?' Magdalen asked.

'He owns half the whore-houses on Bankside,' Marlowe replied, taking the cup from her hand and draining it. 'And half the inns and lodging houses, the Rose Theatre, and three pawn-broking shops and a starch manufacturing business. Oh, and he's a money-lender, too. Half the players are deep in his debt, the thieving, swiving bastard.'

'I'm thirsty!' Magdalen glared accusingly at her empty cup, but Marlowe was grinning to himself.

'I've just remembered! Venus, that's her name, the whore who took his money. She sold herself as a virgin for ten years.'

'What do you mean?'

81

'She had this potion to seal her cunny shut. But one of the younger girls thought it was a beauty potion and slapped it on her face. Her eyes were drawn so close together she looked like a fledgling's arsehole. You couldn't get so much as a little finger in her mouth!'

Magdalen didn't believe a word of it, but Marlowe was laughing so hard she worried he might fall backwards into the river. And then suddenly, he was on his feet.

'Come on. I've saved us the best seats.'

He set off at such a fast pace she had to break into a run to keep up with him. She wasn't surprised he had made no mention of John's passing, or the death sentence that hung above her head like Damocles' sword. She had grown up with his callous disinterest, his rapid mood swings, lurid jokes and devil-may-care attitude. Even so, she longed to tell him she was afraid; longed to tell him she felt her world was collapsing about her ears. Just as she also longed to talk about her grandmother and Father Dawbeney and Anthony Bonvince's cellar.

But such matters were simply too dangerous to discuss with anyone, even Marlowe. Or perhaps *especially* Marlowe, for she had heard whisperings he was a dissembler, ensnaring men in his blasphemies so he might sell their secrets to the Privy Council.

Catching up with him, she asked, 'Is Edward Alleyn playing Barabas the Jew?'

'Yes, he is. What a sanctimonious gob-shite. He married Philip Henslowe's daughter last month and there's no stopping him now.'

Magdalen's laughter died in her throat. Henslowe was holding court by the entrance to the yard. Close to forty years of age, his peasecod doublet disguised a hefty paunch and his beard was flecked with grey. Like Amelia Bassano, he evidently cared little for the restrictive Sumptuary Laws, for his apparel was of the highest quality, no doubt intended to flaunt his wealth. His white damask doublet was intricately pinked using the smallest, sharpest of shears, the slashes on his black jerkin edged with fine thread.

'You still owe me for this play, Philip,' Marlowe said. 'We agreed four pounds.'

'You nag like a wife, Kit,' Henslowe replied.

Magdalen felt Henslowe's eyes sweep briefly over her workaday kirtle and waistcoat, before he quickly dismissed her as not worthy of his attention.

Marlowe winked at her and announced grandly, 'This is Mistress Magdalen Bisset, wardrobe mistress at Burbage's Theatre.'

Marlowe introduced her to Henslowe every time she accompanied him to the Rose. And every time, Henslowe gave the impression they had never met. As far as he was concerned, she was just another whore.

'Come to spy for Burbage I presume?' he asked nastily, addressing the air several inches above the crown of her head.

'You do me wrong, sir!' Magdalen replied indignantly. 'I am come to spy for Shakespeare.'

Marlowe laughed but Henslowe did not. He brushed past them without another word, no doubt seeking to converse with ladies who *were* worth remembering.

'Jumped-up old turd,' Marlowe said, too loudly for comfort. 'Did you know he started life as apprentice to a merchant, then the old man died, and Henslowe married his wealthy widow. He's no better than his whores. He swived that old woman for her coin.'

People were beginning to turn and stare.

'Where are we sitting?' Magdalen asked, hoping to distract him. She wasn't angry with him. She understood the reason for his outburst. Marlowe was the son of a lowly boot-maker but he never denied his humble origins and he eviscerated anyone who pretended to be something they were not.

'Centre, middle gallery. Like I said, the best seats,' Marlowe snapped, and then his gaze alighted on a refreshments stall and his mood instantly brightened again. 'Do you want something to eat?'

'I'll take a cup of beer, because you drank mine. And I'll take a bowl of nuts, if you promise not to throw them at Edward Alleyn.'

Marlowe's eyes lit up. 'What a good idea. Let's get two bowls.'

He bought half the wares on the stall. With their arms full of nuts, fruit, gingerbread and cushions, they took their seats. The Rose was much like the Theatre; three tiers for the bum-cushions, a yard for the one-penny groundlings, a projecting stage and a gallery above for musicians. Burbage couldn't afford any at present, but Magdalen noticed Henslowe had employed five, all dressed as courtly minstrels.

The Rose was filling up, the hubbub of the audience's chatter reverberating around the galleries. And, just for a moment, Magdalen forgot her troubles and shared in their excitement. It was such a joy to watch a whole play, rather than snatched snippets through a stage door.

'Did you ever fancy trying your hand at acting?' she asked.

'Good God, no,' Marlowe replied vehemently. 'What a pain in the arse to learn all those lines! Henslowe puts on five different plays a week.'

A fanfare sounded from the musicians' gallery. As the notes faded, Magdalen leant forward, her eyes sparkling with expectation. This was the moment when the magic struck, when reality was suspended, when invisible bonds were woven between player and audience, binding them together in an alchemical world of make believe. Edward Alleyn, hugely popular with Bankside audiences, drew a collective murmur of anticipation as he strode from the 'tiring house. Large of limb and broad of shoulder, he dominated the stage. Magdalen noted his costume with keen interest, but found it to be unremarkable. Black gown; brimless black cap, and a long, grey beard. A typical representation of a Jew.

Unwrapping the gingerbread, Magdalen watched in awe as the frantic plot unfolded: Incensed by the Christian Governor of Malta's decision to seize all Jewish gold as tribute for the Turks, Barabas the Jew plotted his bloody revenge. The bills described Marlowe's play as a tragedy, but *The Jew of Malta* was streaked through with the blackest of humour. The play was riddled with witticisms, each more outrageous than the last, and Magdalen could hear Marlowe's voice in every one: When Barabas was accused of fornication, he answered, 'But that was in another country, and besides, the wench is dead!'

In truth, Magdalen had never liked Edward Alleyn's acting style. Burbage encouraged his players to seek the truth of a role, but Alleyn was old-school, all sawing arms and exaggerated facial expressions. Or perhaps she had missed the point. Was Alleyn deliberately over-playing Barabas in homage to Marlowe's far-fetched, thundering lines?

Marlowe nudged her shoulder and handed her an orange; a rare, expensive treat. She peeled it with care and ate it slowly, relishing the novelty, the bitter-sweet explosion of taste against her tongue. The play hurtled on at a manic pace, awash with murderous mayhem.

Barabas's daughter, grieving for her dead lover, entered a convent without her father's permission. Outraged by this betrayal, Barabas murdered her, and her fellow nuns, with a pot of poisoned rice-porridge. Her last words were 'I die a Christian' to which a priest replied, 'Aye and a virgin too, that grieves me most'.

Magdalen glanced at Marlowe. He was throwing nuts into his mouth, one after the other. All around him, the audience were laughing uproariously, but he looked irritated and embarrassed.

The final scenes were a Machiavellian orgy of back-stabbing, deceit and betrayal. Magdalen watched in astonishment as a giant cauldron of 'boiling oil' was wheeled onto the stage. Burbage had no props to compare to it. Was it truly as heavy as the players' feigned, or was it fashioned from wood and painted to resemble bronze? She watched in even greater astonishment as Barabas plunged unwittingly through a trap door in the musicians' gallery and fell into the cauldron. Edward Alleyn began to thrash about wildly, giving a spine-chilling performance of a man in mortal agony. It was a long drop, and she prayed he *was* acting.

'Damned Christians, dogs, and Turkish infidels!' he screamed.

As the play drew to a close, the audience leapt to their feet, applauding wildly. Magdalen joined them, but Marlowe stared straight ahead, thunderously ill-humoured.

'What a dunghill,' he muttered.

'You are wrong. It is a triumph,' she replied quietly.

She had promised Will a full report but, in truth, it was not an easy play to define. There was no clear struggle between good and evil. The Jewish, Christian and Turkish characters were all as devious, deceitful and barbaric as each other. Watching *The Jew of Malta* was very much like spending an afternoon with Marlowe himself. He buffeted and challenged and confounded. Above all, he entertained. But when the afternoon was done, you still didn't feel you truly knew him, and that was half the charm.

As they made their way down the back stairs, Marlowe was mobbed by well-wishers offering congratulations, favours, dinner invitations and assignations in various bowling alleys, private houses and pleasure gardens. 'Forgive me, I must speak with Henslowe on a matter of great importance,' he replied repeatedly, slowly edging his way through the crowd. Keeping a firm grip on Magdalen's arm, he swept her along in his wake. Once out of the melee, he made for the musicians' gallery.

'Is Henslowe up here?' Magdalen asked, following him up the stairs.

'No. He's in the banqueting chamber, sucking the cock of anyone he thinks might prove useful to him.'

Accustomed to the players' lewdness, Magdalen didn't even blink. 'What *are* we doing up here then?' she asked, looking about the empty gallery.

Marlowe lowered himself to the floor, and pulled her down beside him. 'We are hiding until the players leave the 'tiring house, and then we're going to raid the 'tire chests. As I said, you'll make a fetching youth.'

Magdalen had briefly forgotten the real reason for her visit to the Rose. 'No,' she groaned. 'I can't.' Women were hanged for the theft of a loaf of bread, and she had rashly agreed to steal an entire suit of apparel.

But Marlowe's eyes were shining. 'Where is your spirit of adventure, girl? All will be well – as long as Rizzley pays you for the commission. The nobility are notoriously tight fisted.' Suddenly, his grin vanished. 'Tell me, will Shakespeare approve of my play?'

'He…' she faltered, caught off guard by his abrupt change of subject, and uncertain how to respond. She had long suspected two hours upon a stage was far too short a time for Marlowe to adequately explore the multitude of ideas writhing in his overheated brain. Consequently, his plays had an air of frantic urgency. She had once heard Will call them 'ill-formed pies, overstuffed and overbaked'. But she had also long suspected that where Marlowe led, Will felt obliged to follow, although she kept such inflammatory thoughts to herself.

'You know he will. It's another masterpiece,' she replied.

'Hardly! The rabble takes delight in watching an old nag and a screaming monkey torn apart by slavering mastiffs, so I am obliged to give them that, in kind.'

'There's more to your play than that!' she said vehemently. But it was hard to know exactly what Marlowe was trying to say in *The Jew of Malta*. Underneath all the violence and pithy witticisms, was the play a damning indictment of religion in general? She prayed the Privy Council would not see it that way, or Marlowe would be back in Newgate within days.

She realised he was staring broodily into space. If he sank further into a quagmire of black bile, she knew from past experience that he might not speak again for days. Racking her brains for a distraction, she remembered the prologue, spoken by a player claiming to be the long-dead Niccolo Machiavelli.

'Is it true Machiavelli's writing was inspired by his years at the court of the Borgia's?'

Marlowe glanced at her, his expression morose. 'I don't give a bull's pizzle about Machiavelli, sweet girl. You must know I can't abide watching my own work, but I couldn't leave you alone with that rabble. They'd be groping for more than just your purse.' Suddenly, he leapt to his feet. 'Come, my fair Hermaphroditus! Let's run a-mock in Henslowe's 'tiring house.'

Music and laughter were drifting along the corridor from the direction of the banqueting chamber, but the 'tiring house was deserted. Magdalen looked about, enthralled, a spy in the enemy's camp. It had the same distinctive aroma as the Theatre's 'tiring house; a hot, airless smell of male sweat and yeasty beer, with undercurrents of bitter wormwood in the costume chests to keep the moths at bay. But there the similarity ended, for

Henslowe's props were far superior to those at the Theatre. Backdrops were stacked haphazardly; sumptuous palaces, forest glades, and the monumental city of Rome. The gaping entrance to Hell painted with the flaming fires of damnation. Here, a life size wooden cow. There, a huge looking-glass of polished steel, its wooden surround carved with intertwining branches, the sprouting hair of a Green Man.

On the opposite wall, a row of hooks held richly decorated religious vestments; cloaks fit for a king; a golden fleece. And in the corner, a gleaming suit of armour. Magdalen thought Henslowe's brothels must be profitable indeed to afford such treasures. Marlowe noticed her gazing at the armour.

'Henslowe has nine more in storage,' he said, carelessly turning out the contents of a costume chest. 'His players are far better equipped than the poor English wretches fighting for Queen and country in the Netherlands.'

Without warning, Magdalen's thoughts turned to her father. The war in France had broken him. The haunted look in his eyes had never faded. A sudden, intense feeling of loss gripped her; for her father, for her mother, for John. That was the trouble with grief, it had a habit of sneaking up when you least expected it.

Desperate for a distraction, she walked over to the cosmetics table and ran envious fingers over a glass bottle of expensive cochineal. She had to make do with humble madder paste to accentuate her players' lips. A vial lay on its side, a trail of fine black powder spilling across the board. Exotic Kohl accentuated Henslowe's players' eyes, whilst Burbage's penury gave her no choice but to use charcoal from the fire. She picked up a bowl of white paste and sniffed it curiously. From its bitter smell, she guessed it was cerise, a mixture of white lead and vinegar. She grimaced and put it down again. She had seen at first hand the awful damage it wreaked on tender cheeks. Even if Burbage's coffers were spilling over with gold, she wouldn't buy such an evil concoction. She blended a harmless face-paint of ash, egg white and talc.

'Enough gawping!' Marlowe said briskly. 'Put these on.'

She turned around to see Marlowe holding out a doublet and hose of the finest silk. 'Yellow?' she queried nervously. Saffron was a highly expensive dye. The suit of apparel must have cost a small fortune. What if she damaged it or spilled something on it?

'Trust me, Rizzley relishes colour,' Marlowe pressed.

Torn with indecision, her eyes darted from Marlowe to the doublet and back again.

'We haven't got all day,' he said irritably.

'Very well. But you must turn around while I undress,' she said shyly.

He grinned wolfishly, but did as she asked.

Afraid someone might disturb them, Magdalen quickly stripped down to her smock.

'Do you need any help?' Marlowe asked cheerily, his back still turned.

'No, thank you. I know how to don men's apparel. I spend my days dressing and undressing the players.'

Marlowe laughed. 'Best keep that to yourself, or Reverend Judd will have you whipped through the streets for harlotry.'

But Magdalen wasn't listening. She had never worn silk stockings before, and she was trying hard not to tear them. She was amazed by how fine they were, how soft, how tightly they clung to her calves. Next, she stepped into the close fitting, knee length breeches. They were attached to the doublet by laces looped through eyelets, hidden beneath an overlapping seam. She fastened the laces at the front but she couldn't reach the rest.

'Are you certain you don't need help?'

Magdalen looked up, and realised he was watching her reflection in the looking glass. 'Damn your eyes, Kit. I took you for a gentleman!'

'That was an ill-conceived notion if I ever heard one,' he replied impishly. 'Here, let me.' Deftly, he attached the laces at the small of her back, then spun her around to face him. Instantly, his expression darkened.

'My master-mistress,' he whispered, staring at her as a starving man might stare at a joint of beef.

Magdalen shifted uneasily. Perhaps sensing her discomfort, he said gruffly, 'We must tame your hair,' and promptly made a show of searching through a tangled heap of ribbons, laces and periwigs on the cosmetics table. '*Et voila!*' He held up a large bone comb with a triumphant air.

A fraught silence fell as he set about plaiting her hair. Coiling it on the crown of her head, he pinned it in place with the comb, then carelessly shoved a tall, black hat over her ears.

'There. That should hold. Now, put these on.' He threw a pair of buckskin shoes at her feet. 'Now, let's be away before Henslowe skins us alive for parchment. Pray God Ben Jonson does not write one of his tedious plays upon us. What a hideous way to be preserved for posterity.'

Magdalen giggled, the awkwardness between them vanishing in a heartbeat.

A thought struck her. 'What am I to do with my own clothes?'

'Put them in here.' Marlowe thrust a canvas drawstring bag into her hand. 'I'll carry it. And don't forget your satchel.'

As she made to follow him, Magdalen caught sight of her reflection in the looking glass. She didn't recognise the skinny youth staring back at her. To her dismay, she realised the doublet barely skimmed the tops of her thighs. The tightly fitting breeches left little to the imagination, and she could clearly see the shape of her calves through the fine silk stockings. She was practically naked. She couldn't walk the streets of London in such unseemly apparel.

'Make haste,' Marlowe said impatiently, holding the door ajar.

Don't be a coward, she told herself. Swallowing hard, she slung her satchel over her shoulder and followed him outside. Accustomed to wearing a full-length kirtle, Magdalen's scantily clad legs felt cold. She had never felt more self-consciousness or more exposed as they walked along Bankside and through the Paris Gardens. The riverbank was still crowded with boisterous groups of cup-shotten young bucks; with well-dressed couples strolling in the sunshine; with children playing tag around the trees. It was a normal Sunday and yet something was different. At first, Magdalen couldn't fathom it, and then it came to her. Despite her garish yellow suit of apparel, only a handful of men were giving her a second glance. She had been rendered invisible and it felt strangely liberating.

'You're walking like a girl. You're swaying your hips and your strides are too short. Watch me,' Marlowe said.

She had never analysed a man's gait before. Marlowe's walk was linear but his arms and shoulders were in motion, matching his long, purposeful strides. She attempted to mimic him, keeping her hips and torso rigid.

'Christ, no! Stop it! You look as if you have a pole up your arse!' Marlowe was bent double with laughter.

Magdalen tried again.

'Worse! Much worse! Now you are a demented windmill. Stop flailing your arms.'

Magdalen thumped him hard across the chest. 'You villain! You're making sport of me!'

'Yes, I am. Why else would I be here?'

They took a wherry across the river to Whitefriars stairs. On a weekday, the streets would have teemed with black robed lawyers but the Temple was quiet today, the gates of the Inns of Court closed against the world. But Magdalen knew what lay behind them, for Burbage's players often performed there. The lawyers lived in rarefied precincts of towering halls, chapels, libraries and tranquil gardens frothed with sweet-scented roses. And she envied their privilege, their learning, their chance to change the world.

Thinking of lawyers reminded her of the inquest.

'How am I to convince the coroner I am not a murderer, when everyone knows poison is a woman's weapon?' she asked plaintively.

Marlowe's expression was unreadable and then, quite suddenly, he quickened his pace.

'Kit?' she called after him. He ignored her.

'Kit!'

He turned around. 'Henslowe gave a performance of *Tamburlaine* at Temple. Ignorant thugs, those damned lawyers. Talked through the entire play. Keep up, will you?'

Not for the first time, Magdalen asked herself why she associated with a man so devoid of compassion, although in her heart, she knew why. It was the same reason the rest of London craved his company. He lived his life without constraints, as if there would be no tomorrow, and just to walk in his shadow was fortune enough. She ran to catch up with him.

'You will ask the earl about John, won't you?' she asked as they turned into Chancery Lane.

Marlowe sighed theatrically. 'Oh, very well. Rizzley is notoriously indiscreet. If he has heard any rumours concerning John, he will not keep them to himself. But don't let his soft looks deceive you. He has a razor-sharp mind. Since his father died, he's invested shrewdly in the family's estates.'

'And he's a patron of the arts?' Magdalen queried, remembering the copy of *Venus and Adonis* in her satchel.

'Yes, he has a taste for the theatre, for art, for poetry. Show him a pretty verse, and his eyes will fill with tears. We were up at Cambridge together, and beneath the furs and the gold thread, there lies a gentle heart.'

The Earl of Southampton's residence in Holborn was a converted monastic building, close by Lincoln's Inn. Magdalen looked up at its ornately decorated gables and finely painted window glass and felt her courage vanishing like Mad Dog spilled into floor rushes. Marlowe must have sensed she was wavering because he grabbed her arm, hauled her up the wide, stone steps, and knocked on the door. Moments later it was opened by an usher in the earl's bright blue livery. He looked down on them with an expression of haughty contempt.

'Tailor to the Lord Chamberlain's Men,' Marlowe pronounced gravely. 'Appointment at five o'clock.'

The usher wordlessly motioned they should follow him. The entrance hall smelled sweetly of beeswax polish; a fragrant haven of plenty. The wall panels were painted with geometric patterns of bright blues, reds and oranges, interspersed with the family's coat of arms. Garlands of ivy cascaded down the banisters of the sweeping staircase and three huge vases of Lenten roses sat upon a carved side table.

The usher marched on; his head held high like a soldier in a military parade. In the ante-chamber beyond, he came to a stop before a wide, oak door. He knocked then stepped aside, gesturing for them to enter.

The dining chamber was huge. A fire crackled in the hearth and the air smelled so strongly of cinnamon, nutmeg and cloves that Magdalen instantly thought of Will's Castile soap. The glazed *fleur-de-lis* floor tiles were a gleaming sheen of reflected firelight, unchanged since the monks had dined here. The ribbed ceiling was ornately decorated. Between gilded pillars, the walls were hung with exquisitely painted cloths. One depicted the Biblical story of Susanna, bathing naked in her garden, spied upon by two lecherous old men. Another portrayed two Greek warriors, wrestling naked, their perfectly honed bodies slick with oil.

The earl was reading a letter at the table, but he stood up as Marlowe and Magdalen approached. He was tall and slim, no more than twenty-five years of age. Magdalen had seen him from a distance at the Theatre but, close up, she was amazed by the delicacy of his features. Shrewd, almond shaped eyes beneath finely plucked, arching brows. Perfect rosebud lips, painted cochineal red. Cerise-white skin, and long auburn hair falling in luxuriant curls over his shoulders.

'Marlowe! Kit Marlowe! What a surprise! I don't recall extending an invitation?' He spoke with the same pretentious, clipped inflection as Lord Hunsdon.

Marlowe waved a hand in Magdalen's direction. 'Your Lordship, I am accompanying Master Bisset, the Tailor to the Lord Chamberlain's Men.'

Magdalen was adrift on a roiling sea. She had watched the players perform the latest, fashionable French bow, but could she emulate it? Taking a deep breath, she slid her right foot towards the earl, bent her back knee and inclined her body forward. After a moment's pause, she straightened up again. She realised the earl's gaze was wandering over her body, and lingering on her long, slender legs. Marlowe had looked at her in exactly the same way in Henslowe's 'tiring house. Deeply uncomfortable, she lowered her eyes to the floor.

'Ah, yes,' the earl said softly. 'Wait here for a moment, Master

Bisset. There is a private matter I must discuss with Marlowe.'

Marlowe winked at her as he followed the earl into the ante-chamber, but his nonchalant air did nothing to calm her trepidation. He had left the door slightly ajar and she could hear the two men talking in hushed tones. She tiptoed closer and watched in astonishment as the earl pushed Marlowe against the wall. They began to kiss vigorously, their lips parted, their tongues entwined. Marlowe's hands slid down the earl's back to his arse, kneading his buttocks, drawing him closer still. Suddenly, the earl grabbed Marlowe by the shoulders. Spinning him about, he shoved him face first against the wall. She caught a glimpse of Marlowe's white buttocks. A momentary fumbling, and then…

Magdalen averted her eyes and backed away, deeply ashamed to have spied on such an intensely private act. It was not long before she realised the two men were in conversation again. She could not help herself. She crept back to the door.

'It is good to see you,' the earl said, flamboyantly pushing Marlowe away as if they were dancing the galliard.

'It is good to be seen.'

'You look in fine form, considering your recent incarceration.'

'I hoped you might visit me.' Marlowe's tone was so bland, Magdalen could not tell if he jested.

'I could have, but I didn't want to,' the earl replied flippantly. 'Besides, I knew you would have your liberty soon enough. You have your allies, do you not?'

Magdalen wondered who those allies might be. Perhaps the rumours were true, perhaps Marlowe *was* an intelligencer for the Privy Council.

'Why are you here?' the earl asked, when Marlowe remained unusually mute.

'I told you, I am accompanying Master Bisset.'

The earl glanced towards the dining chamber and Magdalen stepped back a pace, fearful of discovery.

'Ah yes, I had quite forgotten about young Bisset.' The earl laughed. 'Such a tender fellow, with heavenly legs. And that suit of apparel. He looks like a buttercup. Perhaps I should clasp him beneath my chin and see if I have a liking for butter?'

'Perhaps not, Rizzley. He is soon to be married.'

'I'd wager he's never been kissed. I would enjoy imprinting his sweet seals on my own lips.'

'Leave him be, Rizzley.'

'You care for him, Kit?'

'As much as I care for any rose-cheeked boy,' Marlowe replied artlessly. 'But enough talk of trifles. No doubt you will have heard that John Wood, the player, is dead.'

'A bad business. I hear rumours the wardrobe mistress poisoned him. Was it a lover's quarrel?'

'She is innocent,' Marlowe said sharply. 'She could not harm a fly.'

The earl raised his plucked eyebrows.

'I would not want to see an innocent girl hang,' Marlowe persisted. 'Therefore, I must ask you, can you think of anyone who would wish John dead?'

'You jest, Kit! John had more enemies than I have hunting dogs. Christ's wounds, he was not worth the dust the wind blew in his face!'

'And yet you cared for him, I think?'

'Yes, I cared for him. He was easy to like, was he not? He drank too much and gambled too much, but I've always found something very appealing about a man who lives for the moment without a thought for the future.' He smiled knowingly at Marlowe, and Magdalen sensed tension building between them again, heady and potent. The earl looked away first.

'You were bedfellows?' Marlowe asked.

The earl laughed briefly, a hollow, empty sound. 'Your arrows fly direct, Kit. But what purpose in coyness, eh? We know each other's darkest secrets, do we not? Yes, John and I were intimate for more than a year. At first, I assumed his gambling was little more than a pastime, but I soon learnt he was heavily in debt to all manner of villains. He swore he would stop so I paid his bonds, repeatedly, larger and larger sums each time. But it was a sickness. He couldn't stop and matters reached breaking point last Christmas. I refused to give him any more money.'

Magdalen was fragmenting, shattering like glass. How could she have known so little about a man she considered a brother?

There was barely controlled anger in the earl's voice now. 'I discovered John had many lovers. He was using them, just as he was using me, taking our hand-outs to feed his sickness. Our relationship ended badly.' He paused for a moment then went on bitterly, 'Amelia Bassano was one of John's lovers. She is playing a dangerous game. If Henry Carey suspected the child in her belly was the offspring of a humble player, I doubt he would shower her with such affection.'

Magdalen had watched Amelia collapse at the mention of John's name. Was her swoon due to her delicate condition or was there another, more personal reason, for her distress? Noblewomen, and men, paid handsomely for a dalliance with a player. Could Amelia have been John's lover? Had Lord Hunsdon discovered their affair? Was it possible he had ordered John's death in a fit of jealous rage?

Magdalen jumped at the sound of Marlowe clearing his throat. The two men were almost upon her. She rushed to the fire-side, almost tripping over a small table in her haste. The door opened and the men entered the dining chamber. The earl approached her and, out of habit, she quickly lowered her gaze. She could smell the freshly starched linen of his ruff, and the strong scent of expensive perfume. Her heart began to hammer. Would he guess her secret? Would he see through her disguise?

'Am I so terrifying? Look at me.'

She looked up apprehensively. She noticed his hairline had been plucked, giving him the high forehead favoured by the ladies at court. It served to accentuate his fine, arching brows and his fiercely intelligent eyes which, at this moment, seemed to be boring into her very soul.

'You are of tender years. Scarce out of apprenticeship, Master Bisset?'

'He may be green, but he has proven himself many times over. He made this doublet,' Marlowe lied blithely, holding his arms out and spinning on his heel. 'It is a work of art, to be sure.'

Rizzley gave Marlowe's tawny orange suit of apparel a cursory glance before returning his gaze to Magdalen. A slight frown marred his perfect alabaster brow and she sensed he was trying to decide whether to trust so young a guildsman. The silence stretched on. Her heart was thudding so fiercely now she felt certain he would hear it. What would happen if he guessed her deception? At best, he would ensure she never worked again.

'I want Orsino's cloak, from *Twelfth Night*,' the earl announced at last. 'I found its manner pleasing, and unique.'

Magdalen struggled to hide her surprise. Orsino was Duke of Illyria, a distant kingdom, far beyond France, far beyond Italy. Magdalen had altered his cloak from an existing one, with the express purpose of emphasising his foreignness. She had shortened the cloak to be slung across one shoulder and to skim his waist. It was wildly impractical, and frankly absurd. Why would the earl want to wear such a ludicrous garment?

She could feel Marlowe's eyes upon her, willing her to say something. It was only then that she realised she had no idea how to speak as a man. The earl was eyeing her expectantly. In desperation, she mumbled gruffly from the back of her throat, 'If you would permit me to ascertain your measurements, Your Lordship?' She sounded as if she was suffering from an ague, but the earl did not appear to notice anything amiss.

'Yes. Make haste. I have an appointment this evening.'

Magdalen unfastened her satchel, resolutely avoiding eye contact with Marlowe. She didn't want to see the smirk she felt certain was playing on his lips.

The arrival of the earl's supper was a merciful distraction, for Magdalen's hands had begun to shake. Under the watchful eye of the usher, servants brought platters of spiced meat dishes; finely decorated pies cut into small portions; pickled vegetables and preserved fruits stacked in pyramids as high as the silver candlesticks. The earl washed his hands in a bowl of rose perfumed water then wandered over to the table, eyeing the feast with palpable disinterest.

'Eat, Kit. Just a light supper. You might like to try this.'

He picked up a two-pronged utensil and stabbed a piece of soft, green fruit. Holding the utensil to Marlowe's lips, he proceeded to feed him like a child.

Magdalen did not know which fascinated her most: the strange utensil, which she thought might be called a fork, or the unknown fruit. Clear juice was running down Marlowe's chin. The earl wiped it away with his fingers and licked them lasciviously.

'It is called a melon,' Rizzley said.

'Sweet as honey,' Marlowe replied.

The air simmered between the two men.

Magdalen had not expected the earl to extend her an invitation to taste his supper. A humble tailor was not worthy to eat at an earl's table. As a lowly playwright and poet, neither was Marlowe, but his force of character shone like Spanish treasure, and everyone, whether highborn or low, was entranced by him.

Magdalen pulled a long strip of parchment and a pencil from her satchel, uncertain how to proceed. It would be disrespectful to approach the earl without his permission. How to attract his attention? Mercifully, he noticed her and gestured for her to draw near. She stepped forward.

The earl's doublet was tinsel silk woven with gold thread to create a herringbone effect, and trimmed with enamelled buttons and pearls. The fabric was so exquisite she hardly dared rest the parchment even lightly across his shoulders. His lustrous, lightly-oiled hair fell loosely down his back. It seemed impertinent to move it aside, so she added an inch to her calculations.

Rizzley and Marlowe were discussing the endless skirmishes between English troops and the Spanish army in the Low Countries. They spoke of the hardships suffered by the English, rotting food supplies, rampant sickness and disease.

Tentatively, Magdalen moved round to face the earl. He stopped in mid-sentence, his eyes leisurely roaming across her body again, a slow smile spreading across his delicate features. Magdalen wondered if he would still think her fair if he knew her true sex. Deeply uncomfortable, she swiftly lowered her eyes. She could feel his breath on her cheek. It smelled of sweet wine, Malmsey perhaps, or Muscatel.

'Spare your blushes. I won't bite.' Rizzley's voice was low, sultry. 'Your betrothed is a lucky maid. Tell me her name?'

'Magdalen,' Magdalen blurted wretchedly.

Why wasn't Marlowe putting a halt to this? From the corner of her eye, she saw he was grinning from ear to ear.

'Magdalen,' the earl repeated slowly, as though savouring the name on his tongue. And then he laughed, and she realised he too was relishing her distress.

'I will toy with you no longer,' he said, suddenly brusque. 'Make haste.'

Caught off guard by his rapid change of demeanour, Magdalen's pencil slipped from her fingers and landed with a clatter on the floor tiles. She bent to pick it up, relieved to see it was not broken. It had been a gift from Marlowe, the slender graphite stick encased in juniper wood.

'You may continue.' The earl's left arm fell to his side, and she realised he was giving her permission to mark its length.

Working slowly and methodically, she marked the parchment from collar to sleeve; shoulder to waist; the circumference of his chest; his waist. She repeated each measurement several times, determined not to make a mistake.

Servants brought more platters of tiny marzipans in the shape of piglets and lambs; marmalades; tarts; comfits and wafer cakes. Magdalen had never seen so much food on one table. It seemed a terrible waste because Marlowe and Rizzley barely touched it.

They were discussing Astronomy now, how John Digges's latest almanac supported Copernicus's theory that the celestial planets revolved around the sun and not the earth. How Digges had used his study of a new comet in the sky to show that Aristotle was wrong when he claimed the stars were fixed in their places.

Magdalen made a show of examining her parchments and jotting notes in her workbook, all the while listening to their debate in fascinated awe. She envied their learning. Her education, such as it was, had come from the books in Will's room. There was so much she didn't know; so much she yearned to know.

They digressed to algebra, and talked of Thomas Harriot who had sailed to the New World, learnt the native language, charted the coast of Roanoke, returned safely home and now devoted himself to the study of mathematics. Finally, the earl glanced at the ornate clock on the side table.

'I have an appointment at Greenwich and Her Majesty does not appreciate tardiness.'

'We will detain you no longer,' Marlowe replied smoothly. 'Thank you for your gracious hospitality, Your Lordship.'

Hurriedly, Magdalen gathered up her belongings and fastened her satchel. With her head bowed, she followed the two men back to the entrance hall. It had been a long day and her emotions were as a tangled as a dropped skein of silk.

She felt ashamed she had witnessed Marlowe and Rizzley's love making. She felt angry with the earl for toying with 'Master Bisset'. She felt even angrier with Marlowe for doing nothing to stop him. Worst of all were the revelations about John. A gambler and wastrel, a man who whored himself in exchange for financial reward.

She was exhausted, and she wanted to be gone from this sweet-smelling arcadia of careless plenty, but a small part of her regretted the men's discussion was at an end. She hadn't understood a great deal of their conversation, particularly when they spoke of Mercator and distortions, dimensions and parabolas, but it had been exhilarating none the less. Marlowe and Rizzley hadn't always seen eye to eye, but they had argued logically and with measured reason. In the Mermaid, when men disagreed it invariably ended with fists or daggers.

The men were saying their farewells. They embraced, slapping each other on the back like brothers. And then the earl turned to Magdalen.

'I leave the fabric to your discretion. If the cloak pleases me, you will be paid.'

'Thank you, Your Lordship.'

Magdalen battled to disguise her alarm. She would need at least two yards of cloth for the cloak. Even with hard haggling, it would cost fifteen shillings a yard. And then there was the gold braid, and the lining. She needed payment in advance not in arrears, but such matters were of no concern for one of the wealthiest men in England.

Marlowe nudged her shoulder.

'Are you forgetting something, Master Bisset?' he prompted. 'Will Shakespeare's poem?'

Magdalen reached into her satchel, painfully aware of Rizzley's searching gaze. Holding out the papers, she said, 'You would do your humble servant, William Shakespeare, the greatest honour if you would read his work, *Venus and Adonis*, and, if it pleases you, do Master Shakespeare the even greater honour of allowing him to dedicate the verses in your name.'

The earl took the pages. It was only then she realised she had spoken in her own voice, but he did not appear to have noticed. He was already engrossed in the poem.

'He would not come in person?' he asked, not looking up from the page.

'He would very much like to make your acquaintance, if it pleases you and at your convenience.'

'I am an admirer of Shakespeare's work. I will read his poem.'

Without thinking, Magdalen dropped a curtsey. 'Thank you, Your Lordship.'

Fast as lightning, Marlowe thumped her on the back with such force she bent double, winded and gasping for air. The earl looked up, just in time to see her performing the resemblance of a very deep bow. Marlowe hauled her upright and propelled her towards the door.

'We will not delay you any longer, Your Lordship,' he said smoothly. 'It has been a delight, as always. We wish you a pleasant evening.'

But the earl had already turned away and a moment later, the usher closed the door in their faces, severing them from Rizzley's delicately fragranced world. In stark contrast, Holborn Hill smelled of wood smoke overlaid with the foul miasmas of the river Fleet. Marlowe insisted on seeing her safely back to Silver Street, and so they walked on together, up the steep hill to Newgate and on into the city. They lapsed into silence, not so much companionable, as fraught.

'You are angry with me,' Marlowe said at last.

'Yes, I am angry with you. I was in Hell this evening and you thought it sport.'

'It *was* sport! The earl would have swived you where you stood, if you had given him even a jot of encouragement. And then, by God, he would have had the surprise of his life!'

'How can you jest about such things?' she asked, hurt.

The grin vanished from Marlowe's face. 'I would have killed him before he touched you.'

'No, you wouldn't.' Despairingly, she raised her eyes to the sky. Dusk was falling and bats were darting overhead, making her think of home, of Hampshire.

'I suppose I should thank you for asking Rizzley about John,' she said begrudgingly. 'I didn't know him at all, did I?'

'How did you…' He visibly paled. 'You were listening?'

'No, I wasn't,' she lied. But it was too late.

'So, you… tell me you didn't see…' His voice trailed away. He looked horror-struck.

Magdalen was so mortified she couldn't speak.

'How dare you, Maggie? I would never have marked you for a peeping tom.' Marlowe's voice was cold with fury now. 'It was a private moment… you should not have…'

He quickened his pace, the distance between them increasing rapidly.

'I'm sorry. It was wrong of me, but I would never... I didn't expect...' Magdalen stammered helplessly.

But Marlowe kept walking.

Tears welled in Magdalen's eyes. Surely she wasn't entirely to blame in this unfortunate matter. She hadn't intended to spy. And surely a bed chamber would have been a more suitable place for the men's tryst. And so, rather than running after him, she came to a halt.

'If you valued your privacy so greatly, why did you choose an ante-chamber, where you could have been disturbed at any moment?' she called after him.

Marlowe turned around, eyed her thoughtfully for a moment, then walked back the way he had come. Fishing in his sleeve for a handkerchief, he handed it to her.

'Here, take this.'

'Thank you.' She wiped the tears from her eyes.

'You must know, John wasn't worth a piss in the Thames,' he added carelessly.

Did he assume her tears were for John? A sudden thought struck her.

'Is it possible the earl killed John?' she asked. 'You saw how angry and bitter he was.'

'Adonis's arse, Magdalen. Don't be foolish.'

'Why am I foolish? Isn't it possible John was blackmailing the earl?'

She knew he had grasped her meaning. Sodomy was illegal, punishable by death. But Marlowe brushed the darkness aside, as was his wont.

'John didn't have the brains for blackmail. Now then, you can't walk into the Mountjoys' house dressed like a canary. Come.' Grabbing her hand, he dived into a narrow passageway beside Goldsmiths' Hall. 'You can change here.'

It was gloomy and smelt of piss, but Magdalen was too tired to argue. She would have liked to keep the silk stockings because her woollen pair were so itchy in comparison, but she dutifully pushed Henslowe's apparel into the canvas bag and handed it back to Marlowe.

'Thank you, Kit.'

'It was my pleasure,' he beamed, and she had no doubt he meant it.

At the Mountjoys' door, they embraced briefly. She noticed Marlowe smelt of tobacco smoke, and traces of an exotic scent.

Rizzley's scent.

'I swear on my life no-one will harm a hair on your head,' Marlowe said, and then he was gone, striding jauntily down Silver Street as if they had been laughing about high days and feast days, not talking of murder and the noose.

FIVE

'But let concealment, like a worm in the bud,
feed on her damask cheek'

Monday 30ᵗʰ March

Magdalen awoke with a start. She had been dreaming of the gallows on Tyburn hill, the crowd jeering, hungry for her blood. She buried her face in her pillow and breathed in its familiar, comforting scent of oily down and feathers, but images continued to crowd her mind: John dying in her arms. Edmund Stow declaring her a murderer. Marlowe and Rizzley.

She turned over and stared at the canopy over her bed. Who had reason to wish John dead? The tip of Richard Cowley's rapier had pierced his doublet. Was it poisoned? Was their discord grave enough to warrant murder? She decided she would question Francis Johnson, the landlord at the Mermaid. He was well acquainted with both young men, for they spent half their lives in his tavern.

If Lord Hunsdon knew Amelia Bassano had made him a cuckold, how far might he go for revenge? Joan Coverdale, a distant cousin who worked in Lord Hunsdon's household, might know a few secrets. And Joan had an irrepressible tendency to gossip after a few cups of Rhenish.

And what of the Earl of Southampton? He had made no secret of his bitterness towards John. A man of such power could arrange a lowly player's death with the click of his long, slender fingers. But how to find the truth of any of it?

Her thoughts flew full circle back to the gallows. She had always avoided Tyburn Hill, unlike some folk who took ghoulish pleasure in watching the executions. Dear God, she didn't want to end her days as entertainment for the mob, their cruel taunts the last words she heard on this earth. Flinging aside her blankets, she stumbled to her workbasket and retrieved the pages of *Venus and Adonis*. Sliding back into bed, she sought sanctuary in a sunlit forest where the goddess of love was still attempting to woo a beautiful, but profoundly disinterested, human youth:

'And when from thence he struggles to be gone,
She locks her lily fingers one in one.
'Fondling', she says, 'since I have hemmed you here,
Within the circuit of this ivory pale,
I'll be a park and you shall be my deer;
Feed where you will, on mountain or in dale:
Graze on my lips, and if those hills be dry,
Stray lower, where the pleasant fountains lie.'

Magdalen quickly re-read the last line. There could be no doubt of Will's meaning. In her mind's eye, she could see exactly what the goddess desired, and a thrill of illicit pleasure rippled deep inside her belly.

The bells of Saint Olave's tore her from her wanton daydream. Tumbling out of bed, she pulled on fresh linen and apparel to meet Marie's approval: a bum-roll about her waist; a plain, woad-blue gown with a laced bodice, and a coif to hide her unruly hair. There was no time for breakfast, so she made do with a cup of small beer. If she was not in the workshop by the sixth toll, Marie Mountjoy would make her life a living Hell. In truth, there was much about the workshop that reminded Magdalen of Hell. The obligatory lattice over the window of an immigrant's workplace made the room infernally dark. The air was stale, and the vats of evil-smelling glue stank like Purgatory itself. And then there was Christopher Mountjoy's glowering, satanic presence.

Magdalen paused in the doorway to catch her breath. Christopher was at his workbench, standing over Tom and Rich. They looked tired and pale, squinting in the half light. Magdalen often worried they would be blind as bats long before they completed their apprenticeships.

Like a fox catching a hare's scent, Christopher's nose came up. '*Tu es en retard Maudlin! Viens ici!*'

He was the only person who pronounced her name 'Maudlin', the French way. Her grandmother swore Christopher had once been a handsome man, but that was before a liking for rich food had swollen his belly, the passing years had thinned his hair, and a bout of smallpox had pitted his pallid complexion.

Reluctantly, she joined him at the bench, catching an unwelcome waft of rotting teeth. He was attempting, yet again, to teach the boys how to draw wire. It was the bedrock of the Mountjoys' business; thicker wire for the framework of a head 'tire and much finer wire, woven about with gold and silver thread for its decoration. Christopher was using the largest mill, an iron plate with die holes of different diameters. Magdalen had watched the process many times. Metal rods were drawn through successively smaller die holes, the wire becoming finer with every draw. It was simple enough in principle, but the apprentices were struggling to master the technique. Tom didn't seem to have the strength to pull the wire through the die, and Rich had pulled so hard the wire had snapped in two.

'*Mon Dieu!*' Christopher wrenched the pliers from his grasp. '*Regardes!* First, you must lubricate, *comme ca.*' He ran a cloth soaked in lard around the die holes. 'Second, you must place the wire directly in the centre, or it will not be even. *Comme ça.* And third -'

Christopher's pronunciation of 'third' was unfortunate. Tom and Rich looked at each other, and collapsed in fits of giggles.

'Turd!' Tom spluttered delightedly. 'Turd!'

'*Imbecile!*'

Christopher clouted Tom about the face with such force that his teeth clattered and he fell backwards off his stool. Magdalen bent down to help him up.

'*Laisse seul!*' Christopher snarled.

Magdalen pretended not to hear him. She put an arm around Tom's shoulders and hoisted him back onto the stool. There were tears in his eyes and a red welt blooming across his cheek. She gave him her handkerchief, and squeezed his shoulder in a silent gesture of sympathy.

'I told you to leave him be, you insolent girl!'

Magdalen fought hard to hold her tongue. Outwardly, Christopher Mountjoy was scarred by smallpox but inwardly, she sensed his wounds ran much deeper. French immigrants paid twice as many taxes as their fellow Londoners but they were still hated and mistrusted and blamed for everything, most especially for spreading the plague. It often seemed as if a lifetime of prejudice and abuse had slowly blackened Christopher's heart.

Tom was wiping his tears on her handkerchief. Rich was as tense as a warp thread, suppressed anger emanating from his thin frame. Christopher was staring at Magdalen's breasts, and she shifted uncomfortably. He had swived Anne, the previous maidservant, with such regularity the poor girl had fallen pregnant. When it was no longer possible to hide her swollen belly, he had vehemently denied paternity to the church elders, denounced her as a whore and cast her out into the street. He had then swived Margaret, and only the announcement of her betrothal had eventually spared her his unwelcome attentions. Margaret would soon be leaving the Mountjoys' employ, and Magdalen was very afraid Christopher intended to pluck her next. If she wanted to keep her job, it would not be an easy matter to refuse him.

She was startled from her melancholic musings by the sound of Marie Mountjoy's shrill tones echoing along the corridor. Moments later Marie burst into the workshop accompanied by Mary, and the senior apprentice, Stephen Bellott.

'You stand too close to my husband, you wanton wench!' Marie screeched.

Hastily, Magdalen stepped back, but remained silent. She had learnt from bitter experience that it was best not to rise to Marie's rebukes.

'Stephen! There you are. I want no more of these boys. I am going to find my pipe,' Christopher announced. Glaring at his wife and ignoring his daughter, he strode from the workshop.

Stephen winked at Mary, who smiled shyly in return. Marie pretended not to notice their exchange. Magdalen suspected Marie secretly approved of the young couple's burgeoning romance, but she doubted Christopher felt the same. She could not imagine him willingly parting with any kind of dowry.

Marie bustled over to the head 'tire bench. As if playing a lighting fast game of chess, she tidied bodkins, needles and scissors, ribbons, feathers and nets with brisk, purposeful zeal.

Stephen sauntered over to the workbench, ruffled Tom's hair and patted Rich on the shoulder.

'Now then, boys, watch and learn.'

Rolling up his sleeves to reveal powerful, muscular forearms, he picked up the pliers and drew the wire expertly through the die. Magdalen smiled to herself. She guessed the demonstration was as much for Mary's benefit as for the young apprentices.

'Get over here, Magdalen!' Marie snapped. 'Lady Gerard's head 'tire will not make itself.'

As a child, Magdalen had feared Marie as one might fear an ogre in a fairy tale. But as the years passed, the revelation of Christopher's penchant for bedding the serving girls had altered her perspective. Marie would always be a bully, but she was also flesh and blood; a woman humiliated and betrayed at every turn by her boorish, adulterous husband.

'A player murdered, and upon the stage no less, but what can you expect from a den of ill repute?' Marie's face was pinched, as if she were chewing an unripe plum. 'You should think yourself fortunate I have not cast you and your grandmother out into the street.'

'I am grateful,' Magdalen replied demurely, although she knew Marie's charity had more to do with pragmatism than compassion. The Mountjoys' business was thriving and they could ill afford to lose an experienced 'tire maker.

Magdalen sat down at the bench without enthusiasm. She had little inclination to fashion fripperies to adorn a wealthy woman's head when her own life was crumbling to dust. And then there was the comparatively trifling matter of the Earl of Southampton's commission. She had no funds to buy cloth. Might it be possible to fashion the cloak from the cut-offs in her work basket?

Marie Mountjoy picked up a measuring block and rapped Magdalen's knuckles, hard. '*Depeches-tu!*'

Magdalen stifled a wince. From the corner of her eye, she saw young Mary snigger behind her hand, and a familiar feeling of loneliness unfurled in Magdalen's heart. Swallowing hard, she forced herself to concentrate on the head 'tire, an extravagant fancy floating upon a framework of silver gilt wire. Lady Gerard had requested a nautical theme to celebrate the anticipated home coming of her husband, an admiral, so Magdalen had spent many hours fashioning a tiny ship sailing upon a frothing sea of gauze and lace. Its rigging was of fine-drawn wire; its sails of sarcenet silk.

The 'tire was almost complete. All that remained was to dot the heavens above the ship with 'stars' of pearls to symbolise Lady Gerard's purity and faithfulness. They had been delivered yesterday, the purse now safely under lock and key. Magdalen grimaced at the task ahead. Gluing the pearls to the delicate framework was difficult, painstaking work, made harder by the lack of light. She had no doubt her eyes would soon be bloodshot and sore. And the smell of the glue, a foul compound of boiled horses' hooves, never failed to give her a pounding headache.

Further along the bench, Mary was drawing slender filaments from a sleave of raw silk, in preparation for twisting them into thread. Marie was at the spinning wheel, creating a miniature corded rope by twisting Venice Gold, thin strips of gilded silver spun about with silk thread. Her brow was furrowed in concentration, for the tension of the wheel had to be just right. Too slack and the cord would not hold together, too tight and it would kink.

Sensing Magdalen's gaze, Marie stopped the wheel.

'You want the pearls,' she said flatly. 'I warn you, I have counted them.'

Magdalen, wounded by the implied insult, did not reply.

'Madam?' Margaret stuck her head around the workshop door. 'Mistress Bassano is come.'

Marie shot to her feet, her hands hovering around her head like a pair of agitated gnats, fretting and patting, tucking stray hairs into her coif. Her fidgety fingers darted next to her bosom.

After a rapid assessment, she tugged at her bodice until a decorous hint of cleavage remained on show. Finally, she untied her apron and flung it aside, frantically straightening invisible creases from her gown. Satisfied at last, she hurried from the workshop.

'She wishes to look her best for the customers,' Mary whispered apologetically, looking up from the sleaves of silk and directly into Stephen Bellott's eyes.

'A laudable sentiment,' Stephen replied gently.

'You are kind to say it.' Mary's smile lit up the dark workshop.

Mary and Stephen continued to gaze adoringly at each other until Tom began to noisily kiss the air, and Rich feigned a dramatic, love-sick swoon.

'Magdalen!' Marie shouted from the hall. '*Viens ici!* Bring your workbook.'

Magdalen hastily wiped the grin from her face.

It was fortunate Margaret had recently cleaned the hall, for the scent of lavender beeswax polish went some way towards masking the lingering aroma of boiled eel pie. Amelia Bassano was seated in Marie's best chair, as regal as a queen. Her two ladies-in-waiting stood on either side, like prettily adorned book ends.

Magdalen dropped a curtsey. She thought the Lord Chamberlain's lover looked strained and unwell, despite her perfectly painted face and seductive, belladonna eyes. The Theatre's banqueting chamber was often beautified with her kind; exquisitely dressed dolls with their fluttering fans and yapping lap-dogs. Magdalen had always considered them to be strange, alien creatures but now she found herself wondering if Amelia was not so different from Anne and Margaret after all. Had she been similarly coerced; forced to submit to a powerful man, old enough to be her grandfather?

'Her Ladyship requests a new design,' Marie announced loftily, attempting to emulate Amelia's courtly inflection. Unfortunately, the combination of strangled vowels and a strong French accent rendered her virtually incomprehensible, and Magdalen wished she would stop. Amelia regularly commissioned head 'tires from the Mountjoys' workshop. It did not appear to matter to her whether Marie was French, English or a Barbary Coast Moor.

Magdalen opened her workbook, pencil poised, and waited.

'Jewels. Does Your Ladyship have a preference?' Marie asked deferentially. Amelia Bassano was not entitled to be addressed as 'Your Ladyship'. She was not a lady in any sense of the word, but Marie took great pains to flatter her customers into parting with their wealth.

'Perhaps rubies?' Amelia replied.

'An excellent choice, Your Ladyship. A truly excellent choice. They will compliment your colouring magnificently. Now, for the design…'

Marie turned expectantly to Magdalen, and her heart sank. Her brain was sluggish, as clogged as Houndsditch, and entirely lacking in inspiration. But Marie's gaze was fixed upon her; her stare so pointed Magdalen could almost feel it pierce her skin. Escape was evidently impossible, so she began to tap her pencil rapidly against her workbook, its frantic drumbeat calling her tired brain to muster. This might be the last head 'tire Amelia wore in society with Lord Hunsdon before she entered a loveless marriage with her sodomite cousin. This head 'tire needed to be spectacular, memorable. It needed to encapsulate their time together.

But inspiration proved elusive. Each time Magdalen tried to focus on a head 'tire, she saw the gallows at Tyburn instead. Marie did not hide her growing irritation. Her bosom was rising and falling feverishly; every rapid exhalation a tiny staccato of air.

Her impatience was an even greater distraction for Magdalen than the louring image of the gallows. She turned aside, closed her eyes and concentrated her thoughts on Amelia. How her mesmerising beauty had effortlessly captivated the players. How her hips had swayed as she walked across the yard to join the Lord Chamberlain. How his smile had been for her alone.

Suddenly, it came to her. He had whispered endearments in her ear. He had called her his 'precious sunbeam'. Magdalen opened her eyes and turned to Amelia.

'Rubies bring to mind the beauty of a sunrise, Your Ladyship,' she began. 'If I may be so bold as to suggest a design featuring the sun's beams radiating from a central orb? It would give height to the 'tire, and -'

'Yes.' Tears washed Amelia's eyes. 'That would be…' She visibly gathered herself before continuing, 'that would be suitable.'

Magdalen was taken aback. Was it possible Amelia felt genuine affection for the Lord Chamberlain? Or were her tears for the comfortable, privileged life she was about to lose?

Marie, ever heedful of her clients' delicate sensibilities, feigned not to notice Amelia's momentary distress. '*Tres bien, tres bien.* We will sketch the design for your approval, Your Ladyship. It will be delivered to you later today.'

'There is no need.' Amelia's eyes darted briefly towards Magdalen. 'I am confident the design will be to my liking. I will have the rubies sent to you in due course. And now, I wish you good day.' She stood up slowly, perhaps wary of a swoon. Her ladies, sensing her uncertainty, fluttered closer still.

'Good day to you, Your Ladyship. If you would permit me,' Marie began but Amelia was already half way to the door, her gown sweeping lightly across the boards, a soft murmur of silk.

Marie waited until they were alone before rounding on

Magdalen. 'Another commission! Mark me, girl, you need to work faster. Much faster.'

Magdalen gritted her teeth against the regiment of barbed retorts poised on the tip of her tongue.

'Yes, Mistress Mountjoy,' she replied.

The bells of Saint Olave's had long since struck ten before Magdalen escaped the workshop. She found her grandmother still asleep, the breakfast tray untouched on her night table. Racing downstairs again, she grabbed her cloak and hurried out. It was still raining, the potholes of Shoreditch reflecting a heavy pewter sky. At the Theatre, a fresh graffito had been daubed on the 'tiring house door. The paint was running in the rain, the letters elongating like melting candle wax:

You will rot in Hell.

Magdalen's heart faltered. Was this the work of the Puritans? Had they murdered John? And if so, were all the players in danger now?

In the 'tiring house, Will Shakespeare was sitting cross legged on the floor, ink horn at his side, quill in hand, amending the prompt sheets.

William Kempe was morris-dancing along the top of Magdalen's work bench and singing loudly:

'The woman, the spaniel and the walnut tree,

The more you beat them the better they'll be…'

No-one was paying him any attention, although reels and ribbons were flying in all directions like fireworks over Greenwich Palace.

'Get down from there!' Magdalen shouted angrily but he paid her no heed.

Peter was chasing Slinko about the room, attempting to tip a cup of what Magdalen hoped was small beer over his friend's head. Slinko, wiry and fast, was effortlessly running rings around the smaller boy.

William Sly and Christopher Beeston were standing side by side, Sly's dark curls contrasting with Beeston's shaggy blond mane. They were sharing a pipe of tobacco, and a cloud of smoke hung over their heads. Young Alex Cooke loitered close by, as keen as a puppy, but they were ignoring him. Drawing the smoke into their mouths, they proceeded to snort it out through their nostrils, along with a large amount of snot and phlegm. Henry Condell walked past, coughing and waving his hands in an attempt to dissipate the smoke.

'No more!' he pleaded. 'Don't you know your breath stinks like the piss of a fox?'

'Tobacco weed is good for you,' William Sly said smugly. 'Keeps the French pox at bay.'

'Only because you reek so badly no woman will come within fifty yards of you!' Condell replied.

Magdalen stood, unnoticed, in the midst of the mayhem. A small part of her felt cheered by the players' good humour, a world away from the misery of the Mountjoys' workshop. At the same time, she felt deeply unsettled. John had been dead for less than two days and already the players seemed indifferent to his absence. Admittedly, death was a part of life in the city, where the bloody flux and the sweating sickness carried loved ones away within a matter of hours, but John had been *murdered*.

The door opened and Burbage strode into their midst.

'Enough!' he shouted. Peter and Slinko instantly slid to a halt; William Sly extinguished the pipe, and Kempe brought his jig to a dramatic finale by somersaulting from the work bench and landing on both feet. Peter began to clap enthusiastically but was silenced by a warning shake of the head from Henry Condell.

Magdalen felt herself start to blush with shame. She had made no attempt to control the players' high-spirits whereas Burbage had achieved order in a heartbeat. What would her grandmother make of her negligence?

'John would understand we must continue to perform,' Burbage announced, looking around at the players' sombre faces, daring them to object. None did. 'To that end, I have chosen Richard Cowley to take the role of Beatrice in *Much Ado About Nothing* this afternoon.'

Magdalen watched Richard's eyes light up with delight. Alex Cooke glared at him and she realised he too had been hoping for the role. As the players moved on stage to rehearse, Magdalen pulled Richard aside and looked him and down. He was several inches shorter than John so she stood him on the three-legged stool, dressed him in Beatrice's gown and began pinning up the hem. The task required little concentration and her mind began to drift towards melancholy. John had been the last person to wear this gown.

'Something on your mind, Maggie-kins?' Richard asked.

Magdalen looked up at him thoughtfully. 'You and John were close fellows. Did he ever speak of any problems, or of anyone who wished him ill?'

'What a sly, nasty creature you are!' Richard's plump lips twisted into a sneer. 'You simper and you smile, but truly you are a snake in the grass!' Jumping down from the stool, he tripped over the gown's half-pinned hem in his haste to be away from her.

Magdalen watched him go, bound up with bewilderment. She had supposed her question a reasonable one, so why had he reacted with such venom? With a deep sigh, she sat down at her cluttered work bench. Her gaze settled on Richard the Third's 'hump-back', a stark reminder she had no time to wallow in self-pity. Threading a thick bodkin, she set about fashioning some sturdier straps. Through the open door to the stage, she could hear lazy, dim-witted Dogberry, played by Will Kempe, instructing his fellow watchmen on how best to fulfil their duties:

'I think they that touch pitch will be defiled. The most peaceable way for you, if you do take a thief, is to let him show himself what he is and steal out of your company.'

Magdalen wondered what Edmund Stow must make of Dogberry? Was it possible she was paying the price for Will's blatant mockery of the constables and watchmen of the city?

Someone was knocking on the 'tiring house door.

'Magdalen, are you fucking deaf?' Kempe yelled from the stage.

Magdalen scowled in Kempe's direction. Nevertheless, she stood up and went to the door. The girl standing in the rain looked strangely familiar although she couldn't fathom why.

'Forgive my intrusion,' the girl began, her cheeks flushing. 'I am John's sister, Louisa Du Bois. I am come to give you details about the funeral.'

Magdalen was taken aback. She had been unaware John even had a sister.

'You must be Mistress Bisset?' the girl went on.

Magdalen continued to stare open mouthed at this stranger with John's eyes. She had always supposed John was a Londoner born and bred, so why was his sister speaking with a French accent?

'Perhaps this is not a convenient time? I will leave you.' The girl's huge, blue eyes were wide and apologetic.

'No, please, come in out of the rain. And please, call me Magdalen.'

'Likewise, you must call me Louisa.'

Magdalen led the girl to her workbench and offered her the chair. Pulling up the stool, she sat down opposite her. John's sister was somewhere in her early twenties. She was plainly dressed, with the careworn appearance of a woman who worked hard to put food on the table. Dark hollows encircled her eyes and Magdalen noticed her hands were red-raw.

'May I offer you my deepest condolences,' she began.

'Thank you.' Louisa's eyes were full of suppressed pain. She hesitated for a moment. 'You were with him when he passed away?'

'Yes.' John's last words were echoing around Magdalen's skull: *'this is your fault.'* Guilt tore through her. If she had recognised the signs of poisoning sooner, might he still be alive?

'I have heard the terrible lies Edmund Stow is spreading,' Louisa went on quietly. 'I want you to know I don't believe them. John spoke so fondly of you. He said you were *une amie*, a friend. I know you would never do him harm.'

Her kindness was almost Magdalen's undoing, and hot tears pricked her eyes. 'Thank you. It means a great deal to hear you say that.' She swallowed hard, gathering herself. 'If you will permit me, there is something I must ask you. Do you know why someone would want to hurt John? Did he have any enemies?'

'He didn't make enemies. The Theatre was his life.'

Magdalen hesitated, uncertain how to proceed. Did Louisa truly not know about John's gambling, his debts, his aristocratic lovers? Or was she lying to protect him, even now?

'I understand,' she said tactfully, 'but did you perhaps notice anything different about John in the weeks before he died?'

Louisa thought for a moment. 'Well, there was one matter I found curious. He struck up a friendship with Adam Cooper.'

'The Puritan?' Magdalen asked incredulously.

'Aye,' Louisa replied. 'They were like brothers.'

Magdalen was stunned. Not two days since, Adam Cooper had humiliated her and decried all players as sinful devils. Why would he choose to befriend John Wood? It didn't make any sense.

'Adam is a good man,' Louisa said earnestly.

Magdalen was tempted to strongly disagree. Instead, she asked levelly, 'did Reverend Cooper show you kindness?'

'Aye, he did. You will know John and I are of French descent.' Louisa's eyes were starting to fill with tears. 'We go to church, we work hard, but still we are regarded with suspicion. These last few years, it's become intolerable. People call us dirty foreigners, they throw stones, and worse, through our windows. But Adam was kind to us. He wasn't afraid of the gangs of apprentices who taunted John and me. He threatened them with the wrath of God, and chased them away with his Bible in his hand.'

Magdalen was finding it hard to reconcile this portrait of Adam Cooper with the man who had accosted her in the Stocks Market. Endeavouring to hide her bewilderment, she asked, 'how did John and Adam meet?'

'I couldn't say, but I do know Adam was trying to persuade John to renounce the playhouses. He wanted John to accompany him to his prayer meetings. They spent a great deal of time together and I would hear them laughing. They seemed to enjoy each other's company but a few weeks ago, that all changed. They began to argue and then one evening I heard Adam shout, 'You're a fool, John, don't do it', or some such, and then he ran out of the house. I asked John what they were arguing about. He said they were discussing religious matters. I haven't seen Adam since that day. After John died, I hoped he might call to offer his condolences. I went to his lodgings, but his landlady said he hadn't returned. No-one knows where he is.'

An idea was forming in Magdalen's mind. It was reckless and foolhardy but tempting nevertheless. 'Do you know where these prayer meetings take place?'

'John said they meet in the old, disused pest-house across

Spitalfield, by Saint Andrew's church. The meetings are held in secret, so where better? People tend to give pest-houses a wide berth.' She reached into her cloak, brought out a small cross made from plaited reeds and handed it to Magdalen.

'Adam gave this to John.'

Magdalen turned it over in her palm. It was embroidered with three letters in red wool: 'TGC'.

'What do the initials stand for?'

'I don't know, but Adam told John that if he wanted to attend a prayer meeting, he would gain admittance by the cross.'

'And do you know when they meet?'

'Thursday evenings at seven o'clock.'

'May I keep this?' Magdalen held up the reed cross.

'If you want.' Louisa was fighting to hold back her tears. 'I wish I knew where Adam has gone. I hoped he might help me. I'm all alone now John is gone and I'm afraid that without Adam's protection the apprentices will come back.'

'You're not married?' Magdalen asked gently. 'Your surname is different to John's.'

'I am not married. John changed his name when he became a player.'

'Ah, yes,' Magdalen said, suddenly understanding. *Bois* was French for wood. John Wood.

'I was John's housekeeper,' Louisa explained. 'I also take in wool to spin, and laundry.' She glanced down at her blistered hands, ruined from repeated immersion in unforgiving lye-soap. 'But without his pay from the Theatre, I will not have nearly enough to pay the rent -'

Both girls turned in unison, distracted by the sound of loud knocking.

'For God's sake, Magdalen! Answer the fucking door!' Will Kempe yelled from the stage.

Louisa stood up hurriedly and straightened her apron. 'Forgive me, I have taken up too much of your time. I will leave you. The funeral is on Wednesday, Saint Leonard's church, eleven o'clock.'

'We will attend,' Magdalen promised. 'And if you need anything, we will help in any way we can. May I ask where you live?'

'We live...' her chin wobbled. 'No... *I* live by the sign of the one-legged man, in Tenter Street.'

Magdalen reached out and touched her arm. 'I know it,' she said softly. 'God keep you until we meet again.'

Louisa smiled wanly. 'Farewell.'

Magdalen opened the door and found herself face to face with Matthew Hilliard, who was standing in the rain. Louisa stepped out into the street and he acknowledged her with a small bow, which surprised Magdalen for most gentlemen would have spied her simple apparel, and chosen to ignore her. Blushing, Louisa bobbed him a curtsey and hastened away.

He turned to face Magdalen again. 'Mistress Bisset, do you remember me? My name is Master Hilliard?'

Of course she remembered him. How could she forget such a face, or that slow, deep, mesmerising voice? She thought back to their encounter two days since. So much had happened, it seemed a lifetime ago. His apparel had been of the finest quality then, but he looked markedly different today. His doublet was a plain affair, devoid of ornament. His boots were work-a-day, and there was no sword at his belt.

'How may I be of assistance?' she asked, although she guessed why he had come. He hoped to audition, and his apparel was an attempt to dress the part of a player.

He glanced up at the falling rain. 'Might I come in?'

She hesitated, uncertain. Why was he feigning to be someone

125

he was not? In truth, there were a thousand reasons to turn him away, not least because it was highly unlikely Burbage would employ a man with no experience of the stage, no matter how snout-fair. And yet, Matthew Hilliard had shown kindness to her, when so many others had treated her with contempt.

'Mistress Bisset?' he prompted.

'Yes. Yes. Forgive me.' Stepping aside, she gestured for him to enter.

'I hope you are in good health, Mistress Bisset?' he enquired, looking about the untidy 'tiring house. He was so calm, so self-composed, and she realised she could not imagine him ever losing his temper.

'I am well, thank you. And are you also in good health?'

He gave a small nod. 'I pray you have not been pestered by ranting Puritans since we last met?'

Magdalen thought of the daubs on the 'tiring house door.

'Not personally, no.'

'I am glad to hear it.' He paused. 'I came to *Twelfth Night*. I saw what happened to the player. My condolences to you all.'

'Thank you.' Unwelcome, painful images seared across her mind and she pushed them aside with difficulty. 'You wish to try your hand as a player? Is that why you have come?'

'Yes. The fencing bouts pay poorly, and my landlord grows impatient for his rent.'

He wandered over to her workbench, prodded Burbage's hump-back, and raised a questioning eyebrow.

'Richard the Third,' she explained.

'Ah, yes.'

He turned then, blasting her with the full force of his devastatingly attractive smile, and Nashe's line sprang unbidden into her head: *'He rubbed, and pricked, and pierced her to the bones...'*

She quickly glanced away, mortified.

126

'I am aware this is a great imposition,' Matthew continued, seeming unaware of her discomposure, 'but if I might meet with Master Burbage, I would be eternally grateful. And so would my empty belly.'

He didn't look under-nourished. He had a magnificent figure, sturdy enough to re-take Calais single-handed. She knew he was waiting for her reply, but what to say? The pox-ravaged two-penny whores in the yard would adore him. So too would the ladies in the galleries, the periwigged courtesans, the plump merchants' wives, the be-jewelled noble ladies. Was there a small chance Burbage would also look favourably upon him?

'I will ask Burbage if he will hear you read, but do not raise your hopes too high. Have you prepared a piece?'

'A piece?' he repeated, bemused. 'Ah, unfortunately not.'

Magdalen found it hard to credit he had come totally unprepared. She was at a loss, and then she remembered the prompt books on the back of the stage door. Tattered pages held together by twine, the text barely legible and covered in hastily scribbled stage directions, but she supposed they were better than nothing. Unhooking a particularly well-worn book, she began to rifle through it.

'Have you seen Will's *Henry the Fifth*?' she asked, thumbing to the relevant page. Matthew Hilliard was a tall, imposing figure; he would be perfect for the role.

'No. As I said, I am late come from Oxford.'

So, he knew nothing of Will's plays, and he had never acted before. Burbage would not take kindly to this fool's errand, and she would only have herself to blame. But it was too late to turn back now.

'This is the Saint Crispian's Day speech,' she said, handing him the prompt book. 'King Henry is rallying his troops before the battle of Agincourt.'

'Thank you. Truly.'

There was that smile again, softening his piercingly blue eyes. It took enormous effort to tear her gaze from him.

'Wait there.'

Burbage was not for hearing him, glaring at Magdalen over the prompt book for *Much Ado About Nothing*.

'Tell him to go away.'

'But don't we need of another player, now that John is...' her voice trailed off.

'Does he have experience?' Burbage sounded impatient.

'Yes,' she lied.

'And is he snout-fair?' Richard Cowley asked eagerly.

'Yes.' The truth this time.

Will Kempe sniggered and licked his lips.

Burbage slapped the prompt book against Will's chest.

'Bring him in. I'll give him five minutes.'

Magdalen led Matthew Hilliard to the stage and watched him slowly turn full circle, his gaze sweeping over the Theatre's myriad illusions: The wooden stage pillars painted to resemble creamy pink marble; the gaudy walls mimicking ornate plaster mouldings and, high above the players' heads, a wooden canopy of stars fretted with golden fire.

'Never seen a theatre before, man?' William Kempe asked snidely.

Hilliard's glance of cool disdain rendered Kempe momentarily speechless. He opened his mouth and closed it again several times. With his bulbous eyes and pocked marked cheeks, he looked uncannily like a bull-frog.

'Where are you from Master Hilliard?' Burbage asked.

'I am late come from Oxford, sir, but I was born and raised in Scotland.'

Scotland? That was the first Magdalen had heard of it.

'Aye, that explains it, for you do not sound like a Londoner.'

Burbage glared at Magdalen as if to say, 'why are you wasting my time with this man?'

'He has an audition piece,' she said hastily.

'Very well,' Burbage conceded. 'When you are ready, Master Hilliard, we will hear it.'

Matthew Hilliard walked centre stage, prompt book in his hand. The players gathered in a loose semi-circle around him, their mood reminiscent of a crowd awaiting a public hanging. Surrounded by ten players, whose expressions ranged from blatant hostility to mild curiosity, two sniggering apprentices and a concerned wardrobe mistress, Matthew Hilliard somehow managed to maintain an unruffled air as he gazed out at the empty galleries. The silence stretched on, and Magdalen noticed several of the players rolling their eyes. She stared at him, willing him to say something, willing him to prove his worth. Finally, he turned around.

His rendition was nothing like Burbage's portrayal of the great warrior-king. Burbage declaimed the speech to the audience. They were the massed ranks of his army, and he roused them to patriotic frenzy with his loud and passionate entreaty. But Hilliard had turned his back on the galleries to address the players instead. He looked at each of them in turn with a steady, purposeful gaze. His delivery was slow and mesmerising, his quietly spoken words for their ears alone. He was not addressing the entire army, but a handful of his closest fellows. It was intimate and moving, and tears came unexpectedly to Magdalen's eyes.

'But we shall be rememberèd—
We few, we happy few, we band of brothers;
For he today that sheds his blood with me
Shall be my brother; be he ne'er so vile….'

When he finished, Magdalen began to applaud, before realising no-one else was clapping.

Burbage was shaking his head. 'There's no power, no projection to your voice. I'm sorry lad. I can't hire you.'

Burbage made to walk away but Matthew Hilliard called after him, 'I beg your indulgence, sir!' Without waiting for Burbage's response, he strode to the front of the stage, faced the empty auditorium and launched into the final four lines of the speech again.

'And gentlemen in England now abed
Shall think themselves accursed they were not here,
And hold their manhood's' cheap while any speaks
That fought with us upon Saint Crispin's day.'

This time, he was addressing the entire English army. This time his voice projected loudly and clearly, booming around the galleries, and Magdalen marvelled at the transformation. When he turned around to face the players, a trace of arrogant kingship remained in the set of his shoulders, the jut of his chin, and the glimmer of authority in his eyes.

'I've made my decision. The answer is still no.'

Matthew Hilliard did not falter, but Magdalen could see the disappointment in his eyes.

Richard Cowley groaned. 'But look how snout-fair he is. It's a crime to send him away.'

'Aye,' William Kempe agreed heartily.

'It's true the groundlings would appreciate his fair features,' Burbage replied, 'but we need players for the female roles and he will never pass for a maid.'

Will Shakespeare was eyeing Matthew Hilliard thoughtfully.

'I think we should give him a chance.'

'Are you gone mad?' Burbage snapped. 'It's obvious the man has never acted before, despite his claims. He has no idea how to move on stage, or project his voice, and I haven't the time or the money to train someone from scratch.'

'I'll teach him myself,' Will said. 'Master Hilliard has talent. It's raw and untamed but we should at least attempt to harness it.'

'I have made my decision.' There was something vaguely menacing in Burbage's tone.

'You should reconsider,' Will shot back.

The already strained atmosphere grew glacial. Will and Burbage continued to glare at each other, engaged in a silent battle as fraught as a pistol dual on Shoreditch common. Magdalen sensed there was more at stake here than the hiring of another player. Burbage owned the Theatre, he paid the wages, his word was undisputed. Of late, however, the balance of power had begun to subtly shift, for it was Will's plays that filled the Theatre, day after day, and Will's plays that were chosen for performance before the Queen.

Burbage broke eye contact first. 'Five shillings a week, Master Hilliard, take it or leave it,' he said gruffly.

'I'll take it,' Matthew replied. 'Thank you for this opportunity, sir.'

'But you won't get a penny until you prove your worth, do you understand?'

'Yes, sir.'

Burbage turned to Will. 'He's your responsibility now. He will need to fence, fight, sing, dance and play at least one musical instrument. If he can't, then I have no use for him.'

Burbage stalked off stage, his ill- humour hanging over him like a storm cloud. On stage, the atmosphere remained icy. Magdalen could sense a great deal of resentment. The players had come up the hard way, as dogsbody apprentices, whilst Matthew Hilliard had simply walked off the street and into the role of player. The awkward silence stretched on. Henry Condell

131

finally broke it by shaking Matthew's hand and declaring, 'welcome to the Lord Chamberlain's Men, Hilliard'.

The other players followed his example, particularly Will Kempe, who embraced him for far too long.

Finally, Matthew turned to Magdalen. 'Thank you, Mistress Bisset. I am forever in your debt.'

'You are most welcome. And you should call me Magdalen.'

'Thank you. And you should call me Matthew.'

His smile lit up the stage. It warmed Magdalen's skin and set her heart pounding. Flustered, she retreated to the 'tiring house and made a show of tidying her workbench but she merely stirred the clutter about, her thoughts as tangled as knotted twine. She had been raised in the Theatre, grown up surrounded by handsome players with enough wit and charm between them to deflower all the virgins in London. But none of them had ever reduced her to this state of helpless idiocy.

Why was that? Perhaps it was because she had known the players half her life. She knew their foibles, their hopes and fears. In the space of one day, they could be funny, annoying, selfish, cruel and kind. In short, they were her family. They held no surprises. Matthew Hilliard, on the other hand, was full of surprises, a mystery she longed to solve.

She put a hand to her forehead and exerted pressure, attempting to drive all such nonsense from her head. She thought of the pretty whores in the Mermaid selling their bodies night after night. She had watched them sicken, slowly ravaged by the pox, until Francis Johnson threw them out to die, cold and alone. She did not want to share their fate.

She had sworn, as soon as she had been old enough to understand such things, that her virginity would be surrendered on her wedding night, and not before. But who would marry 'the players' whore'; a penniless girl without any hope of a dowry?

On stage, the rehearsal for *Much Ado About Nothing* had resumed. Through the open door she could see Matthew Hilliard standing to one side, prompt sheets in his hand, following the progress of the play.

'What you staring at, Mags?' Young Peter asked, bounding up to her workbench.

'Nothing.' Hurriedly, she picked up her bodkin and thread.

'Did I tell you Christopher Thomas and his gang of 'prentices burnt down a house full of Huguenots yesterday?' Peter asked excitedly. 'The 'prentices disappeared before the constable came but the Frenchies were burned alive. They say the street smelled like a hog roast, it was lucky the whole of London didn't burn, but it rained and that put a stop to it, good riddance to the dirty Frenchmen, I say.'

Magdalen put down her sewing.

'I want to you to listen carefully to me, Peter. John Wood was French. John, who gave you piggy-back rides. John, who carved wooden soldiers for you.'

'That's not true, Maggie! John was as English as Saint George!'

Magdalen wondered whether she should point out that Saint George was in fact a Turk, but decided against it.

'John was French,' she repeated calmly. 'I am also of French descent. My grandparents fled Paris after the massacre of Protestants on Saint Bartholomew's Day. Just like the Mountjoys. Just like hundreds of other French families.'

Peter looked dumbfounded.

'I was born in England,' she went on quietly. 'So, no-one takes me for a foreigner. No-one called me a filthy Frenchie. I'm lucky. Far luckier than most. Pray tell me, do you still think those poor souls deserved to burn?'

Peter shook his head. He was on the verge of tears but Magdalen was too angry for sympathy. 'The breastplates are rusty. They need sand scouring. Get to it! And no more talk of burning Huguenots, do you hear me?'

She watched him as he skulked away. In truth, she had told him only half the story. Unlike the Mountjoys, Agnes Bisset and her late husband Pierre were not fleeing religious persecution. They were devout Catholics, seeking a better, more prosperous life. Hidden in plain sight amongst their French Huguenot neighbours, the watchers had never given them a second glance.

The rehearsal ended at one o'clock with a delivery of hot pies from the tavern by the Crown and Cushion. The players ate on stage, their fingers glistening with grease, their laps covered with crumbs. By half past one, the audience was flooding in, the hubbub reverberating around the Theatre like cannon fire. Burbage gave Matthew the task of selling the fruit, nuts and gingerbread. The groundlings in particular paid him a great deal of attention, the women flirted prettily, the men laughed at his jokes and he quickly sold all the wares.

Lord Hunsdon and Amelia Bassano took a private box. Magdalen, conscious of the Theatre's need to keep pace with the court's latest fashions, peeked around the stage door and scrutinised Amelia's apparel. In the place of a ruff, she wore a pearl-edged standing collar of the finest lace. Her extravagantly padded sleeves matched her stomacher; creamy velvet silk, embossed and pinked into a pattern of tiny daisies and studded with pearls. Her false, hanging sleeves, so long they almost touched the floor, were a rich tawny orange to match her skirts, and decorated with striking, serrated edges.

A golden phoenix rising from the flames, Magdalen thought in awe.

There was no money in the Theatre's coffers to buy such extravagant attire. She would have to fashion its likeness by altering an existing gown. It would entail a vast amount of labour, and already there were not enough hours in the day. But she could not countenance the idea of Burbage's troupe appearing the poor relation to Henslowe's mighty empire on the south bank.

Magdalen's gaze focussed on Amelia again. Although clearly visible to the rest of the audience, Lord Hunsdon had cast aside all decorum and pulled her onto his knee. It was obvious his hand was up her skirts because she was writhing like an eel.

Once the performance began, Burbage ordered Matthew to copy cue scripts for Will's latest play. Magdalen cleared the end of her work bench and provided him with paper, quill and ink. She watched him pull up the chair, and watched him sit down. She knew she was staring, but she couldn't look away. He was so close now she could smell his distinctive, intoxicating scent, overlaid with clean starch and freshly laundered linen, and subtle hints of an expensive, musky perfume.

'*Romeo and Juliet*. Is this another comedy?' Matthew asked, studying the first page.

'I think not,' Magdalen replied. Will had pronounced it a comedy, but the play's ending was irrefutably tragic.

Matthew looked up then, directly into her eyes. She felt a jolt akin to a thunderbolt, and her face began to burn.

'I am to make ten copies?' He sounded apprehensive at the prospect of such monotonous, repetitive work.

'No, we don't have time.' Magdalen was aware she sounded out of breath, as if she had run from Silver Street to Shoreditch without stopping for a hot pie, but Matthew gave no indication of noticing anything amiss.

'It would take too long to copy out the whole play ten times, so we just give each player his own lines and cues,' she explained. 'Some players take more than one role, so keep an eye out, but Will should have marked them.'

Matthew was examining the script again. 'It's hard to make

sense of it. All these ink blots and crossings out.'

'You'll grow accustomed to his penmanship,' she assured him before springing to her feet to oversee a rapid costume change for William Sly and Christopher Beeston. Returning to the workbench, she picked up her sewing again, but it was impossible to concentrate when Matthew Hilliard's scent filled the air, when his very presence seemed to fill the room. She let out an involuntary cry as the needle pierced her thumb, and blood bloomed like a tiny red rose.

Matthew looked up. 'All well?'

She nodded, sucking her thumb and feeling like a fool.

On stage, she could hear Will Kempe as Dogberry veering wildly from Will Shakespeare's script, adlibbing at length on the pitfalls of drunkenness, how it provoked the desire for lechery, but took away the performance of it.

'It makes him stand to, and not stand to…'

The audience's uproarious laughter was fuel to Kempe's fire. There was little for the players to do but wait in the 'tiring house until he had run his course. Will Shakespeare's face was white with tension, anger emanating from his every pore.

'Get to it. We wait no longer!' he hissed, leaping to his feet and pushing Christopher Beeston and William Sly on stage. Magdalen caught a brief glimpse of Kempe. Holding Dogberry's staff with both hands, he stood astride it like a witch on a broomstick. The pole protruded from between his legs, one moment proud and erect, the next trailing forlornly across the boards. Egged on by screams of laughter from the yard, Kempe began to swing the staff from side to side, missing the top of the groundlings' heads by a matter of inches.

'Give me an excess of ale and I will piss the night away,' he crowed.

Kempe eventually left the stage to much cheering and

applause. In the 'tiring house, he patrolled back and forth like the Queen's caged lions at the Tower. He was grinning broadly, rubbing the top of his bald pate as if hoping a genie might spring from it.

'Did you hear them, Maggie?' he demanded, far too loudly. 'They love me. They fucking love me.'

'Keep your voice down,' she whispered. 'You know how noise travels.'

'Keep *your* fucking voice down, you witless shrew!'

Matthew leapt to his feet. 'That was uncalled for, Kempe!' he whispered furiously. 'I demand you apologise!'

Magdalen was astonished. The players tended to treat her either as part of the furniture, or as a little sister to be mercilessly teased. Such shows of gallantry on her behalf were rare indeed.

'Let it pass,' she said quietly.

Matthew shot her a questioning glance, and she shook her head. It was not worth the trouble of rising to Kempe. He was fired up, but he would cool soon enough.

Matthew sat down again, but continued to glare at Kempe with undisguised contempt.

'Like what you see, pretty boy?' Kempe waggled his arse. 'Gagging for it, are you?'

Burbage put a restraining hand on his shoulder. 'That's enough now.'

'I'm going for a piss,' Kempe announced, and went outside.

Magdalen could sense Matthew's pent-up anger. It seemed to ooze from his every pore. He snatched the quill again, thrusting it into the ink repeatedly as if he were trying to drown it. Magdalen noticed he wrote with a neat script, the exaggerated loops of each letter in perfect uniformity to the next. She didn't have the heart to tell him it wasn't necessary for the cue sheets to resemble legal documents, that speed was the essence, not perfection. The play progressed without further incident, and came to a roistering close with yet another of Kempe's lengthy jigs. Back in the 'tiring house, Will Shakespeare unfastened his sword belt and flung it across her workbench.

'There's a man with more hair than wit,' he muttered, glaring at Kempe's bald head.

Not half an hour later, the players left for the Mermaid, taking Matthew Hilliard with them on a swell of boisterous mirth. In the silence that followed, Magdalen turned full circle and surveyed the chaotic whirlwind of abandoned props and strewn apparel. Sighing, she got down on her hands and knees and put the props back in their boxes. She scooped up the costumes and laid them on her workbench. She treated the furs with fuller's earth. She brushed the finest silk costumes with a soft cloth, sprinkled them with marjoram and wormwood then carefully slid them into their soft linen storage bags. And all the while, her thoughts strayed to her conversation with John's sister.

Louisa had mentioned that Adam Cooper had left his lodgings. But was he still in London, and if so, would he attend the prayer meeting in the old pest house?

She had created a dour, black doublet for Malvolio, Will's parody of a humourless Puritan. Dare she wear it to gain admittance to the meeting? She had fooled the Earl of Southampton after all …

The bells of Saint Leonards were striking six as she left the Theatre. As she turned into Curtain Road, she came face to face with Edmund Stow. He looked more bloated than usual, inflated by his own self-importance. His eyes were squashed by puffy cheeks, his nose a button in a pillow of flesh. His expression oozed malice and her heart lurched with dread.

'I was coming to find you, girl. I have news. The coroner has set a date for the inquest. Friday the tenth of April.'

Magdalen's blood ran cold. April the tenth was less than two weeks away.

'And, I have a witness who saw you poisoning John Wood.'

'No, that's not possible!' she gasped. 'Your witness is lying!'

'He is an honest and reputable man, whereas you are a harlot, a liar, and a murderer. I will prove it, and I will watch you hang.' Magdalen stared at him, aghast. Had she wronged Stow in another life? What had caused this implacable hatred? Angry and afraid in equal measure, she spoke without thinking.

'Constable Stow, how much did you pay this *honest* man to malign me so?'

'How dare you? I will have you whipped, you insolent wench!'

Without warning, Stow raised his right arm, and struck her with the back of his hand. His signet ring tore a gash across her cheek. Stunned, Magdalen staggered backwards with the force of the blow. Through a haze of pain, she realised he was coming at her again. Turning on her heel, she ran, but she did not get far. Huge, paw-like hands landed on her shoulders, wrenching her to a standstill. He spun her about and then his hands were at her throat.

'Vile, sinful whore…'

It was as if he was gripped by madness, his fury sparking like flint. She tried desperately to claw his fingers away, but he was too strong. His grip was tightening. She fought for air but she couldn't breathe. Bright stars burst before her eyes. She had to do something. And fast. Dropping her hands to his shoulders, she kneed him hard in the groin. Instantly, his hands fell from her throat and he bent double. A strange wheezing sound escaped his lips, like a set of leaky bellows. Magdalen did not wait to catch her breath. She ran across Finsbury fields, past the gently turning windmills, and the quietly grazing cattle. Her eyes were blinded by tears and her lungs were aching, but she kept on running, desperate to escape from Edmund Stow and the madness in his eyes. Only when she felt her lungs might burst did she slow her pace to a walk.

'Magdalen?'

She glanced over her shoulder. It was Matthew Hilliard. Dear sweet Jesus, she didn't want him to see her like this. She gave a half-hearted wave, and continued walking. Undeterred, he ran to catch up with her.

'I thought it was you. I wanted to thank you again for the introduction. I am in your debt -' he noticed the gash on her cheek. 'What happened to you?'

'Nothing, I am quite well.' She kept walking, keeping her head down.

'Wait! Did someone hit you?'

She stopped reluctantly and turned around. 'Edmund Stow,' she said flatly, but even as she uttered his name, treacherous tears welled in her eyes again.

Matthew took a long stride and closed the distance between them.

'You should rest for a moment.'

Without waiting for her reply, he put a hand to her elbow, led her to the verge and sat her down. Magdalen closed her eyes and took some deep breaths. The air smelled fresher here than in the city, sweet with the fragrance of daffodils in the hedgerows, of primroses beneath the oak trees. Scents redolent of the wild flower meadows near her parents' farm. She had felt safe and loved there, but it was a long time ago.

'Who is Edmund Stow?' Matthew asked, crouching down beside her.

She opened her eyes. 'He is a constable. He has told the coroner I murdered John Wood.'

'What? Why?' Matthew asked incredulously.

'He says he has found a witness to speak against me. I was so angry, I accused him of bribing the man. And then he struck me...' She put her fingers to her cheek. The cut was still bleeding.

'He struck you?' Matthew sounded appalled. Extracting a clean handkerchief from his sleeve, he held it out.

Magdalen glanced at the fine linen and delicate lace, and shook her head. 'I can't. I would ruin it.'

'Nonsense. Take it.'

'As you wish. Thank you.' She dabbed her cheek gingerly.

'It is common knowledge that constables have no more brains than earwax but even so, this will not stand,' Matthew said forcefully. 'You must bring a charge of battery against him.'

Magdalen sighed. 'It would be a fool's errand. No-one will take my word against his.'

'Then what is Burbage doing to prove your innocence?' Matthew pressed.

'He says he will protect me,' she replied, her voice very small, 'but he is dependent on the patronage of the Lord Chamberlain. I know that if he is forced to make a choice, he will throw me to the wolves to spare his Theatre.' Her chin came up, a small, defiant gesture. 'I am alone in this. But I will find a way through it. I *have* to find a way through it.'

'You are *not* alone, Magdalen. I will help you in any way I can.'

The compassion in his eyes was unmistakeable, and it took her breath away.

'There is an inn nearby, by the sign of the Golden Lion,' he said gently. 'It's a reputable lodging house. You can rest a while, take a cup of wine. Perhaps you will allow me to clean the cut on your cheek before it becomes inflamed?'

He did not wait for her response. He stood up and offered his hand, but she did not take it. In truth, she was in half a mind to decline his offer. She was exhausted and in pain and she longed to crawl into bed and sleep. On the other hand, if she returned to Silver Street bleeding and in disarray, Marie Mountjoy would denounce her as a disgrace. After a long moment's hesitation, she gave a small nod, and allowed him to help her up. His hand closed around hers, and it was comfortingly strong and warm. For a brief moment she felt his grip tighten as if he might warm her cold fingers, but then he let go and stepped aside.

'If you will follow me,' he said courteously.

The inn was a clean and pleasant place, quiet in the early evening. He settled her beside the fire and went to speak to the landlord. Soon afterwards, Matthew returned with a bowl of warm water and a neatly folded linen cloth, and placed them on the low table. He hesitated for a moment, and she sensed his uncertainty.

'Would you prefer I ask for a serving girl to tend to you?'

Their eyes locked and held. Discomforted, Magdalen quickly lowered her gaze.

'It is no matter. You can do it,' she replied.

'As you wish.'

Kneeling down, Matthew dipped the cloth into the water and squeezed it out. His face was just inches from hers, his brow furrowed in concentration as he carefully bathed her cheek. She could smell the tang of beer on his breath, and lingering traces of tobacco smoke. And she could feel his fingertips against her skin. His touch sent tiny, feather-light shivers down her spine. Overwhelmed, she dropped her gaze to her lap again.

'All done. The wound is not deep. It should heal without a scar.' Sitting back on his heels, Matthew dropped the cloth into the bowl. Magdalen watched her blood bloom in the water, drifting clouds of rose red. She felt a strong sense of loss, of emptiness as he drew away from her, and she hid her confusion behind a wall of formality. 'I am most grateful. Thank you.'

Matthew leant forward again and peered at her throat. 'Are they finger marks? Dear God, did Stow try to strangle you?'

She nodded, angry with herself. Stow had shown himself to be unstable, dangerous. So why hadn't she treated him with more respect? Yet again, she had said the first thing that came into her head. She had aggravated the situation, and aggravated Stow. How could she have been so reckless?

'And yet you escaped?' Matthew asked.

'I… I kneed him in the …' Magdalen couldn't meet his eye.

Her blushes were spared by the arrival of a young girl bearing jugs of beer and wine. Matthew thanked her, and she rewarded him with a coy tilt of the head and a winsome smile, but he didn't seem to notice. The girl drifted away, clearly disappointed. Magdalen took a sip of her wine, and caught hints of sugar, cinnamon and ginger.

'Hippocras?' she queried, surprised. Such a drink was usually reserved for special occasions.

'Aye. They celebrated a wedding here recently.' Matthew tried his beer. 'I couldn't decide which to choose, the landlord has so many different brews. I settled on Angel's Food. It was the only one I felt I dare mention in your presence.'

Magdalen thought of the beers Marlowe liked to drink: Father Whoreson, Go-by-the-wall, and Lift-a-Leg. She smiled to herself.

Matthew was studying her over the rim of his cup.

'Let me help you,' he said suddenly.

'But you have helped me.'

'Not this. I mean with Stow.'

'Thank you for your kind offer, but unless you happen to know who murdered John Wood…' She shrugged her shoulders, the gesture heavy with despair. Dragging the jug of hippocras towards her, she refilled her cup and quickly downed it.

'Why doesn't Burbage petition the Lord Chamberlain to clear your name?' Matthew persisted. 'He is patron of the troupe. Surely it is in his best interests to avert a scandal?'

Magdalen shook her head. 'A player died on Burbage's stage. The whole of London is talking about it. Someone must hang for it. Justice must be seen to be done.'

'And you are to be the scapegoat?'

'It would seem so, yes.'

Magdalen poured more hippocras. Matthew refilled his cup of Angel's Food, and they sank into a heavy silence, each lost in their own thoughts.

'You could run away to sea,' Matthew said at last.

Magdalen assumed he was jesting. 'And become a pirate!' she replied, brightening at the thought. 'Attacking Spanish treasure ships and seizing their gold? They do say there are women amongst their crews.'

'You would be a pirate if you kept all the treasure for yourself, but if you donated half of it to the Queen, she would dub you a merchant adventurer and bestow you with a knighthood. It all comes down to perspective, doesn't it?' Matthew ran a hand through his thick dark hair; a quick, irritated gesture. When he spoke again, his tone was confessional. 'I enjoy Oxford. There is great solace to be had in quiet study and I am privileged to be taught by some of the greatest minds in England but, by and large, we study subjects which have little relevance.'

Magdalen glanced at him curiously. Only the sons of the wealthiest sort could afford a university education, although a few scholarships were available for a handful of gifted grammar school boys. Marlowe had benefitted from such beneficence. Magdalen thought back to her first meeting with Matthew Hilliard - his satin doublet, his soft leather boots, and the rapier at his belt. His apparel had spoken of his high status, of his wealth. He was no scholarship student.

The Angel's Food was loosening his tongue. 'Oxford is isolated, inward looking, a finely wrought cage. There is a new world out there, and I want to see it. Can you imagine Virginia, in all its infinite and wondrous variety?' His eyes were glinting with exhilaration. 'John White has sailed to the new world. He sketched the natives, the beasts and birds, the fishes, the plants and trees. It is a land of plenty.'

'Yes, I've read Thomas Harriot's account.'

'You have?' He sounded incredulous.

'I *can* read,' she replied tartly.

He looked embarrassed. 'Yes, of course, I know that. Forgive me.'

She had borrowed the book from Will, and pored over the extraordinary engravings of John White's original watercolours. The dark-skinned people of the new world were nothing like the English. They had black eyes, flat noses and broad mouths. They went barefoot and barely clothed save for flimsy attire made from animal skins. More often than not the women were bare-breasted. They carried their children slung over their backs, whilst the men shaved half their hair and styled the rest in outlandish fashions.

Their world was so alien as to be unfathomable. They danced around circles of upright posts, shaking rattles and worshiping pagan gods. They lived in leather tents. They flayed and sun-dried the bodies of their deceased chieftains, rather than interring them in the earth.

And yet, despite their savage appearance and outlandish customs, White had portrayed dignity and pride in the natives' posture and in their distant, benign smiles. And in the care with which they adorned their dark skins with swirling patterns of

145

paint and tattoos, with necklaces and ear-piercings of beads and feathers.

Queen Elizabeth was encouraging Englishmen to establish colonies in Virginia, and John White had played his part by depicting a land of peace and plenty. But it had proved to be neither of those things for the lost colonists at Roanoke, who had mysteriously disappeared without a trace. Had the collision of two such totally different worlds led to war? Or had starvation and disease brought about the colonists' demise?

She realised Matthew was staring morosely into the flames.

'So, you are disenchanted with your studies at Oxford. Is that why you are in London, seeking the life of a player?'

'I was forced to leave my studies. My father is,' he hesitated, 'my father has suffered a reversal of fortune.'

She noticed his fists were clenched, the rigid set of his shoulders betraying his torment. 'I am sorry, Matthew. Is there any hope of remedy for his misfortune?'

'Perhaps.'

His reply hung heavily in the air between them and Magdalen felt a sudden, inexplicable shiver of unease. Blaming the hippocras, she quickly brushed her disquiet aside but, yet again, Matthew had wrong-footed her. Who would have thought he hankered after the life of an adventurer? In her more fanciful moments, she had mused on such a life for herself, sailing the vast oceans, the thrill of unknown horizons, the exhilarating sense of freedom. What better way to escape Edmund Stow and the hangman's noose?

On the other hand, she had seen countless mariners in the Mermaid with their salt-bleached, toothless grins and their scabbed skin, as wrinkled as last year's apples. And she had listened to their stories; the storms and hurricanes, the floggings, the mutinies, the hangings. The constant danger of capture by

Barbary pirates, the horror of being taken as their slaves. The cramped darkness below deck, the disease. The madness brought on by months of meagre rations, crawling with weevils. And if, by some miracle, they survived to reach that far-flung shore, cannibals lay in wait with their poison arrows and flaying knives.

Matthew was still staring into the fire. It was obvious he was no longer in the mood for conversation. Perhaps he was a maudlin drunkard, like Will Shakespeare.

'The hour grows late,' she said. 'I should make for home.'

But, in truth, she didn't want to leave, no matter how withdrawn or surly Matthew had become. She wanted to stay here. With him. Until the fire died to embers. Until the tavern closed for the night. Until the stars fell from the sky.

'Yes, yes.' He sounded distracted and she wondered if he had forgotten she was there. 'I will see you safely home.'

They stood up in unison, and Magdalen swayed on her feet. She told herself it was the trauma of Stow's assault, but she knew the hippocras was to blame. Matthew did not say a word, but he stepped closer and put a steadying hand under her elbow. Heat rose within her. They came to her from nowhere, Marlowe's wicked lines from *The Amores*:

'…I clung to her naked body, down she fell,
Judge you the rest, being tired she bade me kiss.
Jove, send me more such afternoons as this….'

SIX

'Against knaves and thieves men shut their gate'

Tuesday 31ˢᵗ March
The Strand

Matthew Hilliard had not wanted to accompany the players to the Mermaid again. For the most part, he found prolonged company of any kind exhausting. His privileged upbringing had given him the skills to thrive in polite society, just as his years at university had taught him how to laugh and banter with the tavern crowd. But he much preferred solitude. So, he had matched Burbage's troupe cup by cup before making his escape when the players grew too inebriated to notice his absence.

His journey downriver towards the setting sun was hastened by an incoming tide. The surly wherry-man was in no humour for conversation and so, lulled by the lapping water and the steady plash of the oars, Matthew's thoughts began to drift. He had found himself drawn to Magdalen Bisset from the first moment he had laid eyes on her. He had followed her down Bishopsgate and watched as she browsed in the Royal Exchange, and posted the hand bills along Cheapside.

He had been struck by the shifting shades of colour in her hair. On first impression, it was a deep, chestnut brown but when the sun caught it, it gleamed with flashes of glowing amber. She wore no coif and her locks fell in long, loose waves down her back, like the gypsy girls who handed out sprigs of lavender and offered to tell your fortune.

And he had been intrigued by her striking attire. Most girls of his acquaintance wore apparel to suit their station, their waists nipped in by corsets and bodices, their hips widened by the hoops of a farthingale, their fingers prettified by jewels. But Magdalen's brightly coloured apparel was entirely novel to him. She wore no ruff, the delicate white skin of her throat exposed for all to see. And her kirtle, falling without artifice about those long, slender legs…

In truth, he had never met a girl quite like her before. Most women in his sphere were defined by their relationship to the man legally responsible for them. Magdalen, on the other hand, did not appear to belong to anyone. She was not answerable to a husband or a father or a brother. In many ways, she was free, and he envied her liberty to choose her own path.

Or perhaps he was being naïve? She worked hard, every hour of every day, to keep a roof over her head. In his own hitherto privileged life, he had been fortunate enough to avoid such a precarious state of affairs. Until now. Until the fateful day when his stars had crossed and his life had fallen to rack and ruin.

The bells of Saint Paul's were chiming seven as the boat moored at the landing stage of Essex House. Matthew paid the dour wherry-man and alighted, his gaze instantly drawn to the elegant river frontage with its gilded barge awaiting the earl's pleasure.

A wide, elegant stairway led up to formal gardens surrounding a mansion of vast, perfectly symmetrical proportions. A manservant in the earl's livery stood on sentry-duty at the top of the steps. He cast a scornful eye over the humble wherry, no doubt accustomed to greeting visitors arriving in far grander style.

'The earl is expecting me. My name is Master Hilliard,' Matthew announced, bounding up the steps and feigning a confident air. He noticed the manservant assessing his attire, and was grateful he had had the foresight to return to his lodgings and don a velvet doublet and strap his rapier to his belt. The man produced a sheet of paper and ran a finger slowly down a list of names. Matthew sensed he was enjoying making him wait. After what seemed an age, the man nodded and stood aside.

Sweet scents tickled Matthew's nostrils as he walked along a gravel path running between beds ablaze with tulips and daffodils. The formal gardens were an elaborate, manicured maze of low box hedges, fountains and greening rose arbours, but he had no trouble finding his way, for all routes led to the mansion, its mellow, ancient stonework bathed in the last rays of evening sunshine.

The main entrance was framed beneath an arch of such obvious antiquity Matthew suspected it was a survival from the original Outer Temple, headquarters of the infamous Knights' Templars. Suppressing a nagging sense of trepidation, he drew himself to his full and considerable height and announced himself to the usher.

After the noise and stink of Shoreditch, the earl's mansion had an air of perfumed luxury. A huge vase of tulips and daffodils, evidently freshly cut from the garden, stood upon a long, highly polished table. Hangings of rich, red fabric adorned the walls. The ancient stone pillars were painted red and gold. Matthew was led to a well-proportioned room off the main dining chamber. Nerves soured his gut as his gaze settled first on the stuccoed ceiling, then on the intaglio-embossed leather wall panels varnished to resemble gold, before coming to rest on the portrait hanging above the fireplace. The late Earl of Leicester looked every inch the king he had hoped to become; the arrogant gaze, the haughty stance, one hand on his hip, the other on the hilt of his rapier.

'My step father was a handsome man, was he not?'

Matthew turned sharply.

At twenty-seven years of age, Sir Robert Devereux, the second Earl of Essex, was in his prime. Dark brown curls framed an aquiline nose and a pair of green eyes that glittered with intelligence. Startlingly, his square-cut beard was dyed bright red, Matthew supposed in homage to the Queen.

'Your Lordship.' Willing himself to appear calm, he gave a French bow. As he slowly righted himself, his gaze travelled up a pair of slender legs encased in the finest silk stockings, then a doublet of dazzling white, before coming to rest upon Robert Devereux's handsome features once more.

'I have read your letter, Master Hilliard.' The earl's courtly accent was as clipped as a debased coin. 'I will speak plainly. I chose to receive you today in deference to my dear mother, who speaks highly of your own mater. I believe they were childhood friends.'

'That is correct, Your Lordship.'

'However, it must be said, your father is entirely responsible for his present misfortune. Picking the wrong side never ends well. How convenient you were studying in England at the time, or you would now share your family's fate.'

Matthew fought to maintain his composure. 'My father made a grave error of judgement by offering sanctuary to Francis Stewart. His actions were motivated purely by familial obligation,' he began, but the earl cut him off.

'Your father felt obliged to support a man who led an armed uprising against his own cousin, King James of Scotland? A man who stands accused of witchcraft? A man who, less than three months since, escaped captivity and attempted, yet again, to assassinate King James? A man who is currently in hiding? An outlaw facing charges of treason?'

A shiver of fear ran down Matthew's spine. He should not have come; he was making a terrible situation worse. And yet, how could he walk away? How could he abandon his father to a traitor's death?

Devereux was waiting for his reply. Matthew took a deep breath. 'My English grandfather refused to renounce his Protestant faith, and he was burnt at the stake on the orders of Queen Mary. There is a wood cut of his suffering in Foxe's Book of Martyrs. My family do not share Francis Stewart's political aspirations. We have no desire to avenge the death of the Queen of the Scots. No desire to be part of a Scottish invasion force. I swear to you, we abhor Catholicism, and all its Papist trappings.'

Devereux eyed him shrewdly. 'You enjoy studying at Oxford?'

'I do, Your Lordship,' Matthew replied, caught off guard by the earl's abrupt change of tack.

'How tragic then, that if your father is found guilty of treason, you will not only lose your good name, but also your inheritance. There are very few poor men at Oxford, unless they are exceptionally gifted. Are you exceptionally gifted, Master Hilliard?'

'No, Your Lordship, but I work hard.'

The earl took a turn about the room, encircling Matthew like a wolf closing in for the kill. 'I believe you have already met my man, Barton?'

'Yes, Your Lordship,' Matthew replied. Thomas Barton had made his skin crawl. A huge brute, disconcertingly dead behind the eyes.

'And have you done what Barton asked of you?'

'I believe I have found a way, Your Lordship.'

'You believe you have found a way?' Robert Devereux repeated sarcastically. 'I need more than vague trifles. I need evidence.'

'I have been hired as a player at Burbage's Theatre -'

The earl burst into laughter. 'You jest, surely?'

'I do not jest, Your Lordship.'

In truth, it had all happened so fast, and it had not gone to plan. He had intended to get the measure of Magdalen before approaching her for an introduction to Burbage. But then the weasel Puritan had stamped her playbills into the mud. It had been a spur of the moment decision to help her pick them up and, in retrospect, an unwise one. It was obvious she had noticed his fine apparel, and equally obvious she had questioned why he needed to debase himself as a player.

The earl was still laughing. Determined to prove his sincerity, Matthew said, 'I can dance, sing and fence. I have been taught rhetoric by some of the greatest minds in the land, and I have no doubt I can strut upon a stage. To quote my fellow students, what are players but leaden spouts, that nought do vent what they receive?'

Devereux raised an eyebrow. 'Convenient then, that there is an opening at the Theatre. I hear one of Burbage's players has died, and upon the stage, no less.'

'I swear his death was not of my making. I am no murderer.'

'But let us pray, for your family's sake, that you are an acceptable player. There are whisperings Richard Burbage's playhouse is a nest of Papists and I need to know the truth of it, or at least a form of the truth that will serve my purpose. Look first to William Shakespeare. Before he married, he worked as a tutor in Lancashire, in Alexander Hoghton's household, a Catholic family infamous for breeding traitors to the crown.

There is nothing to suggest Shakespeare has turned his back on his Papist leanings. I want to know everything about him. With whom does he share lodgings? With whom does he share his bed?'

'It will be done, Your Lordship.'

The earl tilted his head slightly. 'You are a hard man to fathom, Hilliard. I cannot imagine you perturbed or vexed. I warrant you will make a passable dissembler.'

If truth be told, Matthew felt a great deal more than vexed. His life in Oxford had been dull at times, but at least it had been safe and comfortable. Days spent in quiet, contemplative study; evenings spent drinking in the town's many taverns with his fellows. But now his life had been turned upside down.

His father should have refused to help Francis Stewart and his followers that night, but it would never have occurred to him to deny a kinsman in need. A lump formed in Matthew's throat. His father was a decent and honourable man. His mother was warm-hearted, strong-willed and full of energy, despite approaching her fortieth year. Edward, his younger brother, was not yet fifteen; a dreamer, a poet. Alice, his little sister, was mischievous, sweet and kind. He could not bear to think of them suffering the deprivations and indignities of captivity.

'Your Lordship, might a petition be made to King James on my father's behalf?'

'I did not take you for a naïve man, Hilliard. Surely you understand how delicate matters such as this must proceed?'

Matthew hesitated for a fraction too long.

'Must I spell it out for you?' The earl sounded impatient now. 'I need intelligence I can take before Her Majesty.'

'But that could take weeks,' Matthew began before he could stop himself.

'You must pray for your family's sake that it does not.'

Matthew's breath caught in his throat. He felt as if he was suspended over the fiery pits of Hell. He knew the earl was locked in a battle for political supremacy against the markedly ugly but fiercely shrewd Robert Cecil, one of the Queen's most trusted advisers on the Privy Council. At a court where the good service of intelligencers was powerful currency for Her Majesty, both men were desperate to establish their own far-reaching web of spies.

'I only need one. Give me one Papist, and he will give up the rest, for no-one can remain silent on the rack. He will squeal and squeal and the entire network will fall, from the lowest in the land to the highest. We will have them all. By God, we will!' The earl was breathless in his ardency.

'I will give you what you need, Your Lordship,' Matthew said quietly.

One way or another, he would provide proof.

One way or another, he would save his family.

He raised his hand to his forehead and wiped away a bead of sweat. Quite suddenly, the chamber had grown uncomfortably hot, as if the flames of Hell were licking against his skin.

SEVEN

'Come away death, and in sad Cyprus let me lie'

Wednesday 1st April

'If you were aware John Wood was unwell, why did you allow him to go on stage?' the coroner asked Magdalen accusingly.

He was a big man, but whereas Edmund Stow was a hill of soft flesh, Walter Wiseman was a giant mountain of hard muscle. He walked like a man wading through deep snow, bent slightly forward, broad shoulders moving in unison with his feet, ploughing all obstacles aside.

'And why did you not tell Master Burbage that the player was indisposed? Think carefully before you reply, because the deposition you give today will be put before the jury at the inquest.'

'He assured me all was well, and I took him at his word,' Magdalen replied nervously.

Walter Wiseman had arrived, unannounced, at the Theatre at eleven o'clock, with three jurors in tow. He had banished the players to the stage before calling them individually into the 'tiring house. One of the jurors, the printer Thomas Thomlinson, had requisitioned Magdalen's workbench. He had opened his writing box, laid out his quills, pen knife and inkpot in perfect alignment with the edge of the bench, and was now painstakingly creating an account of the entire proceedings.

'I am confused. A moment ago, you told me you had no doubt the player *was* unwell.' The coroner squinted over Thomlinson's shoulder to read his miniscule handwriting. 'Let me see, ah yes, you said he was sweating profusely, and his eyes were unfocussed.' He glanced at Magdalen. 'You must have known there a very real possibility he was about to collapse on stage, before hundreds of people. Tell me, was that your intention? Did you hope he would be humiliated?'

'No, sir.' Fear washed over Magdalen, relentless and ice-cold. Had Edmund Stow told Walter Wiseman about his alleged witness? And if so, did the coroner believe the constable's story?

'I ask again, why did you not tell Burbage that John Wood was unwell?'

'Because John told me not to fuss and I was worried he might be…' she broke off, unwilling to speak ill of the dead.

Walter Wiseman let out an irritable sigh. 'I am a busy man. It will not go well for you if you waste my time.'

'I was worried he was in his cups. There are heavy penalties for taking to the stage inebriated. I was trying to protect him.'

'Was he prone to inebriation?'

Magdalen hesitated. If the coroner had made even the most perfunctory enquiries, he would have been aware of John's predilections.

'I have warned you, girl! Your silence does you no favours!'

'No, he was not,' she lied.

'I believe you regularly frequent the Mermaid tavern?'

Magdalen bridled at the implied insult. 'I do, sir, with the players, but never on my own.'

'Then you know how a man acts when he is in his cups. Tell me, did you truly believe John Wood was drunk?'

157

Magdalen hesitated again.

'You *will* answer me!'

The coroner was glaring at her furiously, and she was finding it hard to breathe. Walter Wiseman was the Queen's legal representative. If she lied to him, she lied to God.

'No. I did not believe he was drunk.'

The coroner was just inches from her face now, a menacing gesture, designed to intimidate. 'First you tell me you were concerned the player was gravely ill. Next you tell me you believed him when he assured you he was in good health. Then you tell me you thought he might be inebriated. Next you admit you knew he was not. How can I believe a single word you say when you change your story at every turn?'

'I have told you the truth. I did not know what ailed John.'

'Do you deny you poured him a second cup of wine, moments before he went on stage?'

'I do not deny it.'

'You slipped poison into that cup, didn't you?'

She clenched her fists, her fingernails cutting into her palms. She must not show weakness. She must not show fear because men like Walter Wiseman could smell it a mile away.

She stood up straight, and replied, 'I did not, sir.'

He shook his head sceptically, and she knew he did not believe her. He had caught her scent and he was closing in for the kill.

'You gave John Wood poison because it was your intention to watch him die, slowly and painfully, out there on the stage so all would see his suffering, his agony.'

Don't shout. Stay calm, she told herself. *Don't give him the opportunity to paint you as a witless, hysterical harlot.*

'I had no reason to harm John. I thought of him as a brother.'

Walter Wiseman pursed his lips. 'A brother? Or a lover?'

'You insult me, sir. I am chaste -'

'It is hard to believe you are a chaste maid when you keep such disreputable company. I would never permit my daughter to watch a play, let alone associate with players.'

Magdalen stiffened. 'Your daughter is indeed fortunate to have such a worthy father. I have no such protection, and I must find work where I may. But Burbage's players treat me with respect. They are gentlemen -'

Wiseman laughed scornfully. 'They are *not* gentlemen. Scarcely a day goes by when a player does not stand before me accused of a violent crime. They drink and whore and brawl, and when it goes awry, which it often does, people die.' His expression hardened. 'Did John Wood abandon you? Did he cast you aside for another whore?'

Magdalen gritted her teeth. 'No!'

'Did he break your heart?'

Magdalen knew she had lost the battle. In truth, it had been lost before the first arrow flew. But still, she fought on.

'No, he did not!'

'Your love turned to hate, didn't it? You hated him so much you wanted him dead. So, you poisoned him.'

'A thousand times, no!' she shouted, her composure finally crumbling, but the coroner was no longer listening. She might as well have been back in Hampshire, standing on the hilltop near the farm, her words carried away by the wind.

EIGHT

'Be not amazed, right noble is his blood'

Thursday 2nd April

The moment Matthew awoke, his thoughts turned to Magdalen. Her copper-coloured hair, her charmingly outlandish attire, the way her skirts draped about her long, long, legs.

No, stop. You must not think of her in that way.

Dear God in Heaven, you must not think of her at all.

Keen for a distraction, he sat up and surveyed his chamber. The bed was ornately posted and thickly curtained, a haven of linen sheets, feather pillows and quilted covers. His discarded clothes lay strewn across an intricately carved chest. The walls were wainscoted and hung with fine tapestries. The table before the window was dressed with a Turkey rug, woven in the rich colours of autumn. And upon it, sat a silver bowl filled with lavender heads, their scent sweetening the air.

Matthew closed his eyes for a moment, and Magdalen's image drifted into his head again. He had told her more than he had intended at the inn by the Golden Lion, no doubt lulled into a false sense of security by Angel's Food. Nevertheless, he had lied to her about fencing at the Curtain, and needing the job at the Theatre to feed his empty belly. Indeed, he had lied to her at their very first meeting, and he had kept on lying to her ever since. In truth, he was a guest in the London home of his maternal uncle, Lord Askew. By the sign of the Harp at Whitefriars, it was a grand establishment; a confection of turrets and chimneys, oriel windows and brightly coloured glass. The family were absent, visiting their country estate in Dorsetshire, but the house was his to do as he pleased. The larder and the wine cellar were well stocked, the household servants at his beck and call.

He propped a pillow against the bed-head and punched it into shape. The violent gesture eased neither his confusion nor his guilt. He felt an inexplicable desire to protect Magdalen, but his role at the Theatre was to dissemble and deceive, to find proof of Popery, to ruin the players' lives so his own family might be saved.

What had possessed him to take Magdalen to the inn? He should have walked away and not looked back, for nothing good could ever come of their acquaintance. But he had not walked away. He had stayed exactly where he was, held fast by the sweetness of her smile.

He had watched many of his friends fall victim to Cupid's arrows, but he had always remained immune to the fatal dart. He had met many young women, some fair, some wise, some virtuous, and yet he had remained steadfastly unmoved by their charms. Perhaps one day he might succumb, if he were to find a woman blessed with all those graces combined.

She would also need to be of his own rank and of good dowry, because his father would never agree to a less advantageous match. But most of the young women of his station were so pampered, so shielded from the harsh realities of life. He knew they were not to blame for it, but he found their manners coquettish and simpering, their conversations vacuous and dull.

Magdalen, however, was the very opposite of dull. For a start, she drank like a man, and she was feisty and funny and kind. And full of courage. She was facing the death penalty for a crime he felt certain she had not committed, and yet she was finding the strength to go about her daily affairs. And then there was her smile. It truly was the sweetest smile.

The sound of knocking pulled him from his reverie. Dressed only in his linen undershirt, he got down from the bed and opened the door an inch. 'Yes?'

'Addressed to you, sir.' The steward turned the letter sideways and slid it through the gap between the door and its frame. Matthew recognised the seal. It was from his father.

'Thank you.' He walked to the window seat, broke the seal and started to read.

'My dearest son,

I wonder if you can imagine the torment of guilt and regret I am enduring, day after unforgiving day? I would give my soul to turn back time and undo my moment of utter folly. When I saw Francis in such a wretched, despairing state, I invited him into our home out of charity, out of love. But it was short-sighted of me. Francis is my distant cousin, whilst my wife and my children are my very being. I have brought such terrible suffering down upon you all. There can be no forgiveness for my weakness and stupidity. Even in this our darkest hour, your dear mother raises our spirits with her compassion and her bravery, and Edward and Alice look to her for comfort. No matter how much I blame myself, she tells me repeatedly that God will not view an act of charity as a sin.

The trial has been set for Monday 20th April. You are a grown man, so I will not insult you by spouting false platitudes. You know as well as I that it is rare for the accused to be found 'not guilty' of treason. Francis Stewart's current liberty is a severe embarrassment to King James. He must have had help to escape from Edinburgh Castle and the king is relentless in his pursuit of all those he suspects of aiding and abetting him.

My dear Matthew, I know I will be convicted and I know I will be put to death. I have come to terms with this and made my peace with God. But I fear for your mother, and for Edward and Alice. The king knows Scotland is not safe whilst Francis's rebellion simmers on. Francis can call upon the might of our Catholic enemies, even the Pope himself, for support. And I dread that King James will make an example of not only me, but also our family. I dread hearing the news that he will not grant them clemency.

I had sworn to myself that I would not ask this, but my love for our family has forced my quill to the paper. If there is any influence to be brought at the English court, then, my dearest son, I beg you to try, not for my sake, but for your mother and your brother and sister, who are entirely innocent of these charges.

I will conclude by stating that if you do not succeed, or if there is nothing that can be done, then you must not blame yourself. You are faultless in this matter. I am wholly responsible for the calamities that have befallen our family, and I will go to my grave shamed and dishonoured. But you, Matthew, I would ask you to live on, for your mother's sake, for my sake. Don't look back. Children should not carry the sins of their fathers. You were a good child, and you have grown into a good man. I pray you will be blessed with a long and happy life.

From your loving father,

Ralph Hilliard

Matthew ran his fingers over his father's signature. A sob escaped his throat and his tears began to fall.

NINE

'Dost thou think because thou art virtuous,
there shall be no more cakes and ale?'

Thursday 2ⁿᵈ April

'A TRUE AND HONEST ACCOUNT OF MURDER MOST
FOUL AT THE THEATRE IN SHOREDITCH AS TOLD BY
A PLAYER OF BURBAGE'S TROUPE WHO WITNESSED
AT FIRST HAND THE HORRIBLE DEATH OF JOHN
WOOD, POISONED BY A DOXY.

It is an undisputed truth that all manner of sinful pursuits occur within the
debased and lustful playhouses in the liberties of London. On Saturday 28ᵗʰ
March at Burbage's Theatre in Shoreditch, a wicked doxy of the playhouse
did poison the player John Wood with such foul ungodly potions that he died
horribly upon the stage with great effusions of blood and bile before the entire
audience.

Wherein, this immoral doxy who services the fraternity of players in their
lewd pleasures, confessed to the poisoning, for after John Wood drowned the
member of his virility in the bottomless barrel of her alleged virginity, through
which runs a field of unquenchable, unchaste fire, he did abandon her and
took up with another doxy. Therefore did she take her terrible and unnatural
revenge...'

Magdalen dropped the pamphlet onto her workbench.

Irresistible curiosity had driven her to buy it, but she couldn't bring herself to read any more of its damning, scurrilous nonsense. The quarto claimed the moral high ground but its true purpose was to shock and titillate, at her expense. It spoke of a witness, a player of Burbage's troupe. Could it be Richard Cowley?

She didn't know what to do. She didn't know where to turn, or who to trust. Edmund Stow was taking delight in blackening her name, and these wicked pamphlets were spreading his lies far and wide. The inquest would be held in eight days' time. What hope did she have for a fair trial? Wasn't she already as good as dead? And who would take care of her grandmother after she was gone?

The sound of laughter drifting down the corridor dragged her from her morbid thoughts. Burbage was entertaining the great and good of London in the banqueting chamber, and she was supposed to be serving refreshments.

Standing on tip-toe to reach the shelf above her workbench, she took down six of the best glasses. As she carefully placed them on the tray, the shoddily printed quarto caught her eye again. It seemed to be watching her, its malign presence taunting her. Crushing it into a ball, she threw it into her workbench drawer, out of sight, out of mind. But to no avail. Its cruel words stuck fast, as sharp as pins, 'immoral doxy', 'unchaste fire'.

Picking up the jug, she slowly poured the decanted claret into the glasses. The wine was of the highest quality; clear, without imperfections, pale blood-red. It reminded her of her own blood, slowly drifting through the bowl of water at the inn by the Golden Lion. If she closed her eyes, she could hear the crackle of the fire, and feel the gentle touch of Matthew Hilliard's fingers against her cheek. How might it be to lie with him in the marriage bed? She quickly pushed the thought away, angry with herself.

He had spoken of his family suffering a reversal of fortune; nevertheless, he remained far above her social standing. He would never marry a humble wardrobe mistress without dowry or connections.

She picked up the heavy tray, trying hard not to spill the claret as she walked slowly down the corridor. The sound of animated conversation grew louder as she neared the banqueting chamber. Burbage's gatherings were always well-attended. The nobility, resplendent in their fine clothes and glittering jewels, fawned and fluttered about Burbage's troupe like plain moths to bright, dancing flames. Magdalen never ceased to marvel at the Theatre's ability to turn the world on its head. Was a powerful wizard trapped within its oak frame, with nothing better to do than cast spells of topsy-turvy enchantment?

Magdalen entered the banqueting chamber, and immediately came to a halt. The Earl of Southampton had declined countless invitations to join Burbage and his players for refreshments, and yet here he was, talking to Will Shakespeare. She watched as the earl leant closer to Will, his voice lower than she remembered, husky and sensuous.

'I look forward to our supper this evening, Master Shakespeare.'

'It will be my honour Your Lordship.' She noticed Will had reined in his Warwickshire accent.

'Call me Rizzley.' The earl touched Will's hand, his long, delicate fingers lingering upon pale, ink-stained skin.

Magdalen could feel panic bubbling up like a spring-head. She tried to convince herself she was effectively invisible. With a tray in her hand, she was a humble servant and the earl was unlikely to give her a second glance. But what if he *did* look? What if he enquired about her relation to Master Bisset, the tailor to the Lord Chamberlain's Men?

Weaving her way through the lively throng, she prayed Burbage's guests would accept her proffered claret so she could return to the sanctuary of the 'tiring house. However, she reached the far end of the banqueting chamber with a single glass remaining on the tray, giving her no choice but to make another circuit of the room. She set off again, frowning with concentration. There would be no surer way to attract Rizzley's unwanted attention than to drop the tray, spraying wine over expensive silks, glass shattering in all directions. If the earl recognised her, she could not begin to imagine his fury at being taken for a fool, but she could well imagine Burbage's swift and brutal retribution. Her hands were shaking so much, the one remaining glass quivered on the chased silver.

She passed Matthew Hilliard in conversation with an exquisitely attired young lady. Beautiful in the conventional sense, with pale skin and white-blonde hair, she was smiling prettily, looking up at him through her long lashes. And he was smiling back, staring into her eyes, listening attentively to her breathless, high-pitched chatter. Magdalen walked past with her head held high, irrationally irritated by Matthew's chivalrous display of good manners.

Henry Condell and William Sly were entertaining another finely adorned young noblewoman. Condell was talking at great length about music, and she was hanging on his every word. 'I play the citterne and the bandore, but I most enjoy playing the lute. Music enhances a play, take the opening scene of *Twelfth Night* for example…'

William Sly surreptitiously rolled his eyes at Magdalen.

'Sheep's guts,' Sly interjected loudly.

The noble lady looked politely perplexed.

'Is it not strange that sheep's guts should fill men's souls with such pure delight?' Sly explained jovially.

Magdalen suppressed a giggle. Condell looked mildly put out.

'Ah yes, quite so,' the noble lady said earnestly. 'The strings of a lute are made of such material.'

Sly winked at Magdalen as she moved off through the melee of heavily-perfumed guests. She noticed Will and Rizzley hadn't moved, still deep in conversation. Could she sidle out of the banqueting chamber undetected? Turning around, she found herself face to face with Lord Hunsdon and Amelia Bassano. They were standing side by side but they might as well have been miles apart; unsmiling and rigid with tension.

Magdalen was so close to Lord Hunsdon she could see the bristly hairs protruding from his nostrils. It was not seemly to stand in such proximity to anyone, let alone nobility. She tried to back away but there was no escape. She was hemmed in on all sides by the painted butterflies and dazzling peacocks of Her Majesty's court.

'Whatever are you doing?' Burbage's imposing frame loomed over her. 'The Earl of Southampton is empty handed. Offer him some claret.'

With a sinking heart, Magdalen began to edge her way towards Will and the earl. They were gazing intently at one another, their heads almost touching. Magdalen's blood was pulsing so loudly in her ears she could barely make out their exchange, but she caught the odd word here and there. Rizzley was praising *Venus and Adonis* and Will's 'sugared poetry'. Several moments passed before either man gave any indication of noticing her presence.

'Would you care for a drink, Your Lordship?' Will asked.

'Call me Rizzley,' the earl corrected silkily.

Time seemed to slow as the earl reached for the claret on Magdalen's tray. Would he look at her? Would he demand to know why the tailor to the Lord Chamberlain's Men was masquerading as a serving girl? She watched the earl's fingers close about the glass, and time slowed still further. She watched him raise the claret to his lips and take a polite sip. The action took a lifetime or so it seemed and then, finally, he lowered the glass. Rizzley's gaze remained fixed on Will, his fingers stroking the glass's slender stem, very slowly, back and forth. The smile Will gave him in return was sly and knowing, softening his deep brown eyes. Magdalen realised she had forgotten to breathe. He hadn't recognised her. He hadn't even looked at her. Holding the empty tray against her chest like a shield, she backed away slowly, as if retreating from a beautiful swan that might at any moment transform into a hissing monster.

Back in the 'tiring house, she took her time pouring more claret, for she had no desire to run the gauntlet with the Earl of Southampton again. After the noise and exuberance of the banqueting chamber, the 'tiring house was quiet and empty, and her thoughts scrambled to fill the void. Yesterday, she had paid a visit to Adam Cooper's lodgings in Norton Folgate where his landlady confirmed he had left without providing a forwarding address.

The meeting in the old pest house on Spitalfields was her best hope of finding him now, but only a fool would venture through the liberties alone as night fell. The Upright Men were kings in the hours of darkness, controlling a deadly underworld of cut purses, smugglers, kidnappers and murderers. She glanced at the costume chests. Disguising herself as a man would undoubtedly offer her some protection, if she had the audacity to borrow Malvolio's sombre doublet and breeches. But in Burbage's eyes, it wouldn't be borrowing. It would be stealing. Before John's death, she would never have contemplated taking so much as a pin. It was mortifying to think how far she had fallen in a matter of days.

A peel of laughter rang from the banqueting chamber. It

sounded like Rizzley. She couldn't decide if the earl was genuinely captivated by Will, or merely passing the time with a bout of meaningless flirtation. Just as she couldn't decide if Will truly welcomed Rizzley's advances, for the man was a player after all, adept at feigning smiles. At times such as this, Burbage's entreaty to 'look for the truth of it' was easier said than done. But it appeared the earl *was* genuinely enamoured with *Venus and Adonis*. If he were to become Will's patron, wealth and status would surely follow. In truth, it was all Will had ever desired.

Magdalen yawned, her head swimming with fatigue. Despite quartering the city, she was no nearer to finding John's killer. Francis Johnson, the landlord of the Mermaid, claimed he knew nothing about John's gambling debts. He had insisted he ran a reputable tavern not a dicing den. Undeterred, she had walked to the Lord Chamberlain's mansion on the Strand only to discover her distant cousin, Joan Coverdale, had gone into Hertfordshire to visit her sick sister.

And then, this morning, there had been John's funeral. Louisa Du Bois had cut a pitiful figure, sitting alone in the front pew. She was ashen with grief, her eyes constantly darting towards her brother's coffin, as if she could not believe he lay inside it. On the spur of the moment, Magdalen had walked up the aisle to sit beside her. Louisa's look of surprise had quickly faded to a watery smile. Squeezing Magdalen's hand, she had whispered her heartfelt thanks.

Magdalen had recognised the majority of the mourners; the players, playwrights, poets and pamphleteers who frequented the Mermaid. There was no sign of Marlowe, but he was renowned for avoiding funerals. There was no sign of Richard Cowley either. It was assumed he was lying in a stupor in some ale-house, but when he had failed to appear for the afternoon performance of *The Comedy of Errors*, Burbage's fury had known no bounds.

'Jesu! Do they not have homes to go to?' Matthew Hilliard burst into the 'tiring house, his arms lifted heavenwards in a gesture of exasperation. 'Oh, forgive me. I did not see you there.'

Magdalen froze, the jug of claret poised in her hand. She knew he was as unobtainable as the stars, but she also knew that if he were to walk away now, if he were to journey to the new world and never return, she would always remember him.

'Burbage's guests have been drinking his claret for upwards of two hours. If I wanted to listen to meaningless chatter, I would visit the monkeys in the Tower gardens.' Matthew paused, mesmerised by the girl standing before him. Magdalen looked particularly enchanting today, her cheeks flushed, her eyes sparkling. She was so beautiful and so blameless, whereas he was a two-faced, false dissembler. His thoughts entangled with guilt and shame, he added hastily, 'Please do not suppose I am ungrateful. The players are fine fellows. It is the guests I find tedious.'

'Indeed, they are a race apart,' Magdalen agreed. 'As unfathomable as the creatures drawn at the edges of a map.'

Matthew smiled. 'Quite so. I believe I would rather sit down to dinner with a head-less giant, than spend another moment in the banqueting chamber.'

'Dinner with a headless giant,' Magdalen mused. 'I cannot imagine there would be much conversation, nor need to share your meat.'

Matthew's smiled broadened. 'I was thinking of the monster whose face dwells upon his belly. He has but one giant leg. You know the creature I mean?'

'I do!' Magdalen's eyes lit up. 'How splendid he would look on a hop-scotch champion's coat of arms!'

Burbage appeared in the doorway, and Matthew's laughter instantly died in his throat.

'Don't pour any more claret, Magdalen. They're leaving.' Burbage lowered his voice. 'It seems once the Earl of Southampton makes for the door, they will all follow. They are like sheep.'

'More like wolves in sheep's clothing,' Matthew muttered.

Burbage nodded. 'Aye, Hilliard, isn't that the truth.'

The well-born guests departed, flooding from the Theatre on a tide of claret-oiled bonhomie. The players were not far behind. Christopher Beeston slung a brawny arm about Matthew's shoulders, and propelled him towards the door.

'I cannot drink with you this evening. I have lines to learn,' Matthew protested.

Beeston laughed. 'You must find a better excuse than that! Good God, man, how many lines has Burbage given you? Three?'

William Sly caught up with them. 'The girls in the Mermaid will gladly help you learn your lines. Pay them sixpence, and they'll help you with anything, if you know what I mean.' He grinned wickedly.

Henry Condell pushed past them, frowning.

'Care to join us, Henry?' Sly winked at Matthew.

'No! I am going home to my wife,' Henry replied. 'And you should go home too, Hilliard, if you know what's good for you. The whores in the Mermaid are riddled with the French pox. I would strongly advise you to avoid them like the plague.'

'The young ones are as fresh and unblemished as daisies,' Sly insisted. 'But if you don't want to pay for it, there are ladies aplenty at the 'tiring house door who will scratch any itch for free.'

'Most of those women are married,' Henry Condell retorted. 'Unless you want to be called out for a dual on Shoreditch common by a cuckolded husband, you'd be well advised to give them a wide berth too.'

Magdalen couldn't fathom what Matthew made of all this, for his expression gave little away.

'Enough, Henry, go home to the fair Elizabeth and leave us to our revels!' Beeston's arm was still firmly about Matthew's shoulders. 'Just one drink, Hilliard, just one drink. It will do you good, mark my words.'

Matthew made no further objections, clearly resigned to following the players to the Mermaid. But as he reached the door he turned around and smiled at Magdalen, and she smiled back, a bubble of happiness filling her heart.

The players slammed the door behind them, plunging the 'tiring house into silence and Magdalen's bubble abruptly burst. In her heart, she knew it would be madness to attend the Puritans' meeting; madness to risk her life on a fool's errand. But a persistent inner voice was urging her on, insisting she had no choice, insisting she had to find Adam Cooper.

It sounded uncannily like Marlowe's voice, full of bluster and bravado. Should she go to the lodgings he shared with Thomas Kyd and ask him to accompany her? She had no doubt he would jump at the chance to don sombre apparel and hoodwink a pest house full of Puritans. But Marlowe was not known for his patience or discretion. If he grew bored, he might well throw caution to the wind, and declare the Puritans had 'as much faith as could be found in a stewed prune'.

No, she couldn't risk adding to her troubles. She would go alone. Taking Malvolio's black doublet and knee length breeches from the costume chest, she quickly undressed. Wearing only her smock, she pulled on Malvolio's woollen stockings. They were freshly washed but still sagged about her knees like over-cooked tripe. Next, she donned the doublet and breeches. She laced them together as best she could, but she couldn't reach the eyelets at the back. What if the laces didn't hold, and her breeches tumbled to her ankles? What if she was mistaken for a doxy? Many of the watchmen were in the pay of pimps and would undoubtedly turn a blind eye to her screams.

In the looking glass, a pale, uncertain face stared back at her. Henry Condell was a tall man, and she was drowned in his costume, a child in adult's garb. Opening her sewing basket, she set about pinning excess fabric, trying to focus on the immediate task at hand rather than on her half-witted plan. Finally, she fastened her hair to the crown of her head, pulled on Malvolio's woollen cap and glanced sheepishly at her reflexion again. What was she thinking? No-one would be taken in by her disguise.

And yet, she had fooled the earl of Southampton, so why not a pest house full of Puritans? Swinging Malvolio's cloak about her shoulders, she ventured out. There was not a breath of wind and a fine drizzle hung in the misty air. It was not yet dark but Shoreditch was unusually quiet, the sound of her footsteps echoing about the empty streets.

She headed south, glancing repeatedly to her left and right, as nervous as an apprentice on opening night. Shadows were moving in narrow passageways, sliding along dank wattle walls like wraiths on All Hallows Eve. She quickened her pace, fear heightening her senses, every distant sound an imminent threat.

The damp air sidled about her exposed legs and she shivered. Malvolio's breeches came to her knees, not quite as revealing as the gaudy, saffron yellow apparel Marlowe had chosen for her, but the shape of her calf was still plainly visible through the woollen stockings. Even the Mermaid's whores did not walk the streets in a state of such undress. Ashamed, she drew the edges of the cloak together.

Up ahead, she could see the outline of the former priory and hospital of St Mary Spital, now converted into many fair houses. Wealthy folk called it home. Aldermen, sheriffs and merchants; men who could afford window glazing, and beeswax candles, and Turkey rugs upon their tables. Their leaded windows were gilded with firelight and candlelight and Magdalen imagined them sitting down to supper with their wives and children. She didn't envy them their rich food or their expensive silver plate. But she did envy them the comfort of their family.

Quickening her pace, she turned into Hog Lane. Once part of the tranquil grounds of the old priory, it was now a hotch-potch of cottages and tenements, newly built for the humble sort. A smell of pottage seeped around ill-fitting shutters, overlaid with the noxious miasmas of tanneries, glue-makers and cess pits.

A black cat was on the prowl. It turned to look at her, and she came to an abrupt halt. Her grandmother used to say a black cat crossing your path was a lucky omen. Her mother, on the other hand, had insisted they were the Devil's apprentices. Crossing her fingers, Magdalen spat three times and made the sign of the cross. She held her breath, but the cat did not burst into flames, nor writhe in devilish torment. Instead, it cast her a haughty glance and stalked away. Magdalen sighed with relief. She was about to set off again when the door of the Boar's Head tavern burst open, spilling two inebriated men out into the street. The sound of laughter and music quickly faded as the door was shut in their faces.

The men had spied her. 'What are you looking at?' one of them queried belligerently.

Magdalen shook her head, mute with fear.

'Be gone with you, laddie. You're not my type.' The man was swaying like a sapling in a storm.

'He's no trug-doxy,' the other man said dismissively, grabbing his friend by the arm to keep him upright. 'He's one of them

Puritans. Looks like he has a pole up his arse. Leave the miserable bastard be.'

The men staggered away, heading north towards Shoreditch. Magdalen's courage was hanging by a thread. She was sorely tempted to turn tail and run all the way back to Silver Street, to the sooty warmth of the Mountjoys' kitchen, to the familiar four walls of her bed chamber.

Don't be a coward, she told herself. *You've come this far. You can't turn back now.*

She walked on, and the mean cottages of Hog Lane soon gave way to the open expanse of Spitalfield. When she had first come to London, it had been a place of long swaying grasses and hedgerows frothed with white hawthorn. Homesick and overwhelmed by the crowded city, she had often sought refuge there. Not long after, the fields were dug for clay, and she had watched the journeymen unearth the cremation urns and the bones of ancient folk. They had been laid to rest with wondrous things, with gold treasures that sparkled as if they had been buried yesterday, with beads of coral and jet, and some with mighty swords.

Spitalfield was no longer a bucolic arcadia. By daylight, a few laundry-women still laid out their washing, and the gunners of the Tower still came for target practice, firing their monstrous artillery against great butts of earth, but much of the field was wasteland now, a place for dumping refuse. The clay works had left the ground pock-marked with pits, some as large as a village mill-pond, and some just as water-logged. Magdalen tried to avoid them but the lanterns of the city were behind her now, the light was beginning to fade and it wasn't easy to see where she was going.

The sound of frantic splashing broke the eerie silence.

'Who's there?' Her voice was a whisper of fear.

The splashing stopped.

It's a rat, nothing more, she told herself firmly.

Nevertheless, she anxiously turned full circle. The mist was lending the sodden earth a spectral air, and she imagined the spirits of the long-dead rising up to torment her. A wind sprang up from the east, howling across the flat expanse of Spitalfield. Instinctively, Magdalen tugged at the edges of her cloak and then she faltered, confused. The air was completely still. There was no wind, so what in God's name..?

Lights were flickering in the distance. Were they malignant will o' the whisps, luring her to a watery grave? Or were they the lanterns of Upright Men? Her heart hammering, her throat dry, she stared harder. Not will o' the whisps, but something solid, a structure of some kind.

With a rush of heady relief, she realised it was the pest house, faint slivers of candlelight escaping from its shuttered windows. The howling was coming from within its walls. Magdalen knew little of the Puritans' faith, save that they loathed the Theatre, and all manner of vanity, gaiety and amusement. What was happening in there? What terrible ritual lent itself to such unearthly keening? She crept closer. The howling was louder now, rising to a crescendo of ear-piercing, staccato screams.

Her every instinct was telling her to walk away, but for John's sake and her grandmother's sake, she knew she couldn't. Taking a deep, unsteady breath, she knocked on the pest house door. Moments later, it was opened by a young man with a face of such unusual length that Magdalen was instantly reminded of a cart-horse. Somewhat disconcerted, she held out Louisa's reed cross and willed herself to look him in the eye. To her astonishment, he gave no outward sign of finding her appearance noteworthy or unusual.

'Come in, brother.'

Not trusting herself to speak, Magdalen followed him inside. Nervously pulling Malvolio's cap further down over her ears, she looked about. The pest-house was a small, single-chambered building, devoid of decoration and lit by tallow candles. Three young women were kneeling on the floor and rocking back and forth, their arms outstretched to the heavens. Magdalen didn't recognise the language tumbling from their lips. One moment it was a strange, frantic gabble; the next it rose to a crescendo of plaintive, feverish howling.

Surreptitiously, she began to study the crowd gathered about the kneeling women. They were simply dressed, without ornament or vanity, as befitted those of the Puritan faith. Some had their hands clasped in prayer. Some stared into the distance, their eyes rolled back, disturbingly unseeing. Others were swaying from side to side, their lips moving soundlessly. To Magdalen's intense disappointment, Adam Cooper did not appear to be amongst them.

'Your first time, brother?' the long-faced man enquired.

Magdalen nodded. She had never felt more out of her depth. These people were utterly foreign to her, their bizarre ceremony outlandish to her eyes. How could she possibly hope to pass herself off as one of them? She had no idea what she was supposed to do or say. She looked down at her hands, clasped demurely at her waist. That wasn't right; men did not deport themselves so meekly. She hastily let them fall to her side.

'Do not be troubled,' the young man said reassuringly. 'Sometimes a brother, or sister, attends several meetings before they fall under the power of the Holy Spirit.'

Magdalen fought to hide her astonishment. These people were communing with the Holy Spirit? She pointed towards the women swaying and jabbering on the pest-house floor.

'Do you understand what they are saying?'

'We speak in tongues. It is a language beyond any known philosophy, brother.'

Magdalen couldn't understand why God would choose to communicate in a language no-one could understand.

'When you fall under the power, what do you remember of it?' she whispered.

The young man glanced sharply at her and she realised she was asking too many questions.

'We are not prophets, and nor do we claim to be. The Holy Spirit fills us with His peace and grace, and we are blessed by Him.'

'I understand, brother,' she replied meekly, although in truth, she could make no sense of any of it. If this was a church service, where was the clergyman?

She searched the crowd again. Adam Cooper was definitely not amongst them. This had all been for nothing. The women on the floor were beginning to tire, their wailing fading to strangled mumblings. Magdalen's companion helped one of the girls to her feet. She looked no more than fourteen years old, a hint of mouse-brown hair showing beneath her plain coif. Her head lolled heavily against the young man's shoulder and her eyes were glazed.

A brief, expectant silence descended over the pest-house as an elderly man stepped forward, holding a copy of the Bible. Despite his advancing years, there was no stoop to his shoulders nor shuffle in his step.

'Blessed are the poor in spirit, for theirs is the kingdom of Heaven. Blessed are those who mourn, for they will be comforted.'

Magdalen thought he made a most unusual preacher, his manner as gentle as a lamb.

'Blessed are the meek, for they will inherit the earth -'

His softly spoken words were interrupted by a man who began to bark like a dog. His apparel marked him out as a sober, law-abiding guildsman, but his body was jolting violently with each yelp, as if the Devil was prodding him with red-hot tongs. The preacher tried to talk over him, but the man's guttural cries grew louder. Several members of the congregation followed suit, dropping to their knees and yelping fiercely. A flash of irritation crossed the preacher's face, but he closed his bible, presumably resigned to wait for their fervor to abate.

Magdalen did not know whether to be amazed or terrified. Were these people truly in the grip of the Holy Spirit, or were they struck mad by the moon? Or, God preserve her, were they possessed by the Devil?

'Brother?' The long-faced young man tapped Magdalen on the shoulder. The girl he had helped from the floor was standing by his side. 'May I introduce my sister? My blood relation,' he added for clarification.

The young girl, who looked much recovered, asked shyly:

'And you are, sir?'

'I am a friend of Adam Cooper.'

'No names here!' the girl's brother warned.

'Forgive me, I have much to learn,' Magdalen replied.

Undeterred by her brother's reprimand, the girl tipped her head to one side and smiled coyly. 'Your first meeting, sir?'

Magdalen didn't know what to say. Unless she was much mistaken, the girl was flirting with her. Could this night become any more fantastical?

'Er, yes, indeed,' she replied and then, under her breath, 'I will not speak his name again, but do you know the whereabouts of my friend? I am concerned for his safety.'

'What a dear fellow you are to look out for him,' the girl replied sweetly. 'I believe he has left the city and gone into Hampshire.'

The barking and yelping had died down, and the preacher took the opportunity to resume his sermon.

'They persecute us and they burn us for our beliefs, and yet we follow the word of God. Jesus says, do not resist an evildoer, but if anyone strikes you on the right cheek, turn the other also. And yet we are condemned for refusing to bear arms in Her Majesty's army. And condemned for renouncing violence in all its forms.'

A murmur of agreement ran around the pest-house but Magdalen felt a tremor of alarm. These men and women were not Puritans, they were Anabaptists. No wonder they met here in secret. Her Majesty had decreed them heretics, their views so radical and dangerous they faced the death penalty if discovered.

'And remember, as Paul tells us, neither the sexually immoral, nor adulterers, nor men who have carnal relations with men, will inherit the kingdom of God. Paul also tells us we must not associate with these non-believers. We must not eat with such people. I say unto you, brothers and sisters, do not venture into the taverns, the gaming tables, the playhouses, for all sins and vices are collected there under one roof.'

Magdalen's sense of unease deepened.

'Did not Jesus say, if my kingdom were of this world, my servants would have been fighting, that I might not be delivered over to the Jews. But my kingdom is not of this world.' The preacher looked about the room. 'We belong to God's kingdom. Therefore, we must deny the right of the government of this earthly realm. We must not hold office, nor any rank under government, nor put ourselves at the mercy of the non-believers' courts of law…'

Magdalen had heard enough. She had to leave. Now. This place was dangerous, a powder-keg of anarchy and rebellion. If the watchers carried out a raid and found her here, they would not listen to her pleas of innocence. She would be hung for treason along with the rest of them. As she turned for the door, a tall, blond man elbowed her out of the way, his eyes darting wildly.

'They burn us for following the word of God! They persecute us!' he cried, hissing the final consonant, as if his tongue was glued to the top of his palate by a sugary marshpane. 'And yet you tell us to turn the other cheek? I cannot do it! I will not do it!'

'My brother,' the preacher's voice was full of compassion, 'blessed are the meek, for they shall inherit the earth.'

'I watched my mother burn for her Faith!' The blond man was wringing his hands, his face contorted with anguish. 'I was seven years old and they made me watch. The memory torments me, I can't rid myself of it, I have no peace.'
The preacher put a hand on the young man's shoulder.

'You have known great suffering, just as Christ Jesus suffered upon the cross. Be comforted in the knowledge your mother was a true believer, and now sits with God.'

The blond man tore himself from the preacher's grasp.

'She died for nothing! London is riddled with sin. Worst of all are the playhouses! They are dens of sodomy and non-believers who mock the word of the Lord. Did not the Bible also say, an eye for an eye, a tooth for a tooth? The players must die! They must all die to be cleansed of their sins!'

'Brother, take heed, violence is not the way.'

'No! They must die!' Raising his hands to the rafters the man let out a despairing howl.

Some in the crowd supported him: 'Aye, kill the non-believers!' But the majority shouted him down. The meeting was rapidly descending into chaos.

'Who is he?' Magdalen whispered to her companions.

'No names, brother.'

The blond man was pushing his way through the congregation, heading for the door. Had he painted the slogans outside the Theatre? She had to speak to him. She had to look him in the eye and ask him if he had killed John Wood. She turned to follow him.

'Wait!'

Magdalen spun around. 'Yes?'

'Please don't go,' the young girl pleaded. Lowering her voice so her brother would not hear, she whispered, 'Pay no need to Master Froissart. He is a foreigner. His brain seethes and his wits are distracted.'

Magdalen glanced over her shoulder. Master Froissart had reached the door.

'Where does he live?' she asked urgently.

'Off Cheapside, I believe. Why do you ask?'

'No matter. I must take my leave.'

'Will you come again?' the girl asked, crestfallen.

'I cannot say. I bid you good night,' Magdalen replied distractedly, and hurried after Froissart.

Outside, darkness had fallen, and she could see little further than her feet. Where was Froissart? She closed her eyes and listened hard. She could hear raised voices from within the pest house and the soft pitter-patter of light rain against her cloak, but nothing more. It was as though he had simply vanished into the night.

Deeply frustrated, Magdalen stumbled across Spitalfields in her haste to be home, all the while silently praying Cripplegate was not already locked for the night. It was too dark to avoid the foul-smelling puddles, and her boots and the hem of her cloak were soon heavy with filth. She hurried on, every nerve and sinew taut with fear, her ears straining for any sound of danger. By the time she reached the church of Saint Mary Spital on

Bishopsgate Street Without, her heart was pounding as fiercely as a blacksmith's hammer. She was still a long way from Silver Street, still at the mercy of the Upright Men, but the shuttered houses and taverns felt less threatening than the eerie emptiness of Spitalfield. The rain had stopped, and the clouds had parted to reveal a pale moon. Its brittle light illuminated the city, turning wet rooftops to slick lead-grey, and murky puddles to pools of shining quicksilver.

Somewhere nearby, a watchman called eight o' clock. Magdalen glanced over her shoulder but she couldn't see his tell-tale lantern. Perhaps he was farther away than she had supposed, his voice carrying on the still air. Her eyes narrowed. Someone was loitering in the shadows, perhaps twenty yards away. She tried to tell herself he was most likely a harmless shop-keeper, heading home for his supper. But why had he stopped? What was he waiting for? She looked harder. Could she see one man, or two? The hairs on the back of her neck stood on end. Was it fanciful to suppose they were following her?

She glanced over her shoulder repeatedly as she hurried through Norton Folgate's maze of narrow lanes, searching for any sign she was being followed, but all was quiet. After what seemed an age, she came to a fork in the road. A winding lane led off to her left; a straighter track to her right. She thought she knew this neighbourhood like the back of her hand, but she didn't recognise this place.

She must have taken a wrong turn. She couldn't be more than half a mile from Silver Street, but she might as well have been half a league. She was totally lost. She glanced over her shoulder again, listening for footfall, but it was hard to hear anything above the sound of blood pulsing in her ears.

Without warning, two figures appeared out of the darkness, not ten yards behind her, running fast, their boots splashing through the puddles. For a heartbeat, Magdalen simply stared at them. And then, coming to her senses, she glanced about wildly. She doubted she could outrun the men on the straight track, but she might have a slim advantage along the winding lane. She took the left fork, sprinting through a stream of foul water, her eyes straining for any familiar landmark.

She guessed this was a place of warehouses, for there were no lights glimmering, no smell of simmering pottage, no sound of children's laughter. The store-men, like all Londoners, finished work at dusk. There was no-one here now. Only rats and mice and pigeons. And cut-purses. If she screamed, no-one would come to her aid. If she hammered on a door, no-one would open it to save her. She shot a quick glance over her shoulder. The men were gaining on her, and she realised with a sickening jolt that she couldn't out-run them.

Think! Think!

Could she find her way into a warehouse? Could she hide in the musty darkness amidst bales of wool or sacks of grain? She ran on, but the lane was a seemingly endless, winding tunnel, enclosed on both sides by high, featureless walls.

Suddenly, she caught a glimpse of the iron-work of a gate. She lurched to a stop, her fingers searching frantically in the darkness for a latch.

Nothing.

She looked up at the sky beseechingly but the moon had vanished again behind a thick band of cloud. Turning her shoulder, she flung her full weight against the gate. It creaked on its hinges, but it didn't move. Gritting her teeth, she tried again but it held fast. She had no choice but to keep running.

Strong hands grabbed her shoulders. Her scream died in her throat as the back of her head connected with the gate's ironwork, and jarring pain shot through her skull. Panic-stricken, she tried desperately to break free from her attacker's grasp. In response, he slammed her against the ironwork again with such force that Malvolio's cap flew from her head and fell to the ground. A cloud of pins followed, releasing her long hair to tumble about her shoulders. Strangely, her captor did not seem surprised to discover her true sex.

'Jesus Christ! Hold still, girl!'

It was a Londoner's accent from south of the river. She couldn't see much of his face, for his cloak was hooded and a scarf shielded his nose and mouth, but she could smell stale sweat and the oily tang of hemp. A dock worker perhaps? Did he want her purse, or did he want her body or, God preserve her, was he set on murder?

And what was the other man doing? She turned her head a fraction. He was standing not three yards away. The look-out. She tried again to escape her captor's hold, but he responded by yanking her hair so violently that she cried out in pain. Dear God, she didn't want to die here. What would become of her grandmother? She couldn't bear to think of her spending her final days in Bedlam, surrounded by those pitiful, shaven headed souls.

'I have money,' she lied. 'Take my purse and let me go.'

Her attacker's face was inches from hers. 'I don't want your money. I have a message for you. You must forget John Wood.'

Pain and terror were fighting for space inside Magdalen's head. What had he just said? Had she heard him correctly?

'John Wood,' the man repeated impatiently. 'You must leave it alone. D'you understand me?'

Magdalen's thoughts were spiralling. How did he know about John? Leave what alone? Who were these men?

'I hear something! I think the watchman is about!' A different voice. The look-out.

Her captor grabbed her chin between finger and thumb, forcing her head up. 'D'you understand me, girl?'

'Yes,' she lied again.

From the corner of her eye, she saw the other man step forward, heard him say, 'away, man, we are done here!'

With a grunt of acknowledgement, her attacker released her, and in a heart-beat they were gone, disappearing into the darkness. Magdalen clung to the gate, light-headed and nauseous, the back of her skull throbbing fiercely. She peered into the shadows, hoping to see the watchman but there was neither sight nor sound of him. The accomplice had been mistaken. It seemed she would have to find her own way home. She set off slowly, every step a monumental effort. Fighting waves of dizziness, she trailed her fingers against the cold, damp wall, and an image of Theseus following Ariadne's ball of thread out of the labyrinth swam across her mind.

You are nothing like Theseus, she berated herself. *You are not a hero. You haven't killed a Minotaur. You have been attacked and threatened, and it's likely they'll kill you long before any judge can sign your death warrant.*

In the darkness, she lost track of time. Did hours or minutes pass before she became aware of a faint glow of light up ahead? Soon after, she passed the sign of the White Unicorn on the corner of Milk Lane and Bishopsgate Street Without. She recognised this place. She was no longer lost, and a sob of relief rose in her throat. The streets were quiet, and she saw neither Upright Men nor common thieves on the prowl as she stumbled on towards Silver Street. London had slipped into the shadowy domain of stray dogs and hunting cats, of rats and mice and snow-white owls, swooping silently over the rooftops like guardian angels of the sleeping city.

The Mountjoys' house was in darkness save for candlelight in

Will's bedchamber. He was always late to bed. Magdalen fumbled for her key, her fingers grasping the latch like a sinner seeking sanctuary at a church porch. Inside, drowsy embers warmed the kitchen hearth and air smelled of wood smoke with undercurrents of cured ham and musty cheese in the pantry.

She was greatly relieved the family were abed, for she had dreaded trying to explain why she was wearing men's attire. Wearily creeping up the stairs to her bedchamber, she undressed and carefully folded the costume. To her dismay, she realised she had lost Malvolio's cap, trampled and forgotten in the back lane. How to explain its disappearance to Burbage? Did she have a similar cap in the costume chests?

The back of her skull was throbbing painfully, too persistent to ignore. Cautiously, she probed the spot and her fingers came away wet with blood. Pouring water into the ewer, she bathed the wound then splashed her face repeatedly as if to wash away her memories. But she knew it would take more than a jug of cold water to make her forget this night. What she needed was the comforting familiarity of kin.

Clad in her smock with a shawl draped about her shoulders, Magdalen knocked on her grandmother's door. Agnes was sitting up in bed, staring blankly into the corner of the chamber, but her face lit up at the sight of her granddaughter.

You look weary, Magdalen. Come, sit by me.'

Magdalen was pleasantly surprised by her grandmother's welcome. Of late, it was rare for her to be so hospitable.

'How now, my sweeting?' Agnes asked. A tear trickled from her constantly watering left eye but she did not seem to notice its slow meander down her cheek.

Magdalen took a moment to reply. She felt fragile and afraid, her emotions scattered to the four winds. She longed to fall into her grandmother's arms and sob until she had no more tears left to spill, but she knew she could not. The grandmother who had cared for her, and taught her to read and sew, had gone. In her place was a woman she barely knew. One moment suspicious, hostile and antagonistic; the next, vulnerable, childlike and afraid.

Not so long ago, she would have told her grandmother everything, but now she limited her conversation to banalities because matters of any substance only brought upset and confusion. The tide had turned, and now it was her turn to protect the once formidable Agnes Bisset. And Magdalen felt the loss keenly. It was always there. It had become a part of her. But, unlike the grief she had felt for her parents, this pain never lessened but was renewed with every passing day.

'All is well, Grand-Aggie. And you?'

'Faith, Christopher Mountjoy rages like a tempest, does he not? I have listened to him all day. Most vexing, for I have had many costumes to mend.' Agnes looked vaguely about her spartan bedchamber.

Magdalen nodded sympathetically. 'Has he always been so?'

'Who?'

'Christopher Mountjoy. Has he always been so ill humoured?' Magdalen asked patiently.

'He is not ill humoured, my sweeting. He is a fine young man, and he broke many hearts when he chose to wed Marie. She is an immodest shrew, but I am sorry she lost the child.'

'The child?'

'It died on Tuesday last!' Agnes sounded irritated that Magdalen could have forgotten such a recent tragedy. 'And born just three months after their marriage! The gossips said God was punishing them for their lewdness, but I do not believe God would punish an innocent babe for the sins of his parents. I pray Marie is blessed with a healthy babe one day. She has a cruel tongue, but I would not wish her cursed with a barren womb.'

Magdalen wondered if she should reassure her grandmother that Christopher and Marie were now the parents of a healthy daughter, but decided it would only add to her confusion. Instead, she asked, 'Do you know Edmund Stow?'

Her grandmother raised a hand to her thin white hair, patting it lightly to check for stray wisps, and then she laughed with unfettered delight. Leaning forward conspiratorially, she whispered, 'I should not speak of it, for vanity is a sin, but that man adores me.'

'He does?' Magdalen was astonished.

'Oh yes, even before my beloved Pierre passed away, God rest his soul,' she made the sign of the cross, 'I would catch Edmund gazing at me with lovelorn eyes. And then Pierre died, and scarce three months passed before Edmund asked me to marry him. I said no, of course, and I do believe he has never forgiven me for it. Can you imagine sharing a bed with him?' Agnes winked jovially, and another tear began a slow meander down her cheek. 'The man is spherical like a globe. I could find countries in him.'

Magdalen burst out laughing.

'And besides,' Agnes continued, suddenly wistful, 'Pierre was the only man for me. I knew I would never wed again.'

'Your true love,' Magdalen said, clasping her grandmother's hand.

'Yes, my sweeting. He is.'

With an ache of sadness for loves lost and lives past, Magdalen kissed her grandmother good-night and returned to her own bed chamber. She was exhausted and she longed for the oblivion of sleep, but the Earl of Southampton's half-finished cloak lay on her worktable, mutely reproachful. With her days fully occupied from dawn to dusk, she had been obliged to spend her evenings working late into the night on the earl's commission.

Sitting down, she drew the cloak towards her, and began to sew by the flickering candlelight. The watchman cried 'two o'clock' before she finally put down her needle, and rubbed her sore, aching eyes. Of late, they had become so blood-shot she feared a constable would think her plague-ridden and throw her into the nearest pest-house. Blowing out the candle, she crawled into bed.

Despite her exhaustion, she couldn't sleep, her thoughts hopping about with all the heated frenzy of a Scotch jig. Her attacker had reeked of the docks, of poverty. A lackey then, in the pay of a powerful man? Who might that be? And why?

She knew full well that tonight had been a warning, meant to frighten not harm. Next time, it was unlikely she would escape with just a sore head. But despite the man's threats, she also knew she would not stop searching for John's killer.

What had he become embroiled in? Something so dangerous it had cost him his life? Could Adam Cooper also be involved? And where was he? Had he truly gone into Hampshire or was it possible he had been murdered too? And what of Froissart? The man had spouted a torrent of bile against playhouses, and cried death to all players. Had he murdered John?

Her thoughts hurtled on. Her grandmother's wits were often muddled, but she had seemed entirely rational when she spoke of rejecting Edmund Stow. Was it possible he bore a long-standing grudge? Was it possible his vindictive hatred stemmed from a broken heart?

Magdalen tossed and turned until her dishevelled bedsheets enveloped her like a shroud. Fighting free of them, she groped for her tinder box and lit the candle, eager to escape into the make-believe world of *Venus and Adonis*. Her eyes ached with tiredness but Will's poetry propped up her eyelids, just as the mighty pillars of the Theatre's stage held aloft its star-fretted roof. Her cares slipped away as she entered the greenwood. Adonis had escaped from Venus's arms but before he can climb upon his horse and return to his hunting, his stallion spies a mare and the two animals gallop away together. Venus pleads that he might learn from his courser's passion:

'Had I no eyes, but ears, my ears would love
That inward beauty and invisible;
Or were I deaf, thy outward parts would move
Each part in me that were but sensible:
Had I neither eyes nor ears, to hear nor see,
Yet should I be in love by touching thee.'

Magdalen found herself entranced. Surely those were the words of a woman in love rather than lust? Or were they inseparable; two sides of the same coin? Would her own heart beat faster for Matthew Hilliard if she could no longer see his handsome features, nor hear his dulcet tones? Magdalen had no answers. Perhaps, if she read on, Will's poem would enlighten her. Perhaps that was the purpose of poetry, to hold a looking glass up to life, just as music reflected the sound of the planets moving in harmony in the heavens. She picked up the next page.

In desperation, Venus pretends to faint with grief, and falls to the ground. Fearing she is dead, Adonis wrings her nose, strikes her on the cheek and finally kisses her on the mouth. Venus opens her eyes and cries:

'O, thou didst kill me – kill me once again!
Her arms do lend his neck a sweet embrace,
Incorporate then they seem; face grows to face.
He with her plenty pressed, she faint with dearth,
Their lips together glued, fall to the earth.
Now quick desire hath caught the yielding prey,
And glutton like she feeds, yet never filleth;
Her lips are conquerors, his lips obey,

And having felt the sweetness of the spoil,
With blindfold fury she begins to forage,
Her face doth reek and smoke, her blood doth boil,
And careless lust stirs up a desperate courage,
Planting oblivion, beating reason back,
Forgetting shame's pure blush and honour's wrack…'

Magdalen's skin was tingling; a thousand soft feathers shimmering across her flesh. She could feel her blood thrumming in her veins, her heart pounding fiercely, her every sinew as taut as a tabor. She could see the goddess and the beautiful boy entwined on the forest floor. She could taste the sweetness of Adonis's lips, and smell the reek and smoke of Venus's careless lust.

Perhaps it had been fanciful to suppose Will understood the true meaning of love. Perhaps the purpose of his poetry was simply to set pulses racing with the erotic thrill of the chase. She closed her eyes, and imagined how it would be to lie with Matthew Hilliard. How had Venus enticed Adonis?

'A thousand honeyed secrets shalt thou know…'

What she would give to know just one.

TEN

'How quickly the wrong side may be turned out'

It was hot and airless in the tavern, and Matthew Hilliard stifled a yawn. The evening was proving a waste of time. He had listened to the players as they grew merry on Mad Dog. He had discussed the latest outbreak of pestilence with Will Shakespeare, who was so calm and composed in comparison to his loud fellows. They had spoken of London's rising death toll and how it was only a matter of time before the theatres were forced to close. Will was reluctant to take the troupe into the provinces again because small-town mayors tended to view players as city-dwelling plague-carriers, and barred their gates against them.

The evening drew on, but no-one spoke of religion, Papist or otherwise. The players' concerns were for cue sheets, who had the most lines and why. Who was favoured by Burbage, and why. Which plays were the most popular with the audience, and why. And when would Burbage increase their pay.

Matthew was sitting next to William Sly, but the player had turned his back to talk exclusively to Christopher Beeston. The two men were as inseparable as twins. They were also profoundly in their cups, their conversation an endless stream of anecdotes featuring mishaps with stage props, memorable nights with whores, and blood-curdling street fights.

'…Agnes still attends…'

Matthew supposed Agnes was yet another of the countless doxies of the men's close acquaintance. Only half listening now, he bit down on another yawn and thought wistfully of the quiet comforts of the Askews' house; of fine wine and his uncle's well-stocked library.

'Jesu, what madness,' Sly replied quietly. 'Why hasn't she put a stop to it?'

It dawned on Matthew that the players had lowered their voices. And suddenly, he was listening intently, all the while feigning interest in the conversation between Will Shakespeare and Henry Condell, seated opposite.

'She's tried but, as you will remember, Agnes is as stubborn as a mule,' Beeston said. 'And Dawbeney's the same. He wouldn't listen.'

'Aye. Anthony Bonvince -' Sly glanced furtively along the table then leant towards Beeston and whispered in his friend's ear. 'Bonvince is a dangerous fool to allow that cantankerous old bastard into his cellar.'

It was the stage whisper of a man in his cups, and Matthew caught every word. He realised he was holding his breath, unwilling to move an inch for fear of drawing the men's attention.

'A fool perhaps, but a loyal fool,' Beeston replied. 'The old faith runs deep in that family. Bonvince may be a butcher, but his grandfather was of noble stock. He served the old Queen but fell from grace when Elizabeth took the throne.'

Sly's features contorted into a grimace. 'Fucking Papists. Fucking heretics. If I had my way, I'd string up the lot of them.'

'You don't mean that.' Beeston had turned a pale goose-turd green. He looked as if he was about to vomit. Instead, he belched so loudly that Matthew had difficulty hiding his surprise.

'I fucking do mean it,' Sly snarled bitterly, apparently oblivious to his friend's distress. 'They are responsible for all the troubles in the world. All the wars, the bloodshed, the grief, the suffering.'

'Drink up, brother,' Beeston slapped Sly on the back. 'You grow maudlin and you're making my belly ache.'

'It's the Mad Dog has made your belly ache, not I, you great bucket of lard,' Sly retorted.

'I need to piss,' Beeston replied. He stood up unsteadily, and staggered towards the door.

In response, Sly put both arms on the table, lowered his head into his hands and closed his eyes.

Outwardly, Matthew remained quite still. Inwardly, his mind was racing, trying to make sense of the men's whispered conversation.

Anthony Bonvince and his family were evidently Catholics - of the 'old faith'.

Bonvince had allowed a 'cantankerous old bastard' called Dawbeney into his home. Sly thought that was a dangerous thing to do. Why?

Dawbeney was as stubborn as a mule. So too was Agnes, who 'still attends'. Why did Sly think this was madness?

Anthony Bonvince. Dawbeney. Agnes. Who were these people?

Perhaps he was asking the wrong question. Perhaps he should be asking what was happening in the cellar of Anthony Bonvince's home.

Something so dangerous it seemed like madness to Sly.

Was it possible the cantankerous old Dawbeney was a Catholic priest?

Was it possible he was holding Masses in Bonvinces' cellar?

Sly was snoring loudly now. Sensing an opportunity to make his escape, Matthew got to his feet. Only Will Shakespeare noticed he was leaving. Breaking off his conversation with Henry Condell, he said quietly, 'Good night, Hilliard. Keep your wits about you. The hour grows late.'

Matthew touched the knife at his belt by way of

acknowledgement. At the door he met Beeston heading back inside. The man was swaying like a mariner, his eyes glazed.

'Night, Hilliard,' he slurred.

Matthew was taken aback. He had begun to think himself invisible, for Beeston had not spoken a single word to him all evening.

'Good night,' he replied, and went out into the night.

He had almost reached his uncle's house when a figure stepped out of the shadows.

'Our mutual acquaintance sends his greetings, Master Hilliard.'

Matthew would have recognised that voice anywhere, harsh as a blade over gravel. It was Thomas Barton, henchman to the Earl of Essex. He briefly wondered how the man knew where he was lodging, before remembering a spy ring's purpose was to know everything about everybody.

'What do you want?' he asked curtly.

'I respect a man who gets straight to business.' Barton stepped closer and in the moonlight his face resembled a turnip with a brutally broken nose. 'Our mutual acquaintance awaits your news.'

The air vanished from Matthew's lungs.

'Struck dumb, Hilliard?' Barton's tone was unnervingly jovial.

Matthew's mind whirred frantically. What should he say to this man? Was it possible he had overheard Beeston and Sly talking about a secret Catholic enclave? Or was there an entirely innocent reason for the butcher allowing 'a cantankerous old bastard' called Dawbeney into his home? Could he condemn a family to the living nightmare of interrogations in the Tower without a single grain of proof? Potentially innocent men and women suffering unimaginable pain. Tortured on the rack in the name of God. No, he could not live with such a terrible thing on his conscience. 'I have no news, as yet,' he replied, his voice strained.

Barton cocked his head to one side, eyeing him shrewdly.

'Take a moment and reconsider your answer. Time is running out for your family. King James has been deeply humiliated by Stewart's treasonous betrayal. He has no use for compassion or forgiveness. Your family are going to die. Can you picture it? Can you picture your mother and your sister stripped naked and brought to the gallows?'

'Enough, man!' Matthew said, appalled.

But Barton was not finished. 'Men will leer at their nakedness. They will denounce them as traitorous whores. And your father and your brother will be forced to watch.'

'Enough man, I pray you, enough!'

Barton's smile was sadistic. 'I can see their terror, their humiliation. I can see their pale, naked bodies exposed for all to see. I can see their soft flesh so soon to be despoiled.'

'You bastard, you bloody bastard!'

Matthew launched himself at Barton. His first punch hit the mark. Barton's nose cracked and blood spurted. But the man did not go down. Instead, he let out a bellow like a castrated bull, and drew his dagger from his belt.

Pointing it at Matthew's throat, he said slowly, 'As the noose tightens, your chaste mother and your pure, untouched, sister will piss and shit themselves, and the crowd will laugh -'

Matthew drew his own knife, and came at Barton again. His rage gave him strength he wasn't aware he possessed. With his free hand, he grabbed Barton's wrist and wrenched it sideways, removing the threat of the man's dagger. And then he thrust his own knife hard into Barton's gut. The blade had barely penetrated the man's padded doublet when Barton's forehead butted Matthew's nose with such force that his world exploded in bright lights and agony. Matthew's head jerked backwards, and his knees gave way. He sank to the ground, reeling. Blood poured from his nose, and ran down the back of his throat. Choking, he leant forward and spat red gobbets into the mud.

Barton crouched down and eyed him dispassionately. Matthew tried to stand up, but Barton pushed him to his knees again, bringing the tip of his dagger blade to rest at Matthew's throat.

'You have spirit, Hilliard, and I admire that. I don't want to kill you, but I will, if you give me no choice. Now, listen to me. Our mutual acquaintance is prepared to help you. There is still time for him to intervene on your father's behalf, but you have to give him something in return.'

Matthew realised his punch had broken Barton's already misshapen nose. The cartilage was swollen and twisted, Barton's mouth and chin covered in blood. He mused on whether his own nose was also broken, anything to avoid thinking about the decision he had to make.

'You can save your family from a horrific and dishonourable death with just a few well-chosen words. That is not so difficult, is it?'

Matthew looked into Barton's cold, unfeeling eyes and decided the man must have been born without a conscience.

'If you will not serve your family, then will you serve your Queen? Or is there no loyalty in you? No charity? No compassion?' Barton lowered his dagger and placed the tip of the blade directly over Matthew's heart. 'Does anything beat in this chest, or are you entirely fashioned of stone?'

A strangled, humourless laugh escaped Matthew's throat.

'You speak to me of compassion?'

'Why the reticence?' Barton sounded genuinely mystified. 'Catholics are evil. They are devils incarnate. You know that better than I.'

Matthew thought of his own grandfather, tied to a stake, forced to watch his own flesh melt in the flames, long before his soul fled to God. Bloody Mary was responsible for his grandfather's torment. The Catholic faith, with its hideous obsession with purification, was responsible for his grandfather's terrible suffering. Catholics were evil. And cruel and deluded. They deserved to be punished.

'Well?' Barton asked. 'What have you to tell me?'

Matthew could almost feel the Devil on his shoulder, his claws digging deep into his flesh. He could hear his ugly, jarring voice, urging him to reveal what he had overheard this night. But there was an angel on his other shoulder, speaking softly, pleading caution, pleading mercy.

Barton had the bit between his teeth now. 'Think of your family. What kind of man abandons their own kin to die traitors' deaths?'

Matthew felt bile rise in his throat. He had two choices, but neither was wholly right, nor wholly honourable, and both would most likely torment him for the rest of his days. He wanted to scream to the heavens for guidance, for forgiveness. But Barton was right.

The simple truth was he couldn't abandon his family to die. His loyalty lay with them. He loved them more than life itself. But his heart felt heavy, weighed down by the enormity of the decision he had reached.

'I believe I have found you a Papist,' he said slowly. 'Look to a man by the name of Anthony Bonvince.' The dam broke and the words fell from Matthew's lips, a great outpouring. 'I do not know where he lives. Perhaps Shoreditch? He is a butcher by trade. His grandfather was of the old faith, a nobleman, who served Queen Mary, but he fell from grace when our Gracious Majesty came to the throne. I believe a priest by the name of

Dawbeney is holding Masses in the cellar of Anthony Bonvince's home.'

Matthew's heart was pounding frantically. One part of him was relieved he had shared this intelligence. He had done his duty to the Crown. He had potentially saved his family's life. The other part felt sick and dirty and ashamed. Somewhere close by, he thought he heard the Devil laugh.

Barton was frowning. 'How long have you known of this? Why did you not tell me sooner?'

'I only learnt of it tonight.'

'What connection does this man, Bonvince, have to the Theatre?'

'None that I can fathom,' Matthew replied truthfully.

And you cannot tell me where he lives?'

Matthew shook his head. 'I have told you everything I know.'

Barton eyed him for a long time, and Matthew forced himself to return the man's shrewd, penetrating gaze.

At length, Barton stood up and returned his dagger to his belt.

'You speak true, and it will serve you well. In the meantime, continue your dissembling at the Theatre. Our mutual acquaintance requires proof Burbage is a Papist.'

'Wait! You will convey my intelligence to the earl?'

'Yes, certainly,' Barton replied civilly. 'Good evening, Master Hilliard.'

Matthew watched Barton walk away, and then he leant forward and spat blood into the mud. His nose wouldn't stop bleeding, as if his body was purging itself of all his pain and guilt, and by so doing, absolving his grievous sins.

ELEVEN

'Then come kiss me, sweet and twenty,
Youth's a stuff will not endure'

Magdalen paused in the doorway of the workshop, waiting for her eyes to become accustomed to the gloom. She had barely slept the previous night; her scalp throbbing, her mind churning over the events of the last few days. Her attacker had warned her to 'leave it be'. But how could she? She had decided to take a longer route to the Theatre later that morning, by way of Cheapside, to make discreet enquires about Matthew Froissart. But, even if she did find him, what would she say to him? She could hardly come straight out and ask if he had killed John. She would have to use her wits. Yet again, she would have to dissemble and deceive. And God would know her sin, because God knew everything. Would He forgive her, or was she destined for the fires of Hell?

'Mordlin, viens ici.'

Christopher Mountjoy was beckoning her to join him. She glanced about, and realised they were alone.

'Where is everyone?' she asked nervously.

'Stephen has gone to the blacksmiths, *avec les garcons miserables. Mon Dieu! Je voudrais les jeter dans le puits!'*

There was no trace of humour in Christopher's voice, and a

shiver of apprehension ran down Magdalen's spine. When he was in one of his rages, she could well imagine him throwing the boys down a well.

'*Viens ici!*' he repeated.

Magdalen stayed where she was. 'And Mistress Mountjoy, and Mary? Where might they be?' she asked hopefully.

'They have gone to the haberdashers in West Cheape, for ribbons or some such. They wanted to go to the Royal Exchange but I forbade it. It is full of charlatans who put too high a price on their wares. They think they can hoodwink us because they have one of the finest addresses in the city. Pah!'

Magdalen was unsure how to respond to that, and decided it would be safest to say nothing.

Christopher was examining the mill. 'I have been thinking that I might use the smallest die to craft the wires for Amelia Bassano's latest head 'tire. It is an important commission for us. It must be beautiful, delicate. But I am concerned the wire might be too thin. *Viens ici*, and tell me if you agree. After all, it is you who will fashion it for us.'

Magdalen told herself not to be alarmed. Just because Christopher had swived Anne and Margaret, it did not necessarily mean he intended to swive her too. But recently, he had taken to staring at her bosom. Worse still, he had developed an unnerving habit of creeping up behind her and catching her unawares, his fingers 'accidentally' brushing over her buttocks. And then his breathing would quicken.

'*Viens, Mordlin!*'

With great reluctance, Magdalen went to the work bench and examined the smallest hole in the mill.

'*C'est trop petit, n'est ce pas?*' Christopher asked.

'The wire would be very thin,' she agreed, 'but I could use it, if I was very careful. It would look beautiful, like silver thread.'

'*Exactement.*' He closed the distance between them. Instinctively, she retreated a pace and glanced anxiously towards the corridor, listening for any sound to suggest Marie had returned from the city, or Stephen and the boys from the blacksmith. But the house remained ominously quiet.

Words tumbled at speed from her lips. 'Excuse me, sir, but I must go upstairs. My grandmother is unwell.' She turned for the door, but he grabbed her by the arm and pulled her towards him.

'*J'adore ton cou,*' he whispered. 'White as snow, on display for all to admire. If you wore a ruff, like any respectable wench, you would not entice me so. You are to blame, *Mordlin.* You are a temptress, an evil temptress.' He was breathing heavily, and the smell escaping his lips reminded Magdalen of a stagnant fen. She tried to wrench herself from his grasp, but he responded by tightening his grip about her forearms and then he bent his head and kissed her exposed throat.

'No, stop! I don't want - I beg you, stop!' she pleaded desperately. His wet lips were sucking like a leech. She fought to be free of him, but he held her fast, pushing her against the wall.

'Do not feign chastity, *Mordlin.* Everyone knows you are the players' whore.' His tongue was slithering along her jaw line, and then he fastened his lips on hers. His tongue invaded her mouth. It felt huge, a wet squirming slug, and Magdalen gagged. She could feel him tugging at her kirtle, inching it higher. Through a mist of fear and revulsion, she tried desperately to knee him in the stones but she couldn't move, crushed beneath his huge bulk.

'You whore! You foul, lecherous whore!' Marie's agitated voice rang out across the workshop.

One moment Christopher was everywhere; his lips, his tongue, his hands, his huge, solid frame. The next, he released Magdalen as if she were fashioned from burning coal.

Marie was breathless with rage. 'I want you gone, you harlot!

Bewitching my husband with your evil lechery! I always said we should not give lodgings to players and their whores! I want you gone! Gone from this workshop, and gone from this house! You, and your moon-mad grandmother!'

Magdalen stared at Marie, aghast.

What had she just said? No! Please God, no.

'Did you hear me, harlot? Get out of my sight!'

'I… I… not that… please…' Magdalen stammered.

'Out! Out, you wanton witch!' Marie screamed, her arms flailing wildly.

As Magdalen fled the workshop, she heard Marie shriek, 'How many times have you sluiced her, husband? How many times, you adulterous, virgin-violator!'

In the kitchen, Magdalen placed her palms flat on the table, craving the touch of something solid in a world suddenly without substance. In little more than the blink of an eye, the thing she had dreaded most had come to pass. Dragging the pitcher across the table, she poured herself a cup of small beer, and went out into the yard. She swilled her mouth out repeatedly, spitting the beer into the vegetable patch. But she could still feel Christopher's writhing tongue, still taste his rotting teeth. She sat down on the edge of a raised vegetable bed, and her hand shook as she drained the cup.

What was she supposed to do now? The city's landlords were notoriously greedy. If she had to rely solely on her wages from the Theatre she would be lucky to afford lodgings in a damp and stinking cellar shared with four other families. How long would her grandmother survive in such a place?

Perhaps she could throw herself on the mercy of Henry Condell. He was a family man with a kind wife, perhaps he would take them in. But her grandmother would not be an easy house guest. She could not impose on their charity.

Was this all her fault? Christopher Mountjoy had denounced her as a temptress, and Marie Mountjoy had called her a harlot and a whore. And yet, she had not sought Christopher out. As God was her witness, she had no such designs.

'Come inside, girl. I want to talk to you.'

Marie was at the kitchen door. She sounded strangely calm, and only her red-rimmed eyes betrayed any sign of her previous distress. Magdalen stood up, nervously straightened her kirtle and followed Marie into the kitchen, keeping her gaze fixed firmly on her boots. She waited for Marie to say something but the silence stretched on, heavy and oppressive. Was this how it felt to wait for the executioner's axe to fall?

'If you ever touch my husband again,' Marie said at last, her voice flat, 'I will have you brought up before the church elders, and the entire congregation will know of your lewdness and your sin. And you and your grandmother will be evicted before the sun sets. Do you understand?'

Astonished, Magdalen lifted her gaze and met Marie's cold stare. Had she heard correctly?

'Have you lost your wits?' Marie demanded impatiently.

'Yes, I mean, no,' Magdalen stammered. 'Thank you. Truly. I am sorry. I did not mean… I did not want…' her words trailed away.

For a fleeting moment, Magdalen thought she saw a glimmer of compassion in Marie's eyes before it was quickly suppressed.

'*Suffis! Suffis!* We will not speak of this again. Get back to work. Set aside Lady Gerard's 'tire. She yearns for the Admiral's homecoming, but I hear it could be months before he spies landfall. You will start on Mistress Bassano's 'tire. She must not be kept waiting. She has already sent me the rubies. *Ils sont beau, tres beau.*'

Magdalen walked back to the workshop at a snail's pace. She

felt nauseous, and angry, and afraid. But at the same time, she also felt relieved because her grandmother still had a roof over her head. She peered nervously into the gloom of the workshop, but mercifully Christopher was nowhere to be seen. Sitting down at the bench, she opened her workbook and stared blankly at her preliminary sketches for Amelia's head 'tire, her thoughts elsewhere. What if Marie had not arrived when she did? Christopher Mountjoy was a big, strong man and he had easily overpowered her. What if he had put a babe in her belly? Her life would be over. She would be homeless and destitute, fit for nowhere but Bridewell.

A shudder of dread ran down her spine. Christopher had evidently ignored his wife's pleas for her dismissal. There was nothing to stop him assaulting her again. She had to avoid being alone with him, but that would be easier said than done. Time passed painfully slowly that morning. Magdalen had never been more grateful to hear the bells of Saint Olave's chiming ten o'clock. Quickly gathering her belongings, she left the workshop with unseemly haste.

A low, watery sun glinted on the puddles of Silver Street. After the darkness of the workshop, Magdalen narrowed her eyes against its glare. She turned south along Wood Street and then on into the wide, paved street of Cheapside. Cutting across the city, as straight as a seam, it shone with life and colour; a place where successful merchants displayed their wealth with fine houses, some five storeys high and brightly decorated. A place where humbler country folk sold vegetables and poultry seven days a week from dawn to dusk and the residents, resplendent behind their glazed windows and iron-studded doors, complained of the noise and stink.

She passed flower stalls by the great conduit, and haberdashers' shops, their windows displaying gauzy fabric in satin waterfalls of rainbow hue. The street was filled with noise. The clatter of wagons and coaches; the laughter of goodwives; the raucous shouts of street-sellers offering strings of onions, oysters, sausages, hot codlings. Usually, Magdalen would have paid little attention to the hubbub of familiar sounds, but today she was afraid and on edge, constantly looking over her shoulder for the men who had pursued her the previous night.

And then she thought of Christopher Mountjoy, and her fear became a dense fog swirling inside her head. Quite suddenly, she couldn't breathe. She came to an abrupt stop and put her hands on her knees, willing herself to calm down. Gradually, her dizziness abated, and her heart's frantic rhythm slowed. She righted herself and hurried on.

At the sign of the Black Bear, she turned into Saint Martin's, a district settled by foreign craftsmen, as good a place as any to look for Froissart. The nearby Goldsmiths' Guild regularly accused the immigrants of producing counterfeit goods, and their claims had some merit. When Magdalen needed good quality glass jewels for the workshop's head 'tires, she often purchased them in Saint Martin's.

The narrow streets were crowded and Magdalen slowed her pace, searching the sea of faces for Froissart. Few people were speaking English. Most were chattering in French, but she overheard two men conversing in a language she thought might be Flemish. Froissart had spoken with the same lilting accent, the same distinctive 'hissing' at the end of certain words. She approached the two men and bobbed a curtsey. From their sober attire and tall black hats, she took them for respectable merchants of the middling sort. She decided to address them in French, in the hope of passing herself off as a native of Saint Martin's.

'*Excusez-moi, monsieurs. Connaissez-vous Monsieur Froissart?*'

'*Froissart? Mais oui. Il vit juste la-bas.*' The older man pointed across the street.

Magdalen followed his gaze. '*Il est bijoutier?*' she asked.

'*Oui, bien sur,*' the old man replied, and she realised her question had been a foolish one, for this was a street consisting almost entirely of jewellery workshops.

'*Merci, monsieur.*'

Magdalen crossed the road and loitered outside Froissart's shop for a long while, gathering her courage. The time had come to dissemble once again, and she cursed Edmund Stow for bringing her so low. Taking a deep breath, she opened the door and went inside. The shop was dark and smelled musty, overlaid with faint hints of beeswax polish. The walls were lined with cabinets displaying a sparkling array of necklaces, bracelets and finger-rings. She wondered if they were fashioned from a thin layer of gold over pewter, as the Goldsmiths' Guild claimed.

Without warning, the hairs on the back of her neck began to prickle. She looked about nervously and spied Matthew Froissart standing in the shadows, almost indiscernible save for his mop of thick blond hair. He brought to mind a spider waiting patiently, silently, to catch its prey.

'May I help you, madam?'

Again, Magdalen heard the soft hiss, as if his tongue was stuck to the top of his palate. Fear gripped her and she was rendered momentarily speechless by the alarming possibility that she might be no more than six feet from John's killer.

'Madam?' Froissart repeated.

She found her voice at last. 'Good day, sir. I am looking for a mourning ring, in memory of my late sister. She bequeathed me a small sum for the purpose.' *So many lies. God forgive my sins.*

'May I offer my condolences,' Froissart said, pausing respectfully before continuing, 'I have several items which might suit your needs. One in particular is set with a beautiful piece of jet. May I show it to you?'

'Yes, thank you.' Magdalen was having difficulty reconciling this respectful shop-keeper with the ranting madman she had witnessed in the pest house.

Froissart stepped out of the shadows. He was not an unattractive man, but there was something about his long, gangly limbs and excessively deliberate manner which reinforced her first impression of an arachnid.

He unlocked a cabinet, selected a ring and carefully placed it on a plump, red cushion with all the pomp of a coronation ceremony. His actions were slow and purposeful, and the shop was so quiet Magdalen could hear his every exhalation of breath. Accustomed to the rowdy temperaments of the players, she tried to tell herself that a quiet, methodical nature did not make a man a murderer, yet her every instinct was screaming at her to run.

She picked up the ring and made a show of examining it.

'The jet is from Whitby,' Froissart said. 'We can engrave a memento of your choice on the band.'

Magdalen returned the ring to its cushion.

'It is beautiful, but might I see another?'

'Certainly.'

'I believe you might be familiar with an acquaintance of mine? Reverend Cooper?' she asked as Froissart placed another ring on the cushion with all the reverence due to a Catholic relic.

He gave her a sharp glance. 'Yes, I know him, but may I ask how *you* know him?'

'We share a mutual acquaintance. Louisa du Bois.'

'The player's sister?'

'Yes, the same.'

Froissart stiffened. 'You keep poor company if you associate with such men,' he said coldly.

Magdalen had expected as much. 'My association is not with the late player, but with his sister.' Adopting a doleful demeanour, she added, 'My own sister's death has been grievously difficult for our family, and we prayed Reverend Cooper's teachings and wise counsel might offer us some comfort in our time of grief, but we have been unable to find him. He is not at his lodgings. His landlady said he may have gone into Hampshire.'

'It is unlikely Adam is in Hampshire, for he has no connections there.'

Magdalen took a moment to digest this. Had Cooper lied to the young girl at the Anabaptist's meeting and if so, why?

'My parents would gain great succour from his company. Do you know where he might be?'

'I do not.' Froissart was frowning. 'I pray he has not come to harm.'

'Why do you say that?'

'Because of his association with the player. He swore he was trying to save the man's soul, but I was sorely concerned for his own soul. He was spending so much time with that foul, debauched wretch -' He broke off, glancing over his shoulder as a goodwife bustled into the shop, a basket in her hand and a purposeful look on her face.

It was obvious to Magdalen that she would learn nothing more here. 'I must leave you now. I will return tomorrow to make my final choice. I thank you for your time, sir.'

'I will await your instructions.' Froissart gave her a small bow then turned to his next customer, the goodwife.

'Good day, Mistress Waite, your necklace is repaired…'

Outside, Magdalen took a succession of deep breaths. A brisk southerly wind carried the scents of the river, full of salt and fish and mud; a welcome relief from Froissart's airless musty shop. She paused for a moment to brush her hands over her cloak, an instinctive gesture, as if to rid herself of the sticky threads of a spider's web. Somewhere in the distance, a church bell began to chime. It was eleven o'clock, and she was very late.

As she hurried towards the Theatre, she tried hard to focus on the day ahead, but her thoughts spooled back to Matthew Froissart. He had behaved courteously in his shop, yet in the pest house he had raved like a mad man and called for the death of all players. Which persona was the real Froissart? Had the strange, fervent atmosphere of the prayer meeting triggered an inflammatory outburst from an otherwise peaceable man? Or was he capable of the wholesale murder he had championed? As a child he had been forced to watch his own mother burn to death. Surely such an experience might warp a man? She *had* to find the truth of it, but not today because the company was performing *Richard the Third* in less than three hours.

In the 'tiring house, Christopher Beeston and William Sly were stripped to the waist and bare-fist fighting. Light of foot, they danced and weaved and pulled their punches in a meticulously choreographed display. Taking advantage of the distraction, Magdalen retrieved Malvolio's doublet and breeches from her satchel and returned them to the costume chest. Fearful of discovery, she shot a quick glance about the room but no-one was looking her way. At times such as this, being treated as part of the furniture had its advantages. On her feet again, she realised Joan Coverdale was sitting at her workbench with one of Amelia Bassano's gowns draped across her lap.

'Joan! I have been hoping to speak with you!' Belatedly remembering the reason for her distant cousin's visit to Hertfordshire, Magdalen quickly wiped the smile from her face. 'How fares your sister?'

'She died,' Joan replied. Plump, dark eyed, with strands of rich, chestnut coloured hair escaping from her coif, she would have been a pretty girl but for the cruel smallpox scars.

'I'm so sorry. My condolences for your loss.' Magdalen sat down on the stool, and laid a sympathetic hand on Joan's arm.

Joan shrugged. 'I thank you, Maggie, although my sister was a miserable shrew of a woman. I do believe her husband is mightily relieved she is six feet under.'

'Oh…' Taken aback, Magdalen quickly changed the subject. 'And how do you fare, Joan?'

'Well enough. I expect you know why I've come.'

'Yes, I expect I do,' Magdalen replied, eyeing the gown on Joan's lap.

No doubt Amelia's waistline was expanding and the attire was of no further use to her. No doubt she had gifted the gown to her ladies-in-waiting, who in turn had asked Joan to secure a good price. Magdalen wished she could oblige, for the gown was a thing of beauty, worth at least four pounds. The bodice and sleeves were of fine satin, the gown of baudekin, a wildly expensive fabric woven with shimmering silver threads.

Unfortunately, Burbage had no money for such an extravagance, but an idea was forming in Magdalen's mind. She reached for the jug of Malmsey. 'Will you take a drink with me, Joan?'

Joan agreed without hesitation. 'Don't mind if I do. I've a thirst and no mistake.'

When Magdalen had refilled her cup for the fourth time, Joan's face was flushed and they were chatting as gaily as sisters. 'This is between you and me,' Joan whispered, leaning closer. 'You mustn't tell a soul.'

Magdalen nodded solemnly.

'Amelia had a lover. I always knew when she was due to meet him, because she fair glowed with excitement. She'd see him whenever His Lordship was away at court. They'd meet down in the sunken garden, in a private bower, so they'd not be overlooked. I used to follow her. Not that I was being nosy, you understand. I just wanted to be certain she was safe. Who knows what that boy could have done to her?' She smirked knowingly. 'Between you and me, he did plenty to her. Not that my mistress minded. She mewled like a pussy cat, and that's the truth.'

Magdalen grinned. 'This lover – did you recognise him?'

'Oh, aye, I recognised him right enough. It was John Wood, the player what died. I heard he ate some bad fish, but some folks are saying he was poisoned.' Joan looked at Magdalen expectantly, perhaps hoping she might confirm or deny. When Magdalen said nothing, Joan rattled on. 'Anyways, they had a falling out. One night they was all lovey-dovey, at it, brazen as anything in their pretty little bower, and then the next night they was screaming at each other. She didn't go back to the sunken garden after that. She was right upset.'

'Do you know what they were arguing about?'

'No. I couldn't hear much, just the odd word here and there. I was hiding in a yew hedge, and it wasn't comfortable, not by any means. I tried to get closer but my skirt got snagged.'

Magdalen took a sip of Malmsey, trying to make sense of Joan's revelations. Had Amelia discovered the truth about John's other lovers? Had hurt and jealousy driven her to poison John? Or had there been a more pragmatic reason for his death? Perhaps Amelia believed she had no choice but to kill John, rather than risk losing the Lord Chamberlain's protection? For how else would she, a pregnant, unmarried woman, find a husband without his assistance?

'But I can tell you this,' Joan went on. 'A week later she got into a terrible argument with His Lordship. I heard every word. I put my ear right up against the key hole. Not because I was being nosy, you understand, but because I could hear him throwing things and I was worried for her. He was calling her a whore and a thief, saying he knew all about her and the player, saying he knew all about her stealing his money to pay off the player's gambling debts.'

'What did she say to that?'

'She was sobbing. Swearing he was mistaken, swearing she loved him.'

'When was this argument? Can you remember?'

'Oh aye. It was a Thursday. Thursday the twenty-sixth of March. I remember it, because His Lordship was entertaining that night. There was a huge banquet, very grand, and Amelia was at his side, but it was plain she'd been crying.'

The twenty-six of March. Two days before John was killed.

'Do you think Amelia *was* settling John Wood's debts?' Magdalen asked.

'I wouldn't be surprised. She was in love with that boy. She would have done anything for him. But after that night when they argued, I don't think they saw each other again. And I think it broke her heart.'

'If Lord Hunsdon suspected Amelia had been unfaithful to him, why didn't he disown her?'

'I'll tell you why. She has him wrapped around her little finger. Well, more often he's wrapped around her waist, if you know what I mean.' Joan winked. 'They're fiery and no mistake. One minute they're hurling plates at each other, the next they're cooing over each other. He can't bear to give her up. That's why he's marrying her to a sodomite, so he can go on having her all to himself.'

'Whose baby is she carrying, Joan?'

Joan raised her palms to the heavens. 'I have no idea and I doubt my mistress knows either. One night she swived the player, the next she swived His Lordship. It went on like that for

215

months.' Joan giggled. 'For an old man, he has no problem keeping it up.'

Magdalen could not help but wonder how many hours Joan had spent at the key-hole of their bedchamber to know such intimate details. And while Lord Hunsdon was presumably paying Alfonso Lanier handsomely to marry Amelia, it seemed all the money in the world hadn't stopped her from toying with a lowly player as soon as his back was turned. How would a powerful man endure such betrayal? Would he simply hurl plates to vent his anger? Or would the desire for revenge drive him to commit murder?

Joan poured herself another cup of Malmsey. Magdalen noticed her eyes were glazed, and felt ashamed she had offered her wine for the sole purpose of loosening her tongue. Apologising profusely for Burbage's empty coffers, she suggested Joan try Philip Henslowe's theatre company on the Southbank. Joan did not appear to take offence.

'A fine idea! I'll take a wherry this afternoon. I've a fancy to see Marlowe's *Tamburlaine*. They say it's so thrilling you're likely to piss your linens.' She stood up. 'Best be getting on, Maggie. Not a word to anyone about what I've said, mind.'

'Not a word, I swear.'

They parted with a warm embrace. Magdalen returned to her workbench, her head swimming with Joan's scurrilous revelations. If they were true, it meant both Lord Hunsdon and Amelia had a motive to kill John. But there was no time to think about that now. The performance of *Richard the Third* would begin in little over an hour. She glanced appraisingly around the 'tiring house. The players were drifting about in various stages of undress, but she noticed Burbage had already hoisted Richard the Third's hefty hump-back onto his shoulders. She prayed the stronger straps she had fashioned would hold its weight. Burbage was already in character, his limp pronounced, his body contorted and lop-sided; a monstrously deformed, malevolent presence.

Alex Cooke was hanging on Christopher Beeston and William Sly's every word but, as usual, they were ignoring him.

'Alex! Come here!' she shouted.

With a somewhat dejected air, he left their side and ambled over to her workbench. A long, dark brown wig framed his delicate features, and a thick layer of paint covered an outbreak of adolescent pimples. A cartwheel shaped farthingale was tied about his slender waist. Tilted at the back by a thickly padded bum-roll, it gave him a startlingly cylindrical shape from the waist down.

He was taking the role of Anne Neville, wife of Richard the Third. It would have been John's role, but Magdalen tried not to dwell on that. Frowning with concentration, she began the time-consuming task of pinning Alex's gown into neat, evenly spaced gathers along the wheel frame. After a while, she took a step back, eyed him critically then stepped forward again, her fingers busily perfecting the rounded folds of the skirt's falling pleats.

She looked up at the precise moment Matthew Hilliard walked into her line of sight, as if sensing his approach by some instinct she could not begin to understand. He was reading his cue sheets as he paced back and forth, and she found herself staring at him, a tiny pin poised a hair's breadth from the pleated fabric. True to his word, Will Shakespeare had taken Matthew under his wing and instructed him on stagecraft: how to stand, how to move, how to project his voice. And Matthew had proven his worth, for Burbage had rewarded him with his first, albeit small, role as a courtier to the King.

Magdalen noticed Matthew's nose was swollen, his face bruised. She frowned with concern. It was obvious he had been in a fight, but Burbage was two players short and so, most unusually, it appeared he had allowed the misdemeanour to go unpunished. But who had Matthew been fighting with, and why?

The door to the courtyard burst open and Peter charged in, red-faced, his hair sticking out in all directions.

'Where have you been, boy? I'll have you whipped for running off without my permission,' Burbage snarled, every inch the wicked Plantagenet usurper.

Peter paid him no heed. He ran to Magdalen and tugged at her sleeve. 'Sweet Jesu, you'll never guess, oh, sweet Jesu, I can't believe it...'

Accustomed to the boy's excitable nature, Magdalen spat the pins lodged between her lips into her palm and said calmly, 'Take a breath, then tell me what has happened.'

'He's dead, stabbed to death in that passage next to the Mermaid, the one no-one goes in anymore because the jakes overflowed. He's been there for days, I heard the constable say. The rats have been gnawing at his face.' Peter's face crumpled. 'Oh God, Maggie, it was awful.'

He had her full attention now. 'Who? Who is dead?'

'Richard Cowley.'

For one shameful moment, Magdalen felt only relief. Marlowe lived a life marred by casual violence, and he had so many enemies. It could so easily have been his body left to rot in the noxious alley by the Mermaid.

'There was a piece of paper pinned on his doublet,' Peter went on, sobbing uncontrollably, snot bubbling from his nose. 'It said *sinner and sodomite,* just like the writing on the 'tiring house door.'

You could have heard a pin drop in the 'tiring house.

The players turned to one another, seeking reassurance where none could be found because no-one had any answers, and now they were all afraid.

Burbage broke the silence. 'Grave news indeed. May God have mercy on his soul.'

'Mary, mother of God preserve us.' Will Kempe was crossing himself repeatedly. It was a blatantly Catholic gesture but he didn't seem to care.

Magdalen glanced curiously at Matthew Hilliard. He was standing stock-still, the colour draining from his face, his expression unreadable.

Moments later, Edmund Stow arrived, blundering into the 'tiring house with all the tact and sensitivity of a runaway bull.

Burbage responded with pointed curtness. 'This is not the best time, Stow. I have matters to attend. There is a performance to cancel.'

But the constable appeared determined to revel in the players' misfortune and misery. 'This does not bode well for you, Burbage,' he boomed. 'This does not bode well at all.'

Remembering the grip of Stow's pudgy fingers about her throat, Magdalen attempted to hide behind the muscular bulk of Christopher Beeston but Stow spotted her, and pushed Beeston aside.

'Richard Cowley was poisoned, but you already know that, don't you, Mistress Bisset?'

'I do not, sir,' Magdalen replied unsteadily.

Another player dead. This could not be happening.

'We were told he was stabbed to death,' Burbage said curtly.

'There were wounds,' Stow conceded, 'but his lips were tinged with blue.'

'I don't understand how you could know that, sir,' Peter piped up, 'seen as how his lips were all eaten off by rats.'

Stow turned on the boy. 'You will be silent! You know nothing but tittle tattle.'

'I saw him with my own eyes, sir.' A loud sob escaped Peter's throat and suddenly he was running for the door. Henry Condell made to follow him.

'Stay where you are!' Stow commanded. 'I am not done here.'

He was right about that. His interrogation lasted for several hours, the same barbed questions, the same snide comments.

'Mistress Bisset, we all know you were John Wood's lover. Were you also Richard Cowley's lover?'

'No, sir,' she replied furiously. 'I am a virtuous maid. I have no lovers.'

She noticed there were large beads of sweat standing out on the constable's forehead. The man was in a continual state of thaw.

Once again, he ordered the players to take up a quill-pen, this time to write the words, '*sinner and sodomite*'. He examined Magdalen's handwriting for a long time.

'Remarkable similarity,' he said at last.

Burbage snatched the paper from him, and scrutinised Magdalen's penmanship. 'No more than the rest. Take care, sir, or I will be obliged to report your lack of impartiality to the coroner.'

Stow's rotund chest inflated indignantly. 'And *you* should take care, or I will be obliged to report your disrespect for an officer of the law.'

Magdalen clasped her arms tightly about herself; a make-shift shield against the constable's unyielding malevolence. She thought back to their previous encounter. Would he have actually throttled her to death, if she had not kneed him in the stones?

'The same words have been painted on the 'tiring house door several times of late,' Will Shakespeare said quietly. 'It suggests the Puritans are responsible for Richard's death.'

'More likely the murderer is dissembling,' Stow replied

disparagingly. 'What better way to hide the truth than to lay the blame at the Puritans' feet.' He shook his head sanctimoniously at Burbage. 'You may expect a visit from the coroner in the next day or so. By the heavens! I did not believe the Theatre's reputation could sink any lower, but it seems I was mistaken.'

Burbage's eyes narrowed but he wisely kept his silence.

Perhaps realising he had exhausted every conceivable means of humiliating Burbage and his players, Stow made to leave, but at the door he turned around and fixed his gaze upon Magdalen.

'I have proof you poisoned John Wood and, as God is my witness, I will prove you killed Richard Cowley too. And I will see you hang for your unnatural crimes, you wanton, wicked whore.' And with that, he stepped out into the street, slamming the door behind him with such force that a handful of Magdalen's 'tire pins leapt clean from their tin.

The sense of shock in the 'tiring house was almost physical, even the air felt weighed down by it. For several moments, no-one spoke until William Sly said quietly, 'To the Mermaid?'

'Aye,' Christopher Beeston agreed solemnly. 'It would be for the best.'

In the Mermaid, the players dragged two tables together, and told Francis Johnson to add the barrel of Mad Dog to Richard Cowley's account. Magdalen pulled up a chair and joined them. She noticed Matthew Hilliard was staring at the contents of his cup. His brooding intensity was in sharp contrast to the rest of the players, for the atmosphere in the Mermaid already had an air of desperate abandon.

Magdalen was struggling to make sense of another player's death. It was all too much to comprehend. Laying claim to the jug of Rhenish, she refilled her cup, downed the wine, and refilled it once again.

The afternoon slipped into an evening lit by fire flame and candle light, and loud with raucous laughter. Another player was lost, the plague was rife, and perhaps the company felt their days were numbered. Francis Johnson rolled out more barrels of Mad Dog, the serving girls poured more Rhenish, and filled platters with game pies and saffron cakes, and the players drank and feasted as if there would be no tomorrow.

As will happen when men come together in one place with an unlimited supply of alcohol, the evening developed a competitive edge. Urged on by William Sly and Christopher Beeston, the players rested their foreheads on the end of a broomstick, ran around it five times then raced each other to the far wall of the tavern. No one could run in a straight line. William Kempe crashed onto the table and slid along its length, like some giant, ungainly bird landing on water, pewter drinking cups spraying in his wake.

When it came to Magdalen's turn, she took three steps, and fell over. Robert Greene, the poet who so hated Will, tried to pick her up off the floor, fumbling her breasts in the process. His long red quiff of unwashed hair was dangling in her face, and he smelled of piss, but Magdalen was so dizzy it wasn't easy to fend him off. From the corner of her eye, she saw Matthew Hilliard on his feet, running to her aid, but Greene's wife, Cutting Ball Cath, beat him to it. A renowned thief, she cuffed Greene about the head and dragged him away.

Matthew watched as Will Shakespeare stepped in, taking Magdalen by the arm and lowering her into a chair. Judging by his solicitous manner, he guessed the playwright was asking if she was hurt. Matthew watched their exchange and found himself wrestling with an unsettling mix of emotions.

He felt angry with Robert Greene for treating Magdalen with such disrespect, and angry with the players for making no effort to protect her from such a man. It was much harder to fathom why he also felt angry with Magdalen. Perhaps, if he was honest with himself, he didn't like to see her behaving with such abandon in the company of lowly players, in an equally lowly tavern. And yet, wasn't it her recklessness, her feistiness, that had attracted him to her in the first place?

And he felt angry with Will Shakespeare for…

For what exactly? For showing Magdalen kindness? Was he angry with Shakespeare, or was he jealous? Matthew shook his head, driving away such treacherous notions. His thoughts turned to his encounter with Thomas Barton, and his emotions darkened.

The names Dawbeney, Agnes and Bonvince meant nothing to him. How much harder would it have been to offer them up like lambs to the slaughter if he had known them personally?

And had Barton delivered his intelligence to the earl? If so, would the earl honour his promise and write to the King James on his father's behalf? How much longer must he wait for news, when every minute felt like an hour, and every day an eternity?

Pressure was building inside his head; unbearable pressure that only a surfeit of Mad Dog could alleviate. Countless cups later, he borrowed Francis Johnson's set of bagpipes and, for some unfathomable reason, decided they would sound better if he played them outside or, better still, from a great height. With grim determination, he climbed onto the out-house roof, and then onto the roof of the Mermaid itself. A large crowd, including Magdalen, quickly gathered below to cheer him on. He had almost reached the apex when a tile cracked beneath his weight, and he almost lost his footing. A gasp of horror ran around the assembled crowd before he managed to regain his balance.

Robert Greene was taking a piss against the wall. 'That's a

fucking big pigeon,' he said before recognition dawned. 'Ah, it's you. Play us a tune, you daft prick.'

The tune Matthew played was a haunting one, so beautiful it brought tears to Magdalen's eyes. During the impromptu performance, Marlowe arrived. He looked spectacular, the ornate gold buttons of his doublet reflecting the moonlight, a braided cloak slung jauntily over his shoulder.

'What is that terrible noise? Is someone buggering a cat?' he yelled, glaring at Matthew, who studiously ignored him and continued to play.

Magdalen giggled.

'Adonis's arse, Magdalen. Are you drunk?' Marlowe asked sternly.

'Only a little.' She giggled again.

'Then dance with me, my sweet girl!'

Putting both hands on her waist, he lifted her high into the air, twirling her around then setting her back to earth. Magdalen had skipped around the May pole in her childhood, but she had no idea how to dance the courtly galliard. She stood on Marlowe's toes countless times before they staggered to an ungainly halt. Marlowe was laughing so hard he could barely stand up.

'I will teach you how to dance one day, but not now. Ganymede's stones, I need a drink,' he gasped and pulled her back inside the tavern.

A game of indoor football was in progress, two teams vying for a pig's bladder ball. Players, playwrights and poets were scrambling over the furniture, chair legs splintering, trays of beer flying. Magdalen expected Marlowe to join in, but he seemed more interested in finding a keg of Mad Dog.

'I recognise that fellow on the roof,' he shouted above the mayhem. 'Who is he?'

'Burbage's new recruit,' Magdalen shouted back.

'I saw how you were looking at him. Have a care, Maggie.'

It was most unlike Marlowe to show any concern for her wellbeing. 'I don't know what you mean,' she replied but her blush gave her away.

'As you wish. In faith, speaking of such matters makes my teeth hurt.' Righting two upended chairs, he bade her sit down with him. As was his want, he did not indulge in common courtesies. He did not ask how she fared, nor offer his condolences for Richard Cowley's death, nor comment on how it might affect her chances at the inquest. Instead, he produced a couple of dice from his pocket.

'Lady Fortune favours me tonight, I am certain of it! Double sixes!' he crowed, tossing them across the sticky table.

As they came to rest, Magdalen peered at them. Two sixes. She shook her head and laughed. 'You are a scoundrel. False dice to be sure. I will not play with you.'

'Would you break a poor man's heart?'

'For one, you are no longer poor. Your attire tells me you have come into money, yet again. And two, you have no heart to break.'

'It's true.' He thrust the dice into her palm. 'But humour me.'

Magdalen sighed and drained another cup of Rhenish.

'Oh, very well.'

The next day, she had only the vaguest recollection of their game. But she did remember Marlowe growing bored after a while and wandering off. Sometime later, he brought the evening to a dramatic close by dragging the ancient harpsichord out into the street. Announcing loudly that it was an 'affront to the music of the spheres', he promptly set fire to it. Francis Johnson lost his sense of humour at that point, and who could blame him. Fire was the city's deadliest enemy. He banned Marlowe for life and told the rest of them to leave.

TWELVE

'My thoughts are ripe in mischief'

Saturday 4th April

The next morning, Magdalen awoke to yet another head-ache, this time brought about by a surfeit of Rhenish rather than the wound at the back of her skull, which had mercifully begun to heal. Her pain was somewhat lessened by the realisation that it was Saturday, a day of rest from the workshop. She opened her eyes, and the events of the previous week came flooding back, not least Peter running into the 'tiring house with news of Richard Cowley's death. She had never much liked Richard and it was strange to realise she felt no grief for his passing. Richard had never much liked her either. Could he have been the witness Edmund Stow had boasted about?

A note was tied around Richard's neck, *'Sinner and Sodomite'*. If the Puritans *were* responsible for John's death and now Richard's, why would they blatantly incriminate themselves? Perhaps Stow was right about one thing. Perhaps the real killer was dissembling, but how to find the truth of it with the inquest only six days away?

Magdalen tossed and turned, and all the while, her head

pounded and her mind seethed over the nightmare her life had become. Finally, when she could bear it no longer, she leapt from her bed, opened the shutters, retrieved the pages of *Venus and Adonis* from the bottom of her work basket and slipped beneath the blankets again:

Holding Adonis fast, Venus beseeches him not to hunt the ferocious boar because she has had a premonition it will lead to his death. She implores him to give up his fruitless chastity, but Adonis replies it is not love he hates, but her reasoning…

'Call it not Love, for Love to heaven is fled,
Since sweating Lust on earth usurped his name…'
'Love comforts like sunshine after rain,
But Lust's effect is tempest after sun;
Love's gentle spring does always fresh remain,
Lust's winter comes 'ere summer half be done;
Love surfeits not, Lust like a glutton dies;
Love is all truth, Lust full of forged lies.'

Magdalen was mesmerised. She had read the poem in the hope of understanding the difference between love and lust and now, at last, she did. How could Will have found the truth of it, and distilled it into such exquisite poetry? How could he have encapsulated so much in so few words? Where did such genius spring from? Did it pour, fully-formed, from his quill? Or was it hard won, for he spent many hours in his chamber, hunched over his desk, finger nails stained with ink. Perhaps she should make allowances for such genius? Perhaps she should forgive him his obsession with advancement; for not thanking her for taking *Venus and Adonis* to the Earl of Southampton; for not enquiring how she had endured the excruciating deception of playing the Lord Chamberlain's tailor; for seeming not to care that Edmund Stow was determined to see her hang.

Christopher and Marie were shouting at one another, their

voices carrying up the stairs. Reluctantly, Magdalen flung back her blankets and climbed out of bed. She was about to return the pages of *Venus and Adonis* to the bottom of the workbasket when she remembered her landlady's increasing tendency to pry, and decided Will's poem, and *Nashe's Dildo,* might be safer in her workbench drawer at the Theatre. Slipping the pages into her satchel, she washed, dressed and went downstairs. She was relieved to discover the Mountjoys had finished breakfast and moved into the workshop. She had no wish to see Christopher today, or any other day for that matter.

Filling a tray with slices of bread and a wedge of cheese, two cups and a pitcher of small beer, she went back upstairs. She was not due at the Theatre until ten o'clock, which gave her ample time to breakfast with her grandmother. But Agnes was having a bad day.

'Who are you, and how did you get into my chamber?' she demanded, her eyes darting about her chamber as if she expected to see a gang of Upright Men lurking in the corner.

'It's me, it's Magdalen, your granddaughter.' Magdalen sat down on the edge of the bed and mustered a reassuring smile, but Agnes's stick-thin arms were flapping wildly.

'Pierre and I have not yet been blessed with children, so how can I have a granddaughter? Get out! Get out of my house, before I call the constable!'

'It's me, Magdalen, your granddaughter,' Magdalen repeated.

'Get out, you thieving harlot!' Agnes snatched a cup from the tray and hurled it at her.

Magdalen caught it before it fell. She picked up the tray and retreated downstairs. Sinking into a chair at the kitchen table, she put her head in her hands. Old age was cruel, stripping away dignity and compassion and reason. She prayed she would not live long enough to endure such infirmity. She sat there for a long time, wallowing in grief and self-pity, until Tom bounded into the kitchen.

'He's let us out for five minutes 'cos he wants to smoke that stinking pipe in peace. What's the matter, Mags?' he asked, belatedly noticing Magdalen's crumpled form.

'Nothing.' She wiped her eyes with a handkerchief hastily retrieved from her sleeve. 'I had something in my eye.'

Tom, not renowned for his empathy, accepted her explanation without question. 'You eating that?' he asked, eyeing the tray of untouched food. Like most twelve-year-old boys, he was perennially hungry.

'You can have a slice of bread. I'm taking the rest to a friend in need,' she replied, making a spur of the moment decision to visit Louisa du Bois. John's sister had appeared painfully alone at the funeral. Perhaps she might take solace in some company.

Putting the bread and cheese into a basket, Magdalen grabbed her cloak and went out. The streets of Shoreditch were busy with wagons and carts, some laden with sacks of grain from the countryside, others with spices from the city docks, still more with freshly hewn wood from Epping Forest. The noise did nothing to alleviate Magdalen's headache, her mind seething like the contents of an apothecary's cauldron. She had meant the basket of food to be an offering of friendship, but what if Louisa saw it as unwanted charity?

As Magdalen approached Tenter Street, she heard the sound of shattering wood followed by screams. Alarmed, she quickened her pace. Turning the corner, she was faced with a gang of blue-cloaked, axe-wielding apprentices tearing shutters from windows, breaking down doors, and chanting all the while, 'Filthy foreigners!' 'Devil's spawn!' 'Plague carriers!'

Magdalen recognised their ring-leader. Christopher Thomas was a carpenter's apprentice, fast gaining a reputation as a rabble rouser. Burbage had ordered Peter and Slinko to have nothing to do with him, on pain of dismissal. Another door fell, and a group of apprentices surged inside. They reappeared moments later dragging a man, a woman and two small children out into the street. Hurling the family into the mud, they set upon them, some with their bare fists, others wielding clubs.

Magdalen looked about in shocked disbelief. The apprentices were hurling bricks through gaping windows and forcing more families from their homes. Christopher Thomas was dragging a young woman by the hair. To Magdalen's horror, she realised it was Louisa Du Bois, her coif gone astray. She was fighting to be free of the apprentice, and screaming in pain and terror.

Magdalen's mind was reeling. The crowd of onlookers was growing, but no-one was trying to stop the violence. Damn them! In desperation, she turned and shouted, 'Don't just stand there! Fetch the constables! Make haste!'

Louisa was on the ground now. She had curled herself into a ball, her arms over her head, a futile attempt to protect herself from the apprentice's savage blows. Fury boiled inside Magdalen. Louisa and her neighbours would most likely be dead by the time the constables arrived. She had to do something, but what?

With no clear idea in her head, she put down her basket and ran to Louisa's side.

'Stop this madness!' she yelled at the apprentices. 'Leave these good, Christian folk alone! Shame on you all!'

Christopher Thomas pushed Magdalen aside with such force that she fell backwards into the mud. She was on her feet again in an instant.

'For God's sake, leave her be! You're killing her!' she pleaded.

Magdalen tried to wrestle the club from the apprentice's hand, but he wrenched it from her grasp with ease. Winded, she tried again. This time, he swung the club at her head. She ducked, and the weapon missed her scalp by inches.

'This isn't your fight, girl. Stop this before you get hurt.'

'You're wrong! This *is* my fight!' Magdalen shouted, addressing both the apprentices and the crowd of onlookers. 'These people are our neighbours. They shop in the same markets. They worship in the same churches. They are decent Christian folk. They do not deserve your hatred.'

'There is nothing decent about Huguenot filth!' the apprentice sneered.

'Christopher, enough. We must away. The constables are close.' An older man, too old to an apprentice, was pointing in the direction of Milk Street.

'Aye, I'm coming. But there's one thing I must do first.'

Christopher Thomas crouched down and brushed Louisa's hair from her forehead; a strangely intimate, tender gesture. And then he moved closer still, and spat in her face. A large gobbet of saliva slid down her cheek and fell into the mud. Righting himself, he winked at Magdalen. 'Time to go, brothers!'

In a heartbeat, he and the other apprentices were gone, vanishing into the narrow lanes of Shoreditch like cockroaches scuttling from candlelight. Magdalen dropped to her knees, so intent on helping Louisa that she barely noticed the arrival of the constables.

'Can you hear me? Are you badly hurt?'

Louisa sat up slowly, wincing with the effort. 'No, I don't think so. Just bruises.'

Magdalen used her handkerchief to wipe Louisa's face. 'You're safe now. They've gone,' she said gently.

Louisa was shaking, her complexion grey as dust. 'You should not have done that. It was foolhardy. He could have killed you.'

'But he didn't,' Magdalen replied matter-of-factly, although in truth she felt so shocked and so angry she could barely catch her breath. Putting an arm about Louisa, she helped her to her feet.

Louisa clung to her, gazing horror-struck at the devastation on Tenter Street. The house she had been sharing with three other families was now a hollowed-out shell, its door demolished, its window frames hacked to firewood, the meagre furniture of its Huguenot tenants cast out into the street and shattered into kindling.

'My father was a tapestry weaver,' Louisa's voice wobbled. 'He was highly skilled. The City employed him to teach the poor orphans at Bridewell, so they might learn his craft. He paid his taxes and he was a God-fearing, generous man. I thank God he is not alive to see this day.'

Magdalen felt a lump forming in her throat. Louisa had lost her brother just seven days since. She did not deserve this.

'My father was the kindest soul,' Louisa went on, her voice a whisper. 'He taught me my letters with such patience. He said it wasn't right that John could read the Bible yet I could not...' Without warning, her knees buckled.

Magdalen caught her, and hauled her upright again.

'I brought you some bread and cheese. I had hoped we might take breakfast together.' She glanced ruefully at her overturned basket, the food trampled underfoot. 'Never mind. Come back with me to Silver Street. We can eat something there.'

'No, no, I could not impose on you. I don't want to be any trouble.' Louisa's eyes were as glassy as fake jewels.

'I insist,' Magdalen replied. She had not saved John, and she had to live with her guilt and regret each and every day, but perhaps she could save Louisa.

Louisa was shaking her head. 'You have done enough, Magdalen. I would not have you late for the Theatre.'

'I am not leaving you here. Come, let us away to Silver Street.'

232

In the Mountjoys' kitchen, Marie Mountjoy wiped her hands on her apron, and pursed her lips disapprovingly. 'And you chose to bring her here? *Pourquoi?*'

'The apprentices have destroyed her lodging house,' Magdalen explained. 'Louisa is an honest, hard-working, God-fearing woman, but she is of Huguenot descent, and so the apprentices set upon her and her neighbours, beating them most cruelly and calling them the foulest of names.'

Marie glared at the two young women in her kitchen. She felt loathing for one, and pity for the other. Her dislike of Magdalen was deep and unyielding. The girl's disreputable employment at the Theatre was beyond the pale.

And then there was the matter of her husband and his lechery. She baulked at the memory of Christopher and Magdalen, their bodies touching, his tongue in her mouth. She was a whore, nothing more than a dirty whore.

Marie's thoughts shifted to the early days of her marriage, when Christopher had desired her with an intensity that had taken them both by surprise. It had made her feel beautiful, and happy, and proud. But then came the stillbirths, and life's repeated tragedies had gradually taken their toll. Each time she followed a tiny coffin to the churchyard of Saint Olave's, she buried a piece of her heart beside it.

Christopher never openly expressed his grief for their lost children. Instead, he grew surly, blaming his anger on the injustices of a city where he was seen as a filthy, thieving foreigner, but Marie knew he mourned those tiny, perfectly-formed babies. She knew why he refused to look in the cradle when Mary was born, a healthy babe, crying lustily. She knew he dared not risk opening his heart to such agonising loss again. Even now, with Mary approaching her sixteenth birthday, Christopher kept his distance from their daughter, regarding her warily as if she might disappear in a puff of smoke at any moment. Marie's expression soured. Why did Christopher no longer look at his wife the way he looked at Magdalen? She knew she was still an attractive woman; she saw the appreciative glances other men threw in her direction.

Some part of her wanted to turn the Huguenot girl away, purely to spite Magdalen. To hurt her, as she was hurting, every moment of every day. But when she looked into the frightened face of Louisa Du Bois, she saw a younger, albeit markedly less attractive, version of herself. A young woman, far from home, despised for being different. An outsider, doomed never to belong no matter what she did, no matter how hard she tried.

She noticed there were red splotches spreading up the girl's neck and across her cheeks. It really was most unattractive.

'There is hot water in the saucepan,' she said coldly. 'And there is a little marigold salve left in the pantry.'

'Thank you,' Magdalen said, both surprised and relieved.

'*Merci, madam.*' Louisa curtseyed, wincing as she righted herself. Her cheeks were scarlet now, a painful bruise of self-consciousness.

'*Oui, oui.*' Marie made a show of bustling towards the workshop then came to a stop and turned around.

'My previous girl left us to marry. Most inconvenient. I find myself in need of a maidservant. The pay is three pounds per annum. Would such a position interest you, Louisa?'

Magdalen had secretly hoped Marie might make such an offer, but she suspected Louisa might think the role demeaning. Louisa, however, did not hesitate.

'*Mais oui, Madam Mountjoy. Ce serait bien. Tres bien. Merci, merci beaucoup.*'

'*Oui, oui,*' Marie said dismissively. 'You can start today. Magdalen, show Louisa to Margaret's old room.'

The bedchamber reserved for the maidservant was on the top floor, next to Will's. The plaster was damp and stained where the roof had leaked and the room smelled of mice and musty mattress straw. Magdalen hurriedly opened the shutters and cool, fresh air flooded in, accompanied by the perennial sound of pigeons cooing on the roof ridge. She turned around to find Louisa staring blankly into space.

'Would you like to rest a while?' she asked gently.

Louisa physically jumped and glanced apprehensively about the room. She appeared unsure how she had come to be there.

'You should rest,' Magdalen said, more firmly now. 'But first, would you let me put some salve on your bruises?'

'I don't want to be any trouble,' Louisa said fretfully.

'It is no trouble, I assure you.'

Louisa was blushing again. She shook her head and averted her eyes. Magdalen hesitated, bemused by her reticence before remembering that whilst the players thought nothing of stripping down to their linens in the 'tiring house, not everyone was so uninhibited. She placed the salve on the table beside the bed. 'I will leave you to rest a while.'

She had reached the door before Louisa said softly, 'thank you Magdalen. I am forever in your debt.'

Magdalen turned around. 'John was kind to me. He looked out for me. It is *I* who is in *your* debt.'

A feeling of guilt enveloped her, hot and uncomfortable, and she found she could no longer hold Louisa's gaze. She wanted to apologise; to tell her how she blamed herself for John's death, but she could not find the words. Instead, she found herself spouting a string of platitudes.

'You must be exhausted. Try and sleep. We'll talk later.'

Louisa was staring at the floorboards. She looked broken and vulnerable, her thin frame trembling like a greyhound, and

Magdalen felt a sudden twinge of foreboding. John's sister was safe from the apprentices in this attic room, but danger still lurked in the shape of Christopher Mountjoy. She prayed that bringing Louisa to Silver Street would not prove to be a tragic mistake.

On the floor below, her grandmother was snoring loudly, her bottom jaw dropped to her chest. Loose skin hung slackly from her sunken cheeks, reminding Magdalen of the skeletal effigies on the tombstones in Saint Olave's Church.

Burdened with sadness, she walked to the Theatre with as much enthusiasm as a small boy heading to school. Her route took her past the lodgings Marlowe shared with Thomas Kyd in Norton Folgate. A recently constructed, three-storey property, it had evidently been thrown up in haste by unscrupulous landlords looking for a quick profit. Magdalen suspected it lacked foundations, for it was already listing, and cracks were appearing in the plasterwork.

She could hear shouting from within. A heartbeat later, the door opened and Thomas Kyd ran out into the street, closely followed by Marlowe, his rapier drawn. His social status did not merit carrying such a weapon, but he had never paid the slightest attention to convention.

'Turn and fight me you coward!' Marlowe yelled at his friend.

'I don't want to fight you, Kit,' Thomas retorted. 'I want you to grow up!'

Marlowe slashed his rapier back and forth, missing Thomas' doublet by inches. Remarkably, Thomas held his ground.

'Grow up?' Marlowe jeered. 'To what end? To die? I'll have none of that!'

'Coining is punishable by death, Kit. How you escaped the hangman's noose I'll never know, but your luck will run out one day and I'll be damned if you take me down with you!'

Magdalen's eyes widened with alarm. Why was Thomas accusing Marlowe of making counterfeit coins? What the devil had he been up to now?

'Adonis's arse, Tom! Don't speak of what you don't understand!' An ugly look came over Marlowe's face. 'Of course, you do not enjoy the benefits of a university education, so there's much you don't understand.'

'I understand well enough that I am insane to share chambers with you.'

'My dear Tom, you are being wildly over-dramatic, but that is your forte, is it not?' Marlowe launched into verse, sighing excessively and wringing his hands.

'O eyes, no eyes, but fountains fraught with tears;
O life, no life, but lively form of death.'

Magdalen recognised the lines. He was quoting from Thomas's play, *The Spanish Tragedy*, where Hieronimo discovers his son's hanged body.

'You whoreson villain! You filthy bung!' Thomas drew his dagger from his belt and launched himself at Marlowe.

It was a terrifyingly uneven fight, Thomas on the back foot constantly retreating to avoid Marlowe's slicing rapier. Magdalen was horrified. How would the Justices of the Peace react to the news Marlowe had been fighting in the street again?

'Enough! Both of you!' she shouted.

Marlowe took no notice but Thomas's eyes briefly flicked in her direction. It almost cost him dear, for Marlowe took advantage of his momentary lapse in concentration, and lunged. Thomas side-stepped and the blade missed his shoulder by a hair's breadth. And then they were fighting again, grunting with exertion, their faces streaked with sweat.

Magdalen tried again. 'Do you want to return to Newgate, Marlowe? Pestilence is rife in there. You'll die for certain.'

This time, both men looked at her.

Marlowe lowered his blade a fraction. 'Truce?'

'Aye, truce, but I mean it, Kit. I won't share chambers with you any longer. I want you gone.'

'Why must it be me who goes? We are joint tenants here.' Marlowe sounded like a petulant child.

'No more, Kit. No more, I say,' Thomas pronounced breathlessly. Striding back to their lodgings, he slammed the door behind him with a mighty flourish.

'Well, that was some keen sport!' Marlowe's smile was guileless, his soft brown eyes sparkling.

Magdalen didn't return his smile. She knew full well he hadn't been play-acting. He had come close to killing Thomas Kyd. There were times when Marlowe reminded her of the protagonist in his much-lauded play *Tamburlaine*. She knew the thundering lines off by heart:

'I hold the Fates bound fast in iron chains
And with my hand turn Fortune's wheel about
And sooner shall the sun fall from this sphere
Than Tamburlaine be slain or overcome.'

But Tamburlaine's over-reaching pride and ambition had ultimately led to his downfall and death. She eyed Marlowe uneasily. There was something ugly about his manner today. He was often callous, but it was unlike him to crow about a man's lack of education, or to mock a friend's work so cruelly.

'Do you think Richard Cowley *was* poisoned?' she asked. 'In the Mermaid they are saying he died from stab wounds.'

Marlowe shrugged. 'The man was a fusty nut with no kernel. We are fortunate to be rid of him. No-one cares whether he was snatched from the street by the Devil himself and carried screaming down to Hell.'

Magdalen put her hands on her hips. 'I care! I have no wish to hang for two murders, neither of which I committed!'

But Marlowe was already walking away. 'They can only snap your neck once, so what does it matter?' he called over his shoulder.

Appalled, she chased after him, wrenching him around to face her. 'Stop it!' she hissed. 'You don't mean that. What is wrong with you?'

She did not like the look on his face. It was dark with despair, and when he spoke there was deep melancholy in his eyes.

'Clotho spins the thread of life. Lachesis measures its allotted length and Atropos cuts it with her shears. It is Lachesis we must fear.' He reached out to touch her cheek but seemed to change his mind, and his arm fell to his side again. He turned and walked away.

'You said you'd keep me safe,' Magdalen called after him. 'You swore to me.'

He did not look back. Magdalen watched him until he rounded a corner and disappeared from sight. He had sworn he would not allow anyone to harm so much as a hair on her head but, in truth, she had always known he would abandon her.

Magdalen walked into the 'tiring house more than two hours late. She noticed several players were wearing toadstones about their necks. Apothecaries swore the tiny, magical stones were extracted from the head of a toad and glowed hot in the presence of poison, but she had long suspected they were simply pebbles plucked from the river shore at low tide.

The atmosphere in the 'tiring house had changed overnight, and Magdalen sensed it had little to do with the three barrels of Mad Dog the players had consumed the previous evening. Death from illness and the plague was a part of life, but death by murder was less common. It had visited the Theatre twice, and there was no way of knowing when it might strike again. The players were afraid; their banter muted, their sombre discussions repeatedly returning to the murders of Richard and John. Were the two murders connected and if so, how? Was a madman planning to systematically kill Burbage's entire troupe? Or merely the players who cross-dressed and took women's roles? Or, in hushed tones, was it a vendetta solely against sodomites?

Magdalen's sense of despair deepened. She had known the players since childhood. She thought of them as her family, but the events of the last few days had proved they did not feel the same way about her. They didn't seem to care she was going to be indicted for John's murder. They didn't seem to care Edmund Stow intended to lay Richard Cowley's death at her feet too. They had not asked how she fared, and so they knew nothing about Christopher Mountjoy's assault, or the night she had thought she would die in Norton Folgate. They were all far too wrapped up in their own lives to notice that *her* life teetered on the edge of ruin. But it was Marlowe's throw-away comment that had hurt the most, cutting to her soul with its breath-taking betrayal.

'They can only snap your neck once, so what does it matter?'

Fury and frustration bubbled inside Magdalen. This time tomorrow, any one of the players might be lying on the searcher's slab. Couldn't they see it was in their best interests to help her find John's killer? For a brief moment she considered berating them for their selfishness, but she needed this job. She could not afford to anger Burbage with a show of unwomanly, brazen behaviour. And so she chose to suppress the part of her that longed to shout and scream, and rebel against all the ways her life was confined and controlled and judged; the part of her she had struggled to control for as long as she could remember.

'I am aware of your tardiness, Magdalen!' Burbage shouted

across the 'tiring house. 'Take the broom and sweep the stage.'

Sweeping was a job for the apprentices not the wardrobe mistress, but Magdalen knew she had no choice but to obey. With her head held high, she snatched the broom and walked out onto the empty stage. Once, the Theatre had been her sanctuary from the troubles of the world, and then death had crept inside and it no longer felt a safe haven. Nevertheless, she breathed in the familiar scents of hewn oak and tobacco smoke; of bruised apple cores and spilled, souring ale, and she knew she would always love this place.

Despite everything that had happened, the air still glimmered with dreams and magic. The same magic that brought thousands of Londoners flocking to the Theatre, day after day, year after year. They came to escape the cares of their own lives, to share music and laughter, to be transported to far off lands, to witness treachery and betrayal, to see lovers meet, and battles fought and won. In short, they came to be entertained. And, of late, they came to be challenged, for Will's plays were no longer so straightforward, his characters neither wholly good nor wholly bad but full of contradictions, enigmas and flaws, as if Burbage's oft-said words had taken root in Will's fertile mind:

'*Look for the truth of it. Hold a looking glass up to life.*'

And she knew she would sweep the stage a thousand times if it meant she could remain a part of this world within a world; this kingdom peopled by infuriatingly selfish but staggeringly talented players. Because the 'tiring house was her home, the one place she felt she belonged. The one place where no-one saw her as a wicked, worthless whore.

The players were drifting on stage to rehearse for the afternoon's performance of *Twelfth Night*. Alex Cooke was to play Viola. Magdalen watched him as he took centre stage. His bearing and manner had subtly altered, his confidence growing

241

by the day. Burbage had given him all John's roles, and he had effortlessly made them his own. There was no doubt he was a fine player, just as there was no doubt he had benefitted most from John, and Richard Cowley's, death.

'Magdalen? Are you quite well?'

Matthew Hilliard's unmistakeable, velvet tones drew her from her reverie. She turned around. The bruise on his left cheek was mottled purple now, but it did not diminish his smile, and tiny muscles she didn't know she had clenched deep inside.

'Yes, yes, thank you.' She was so distracted it took her a moment to realise there was a cue sheet in his hand. 'What role?'

'Antonio. Is he… how should I…?'

Magdalen knew what he was trying to ask, but it was not an easy question to answer. In *Twelfth Night*, despite all the cross-dressing and subsequent misunderstandings, Antonio was the only character who appeared to have deep, genuine feelings for someone of the same sex. Many of his lines burned with passion for Sebastian, Viola's twin brother:

'If you will not murder me for my love, let me be your servant.'

But there would be no happy ending for Antonio's unrequited love and nor could there ever be, considering sodomy was punishable by death.

'The Master of the Revels will come to hear of anything scandalous so I would suggest subtlety, for all our sakes,' she replied carefully.

'Hilliard What are you? A gossiping fishwife? Get over here!' Burbage's voice boomed across the stage.

'Coming.' Matthew raised a hand in acknowledgement, and then, under his breath to Magdalen, 'Sage advice. My thanks. Wish me luck.'

'A sack full of rabbits' feet,' Magdalen replied.

'Rabbits' feet?' Matthew repeated curiously.

'You have not heard the expression?' It was something her grandmother used to say.

'I have not, but then I was born and raised in Scotland where we have our own superstitions. I could tell you many a dubious tale about black sheep, white heather, and lucky horseshoes.' He paused. 'Rabbits' feet. Good luck for some, but presumably not the rabbits?'

Magdalen laughed. 'I suppose not.'

'Hilliard!' Burbage bellowed.

'Coming, sir!'

Magdalen returned to the 'tiring house and set to work on a task she had been putting off for weeks: repairing Crab, the stuffed dog originally purchased for *The Two Gentlemen of Verona*. Despite the fact Crab had no lines, he never failed to bring the house down, partly due to Will's witty script, and partly due to the comic genius of Will Kempe. Crab had once been a real dog, but now he was coming apart at the seams. Magdalen threaded a sturdy needle with some reluctance. Beneath Crab's dirty, moth-eaten fur had once dwelled lungs, belly, and a beating heart. Surely he had deserved a decent burial? It didn't seem right he should spend his eternity as a laughing-stock, dragged about a stage as entertainment for the masses.

On stage, Burbage, as Count Orsino, was asking Viola, in disguise as Ceasario, if she had ever fallen in love. Orsino believed Viola to be a man, and Viola was secretly in love with Orsino, so it was a delightfully playful scene.

'I bet my life that young as you are, your eye has fallen upon some favour that it loves? Has it not boy?' Burbage asked.

'In truth, a little,' Alex Cooke replied.

'What kind of a woman is she?'

'Of your complexion.'

'She is not worthy of you then. What years, in faith?'

'About your years, my Lord.'

Magdalen stuffed Crab's straw innards back into his belly and began to repair the seam, all the while keeping half an ear on the rehearsal. Viola was telling Orsino of her fictional sister who had loved a man but never found the courage to tell him.

'A blank, my lord. She never told her love,
But let concealment, like a worm in the bud,
Feed on her damask cheek. She pined in thought,
And with a green and yellow melancholy
She sat like patience on a monument,
Smiling at grief. Was not this love indeed?'

Magdalen sympathised with Viola. A smile was all she could ever share with Matthew Hilliard and, like patience on a monument, she had no choice but to accept her fate.

After the performance, Magdalen spent the evening in the banqueting chamber, serving claret to a glittering assembly of pearls and privilege. The Earl of Southampton took centre stage, gloriously outlandish as usual. His doublet was startlingly short; his lack of breeches serving to accentuate his shapely thighs, clad only in the finest hose. His lustrous hair fell in long tresses over one shoulder whilst on the crown of his head a tuft had been cut and oiled, standing vertically to a height of some three inches.

Magdalen gave the earl a wide berth, but she need not have worried, for he never took his eyes off Will Shakespeare. They were standing so close together she could not have slid a cue sheet between them. They hung on each other's every word, as if the world around them had ceased to be. Will said something, and the earl laughed delightedly. The earl replied and Will returned a coquettish smile, looking up at Rizzley through dark lashes. And so it went on, a masque of knowing eyes and lingering hands. Magdalen didn't know what to make of it.

She didn't know what to make of Amelia Bassano and the Lord Chamberlain either, for there was no sign of their previous rift. Amelia's hand rested possessively upon his arm and in return he was openly affectionate, kissing her on the mouth and patting her rounded belly with unbridled pride.

Burbage's guests lingered, eventually departing a little after seven o'clock. After tidying the chamber and washing the glasses, Magdalen was the last to leave the Theatre, walking home alone. The streets were quiet and she jumped at every shadow. If she closed her eyes, she could still see the narrow, moonlit alleyway; still feel her attacker's hands landing on her shoulders; still smell the dirty tang of hemp oil on his jerkin.

As she approached Silver Street, she broke into a run, her fingers fumbling in their haste to turn the key. Once inside, she quickly locked the door behind her and let out a ragged sigh of relief. The Mountjoys had already retired for the night, and she climbed the stairs in darkness, her feet feeling for each step. Much as she longed for sleep, she lit a candle and sat down at her work table. The Earl of Southampton's cloak was almost finished; all that remained was to sew braiding to the collar. In such a prominent position, the stiches needed to be very small. Threading a needle, she remembered a conversation with her grandmother, many years ago:

'Sew the tiniest of stiches, Magdalen, as if you are transformed to a mouse, but not any old common or garden mouse. Sew as if you are Master Tailor to the court of the Mouse King.'

'And what is the name of this Master Tailor, Grand-Aggie?' ten year old Magdalen had asked.

'You can decide, my sweet.'

'I will call him Malcolm the Magnificent, the cleverest mouse in all of London.'

Magdalen smiled to herself, warmed by the memory.

The watchman had long since called two o'clock before she finally put down the needle and thread. Her shoulders ached and her eyes were sore but the commission was finally complete. With great care, she placed the cloak inside a linen clothes-bag, added a pomander of rose and lavender, and pulled the drawstrings together.

Leaving her own clothes where they fell, she blew out the candle and crawled into bed. For a few troubling moments she wondered how she would deliver the cloak to the earl's house, and if he would ever pay her for it. What had he said? *'If it is to my liking.'* And on that worrying thought, she sank into a deep, exhausted sleep.

'Wake up! Magdalen! Wake up!'

She had been dreaming of an army of mice, dressed in cloaks with collars so high only their pointy ears protruded above the braiding. She was asking them for payment but they merely squeaked in response, scuttling between her feet and disappearing into mouse-holes in the wainscoting.

'Magdalen! Wake up! Your grandmother has been taken!'

She opened her eyes, the dream receding.

'Taken?' she repeated groggily.

'By the watchers!' Louisa's cheeks were red with anguish. 'A house on Noble Street. A Catholic priest was hiding in the cellar!'

THIRTEEN

'My stars shine darkly over me'

Sunday 5th April

'Are you certain she is taken?'

Yes, Louisa is certain. Look at the misery etched on her poor, purple face.

'What time is it?'

Dear God, it doesn't matter what time it is. I have overslept.

'It's seven o'clock, the watchers raided a butcher's house, Bonvince, I think that was his name,' Louisa was gabbling in her distress. 'A Catholic Mass, they took them all away, Madame Mountjoy says they took them to the Tower, even the women and children.'

Magdalen sat up, her thoughts reeling. In what kind of world were old women and children taken to the Tower?

'But they took your grandmother to Bridewell.'

'What?' Magdalen couldn't concentrate. 'That doesn't make sense.' Bridewell was not a prison for heretics, but for debtors, vagabonds and prostitutes.

'She was outside the butcher's house. Madame Mountjoy says the watchers took her for a homeless beggar.'

Magdalen fell out of bed, her fingers fumbling to don kirtle, bodice, jacket and boots. She had planned to lock her grandmother's door last night, effectively putting a stop to her wanderings, but she had been so preoccupied with finishing the earl's cloak, she had clean forgotten. This was her fault. She was supposed to look after her grandmother. She was supposed to keep her safe.

Instinctively, she raced up the stairs to Will's chamber, knocked, and entered without waiting for a response. He wasn't there, and his bed hadn't been slept in. She turned on her heel and ran back downstairs. In truth, she had not expected him to come to her aid in any remarkable way. Their friendship, if it could be described as such, was marked by his quiet detachment, but at the very least, she had hoped he might offer some advice.

Louisa was waiting for her on the landing. 'What can I do?' she asked plaintively.

Magdalen shook her head and pushed past without a word. All that mattered was bringing her grandmother home. She hurtled downstairs, her leather soles slipping on the polished oak. In the kitchen she could hear Marie shouting at Christopher.

'*Mais non*! She has to go! *Dieu nous sauve*, we are all in danger now!'

Magdalen tiptoed closer.

'They have taken Agnes to Bridewell, not the Tower. Anyone can see she is a harmless old crone.' Christopher's tone was dismissive. 'They will release her soon enough. And besides, we need Magdalen. She is a talented 'tire maker.'

'It is *you* who needs her, for your foul debaucheries! How can you humiliate me so, in our own house?'

'She seduced me. She will not do so again.'

'You can swear on your mother's grave and I would not believe you. You are a wicked lecher! I know Anne's babe was yours. The church elders knew it too, but they chose to take your word over that of a serving girl -'

Magdalen heard the slap and then she heard Marie's cry; a tiny, muffled thing.

'*Je suis ton mari*, and I will be obeyed, or the church elders will hear of your shrewish tongue.'

There was a long silence and then Marie's small, frightened voice: 'How many names will that old priest give up as he is torn apart on the rack? He will accuse anyone in the futile hope of saving his scrawny neck. There will be raids, arrests, innocent lives destroyed! I tell you, if that girl remains under our roof, she will lead us to the Tower. There are many 'tire makers in London. We can find another.'

'We are Huguenots!' Christopher snapped impatiently. 'Protestant to our very souls. No-one could ever take us for Catholics. A lunatic old woman will not be our ruin.'

'*Mon Dieu!* Why are you being so stupid, so stubborn? You know as well as I that Agnes was not on Noble Street by chance. In all the years she lodged with us, she never once attended church. And we turned a blind eye to her Popery because it suited us, because Magdalen can fashion a head 'tire in the time it takes most to choose the wire. *Dieu nous sauve*, we have housed a Catholic under our roof! A traitor!' Marie was shouting again. 'Our Huguenot blood will not save us. *Mais non*, it will damn us! *Nous sommes etrangers.* No-one trusts us. No-one will believe we didn't suspect Agnes was a Papist. The only thing that can save us now is our reputation. We must be seen to be above reproach. You of all people should understand that. Think of your daughter, Christopher. For once in your life, think of her!'

'What do you mean by that?' Christopher sounded genuinely bewildered.

And then Marie's voice again: 'I know you are listening, Magdalen. *Viens ici*.'

Filled with trepidation, Magdalen stepped into the kitchen.

Christopher's anger was palpable, his jaw tightly clenched. Marie was glaring at her husband with a look of such penetrating fury Magdalen half expected to see him to flinch.

'Husband?' Marie pressed.

Magdalen could almost hear the battle of wills raging within the smoky confines of the kitchen.

'Think of Mary,' Marie begged plaintively.

Christopher's eyes were darting this way then that, a sure sign he was thinking hard. The fraught silence stretched on. At last, addressing a point several inches above Magdalen's head, he announced stonily, 'You are to leave this house. You will no longer work here and you will no longer lodge here, with immediate effect.'

He collided with Magdalen's shoulder as he left the kitchen, his hefty frame knocking her sideways. She tried to regain her footing, but it was as if she had fallen into a fast-flowing river; the strong current sweeping her away from everything familiar, everything safe. Marie Mountjoy had wanted rid of her for so long, and now the perfect excuse had presented itself. This time Marie was afraid; afraid for her family, afraid for their very lives. This time, the Devil himself could not persuade her to change her mind.

'I have to go to my grandmother. She will not understand…'

Disorientated with shock, Magdalen reached for her cloak from the hook in the passageway, opened the front door and stumbled out onto the street. The cold morning air hit her in the face, as sharp as a slap.

'Wait!'

Magdalen turned around.

Louisa was running after her. 'Some bread and cheese for your grandmother,' she explained, thrusting a basket into Magdalen's hand. 'What can I do to help?' she added earnestly.

'Nothing. I thank you for the food, truly, but this doesn't concern you.' She could not, in all conscience, draw John's sister into her troubles.

Louisa reached out and touched her sleeve. 'Please, there must be something I can do?'

Magdalen was moved by the genuine sympathy and kindness in her eyes. 'As you wish,' she relented. 'I would be grateful if you would go to the Theatre and explain to Richard Burbage what has happened.'

Louisa nodded. 'I can do that.'

'Thank you. You are a good friend.' Instinctively, Magdalen enveloped her in a warm embrace, but she felt Louisa tense, and instantly regretted her lack of decorum.

'Forgive me.' She made to pull away, but Louisa held on tightly and Magdalen took comfort in her closeness, her warmth. When at last they drew apart, Louisa's eyes were filled with tears, and Magdalen surprised herself by saying, 'all will be well.' It was one of Will Shakespeare's annoying platitudes, but it was nonsense, for how could anything ever be well again?

And so they parted; Louisa for the Theatre, and Magdalen for Bridewell. Silver Street was crowded with parishioners making their way to Saint Olave's Church. News of the raid on a Catholic Mass had spread like wildfire, and Magdalen could sense fear in the air. Everyone knew that a long-forgotten crucifix or a string of rosary beads hidden away at the back of a dusty cupboard could lead to the gallows.

Keeping her head down to avoid eye-contact with neighbours who had never become friends by dint of the Mountjoys' 'foreignness', Magdalen left the city through Ludgate, crossed the bridge and turned south. To her left, the foul-smelling Fleet River ran towards the Thames, bounded by the old city walls and beyond, the derelict priory church of the Blackfriars. To her right, loomed the forbidding presence of Bridewell, once a king's palace, now a prison. A young woman was begging for bread, her thin arms reaching out through a small, barred window, and from somewhere within came the pitiful wail of a sick child.

Magdalen had bread to spare, for her grandmother had the appetite of a sparrow. Approaching the window, she took a loaf from her basket and passed it through the bars. In an instant, it was snatched from her hands. She peered into the gloom, unnerved by the fight that ensued for possession of the bread. The women were vicious in their desperation; scratching, tearing, gouging. Her grandmother could not survive in such a place. By whatever means, she had to bring her home.

Magdalen faltered, pulled up short by the realisation that, as of today, they had no home.

Swallowing hard, she walked through the archway of Bridewell's gate-house; a double-towered and ornately castellated structure, reminiscent of the fortresses of old. In the vast courtyard, the initial impression of opulence was marred by the pervading stench of the Fleet, the scatter of broken roof tiles across the cobble stones, and the unkempt ivy smothering the red-brick walls and glazed windows.

Magdalen turned full circle. The courtyard was deserted. Perhaps the prisoners and gaolers were at prayer? The four identical wings loured over her, menacing and oppressive. Everyone knew Bridewell had been founded on good intentions. The old palace had been given to the City by King Henry's son, King Edward, to be used as a house of correction for disorderly women, a hospital and an orphanage. Charitable donations meant many of the orphans were trained in apprenticeships; Louisa's father had taught tapestry weaving in Bridewell.

But everyone knew there were more prisoners than apprentices now, more leg irons and gallows than hospital beds.

And everyone knew it was over-run with rats and pestilence.

'What are you doing out here?'

A huge bull of a man was striding towards her across the courtyard. He appeared to have no neck, his head sitting directly atop muscular shoulders. His scalp had been roughly shaved, giving it the resemblance of a plucked chicken. Clad in a leather jerkin and breeches, and wearing sturdy, knee-high boots, he would not have looked out of place in a smithy.

'I am looking for the warden,' she replied, squaring her shoulders and attempting to sound more confident than she felt.

'Forgive me. My eyes are bad. I thought you was a prisoner, but now I am close, I sees I was mistaken. The warden, you say?' He sucked air between stained teeth. 'Might be difficult, being a Sunday an' all. Master Baldry won't want to be disturbed.'

Magdalen had expected as much. Opening the purse at her belt, she removed five precious pennies.

'For your trouble, sir.'

He took them without acknowledgement. 'This way.'

She followed him to the north range and up a short flight of steps which led to a gloomy passageway. The roof evidently leaked because they passed several buckets full of rain-water. The passageway led out onto another, larger courtyard. Magdalen guessed this inner sanctum had once housed the king's private quarters, for the architecture was markedly grander than the first, with ornately patterned brickwork and delicately domed oriel windows. A huge fountain stood in the centre of the courtyard, but water no longer flowed from its fluted taps, its basin clogged with dead leaves.

The guard led her to an imposing door carved with Tudor roses, and gestured for her to follow him inside. Their footsteps echoed around an empty entrance hall, up a sweeping flight of dusty stairs, and on through a succession of equally empty chambers that smelled of damp and rot. At last, he stopped at a pair of double doors.

The office of Bridewell's warden had an air of faded grandeur. In places, the decorated ceiling plaster had cracked, and clouds of fine, white dust had settled on the dark floor boards like a sprinkling of frost. The silk fabric upon the walls was an intricate repeat of tiny fleur-de-lis. Perhaps once the colour of rich burgundy, it was now faded and frayed. A huge fireplace dominated one wall, its mantel held aloft by pillars carved to resemble Greek columns and above it, a massive stone relief of King Henry's coat of arms. Magdalen guessed the chimney was clogged with dead pigeons, for the fire in the hearth was slowly filling the room with smoke. If they didn't sweep the chimney soon, the palace would surely burn to the ground before the year's end.

Ralph Baldry, the warden of Bridewell, was seated at his desk, a ledger open before him. He was a young man; so thin and gaunt Magdalen thought he must be recovering from a serious ailment. His hair was brushed back from a high forehead and his hollow eyes were so close together he gave the appearance of a startled owl.

'This had better be important, Pargitar.'

The guard looked taken aback, and Magdalen realised he had not thought further than the five pennies now lodged in his purse, and thus had no notion of the purpose of her visit.

Magdalen stepped forward. 'Sir, my name is Mistress Bisset. I believe my grandmother, Mistress Agnes Bisset, was brought to Bridewell this morning?'

'That is correct.'

'There has been a misunderstanding. My grandmother is -'

'There is no misunderstanding. Your grandmother has been accused of Recusancy.'

Magdalen was so stunned she barely registered that Baldry's gaze had settled on her breasts. Why was he talking of Recusancy?

'But I was told…' she began faintly.

The warden tore his gaze from her bosom, looked down at the ledger and proceeded to read aloud:

'According to the testimony of Reverend Judd, the accused has been absent from the congregation of Saint Olave's church in Cripplegate ward for the last two years, seven months and three weeks. The total amount of the fine owed by Mistress Agnes Bisset of Silver Street is therefore six hundred and thirty-five pounds.'

Magdalen stared at him incredulously. In ten lifetimes, she could not earn such an inconceivably large sum of money. Why had Reverend Judd betrayed her grandmother? She had always believed him to be a compassionate man.

'Such an amount is far beyond my means, sir. I have heard the courts are sometimes willing to significantly reduce the fine, and draw up a schedule for payment by instalments -'

The warden shook his head. 'I have been instructed there is to be no reduction, and no inducements. Until the entire amount is paid, Agnes Bisset is to remain in my charge.'

'But that's not … I cannot…' Magdalen's voice trailed away.

Baldry smiled unpleasantly. 'Whilst I would be content to spend the rest of the day admiring your pretty features, I have business to attend to. I must ask you to leave now.'

No. She couldn't leave. Not without her grandmother.

'But she is innocent of any crime, sir. Surely she should not be punished for a misunderstanding?'

'Mistress Bisset,' the warden said impatiently, 'your grandmother was found loitering outside a household giving shelter to a Catholic priest. You should be thankful she is not in the Tower. The rest of those taken from Noble Street this morning are not so fortunate. In all honesty, she has been

255

granted more clemency than many would argue she deserves.' He nodded at the guard. 'Pargitar, take Mistress Bisset back to the gate.'

'No wait!' Magdalen approached the warden's desk. 'I beg you for clemency, sir. My grandmother is old and sick, and her wits are confused. Bridewell is no place for her.'

'On the contrary, she will feel much at home here. Bridewell is full of prisoners who are old and sick, and we have more than our fair share of lunatics.'

The colour was draining from Magdalen's face. Pargitar was almost at her elbow now, the ancient floorboards creaking beneath his substantial frame. She sensed she was about to be forcibly removed from Baldry's office.

'Wait!' she repeated urgently. 'I want her to be comfortable. I have money.'

Baldry held up his right hand, stopping the guard in his tracks. 'How much money?'

Magdalen took the leather coin-purse from her belt. Like a hawk swooping on a mouse, the warden leant across the desk, snatched the purse and gave its contents a cursory inspection.

'That will pay for her lodgings for a week,' he said carelessly.

Magdalen watched him drop her purse into his desk drawer and slide it closed with his knee. Every penny she currently possessed had vanished in a heartbeat, and her voice wobbled with distress.

'Will that be sufficient for a private room, sir?'

'No.' The warden laughed derisively. 'Private rooms are far beyond the means of someone of your station. Your grandmother will be held in one of the common wards. Board and lodgings, five shillings a week, and I'll need payment again in seven days, or she will be moved to the cellars.'

'The cellars?' Magdalen repeated warily.

'Let's just say it would be in your grandmother's best interests if you were prompt in your weekly payments.'

Shock rendered Magdalen mute. She could no longer rely on an income from the workshop, and it would take every penny she earned at the Theatre to keep her grandmother in the common wards, but it would be another two weeks before Burbage paid her wages. She realised she had forgotten to breathe. Gripping the edge of the warden's desk, she inhaled raggedly.

'Are you unwell?' Baldry enquired, his gaze dropping from her bosom to peer into the basket hanging from her wrist.

'I am quite well, sir.' Magdalen straightened up and hastily stepped back, praying he would not snatch her basket as well as her purse.

'If you are unable to provide your grandmother's lodging fees, it might be possible for us to come to some sort of arrangement. Services rendered in lieu of payment? I have no doubt you understand my meaning, for you are in the employ of the Theatre, are you not?' The warden smiled knowingly.

'You are mistaken sir. I am the players' wardrobe mistress, not their doxy,' she replied coldly.

'If you say so.'

The bastard didn't believe her. And she had no more cards to play. She had promised herself she would not leave this place without Grand-Aggie, but she had failed her, yet again.

'Will you at least permit me to see my grandmother?' she asked bleakly.

'That will not be possible. Only prisoners with private chambers are permitted guests.'

A scream was building inside Magdalen's head, pressing against her skull. 'For pity's sake, sir, what harm will it do?'

Baldry's gaze focussed on her breasts again. In the long silence

257

that followed his eyes glinted lasciviously. 'Indeed,' he said at last. 'What harm will it do? Pargitar, take Mistress Bisset to Mary Ward.'

Magdalen did not like the look of undisguised anticipation on Baldry's face. Surely he did not think an understanding had passed between them? Unnerved, she followed Pargitar back to the outer courtyard. He opened a heavily studded door in the west range, and led her down a long, dark corridor. It was unsettlingly quiet. Their footsteps echoed around the bare walls, the malodorous air so thick you could almost slice it, but the guard seemed oblivious to the stench.

'Mary Ward,' Pargitar announced gruffly, and began to walk back the way he had come. As an afterthought, he called over his shoulder, 'door's not locked.'

Magdalen frowned, confused. If this was a prison, why was the door unlocked? She reached for the handle then hesitated. It was her fault Agnes was in this ghastly place, and she felt so guilty and so wretched that a small part of her wanted to walk away and pretend none of this had happened, because how could she face her grandmother now?

But she couldn't run away. This wasn't a nightmare, and there would be no merciful awakening. This was reality, and somehow she had to find the strength to face it. Resorting to her trusted failsafe, she asked herself what the redoubtable Agnes Bisset would do in such a situation. The answer was obvious. Squaring her shoulders, she opened the door.

FOURTEEN

'If this were played upon a stage now,
I could condemn it as an improbable fiction'

Matthew Hilliard was going over his lines in his head. Consequently, the church service washed over him, largely unheard. He found it hard to believe that gentle, reasoned Will Shakespeare had written such a distasteful work as *Titus Andronicus*. As far as he could make out, the plot hinged on the eponymous Roman general's return from war with five prisoners: Tamora, queen of the Goths, her three sons and Aaron the Moor. Titus sacrifices Tamora's eldest son as part of the funeral rites for his own sons, and thus begins a revenger's tale of appalling violence. Titus's daughter, Lavinia, is raped, mutilated and murdered. In swift retribution, Titus orders Tamora's sons to be murdered and cooked in a pie, which their mother unwittingly eats.

Astonishingly, the good citizens of London did not appear to share Matthew's revulsion for a play featuring the torture of a young woman, cannibalism and fourteen brutal murders. According to the players, *Titus* was one of Will's most popular works and audiences returned again and again to gasp with outward horror and inward delight. Their attitude reminded Matthew of the amphitheatres of the Roman world. England saw itself as an enlightened Christian realm, but at times the veneer of civilisation was very thin indeed.

Matthew did not linger after the service for he had no desire to speak to the wealthy parishioners of Whitefriars. He could well imagine their ill-disguised curiosity: *'How long will you be staying with your uncle? When do the family return from Dorsetshire? What is your business in London?'*

Instead, he gave his thanks to the vicar and hurried away. He was so lost in his thoughts he did not notice the sparrows flitting busily across the graveyard with twigs and moss in their beaks. And he did not hear a blackbird's warning cry from an apple tree, its boughs frothy with pale pink blossom. He had been given four parts in *Titus*. The largest role was Bassianus, who met a violent end, stabbed to death by Tamora's sons. A knot of anxiety tightened in Matthew's chest. Despite Will's patient guidance, he knew he remained woefully lacking in stagecraft. He had studied rhetoric at Oxford and consequently he knew how to project his voice, but to credibly portray a noble son of Rome called for entirely different skills. And he still hadn't decided whether Bassianus would expire quickly or die a prolonged and dramatic death.

The sun was shining by the time he reached Cheapside, absently sidestepping the crowds of Londoners let loose from church, his thoughts still focussed on the play. Did Bassianus truly love his betrothed, the doomed Lavinia, or did he see her solely as a trophy, *'Rome's ornament'*, to be wrestled from the hands of his elder brother?

Beyond Bethlehem hospital, he stopped to buy a hot pie from a street vendor, enticed by the appetising aroma of freshly baked pastry and the realisation he had not yet eaten today. Wolfing down the pie and burning his tongue, he decided it was impossible to determine Lavinia's feelings for Bassianus because

Will had written a bland stereotype of a virtuous woman: chaste, obedient and largely silent.

Magdalen is rarely silent, Matthew thought. *She is feisty and brave and she says what she thinks. Perhaps that's why I love her.*

Matthew came to a sudden halt.

Love? What in God's name…?

The 'tiring house was as loud as Billingsgate quay. Will Kempe was clad in his morris-dancing attire, his face emblazoned with stripes of red, blue and white paint to match its gaudy hues. He was wearing outrageously long, pointed shoes and twirling about the room like a spinning top, his long false sleeves taking to the air in a dizzying blur. For reasons known only to himself, he had strapped bells to his knees, elbows and wrists, whilst from his hat hung a bell so huge it would not have looked out of place about a prize cow's neck.

Young Peter was following in Kempe's wake, spinning on his heels and grinning like a monkey. Henry Condell caught the boy by the waist, flung him easily over his shoulder and began to tickle his ribs.

'Peter! Peter!' he chanted. 'Watch where you're going, my pretty, prattling, parley pig!'

The boy was laughing uncontrollably and his screams for mercy were ear-piercing. Henry set Peter down, and shouted over the discordant cacophony of chiming bells, 'Hilliard, come here!'

Matthew joined Henry at Magdalen's workbench. 'Why is Kempe so attired?' he asked. 'Are we abandoning *Titus* in favour of a two-hour jig?'

'Kempe would like that, but no, he is to play the clown. But I'd wager no jester of ancient Rome ever made such a racket nor possessed so little sense,' Henry replied.

'Be silent, you beetle-headed, flap-eared knave!' Will Shakespeare admonished, and threw a well-aimed cushion at Kempe's head. It hit him with force, sending him off-kilter. Tripping over his long, pointed shoes, he careered into Magdalen's workbench in an explosion of clanging bells and curses.

Several players broke into applause, although it was unclear to Matthew whether they were clapping for Kempe or for Will Shakespeare. Kempe's hat was askew, the giant bell resting on his bulbous nose. Flicking it to one side, he bowed, soaking up the applause which quickly tapered towards desultory.

Distracted by the mayhem, no one noticed Burbage's arrival.

'What in God's name are you wearing, Kempe?' he demanded. 'You make a mockery of our play. Remove those damn bells at once!'

Kempe shrugged his shoulders, to tinkling accompaniment.

'Surely the audience deserves a little light relief from two hours of relentless, degenerate barbarism without any obvious redeeming features?' he asked belligerently.

A hush fell over the 'tiring house.

'I give them what they want,' Will Shakespeare said quietly. 'I am not to blame for their low tastes.'

'Quite so,' said Henry Condell, ever the peace-maker. Turning to Matthew, he waved a pig's bladder pouch in his face. 'You'll be stabbed today, Hilliard, so here's your blood. Ever died on stage before?'

'Metaphorically, many times I'd wager,' Kempe sniped.

Matthew ignored him. 'No, it's my first time.'

'A virgin,' Kempe grinned. 'How appropriate there will be blood.'

Condell rolled his eyes. 'Pay no attention to him, Hilliard. I need to show you how this works. You attach it to your chest, like so.' He was frowning with concentration. 'Magdalen usually takes care of the props and gore.'

Matthew looked about. 'Where is she?'

'You haven't heard?'

'Heard what?'

Condell hesitated.

'Heard what?' Matthew repeated.

'Anthony Bonvince has been caught harbouring a Catholic priest. The watchers found Agnes loitering nearby. They've taken her to Bridewell, but I fear she'll be in the Tower before the week's out.'

'Agnes?' Matthew queried.

'I forget, you are not acquainted with Agnes,' Condell replied gravely. 'She was our wardrobe mistress. Magdalen's grandmother...'

Condell was still speaking but his voice sounded very far away. Matthew turned away blindly.

'Hilliard? Where are you going?'

'I need some air.'

Outside, Matthew leant against the wall and closed his eyes. He could still hear Henry Condell's words echoing inside his head:

'She'll be in the Tower before the week's out... She was our wardrobe mistress. Magdalen's grandmother...'

He was vaguely aware that the wall was cold and damp, the chill seeping into his doublet, but he couldn't move. His limbs had turned to lead. He was finding it hard to think, finding it hard to breathe, and darkness was closing in.

What had he done?

May God forgive him, what had he done?

FIFTEEN

*'In nature there's no blemish but the mind,
None can be called deformed but the unkind'*

Mary Ward, Bridewell Prison

The stench was overpowering; unwashed bodies, disease, piss and shit. Magdalen clamped a hand over her nose and mouth, and looked about. The ward was a well-proportioned room, rectangular in shape and some twenty yards long. Any fine decoration had long since been removed and the whitewashed walls were mottled with mould. Bars had been bolted to the tall windows and the leaded glass was streaked with pigeon shit. There was little in the way of furniture save for rows of filthy straw mattresses and a few meagre possessions: a threadbare blanket, a frayed linen shawl, a wicker basket with a broken handle.

Magdalen's emotions were scattering. The warden might call these cells 'wards,' but she could see nothing in the way of physicians or medicine. There must have been thirty or more prisoners in this one room, all female, all painfully thin and sickly. Many of them had children at their side, listless little souls, thumbs in their mouths. And in their midst was her grandmother, sitting on the edge of a stained, threadbare mattress, legs straight out in front of her like a rag doll. She was gazing about the ward, and her curious, bemused expression tore at Magdalen's heart. Running across the room, she fell to her knees and gathered Agnes into a close embrace.

'Get off me! Who are you? What is wrong with you?' Agnes pushed her away angrily.

'She's not right in the head, is she?' A young girl was huddled at the other end of the mattress. She might have been pretty once, but her blonde hair was thinning and her skin was pocked with open sores. A small boy sat in her lap, nuzzling against the bodice of her gown and whining piteously.

'Don't mind Tommy.' The girl batted the child away. 'He's always hungry but my titties are dried up.' Tommy wiped his runny nose on his sleeve and then scratched his scalp. When he lowered his hand, Magdalen noticed fresh blood beneath his dirty fingernails. 'My name's Arabella, everyone calls me Belle,' the girl added. Her teeth were rotten and loose, rattling in her gums as she spoke. 'Who are you?'

'I'm Magdalen and this is my grandmother, Agnes.'

'Not right in the head is she, poor old soul,' Belle repeated, not unkindly.

'Who is not right in the head?' Agnes queried, looking about expectantly.

A lump was growing in Magdalen's throat. With a show of brusqueness, she reached into her basket for the remaining loaf. Breaking it in two, she offered half to Belle and the rest to her grandmother. Agnes pulled a face and refused to take the bread. Belle, on the other hand, broke her share into tiny pieces and slowly fed them to Tommy. With food in his belly, he perked up and began to play with his mother's hair. Magdalen noticed Belle ate nothing herself.

'Not seen you in here before,' Belle said, looking Magdalen up and down quizzically. 'This your first time? What did you do?'

'I… I…my grandmother…' Magdalen faltered.

'Not to worry,' Belle patted her knee. 'I knows it's not easy talking 'bout it. But you get used to it. Lord, you get used to anything, ain't that the truth. You'll have to get your own mattress. Is there someone on the outside could bring you one, cos you don't get nothin' in here for free - I don't mind sharing for now, not after you gave us the bread, but not forever, mind. You'll need to find a pot to piss in too -you get used to the stink.' She gestured to a wooden barrel in the corner. 'They only empty it once a day, and sometimes they forget, on purpose, the fuckin' bastards.'

Magdalen stared at her, dumbstruck.

Belle was still talking, at speed. 'It's Sunday, day of rest, so make the most of it. Tomorrow, you'll most likely be working in the hemp sheds.'

'I want to go home now,' Agnes tugged at Magdalen's arm. 'Take me home now.'

Tears blurred Magdalen's eyes and she hurriedly brushed them away. Forcing a smile, she squeezed her grandmother's hand. 'Soon. We'll go home soon.'

'No need to be shy,' Belle pressed. 'Lord, I've heard it all before. What you in for?'

'My grandmother is in debt,' Magdalen replied unsteadily.

'Who is in debt?' Agnes asked, concerned.

'You mean *you* don't need to be in here?' Belle asked in amazement.

'No, I don't…' Magdalen dug her fingernails into her palms, fighting to keep her emotions in check. How was she going to leave her grandmother alone in this terrible place?

Belle was eyeing her ring-less fingers. 'You're not wed? Who keeps you? Are you a whore?'

'No, I am the wardrobe mistress at the Theatre,' Magdalen replied, glancing with concern at Agnes. Her eyes were drooping, her head beginning to nod to her chest. 'Belle, can Agnes lie down for a while?'

The girl shrugged. 'S'pose so.'

Magdalen lowered her grandmother onto the mattress. In a matter of moments, Agnes's jaw fell open and she began to snore loudly.

Magdalen turned back to Belle. 'So, why are *you* here?'

'I'm here 'cos of Tommy.' Belle sighed wearily. 'I'm an unmarried mother without family or means. I beat their hemp, Lord, its brutal work,' she held out a red, raw palm, 'and if I spread my legs for the guards, sometimes I can get more food.'

So many emotions were fighting for space inside Magdalen's head: disbelief, rage, pity and a profound feeling of helplessness. This place was worse than Hell. Were the governors of Bridewell aware of what went on here? Were they turning a blind eye in return for a share of the ill-gotten takings?

'You work at the Theatre? I went to a play once.' Belle was picking listlessly at tufts of straw protruding from the frayed mattress, whilst Tommy began to nuzzle at her breasts again.

'Which play?' Magdalen asked.

Belle shrugged again. 'Dunno. Weren't listenin'. Me pimp 'ad me lifting purses in the yard - fuck! I shouldn't have said that. Me and my big gob.'

'It's no matter,' Magdalen said gently.

Everyone knew pimps sent their doxies into the yard to rustle up trade and loose purses. Tommy gave his mother's hair a sharp tug and Belle batted him away again. Magdalen glanced about the ward. It had an air of hopelessness, of despair. The prisoners were either asleep or too sick to leave their mattresses, their children too hungry to play.

267

'The door is unlocked. Why isn't anyone taking some air in the courtyard?' she asked.

Belle gave her a strange look. 'Best to stay here. Safety in numbers.'

'What do you mean?'

'Fuck me with a feather, aren't you the innocent. They all want their entertainment - the guards, the warden. How do you think we afford to stay out of the cellars?'

'But that's -'

'Unchristian? Unlawful?' Belle said mockingly. 'Aye, it's all of them things. But every one of us girls has the French pox, and now they have it too. We watch 'em scratching their itchy cocks and it gives us something to laugh about and believe me, there ain't much to laugh about in this place.'

Dinner arrived. The guards placed the trays of food on the floor and stepped back, arms folded across their chests. And suddenly the women of Mary Ward were no longer listless. They were on their feet, sprinting across the ward, pushing each other out of the way, tearing bread from each other's hands in their desperation to feed their children.

There wasn't nearly enough food to go around. Magdalen suspected there was never enough food to go round. Her grandmother would not understand that she had to fight in order to survive. And no-one would take pity on her; not when they had their own starving children to feed.

She would have to bring food for Agnes every day, after she had finished her work at the Theatre. Come winter, it would mean crossing London alone as darkness fell, assuming Grand-Aggie was still alive by then.

Assuming I am still alive by then.

Tommy was trying to undo the laces of his mother's dress, his mouth puckered expectantly.

'I've no milk, Tommy love.'

His face crumpled and he began to wail pitifully. Magdalen reached into her pocket and pulled out a silk pincushion, fashioned to resemble five girls holding hands, their plaits woven from yellow thread. Her grandmother had shown her how to make it when she had first come to London, and she had carried it with her ever since, her lucky charm, her protection against all adversity. She held it out to Tommy.

'Would you like to play with this?'

Tommy's eyes lit up and he snatched it from her.

Belle smiled fondly at him. 'I didn't set out to be a whore,' she said quietly. 'I was in love with an apprentice. We were to be wed, so I lets him put his date in my pie, if you know what I mean. But then the plague took him and then it took my parents. And then I find I'm carryin' his child. Tommy's all I have now.' She looked Magdalen in the eye. 'I'll give you some advice for free. If you need coin - and you surely do, or your grandmother wouldn't be in here - there are stews in every street round here. You can earn good money, and the constables turn a blind eye. It's outside the city walls, outside the city's grip, you see.'

'I don't think I -' Magdalen began but Belle interrupted her.

'No, none of us do, duckie, but when your babe's cryin', so hungry he can't sleep, well, what choice do you have? Listen, I like you. You're kind. So, I'll tell you a secret. There's a gate in the city wall, at the back of Blackfriars, leads out to the old bridge across the Fleet. The monks built it so they could sneak out and take their pleasures in the stews - the godless old farts. And I used it too, to come and go after dark, to work in them very same stews. Not many folk know about that gate, it's hidden beneath the ivy -'

Agnes let out a particularly loud, rumbling snore, and Belle raised an amused eyebrow. 'It's my fault we're in here. I was stupid. I tried me luck in St Paul's, but the constables were roundin' up beggars and whores that day. I tell you, Magdalen, use the Blackfriars gate. You'll not get caught in them stews by the Fleet. A man could fuck a horse in broad daylight beyond the city walls and the constables wouldn't bat an eyelid.'

'I'll remember that,' Magdalen said quietly. In truth, it was an image it would be difficult to forget.

Tommy was chewing the pin cushion. 'It's not to eat, you daft duck,' Belle said, forcibly removing it from his mouth.

He let out a howl and Magdalen's heart lurched with pity. At first glance, Belle's predicament was identical to Amelia Bassano's. Both women had fallen pregnant out of wedlock but in reality, Fate had dealt them entirely different hands. Belle and Tommy were in Bridewell because they had no money, no family and no connections of any kind. Amelia Bassano, on the other hand, was under the protection of the Lord Chamberlain, one of the wealthiest, most influential men in the land. 'Connections' did not come any better than that.

'Anything left in there?' Belle asked, peering into the basket.

Magdalen nodded. She took out the crumbly white cheese and carefully unwrapped it. She kept a portion for Agnes when she awoke and shared the rest with Belle and Tommy. They drank the small beer straight from the bottle. It made Tommy burp, which in turn made him giggle. He evidently didn't giggle very often because Belle hugged him, tears welling in her eyes.

The day drew on, and an icy draft crept across the floor. Agnes continued to snore, and Tommy fell asleep clutching the pincushion. Magdalen looked around at the prisoners curled up on their mattresses, their few, threadbare belongings neatly arranged about them. She realised the mattresses were all the women had left. Their tiny, pitiful patch of home; their last, frayed shreds of dignity.

Daylight was fading when the guards returned.

'Mistress Bisset. We're locking up. It's time to go.'

Pargitar's bulky frame loomed over Belle's mattress, a menacing presence. Magdalen looked up at him, cold dread coiling about her heart. How could she leave her grandmother here? How could she walk away?

'Can I stay with her tonight?' she asked beseechingly.

'This ain't a fuckin' tavern. On your feet. Now.'

Magdalen carefully tucked her grandmother's cloak about her thin frame, a makeshift blanket against the icy chill. Agnes did not stir, not even when she kissed her forehead.

She stood up shakily. 'I beg you to have pity on her. She is old and weak. She's not strong enough to work hemp, and besides, she won't understand what's expected of her. Is there something else she could do?'

'No special treatment,' Pargitar sniffed. 'Like I said, this ain't a fuckin' tavern. I've got orders to take you to the gate.'

Magdalen felt as if her heart was being torn in two. She looked down at her grandmother again.

'Don't you worry, duckie, I'll keep an eye out for her,' Belle said quietly.

Her kindness was almost Magdalen's undoing, and her voice wobbled as she spoke. 'Thank you, Belle. I'll bring more food tomorrow.'

'I ain't got all day,' Pargitar said gruffly.

'I'm coming.' Magdalen made to follow him but Belle tugged her sleeve and whispered in her ear. 'You'll need money, fast, or your grandmother will end up in the cellars and believe me, she won't last more'n a few days down there 'cos the plague's taken hold. If the warden wants to fuck you, tell him it'll cost him a sovereign. Don't sell yourself short, you're a pretty lass.'

Magdalen's eyes widened, and Belle laughed. 'Who you savin'

yourself for? A handsome prince? Now go, and bring us a pie next time. Can't remember the last time I ate meat.'

Pargitar took Magdalen back to the gate house and left her there without a word. She stood in the growing darkness, suffocating beneath a landslide of guilt and misery. In the confines of Mary Ward, Agnes had not understood Bridewell's true nature and perhaps there was some mercy in that. But tomorrow she would be sent to the hemp sheds. Pargitar had made it clear no allowances would be made, and she was surely too old and too frail to endure such brutal work. Her grandmother was one of the kindest people she knew. She did not deserve such an end.

Magdalen looked up at the sky. It was pinpricked with stars, as if an endless expanse of indigo blue silk had been embossed with twinkling pearls. But where was God in all that vastness? She could not feel His presence. Wearily, she turned towards the city, but each step was a monumental effort. Her head was throbbing, a knife-point of pain stabbing her temples. She had to secure Agnes's release. But how? The Recusancy fine was far beyond her reach, and far beyond the reach of anyone she knew. Of more immediate concern was the five shillings a week the warden had demanded to keep her grandmother out of the cellars. Instinctively, Magdalen reached into her cloak pocket for the tiny pincushion, seeking the reassuring sensation of silk against her fingertips. And then she remembered she had given it to Tommy. For a brief moment she felt its loss keenly, before telling herself that Belle's little boy had far more need of it than she did.

Skirting the city walls, Magdalen turned north, towards Norton Folgate, towards Marlowe, towards the man who had always sworn he would not allow any harm to come to her. She tried not to dwell on their last meeting when he had turned his back on her and walked away. She tried to tell herself he was as changeable as the weather, and tonight he would welcome her with open arms.

And yet, even if he did greet her with a blast of his outrageous, devil-may-care charm, what did she hope to achieve? She had far too much pride to ask him for money and besides, even Marlowe with his new-found wealth could not afford to lend her the staggeringly large sum of six hundred and thirty-five pounds. But unless she wanted to sleep in the street, at the mercy of pimps and Upright Men, she needed a bed for the night.

She quickened her pace across Moorfields and on into the maze of Norton Folgate's narrow lanes. She kept her head down and her hood pulled up, ever mindful of the two men who had pursued her through these same narrow lanes not three nights since. Her senses heightened, she jumped at every sound and shadow.

As she ventured deeper into the dark alleyways, the stink of poverty and pestilence filled her nostrils. Thin, barefoot children appeared out of the darkness, holding out their hands for alms. She reached into her pocket for her purse before remembering the warden of Bridewell had taken it. Shaking her head apologetically, she hurried on. She felt a flutter of apprehension as she knocked on Marlowe's door.

Surely he would not turn her away? Or would he? A window opened above, and a voice called out, 'Who's there?'

Magdalen stepped back and looked up. Thomas Kyd held a candle in his hand, its flame quivering in the breeze. He was pale and dishevelled and she wondered if she had woken him.

'Good evening, Thomas. Is Marlowe at home?'

'The bastard's gone, thank Christ.'

'To the Mermaid?'

'No. Overseas. He didn't say, but my guess is the Netherlands.'

The Netherlands? Marlowe would be gone for weeks or, more likely, months.

Kyd must have noticed her distress. 'What's wrong Maggie?'

'Nothing is wrong,' she lied. 'I'm sorry to have disturbed you. Good night.'

'Good night, Maggie,' Kyd replied, stifling a yawn as he ducked back inside and closed the shutters behind him.

The moon had not yet risen and Magdalen peered uneasily into the darkness, her eyes prickling with exhaustion. What in God's name should she do now? Norton Folgate was full of noise even at this late hour. Barking dogs, wailing babies, men's laughter, and music. And if she closed her eyes, she imagined she could hear other sounds too. Men's footsteps in the shadows; thieves, murderers and rapists. Instinctively she reached into her pocket again, searching for the silk pincushion. Instead, her fingers found the set of keys she carried for the Theatre.

Her thoughts focussed. Burbage had stipulated the Theatre was out of bounds after sunset, but he need never know and, in truth, what choice did she have? She broke into a run as she turned north, anxious to leave Norton Folgate behind. It was too dark to avoid the deep puddles that pitted Hog Lane and she splashed through them, spraying foul water into the air in her haste to reach the Theatre. Unlocking the 'tiring house door, she stumbled inside, quickly locking it again behind her.

She turned around slowly. The 'tiring house was in total darkness and eerily quiet. She tried to tell herself she had no reason to be afraid, but her heart was pounding as she felt her way to her workbench, found the tinder box and lit a candle. The flame caught, and she let out a gasp of horror. Beyond the pool of candlelight, veiled and menacing wraiths were creeping towards her across the floor. What manner of otherworldly devils were these? Backing away, she felt something hard ram into her ankles. She cried out in pain, her thoughts scattering. She had made a terrible mistake. She should not have ventured here after dark, when the world no longer belonged to the living, but to the spirits of the long dead.

She turned and ran for the door, her heart hammering, her hands shaking so violently she almost dropped the candle-holder. Where was the key? She was sure she had left it in the lock. Or was it on the workbench? She shot a terrified glance over her shoulder, her breath coming in short, painful gasps.

The candle flame flickered, and the wraiths retreated from the light as if it were poison. Suddenly, Magdalen could see clearly. She had backed into nothing more menacing than a costume chest. And the wraiths were merely shadows belonging to Crab the stuffed dog, and the old wax severed head propped against her workbench. A strange sound escaped her lips, a cross between a sigh of relief and a strangled laugh.

Shaking her head at her own foolishness, she got down on her hands and knees, and set about making a nest beneath her workbench using furs and cloaks from the costume chests. It was cosy if a little cramped; a miniature simulation of a four-poster bed. She lay down but despite her exhaustion, sleep did not come. Instead, her thoughts jostled each other for attention, beating against her temples and stabbing her left eye with such relentless ferocity she thought she might be sick.

What to do about Grand-Aggie in Bridewell, and the Recusancy fine, not to mention the five shillings she must find for the warden every week?

What to do about Edmund Stow, and the madness in his eyes as his hands closed about her throat?

What to do about the inquest?

There would be an inquest into Richard Cowley's death too. And then a hasty trial, over in a matter of moments, wretches hung so jurymen might dine. A feeling of pure terror shot through her, as sharp and brutal as a cross bow bolt.

Abandoning all hope of sleep, she retrieved the last few pages *Venus and Adonis*, now safely hidden in her workbench drawer. She craved distraction and she hoped the poem would end happily, but Ovid's account of the story had ended tragically and she suspected Will's version might too. Placing the candle at her side, she pulled a heavy, fur trimmed cloak about her shoulders and braced herself for what was to come:

Venus, distraught with worry after her premonition of Adonis's death, hears the sounds of his hunting party and the terrified yelping of his dogs. Entering the clearing, she finds him dead from a wide wound the boar has inflicted.

'Alas poor world, what treasure hast thou lost!
What face remains alive that's worth the viewing?
Whose tongue is music now? What canst thou boast
Of things long since, or any thing ensuing?
The flowers are sweet, their colours fresh and trim,
But true-sweet beauty lived and died with him.'

Venus goes on to curse all those who fall in love:

'In his prime Death doth my love destroy,
They that love best their loves shall not enjoy.'
'By this, the boy that by her side lay killed
Was melted like a vapour from her sight;
And in his blood, that on the ground lay spilled,
A purple flower sprung up, chequered with white,
Resembling well his pale cheeks, and the blood
Which in round drops upon their whiteness stood.'

What did Will know that she did not? Was love truly cursed, to be feared rather than cherished? She had no answers. She didn't recognise the flower he was describing either. Was he thinking of the exotic bulbs she sometimes saw in the flower markets, brought all the way from Constantinople by the dark-skinned merchants whose colourful attire she so admired? Dropping her gaze to the page again, she read the last six lines of the poem.

'Thus weary of the world, away she hies,
And yokes her silver doves, by whose swift aid
Their mistress, mounted, through the empty skies
In her light chariot quickly is conveyed;
Holding their course to Paphos, where their queen,
Means to immure herself and not be seen.'

Magdalen envied Venus her escape from the troubles of the world. But did the goddess truly love Adonis, or was she simply enamoured of his beauty? Matthew Hilliard was fair of face to be sure...

A loud bang jolted her from her thoughts. She sat bolt upright, and hit her head on the underside of the table. Cursing aloud, she peered into the shadows and listened hard, but all she could hear was her own blood pulsing in her ears. She held her breath, trying to concentrate. There was someone on the stage, she could hear the boards creaking. Her blood's rhythmic pounding grew louder; a pulsing manifestation of her fear.

It's nothing, the rational part of the brain told her. *It's just the Theatre settling for the night, just like the house on Silver Street.*

But she had been raised in the countryside, where it was common knowledge that fairies lived in the hills, and sprites guarded the greenwood, and water nymphs watched over the springs. Just as it was also common knowledge that tormented souls might cling to the place of their death until their murders were avenged.

She was sorely tempted to burrow beneath the furs until the noises stopped and daylight returned, but reckless curiosity drew her out from beneath the workbench. With the candle holder clutched in her hand, she crept to the stage door. At first, she could hear nothing except her beating heart, but then the hairs on the back of her neck stood on end. There *was* something on the other side. She could feel it. Or rather, she could feel *him*.

Did John blame her for his death? Would she feel his cold fury snaking over her skin? She almost lost her nerve, but she had let John down once before. She couldn't do so again. She opened the door. Instantly, the temperature plummeted, the icy air coiling around her.

'John? Is that you?' she whispered.

A hair's breadth of silence and then her voice echoed back to her. The stage and galleries were bathed in moonlight. She could see no-one and all was quiet, but she had the strangest feeling she was not alone.

'Hello?' she called and her echo mimicked her fear once more.

Movement caught her eye and she looked up. An owl was flying overhead on silent wings, a gliding silhouette against a night sky dotted with stars.

'John?' she whispered. 'I haven't forgotten you. I will find your killer. I will give you the justice you deserve, I swear.'

'I swear, I swear, I swear…'

Her echo swirled around her; hissing, threatening, closing in like unseen Furies. Her nerves at breaking point, Magdalen felt something brush against her calf. She screamed, and in response, a hideous howl rent the air, as if Hell's hounds had been released upon the earth. Turning on her heel, Magdalen fled to the 'tiring house.

She was about to slam the door behind her when Brutus, the Theatre's tabby cat, stalked past. After examining the nest she had made beneath her workbench, he found it to his liking and curled up amidst the costumes.

Magdalen awoke the following morning to find Brutus asleep beside her, his fur tickling her cheek. For a fleeting moment, she floated on blissful oblivion until the reality of her predicament rushed in, a hurly burly of troubles. She turned over wearily. The sun was already high in the sky, spilling through the high window. She had overslept. Not wanting Burbage and the rest of the players to know where she had spent the night, she pushed the sleeping cat aside and hastily returned her makeshift bedding to the costume chests.

In the daylight, the 'tiring house no longer appeared menacing and the wax severed head looked positively benign. Nevertheless, her gaze was drawn towards the stage, her mind reliving the previous night; the eerie, terrifying sense that she was not alone. She opened the stage door cautiously, and peeked out. The Theatre looked entirely different now; commonplace and unthreatening. If John's ghost had walked abroad in the darkness, he had vanished at the coming of the light. She walked slowly across the boards. The sounds of the city were muffled and the cocooned silence wrapped around her. It was not an empty silence, but filled with memories. Was it fanciful to suppose the poetry and music and dancing of Will's plays had somehow infused the boards and pillars and galleries to become part of the Theatre itself?

She glanced over her shoulder. Familiar voices were drifting from the 'tiring house. The players were arriving for the morning rehearsal. She knew full well her position at the Theatre was hanging by a thread. In all likelihood, Burbage had already decided she was a liability; already decided he wanted her gone. Filled with apprehension, she returned to the 'tiring house.

Peter and Slinko were firing dried peas at each other from opposite ends of the room. Their pistols were short straws, no doubt pilfered from the nearest stable. Fresh supplies were wedged into their belts, giving the boys an air of pugilistic scarecrows. Peter had barricaded himself behind a costume chest, raising his head above the parapet just long enough to put a straw to his lips, puff out his cheeks, and launch another volley. In response, Slinko was strutting about the room with a devil-may-care bravado as peas flew past his ears.

In Magdalen's brief absence, William Sly appeared to have dyed his hair. His dark locks were now tinged with purple, the colour of an emperor's robes. Only hibiscus powder resulted in such a hue, and Magdalen wondered who had tricked him into using it.

'Jesu, Sly, did you boil your head in a pan of beetroot?' Christopher Beeston was bent double with laughter.

'He looks like one of Henslowe's whores,' Will Kempe laughed. 'The ones you pay extra for, seeing as they are *exotics*.'

'Nothing exotic about you, Sly,' Beeston guffawed. 'You look a right clod!'

Sly was bearing their ridicule with good-natured fortitude.

'Say what you will, but I am pleased with the effect,' he lied. 'What is life without colour? Isn't that what you always say, Maggie?'

As one, the players turned to look at her, but she felt fragile and unusually lost for words. They all seemed strangely blurred, save for Matthew Hilliard who remained vividly in focus. She noticed he looked pale and drawn. Pray God he was not sickening with the plague. Her heart missed a beat. Pray God he had not been poisoned like John.

Stop it. You are staring at him like a fool.

No-one noticed Burbage until it was too late. The world seemed to slow as he walked unwittingly into Peter's line of fire and a small, dried pea, travelling at speed, struck him in the eye. Startled, Burbage swore loudly, then he marched across to Peter, grabbed him by the ear and hauled him to his feet.

'You stupid, ungrateful boy!' Each word was perfectly in time with a stinging slap aimed at Peter's backside. 'Mark my words, you are on borrowed time. If you put so much as a foot out of line in future, I will send you back to your parents in disgrace.'

Peter was sobbing, his face a picture of misery and humiliation. Henry Condell made a move to comfort him, then appeared to change his mind. Perhaps even he had sensed it was time Peter learnt to rein in his excessively high-spirits. Magdalen sat down at her workbench and made a half-hearted show of examining her mending pile. Gradually, a low hum of subdued chatter resumed in the 'tiring house.

'How fares your grandmother?' Will Shakespeare asked, pulling up the stool and sitting down beside her.

'She is…' Emotion tightened Magdalen's throat and she found herself unable to continue, but if Will had noticed her distress, he gave no sign of it.

'The Mountjoys asked me to tell you that you must collect your belongings today or they will throw them out onto the street. Their Christian charity is boundless is it not?' He pulled a face.

Magdalen had known him long enough to recognise his outward show of disgust did not reach his eyes. He was as detached as ever, a witness not a participant in the troubles of others.

'Where did you sleep last night?' he asked.

'Here.' Her voice was a whisper. She was ashamed of her homelessness; ashamed of how far she had fallen.

Will's response was predictably understated. He merely raised an eyebrow, and changed the subject. 'Is it true Agnes has been accused of Recusancy?'

Magdalen nodded wordlessly.

Will leant forward. 'I am aware I offer cold comfort, Maggie, but treason brings the death penalty whereas the penalty for Recusancy is merely a fine.'

Exasperated, she finally found her voice. 'A fine so huge I can never repay it! My grandmother is condemned to live out the rest of her days in Bridewell!'

Will fell silent, his expression unfathomable.

Magdalen took a deep breath, gathering her courage.

'I believe you are…' she hesitated, remembering Will's empty bed, 'acquainted with the Earl of Southampton. Might you put in a good word for my grandmother? Her age and infirmity, they are exceptional circumstances, are they not? If the fine were to be reduced -'

'I'm sorry, but cannot help you, Maggie. Agnes is fortunate not to be in the Tower. You know as well as I that the Queen has hardened her attitude to Catholics. The earl could kneel at her feet for a year and a day and she would not yield.'

In an attempt to hide her bitter disappointment, Magdalen feigned a sudden interest in a fallen hem on her mending pile. When she looked up again, she half expected Will to have gone but he was still there, still staring into the middle distance. There was no way of knowing if he was musing on her predicament or on the afternoon's performance of *The Merry Wives of Windsor*.

A feeling of desperation settled heavily on her heart. So many doors were closing in her face. First the Mountjoys, then Marlowe and now Will. She glanced about the 'tiring house and her gaze fell on the green-glazed money pots. They were full of pennies, the takings from yesterday's performance; enough to pay the warden of Bridewell for many weeks to come. Appalled she had even considered committing the deadly sin of thievery, her eyes darted guiltily to Richard Burbage. It was fortunate he could not read her mind.

'Ask him, by all means, but his answer will be the same as

mine,' Will said, seemingly equally unable to read her mind. 'Burbage has no sway with the Lord Chamberlain,' he added. 'We are his playthings, nothing more. As soon as he tires of us, he will cast us aside, and so Burbage does everything in his power to please him.'

'I know,' Magdalen said softly. 'But I have to try.'

She stood up and straightened her skirts, a tense, nervous gesture. Burbage was surrounded by players but their conversation ceased as she approached.

'Might I have a word with you, sir?'

Burbage's expression was unwelcoming. 'Yes?'

'I…' Magdalen glanced apologetically at the players. 'May I speak to you in private?'

Burbage tutted irritably but led her to one side. 'Yes?'

'I know you would not normally give an advance of wages but, as you are aware, my grandmother is in Bridewell.' Her throat was dry, her voice not her own. 'The warden has taken my purse, and I find myself entirely without funds. He is demanding further payment -'

Burbage raised a hand to silence her. 'If I give an advance to one, then the rest will see it as their right. I am sorry, Magdalen, but you have only yourself to blame for your grandmother's misfortune. For the love of God, why didn't you stop her attending a Catholic Mass?'

'She wasn't… she didn't… she was outside, in the street -' Magdalen began, but Burbage cut her off again.

'My hands are tied. I am sorry, but I cannot help you.'

Shaking his head disapprovingly, he returned to the players. Magdalen, however, remained rooted to the spot with shame. In truth, she had always known Burbage would not jeopardise his fragile association with the Lord Chamberlain to save his old, moon-mad wardrobe mistress. Just as she had always known

Will would not risk damaging his potentially lucrative relationship with the Earl of Southampton.

'What did you say to him?' Will was at her shoulder.

'I asked him for an advance. He refused.'

'And yet you remain in his employ, despite Agnes's present misfortune?'

'It would seem so.'

'Then the bastard does have a heart after all.'

Magdalen glanced at Will, torn with indecision. Her sense of pride was urging her to say nothing, but another more powerful instinct was begging her to throw decorum to the wind.

'Would you be able to lend me some money, just until the end of the month?' she blurted.

Will's features twisted slightly. She recognised that look. It meant he was uncomfortable.

'Forgive me, but I cannot. My wages go to Stratford.'

She thought fleetingly of the banter in the Mermaid, the barbed taunts that Will was tight with money, but she quickly rejected the idea as uncharitable. Stratford was Will's home. The home of his wife and his three children. The family he rarely mentioned.

'I apologise. I shouldn't have asked,' she said, mortified.

'It is I who should apologise, but worry not. All will be well,' Will said, as casually as if she had dropped a handful of pins.

Giving her shoulder a quick squeeze, he headed for the stage. Magdalen made to follow him but she did not get far. She came to a stop, her hands balled into fists, her knuckles white.

What was Will thinking? How could anything ever be well again?

The players were following Will onto the stage. They parted to avoid her, like a river flowing around an island, and in the crowded 'tiring house, she had never felt more alone.

'I'm sorry… about your grandmother… I'm so sorry…'

Magdalen turned around. On closer inspection, Matthew Hilliard looked very ill indeed, the blue smudges of fatigue beneath his eyes blending with the purple bruises on his nose and cheek.

'What's wrong?' Without thinking, she placed a hand lightly on his arm but he recoiled as if he had been struck. She hastily retreated a pace. 'Forgive me.'

'No…that's not… I…' His expression was tormented. Gone was his air of aloof self-confidence.

'Have you received bad news about your family?' she asked apprehensively.

Waving away her question, he took a purse from his belt.

'I want you to have this. For you grandmother.'

Magdalen was astonished. 'That is most gracious of you, Matthew, but I cannot take it.'

Asking Will and Burbage for money had been shaming enough, but she had known them forever. Over the years she had come to think of them as father figures (albeit distant in Will's case, and stern and unyielding in Burbage's), whereas she had known Matthew Hilliard for little over a week. He made her heart beat faster, and he took her breath away. He was handsome and wealthy, and far beyond her reach. If she accepted money from a man who would never offer her the respectability of marriage, she would become the whore the world had always presumed her to be.

'Consider it a loan then,' he pressed.

Their eyes met and held, and as she gazed at him, Belle's words came back to her:

'*You'll need money, fast, or your grandmother will end up in the cellars. When the warden wants to fuck you, tell him it'll cost him a sovereign…*'

No. That would not be her fate. There had to be another way.

'Thank you, Matthew, but I cannot accept your money.' Her voice sounded cold and formal and she hated herself for it because she sensed he was nothing like the warden of Bridewell. In her heart, she knew he would have expected nothing in return.

She watched the hurt bloom in his eyes but he must have heard the finality in her words because he gave a small bow.

'As you wish, Magdalen,' he said, and walked away.

SIXTEEN

'I say there is no darkness but ignorance'

In the Mountjoys' kitchen later that day, the delicious, welcoming aroma of freshly baked bread did little to improve Magdalen's humour. There was much she hated about this house: the gloomy, oppressive workshop; Marie's relentless hostility; Mary's vicious spite; Christopher's rages and, of late, his unwelcome advances. But there were good memories too, treasured memories, and her grandmother loomed large in each and every one.

Louisa was reading her Bible at the kitchen table. Spying Magdalen, she leapt to her feet. 'Oh, I can't believe it. Your grandmother is an old woman. How can they be so cruel, so heartless?'

'In faith, I do not know.' Magdalen clasped Louisa's outstretched hands and took comfort in their warmth.

'They've gone out. They didn't want to see you. Oh, Magdalen, first Edmund Stow accuses you of -' Louisa faltered, her eyes huge with sorrow, 'of John's death, and now this. Where will you go? What are you going to do?'

Magdalen swallowed hard and said briskly, 'I still have my job at the Theatre, and I'll find somewhere to live. I have to find a way through this, for my grandmother's sake.'

'Madame Mountjoy has already found new tenants. She wastes no time, does she?' Louisa grimaced. 'Did Master Shakespeare tell you she wants your rooms emptied? Would it help if you stored your belongings in my room? Madame Mountjoy rarely goes up there. She would never know.'

Magdalen's face lit up. Generosity in the Mountjoys' house was rare indeed. 'Thank you,' she said warmly. 'I am truly blessed to have such a friend.'

Louisa blushed and smiled. 'Are you hungry? I baked bread this afternoon, and there is some pottage on the stove.'

Magdalen *was* hungry, but she couldn't contemplate even the thought of food. 'Thank you, but no. I should make haste. I should like to be gone before the Mountjoys return.'

'I understand. I will help you.'

Magdalen followed Louisa up the stairs, fighting her misery with every familiar, creaking step. In her bedchamber, her mattress was upended, her clothes and linens scattered across the floor. It felt like a desecration, a final insult to add to all those that had gone before.

'Madame Mountjoy was looking for relics of the old religion, rosary beads and the like.' Louisa's voice was a whisper of desolation. 'She is afraid the watchers will come.'

Magdalen looked about, drowning in memories. So much had happened in this small room. Here, she had mourned the loss of her parents, and yearned for the changing seasons and sweet scents of the countryside. Here, her childhood had slowly, indiscernibly slipped away. Here, she had sewn doublets and gowns, fairy wings and cloaks for kings, and here, as the years passed, she had taken delight in Will's library, reading late into the night until her eyes grew gritty and sore.

She would miss the way the room creaked at night as the house settled. Its grumblings had frightened her at first, but she had learnt to find comfort in them. She would miss how the sunlight played across the unevenly plastered walls, how it warmed the floor boards, soaking into the wood until she could almost believe the ancient oak still breathed. Her gaze fell upon the small hearth. Here she had sat upon Grand-Aggie's knee and listened to her stories of the little-folk and watched fire fairies dancing in the flames.

'Are you quite well?' Louisa asked gently.

Not trusting herself to speak, Magdalen nodded and began to bustle about collecting her strewn belongings. She took the Earl of Southampton's cloak to Will's room. He wasn't there, so she laid the linen bag on his bed. Dipping a quill into the ink pot, she left him a short note.

'This is the cloak I fashioned for the Earl of Southampton. Please could you see it to him?

Thank you.

Magdalen.'

She felt deeply uncomfortable emptying her grandmother's bedchamber; an intruder in a foreign land she had no right to invade. She had always respected Grand-Aggie's privacy so it came as a surprise to discover she had very few personal belongings, but one in particular caught her eye. It was a miniature portrait, barely larger than her palm, set in a gilded, circular frame. Against a background of deep, azurite blue, the sitter's sober clothing proudly marked him out as a member of the merchant class. Fine featured, a mischievous gleam in his eye, and a hint of a smile. His was not a haughty face; if anything, he seemed to be inviting her to join him in his mirth.

Around the man's image, in striking gold lettering, ran the words, *Ano Aetatis Pierre Bisset 60 Ano Dni 1580.*

This was Grand-Aggie's beloved husband, Pierre, the grandfather she had never met. His image was exceptionally well painted and brimming with life. She trailed a finger over his cheek, half expecting to feel the harsh bristles of his greying beard.

'What is it?' Louisa asked, peering over her shoulder.

'A keep-sake,' Magdalen replied and slipped the portrait into her pocket.

Agnes and Magdalen's Bisset's entire worldly goods filled but a small corner of Louisa's attic bedchamber. Magdalen stared at the meagre boxes and baskets and wondered how there could be so little to show for their lives. How insignificant they seemed. How pitiful. And how quickly they would turn to dust and be forgotten.

'Magdalen, sit for a moment. You look worn out. Drink this.' Louisa handed Magdalen a cup of small beer and gestured for her to take the spindly chair whilst she perched on the edge of the bed. 'What can I do?' she added gently.

Magdalen shrugged her shoulders. Her life had fallen apart so drastically, she sensed only a miracle could put it back together again, and why would God waste his miracles on her, a lowly nobody? On the other hand, she reminded herself, Louisa was only trying to be kind.

'You should avoid spending time alone with Christopher Mountjoy, if you understand my meaning?'

Louisa looked momentarily shocked, and then she nodded soberly. 'Yes, I understand.'

'And will you swear to it?'

'I swear.' Louisa paused for a moment. 'The inquest is soon, is it not?'

'Yes. This Friday, the tenth.' Saying it out loud made it all the more real, all the more terrifying. Only four more days.

May God have mercy on my soul.

'And Edmund Stow hates me.' Magdalen's voice trembled.

'So it seems. But do you have any idea why?'

Magdalen shook her head wearily.

But perhaps she *did* know. Her grandmother had claimed, *'that man adores me'*. Had Agnes's rejection warped Stow's love into a terrible desire for revenge? She brushed the thought aside. Even if it was true, it could not help her now.

'Whatever his reasoning, he has sworn to see me hang. But I have to live, because I want justice for John, and because my grandmother cannot remain in Bridewell. Believe me, Louisa, it has changed beyond all recognition since your father taught there.'

Louisa placed a comforting hand on Magdalen's arm, and then a thought struck her, and her eyes lit up.

'A neighbour on Tenter Street, a good, kindly soul, loaded my belongings onto a hand cart and brought them to me. I want to show you something.' Dropping to her knees, she retrieved a small wooden box from beneath her bed. 'After John died, I was clearing his bedchamber, and I found this.' She placed the box in Magdalen's lap.

Magdalen turned it over in her hands. It was a fine piece of craftsmanship, the face of a green man carved upon the lid, the remaining sides adorned with the intertwining tendrils of his leafy hair.

'I don't know what's in it. I've tried to open it, but it's locked and I can't find a key that fits,' Louisa explained. 'It could well contain nothing of importance but then again, it might. I think we should try and prize it open.'

Magdalen looked up at her friend. 'Are you sure?'

'Yes. Your life is at stake and I know John would want me to do everything in my power to help you.'

'Would you like me to try and open it?' Magdalen asked.

Louisa nodded. 'Yes, please.'

Magdalen took the small pen knife from the work purse at her belt. With the box in one hand and the knife in the other, she carefully inserted the tip of the blade into the key hole. Her lips pursed with concentration, she began to manoeuvre the knife back and forth, slowly edging the bolt away from the keeper, a hair's breadth at a time. After what seemed an age, she felt the latch spring free. She returned the box to her friend.

With a quick, nervous glance at Magdalen, Louisa lifted the lid. The box was full of papers, and Magdalen felt a pang of sudden disappointment. What had she hoped to see? Gold coins? Pirate's treasure? Slowly, reverently, as if it were an exquisite swatch of cloth-of-gold, Louisa picked up the first paper. As she read it, a look of confusion clouded her face. She handed the paper to Magdalen, and picked up another.

Magdalen was a fast reader, and it did not take her long to understand that John owed money to half of London. Many of the papers were final demands for payment going back several years. She knew some of the establishments to be taverns, gaming and dicing rooms, others were brothels, still more were signed by individuals whose names she did not recognise.

'There must be some mistake? John wasn't in debt. Why are all these people demanding payment from him?' Louisa was picking up the bills and putting them down again with increasing agitation. 'I've never heard of Stodie's, or Mackworth's Inn, or any of these places. What is all this?'

'Stodie's is a gaming house, and Mackworth's Inn is a tavern, obviously.' Magdalen couldn't bring herself to add that it was also a brothel, renowned for the depths of its depravity.

'I don't understand. John had no business in such places!'

'John was known to enjoy throwing the dice on occasion,' Magdalen replied cautiously.

'Who told you that? It is not true!' Louisa said indignantly.

Magdalen's heart sank. It seemed Louisa genuinely knew nothing about John's private life. She suspected this was going to be an extremely difficult conversation. 'Your brother was a good man, a kind man,' she began slowly, 'but he enjoyed a drink and sometimes he drank too much and then he threw the dice and then he got into debt.'

'No! Why are you saying such things? These bills cannot possibly belong to John!'

Magdalen didn't know what to say to that, because John's name was writ large on every paper. Louisa reached out to close the lid, as if by shutting the box she could deny its contents had ever existed, but something caught her eye. With an air of great reluctance, she drew out another paper.

'This is written in John's own hand, but I don't understand… this can't be right.' Louisa thrust the letter at Magdalen. It was addressed to Henry Wriothesley, the Earl of Southampton:

'My dearest Rizzley,

Know that I write to you out of love and devotion to your most honourable self. I humbly beseech you to remember our friendship, which I value above all else in my worthless life. I am a weak vessel compared to your grace and strength and compassion. My weakness is but a symptom of my humanity and it is with my humanity that I beg you to listen to my humble request. You have spurned me this far. I beg you not to do so again. You have so much and I have so little, but if you were to find the charity to forward me the sum of twenty guineas, I would indeed be blessed by your compassion and find the strength to turn away from my affliction and weakness.

But if you continue to harden your heart towards me, I will feel obliged to reiterate my intention to speak freely of your choice of bedfellows and your heretical support for the old religion. I pray to God you do not force me down such a dangerous path, for you are too worthy for such an ignominious end.

Your humble servant, and devoted friend, John Wood.'

'It's blackmail,' Louisa whispered, horrified. 'I don't understand. I can't believe John would do something like that. His language suggests he is a friend of the earl, but that doesn't make sense either. John was just a lowly player…'

Magdalen put the letter down, her mind spinning. It appeared John had not sent this particular letter to the earl, but he *had* sent others in a similar vein, threatening to expose Rizzley's *'choice of bedfellows'* and his *'heretical belief in the old religion'*. She knew from her visit to Lincoln Place that John had shared Rizzley's bed, but she hadn't realised the earl secretly adhered to the Catholic faith.

'Surely this is a forgery because I can't believe … Magdalen, please say something…' Louisa was ashen faced.

Magdalen's gaze slid sideways and she shifted in her chair.

'You don't seem particularly surprised by any of this,' Louisa said slowly, accusingly.

Magdalen bit her lip. How to explain John's relationship with the earl? 'I don't think it is a forgery because, like you, I recognise John's hand,' she began slowly, taking time to gather her thoughts. 'I know the Earl of Southampton befriended John, but it didn't last because the earl grew tired of John's love of the dice, and refused to lend him any more money -'

'No, that can't be true! This letter is some kind of poisonous trick, designed to malign my brother. Why are you saying it's genuine? I had no idea you hated John so much!'

Magdalen forced herself to speak calmly and rationally. 'I don't hate him. I was very fond of him, and I still miss him, every single day, but there was a side to your brother that I knew nothing about until after his death. And I'm truly sorry this is so painful for you to hear.'

In the long moments that followed, Magdalen watched her friend's anger and denial slowly fade to sullen, exhausted resignation. 'You had better continue,' Louisa said flatly.

'As you wish. John never sent this letter to the earl, but it appears he's been threatening to blackmail him for some time. So, it is possible the earl had John killed to silence him.'

Louisa looked dumbfounded.

Magdalen willed herself to go on. 'I don't know if you were aware, but John... enjoyed the company of other men.'

Suddenly, Louisa was on her feet, her muted acquiescence vanishing in an instant, her cheeks no longer pale but flushed with fury. 'First you tell me my brother was a drunkard who frequented gaming houses. Next you tell me he was a blackmailer, and now you accuse him of sodomy? Why would you say such a terrible thing?'

'Because it's the truth. John and the Earl of Southampton were lovers, but John had other lovers too, and when the earl found out about them, it's possible he felt so betrayed he murdered John.'

'No... no... this is... I can't...' Louisa sat down again, put her head in her hands and began to sob.

Consumed with remorse, Magdalen fumbled in her sleeve for a handkerchief and placed it in Louisa's lap. What had possessed her to be so cruel? She had achieved nothing by this frank and brutal admission. It would have been far kinder to leave Louisa in blissful ignorance of her brother's true nature.

'I'm sorry, I shouldn't have said anything,' she said quietly.

Louisa took the handkerchief and dabbed her eyes.

'You are not to blame. It's just... so hard... to hear...'

She blew her nose repeatedly and then, finally, she sat up straight, visibly gathering herself. 'But if the earl did have John killed, how will we ever prove it? He is so far above us and the laws of the land do not apply to men like him.' She paused for a moment, lost in thought. 'Perhaps there is someone else who might have wished to hurt John?'

Magdalen had a lengthy list of suspects, but she doubted Louisa was in the right frame of mind to hear it.

Louisa cocked her head to one side, eyeing her speculatively.

'I think there is something else you are not telling me. You have come this far. You can't stop now.'

'Perhaps another day. You must be exhausted.'

'I would like to hear it now.'

Louisa's expression reminded Magdalen of John; the determination in his eyes when he had made up his mind about something and would not be deterred.

'Very well. Let me see. Firstly, there is Amelia Bassano. She is Lord Hunsdon's mistress, and she was also John's lover. I know she was stealing money from Lord Hunsdon to pay off John's debts. I also know she is with child. By all accounts, she has told Lord Hunsdon that he is the father, and from what I can tell, he believes her. But the child might be John's, although I have no proof. Either way, in order to avoid a scandal, Lord Hundson has arranged for Amelia to be married to Alfonso Lanier, a court musician.'

'From what I have heard, Amelia truly loved John. She may have asked him to acknowledge the child, perhaps hoping he would marry her, but if he refused, she may have felt she had no choice but to kill him to keep their affair secret. I have also been told that Lord Hunsdon found out about the affair, so he might have murdered John out of jealousy and a desire for revenge.'

Louisa was staring at her open-mouthed, but Magdalen ploughed on, relieved to finally give voice to her speculations, even if she had no proof to support any of them.

'I saw Richard Cowley arguing and duelling with John the day he died, and it's common knowledge Richard was jealous of your brother. I know one should not speak ill of a dead man, but at the time, I did suspect Richard. But it's Alex Cooke who benefits from both John and Richard's deaths now, because he has secured all the best female roles.'

'And then there's Christopher Thomas. John changed his name, but he lived with you in a Huguenot enclave, so it's likely Thomas knew John was a Huguenot by birth. And you know at first-hand how much that man hates foreigners. And then there's the Puritans, and Adam Cooper in particular. He goes about the city decrying the theatres as dens of vice. On the day John died, I was posting hand bills by the Stocks Market and Adam Cooper was just as quickly tearing them down. He shamed me in front of the crowd, calling me the players' whore. So why did Adam Cooper choose to befriend John, a player? It doesn't make sense. Did he kill John? Is that why he has disappeared? Or, perhaps he has been murdered too?'

Louisa had begun to cry again. Magdalen sat down beside her on the bed, and put an arm about her shoulders. There were more names on her list, but she had said more than enough. Matthew Froissart, the ranting Anabaptist, would have to wait. So too would Matthew Hilliard - mysterious, evasive Matthew, who had appeared from nowhere to save her from Adam Cooper. Had Matthew killed John so he might audition to fill his place at Burbage's Theatre? It seemed wildly far-fetched but, in truth, she didn't know what to believe any more.

'He was my brother,' Louisa gulped. 'But I didn't know him at all.'

'Everyone has their secrets,' Magdalen said gently. 'The important thing to remember is that John loved you very much.'

In the long silence that followed Louisa wiped her eyes until the handkerchief resembled a sodden rag. At last, she said, 'If Amelia Bassano *is* carrying John's child, then I would be the babe's aunt.'

Magdalen could hear the yearning in Louisa's voice, the ache for a part of John to live on. But, even if that were true, she could not envisage a world where the Lord Chamberlain, or Amelia's future husband, Alfonso Lanier, would permit Louisa to go anywhere near the child. But now was not the time to shatter her fragile glimmer of hope.

'I don't know for certain if the child is John's. Perhaps, in time, we might know the truth of it,' she replied tactfully.

Louisa fell silent, seemingly digesting this. Eventually, she said, 'I'm sorry Adam shamed you. I always sensed he was a troubled young man, but I had no idea he could be so cruel. Do you really think he might be dead?'

'I don't know. He might have simply left London. He's dangerously outspoken and he might have decided he needed to lay low for a while.'

Louisa nodded earnestly. 'Pray God he is not dead, for I have a feeling he knows the answers to all our questions.' She picked up the last sheet of paper tentatively. She read it then handed it to Magdalen. 'What do you make of this?'

Written in John's hand, it was a list of names and addresses, scattered across London. Five were within the walls: Poultry, Lombard Street, Hart Street, Aldgate Street and Thames Street. And four were without: Bank Side, Fleet Street, Charing Cross and Long Lane.

At the bottom, there were three more names, presumably added later for the quill was thicker and the ink a different shade of black: *Adam Cooper. Richard Cowley. Nicholas Alwine.*

'We know Adam Cooper and Richard Cowley,' Magdalen said thoughtfully, 'but who is Nicholas Alwine?'

'I've never heard of him,' Louisa replied. '*Mon Dieu*, is it possible John owed money to these people too? Will they come looking for me, expecting me to honour his debts? I have nothing to give them, no savings, nothing!'

'Let's not cross our bridges before we come to them. We don't know why John made this list. It may well have had nothing to do with money.' Magdalen's tone was reassuring but her thoughts were whirring frantically. She had to find these people. Perhaps they knew something she did not. Perhaps they could lead her to John's killer.

Louisa had read her mind. 'I'll go with you. I will meet you outside the Theatre tomorrow morning at eight 'o clock, and we can make a start. I will tell Madame Mountjoy I am going shopping.'

But Magdalen was thinking of the two men in the alley, the sound of their footsteps growing louder in the darkness.

Their warning had been stark. *'Leave it alone.'*

She shook her head. 'No. It's too dangerous. I won't put you in harm's way.'

But Louisa was adamant. 'He was my brother, which gives me as much right to search for his killer as you. I want you to have this.' She thrust a small purse into Magdalen's hand. 'It's not much, but you and your grandmother have to eat, and I will not take no for an answer.'

Magdalen smiled sadly. 'You remind me of John. He was bull-headed at times. But my troubles are not your troubles. I will not draw you into them, and nor will I take your money.'

'I will not take no for an answer,' Louisa repeated firmly.

Magdalen looked into Louisa's huge, earnest eyes and sensed she was beaten. 'Very well, if you insist. Thank you for your kindness and your generosity. I will be forever in your debt. And now, I should go, before the Mountjoys return.' She squeezed Louisa's hand. 'I'm sorry I upset you tonight. Will you be all right?'

Fresh tears pricked Louisa's eyes, but her gaze was resolute.

'Yes, I will be. In time.'

SEVENTEEN

'Alas, the frailty is to blame, not we
For such as we are made of, such we be'

Matthew Hilliard was waiting for an audience with the Earl of
Essex at his sweet-scented residence on the Strand. As he
patrolled about the chamber, the eyes of the Earl of Leicester's
portrait seemed to follow his every step. The late earl's
expression was one of such haughty disdain Matthew sensed the
great man had judged him and found him wanting.

Dismissing the foolish notion, he went to the window and
looked out at the well-manicured gardens with their secret
arbours and neatly clipped hedges. He thought how perfect it
would be to walk beside Magdalen Bisset through such a garden;
to catch the scents of rosemary and lavender on a tranquil
summer's evening; to watch the last of the sun's rays transform
her auburn hair into flowing amber; to feel the warmth of her
smile; to see her happy again.

What a fool he was. How could Magdalen ever be happy again
when her grandmother was enduring the deprivations and
misery of Bridewell? A few desperate words whispered to that
bastard Thomas Barton had been enough to destroy Magdalen's
family. Today he would find out if those same words had been

enough to save his own. He listened for the sound of footfall, but all was silence. What was keeping the earl? Impatient and ill at ease, his treacherous heart continued to conjure up Magdalen's image. He had yearned to protect her, and instead he had thrown her to the wolves.

Sick with remorse, he refocussed his attention on the view from the window. The landscaping had been cleverly designed to lead the eye down to the river, to the bustling, watery metropolis of sailing ships and tug boats and wherries. At first glance, they appeared to be steering their own course, but in reality, they were at the mercy of the river, carried upstream or down by the endless pull of the tides. They had no more control over their fate than he did.

'Master Hilliard.'

Matthew turned around. Robert Devereux, the second Earl of Essex was a vision of opulence, the satin of his black doublet and breeches slashed and pinked in an intricate chequer board pattern to reveal a dazzling white lining beneath.

Matthew bowed. 'I am at Your Lordship's command.'

In truth, when that bastard Thomas Barton had informed him the earl demanded an audience, not even the twelve horsemen of the apocalypse could have slowed his journey to the Strand. And now, he was desperate to know what the earl had to say, but at the same time, he didn't want to know, for how would he bear it if all hope was irrevocably lost?

'I wanted to thank you in person.' The earl spoke quickly, his eyes darting from Matthew to the documents awaiting his attention on the table. His manner was that of a busy man, and Matthew sensed their meeting would not be a lengthy one.

'Your intelligence has led to the capture of a Catholic priest whose detainment in the Tower is already proving fruitful. Her Majesty has welcomed this new development.' Perhaps subconsciously, the earl began to stroke his neat beard, still dyed the same vivid red hue. 'I agreed to secure the release of your family, in return for a small favour. You have fulfilled your side of the bargain, and I am a man of my word. This morning I wrote a letter to King James of Scotland, entreating him to pardon your father. Suffice to say, the King is in my debt, and I trust he will grant me this request.'

The earl's words were disparate entities floating like dust motes inside Matthew's head. As they slowly aligned to form a string of coherent sentences, Matthew felt no overwhelming sense of elation. Instead, his feelings were strangely muted. There was tangible hope now, but the terrible uncertainty of the last few months had worn him down, embedding melancholy deep in his soul. He found himself momentarily lost for words.

'I must make haste. I have another engagement,' the earl said briskly.

With considerable effort, Matthew gathered himself and squared his shoulders. 'Forgive me, Your Lordship. I thank you most sincerely for your gracious and generous actions with regards to my family. I am forever in your debt.'

'Yes,' the earl replied. 'You are.'

Matthew tensed, caught off guard.

'I knew it from the first moment I met you,' the earl continued. 'You are a fine dissembler. Your talents are too profound to be wasted in the dusty halls of Oxford. I will call on you again when I have need of you. I presume I can rely on your service when the time comes?'

A feeling of dread crept over Matthew.

'Yes, indeed, Your Lordship,' he replied, bowing low. 'I am, and always will be, at your command.'

EIGHTEEN

'Oh time, thou must untangle this, not I'

Tuesday 7th April

Magdalen awoke at dawn, her back aching from a second night spent on the 'tiring house floor. Once again, Brutus was curled up beside her, his fur tickling her nose. She sneezed and pushed him away. Incensed he had been disturbed, the cat gave her a scathing look and stalked off.

Crawling out from beneath the workbench, Magdalen returned her improvised bedding to the costume chests. She had bought water from a carrier the previous day, so she stripped to her linens and endured a bracingly cold wash. Dressing in haste, she pulled a comb through her unruly hair and drank a cup of small beer, all the while worrying about her grandmother. Was she cold? Was she afraid? How had she fared in the hemp sheds?

Her head pounding with anxiety, Magdalen set out for the bakers on the corner of Hog Lane where she bought a loaf of bread for Agnes and a chicken pie, still warm from the oven, for Belle and Tommy. Hurrying towards Bridewell, Magdalen barely noticed the windmills of Finsbury Fields, or the cattle stalls of Smithfield market, or the towering scaffolding on either side of Pie Corner Street. After a recent devastating fire, reconstruction

303

had begun in earnest. High above Magdalen's head, carpenters, joiners and journeymen perched like sailors on the rigging of a ship. Some balanced precariously atop ladders, others strode brazenly across wobbling planks. Hammering nails and daubing walls, they laughed and bantered, seemingly oblivious to the fact that if they fell, they would most likely never walk again.

Passers-by were giving them a wide berth because journeymen were notorious for carelessly dropped hammers. But Magdalen was so distracted she walked directly beneath their scaffolding, scarcely aware of her surroundings. As she neared Ludgate, however, the stench of the river Fleet pervaded her senses, dragging her from her dark thoughts.

The guard at Bridewell's gate house was a stocky fellow with a swollen black-eye. Armed with a long pike, he used the weapon to bar Magdalen's way.

Undeterred, she stepped closer.

'I am here to visit my grandmother, Mistress Agnes Bisset. Let me through.'

'No visitors. There's pestilence inside,' he said laconically.

Magdalen stared at him, aghast, struggling to comprehend the enormity of his words.

'On your way,' the guard added, not unkindly.

'No! I have to see her.'

Again, the guard barred her way. 'I said, no visitors.'

Magdalen had been so preoccupied with securing funds for the warden, she had given little thought to the ever-present threat of pestilence. Grand-Aggie was frail, and plague was a coward; it always attacked the weakest. She squared her shoulders, resolute.

'She won't understand why I haven't come to see her. She will think I have abandoned her. You must make an exception, just this once. I have money -'

'I've been given strict instruction there's to be no exceptions, mistress.' The guard was addressing a point several inches above her head. Perhaps he had discovered it was easiest to avoid eye contact when delivering bad news.

Magdalen didn't know what else to do or say, but she knew she couldn't walk away. In desperation, she peered over the guard's shoulder, wondering if she could dodge around him and make a run for Mary Ward. But it seemed Fate had other ideas, for a man was barrelling towards her across the courtyard. She narrowed her eyes. There was something familiar about his bulky frame and his distinctive, rolling gait.

Christ in Heaven, it was Edmund Stow. His expression blazed with anger; his chest was puffed out like a giant bullfrog. The guard followed Magdalen's horrified gaze, took one look at Stow, and retreated to warm his hands at the brazier.

Stow came to a breathless halt just inches from Magdalen's face. 'You are a worthless whore!' he thundered. 'Bad blood will out! Why she married that worthless man I will never know.'

Intimidated, Magdalen hastily retreated a pace, her thoughts tied up with confusion. Who was he talking about? Did he mean Agnes and her grandfather, Pierre?

'Your days are numbered, and I am glad of it!' Stow closed the gap between them, so close now she could see the stitchwork of tiny veins threaded across his nose. 'You'll either hang as a murderer, or as a traitor to the crown, because that foul priest is talking now, and he knows your name.'

'I... I...' Magdalen stammered, his malevolence rendering her incoherent.

Stow was glaring at her, his eyes filled with hatred. She watched him draw the club from his belt and bounce it in his palm. He was breathing heavily, and she sensed the rage welling up within him, fighting for release.

Over his shoulder, the guard coughed; an unpleasant rattle of sticky phlegm. Perhaps Stow had not noticed him before, because he shot him a startled glance. When he looked at Magdalen again, she knew the danger had passed for she could no longer see madness in his eyes. He continued to glare at her for a long moment before he finally turned his back and lumbered at speed towards Ludgate as if a pack of English mastiffs was slavering at his heels.

Magdalen had begun to tremble. How could she reason with such a man? How could she hope to prevail against such relentless, vindictive hatred?

Black smoke was drifting from the brazier. Its acrid fumes stung her eyes and caught in her throat, but the guard appeared oblivious to the noxious cloud. He was casually picking his teeth and giving every indication that Stow's tirade was an everyday occurrence.

Magdalen took the pie from her basket. 'This is for my grandmother, Agnes Bisset, and for Belle and her son Tommy, in Mary Ward. In the name of Christian charity, I pray you will see they get it.'

The guard pursed his lips. 'Why would I help a doxy?'

'I swear to you, I am no whore. The constable has taken against me.' She hesitated. 'And God is watching.'

The guard shot a startled glance over his shoulder, as if expecting an angel to be lurking in the shadows taking notes. And then his expression softened.

'If truth be told, Stow's a nasty piece of work. Got something against women, so he has. Give me the pie. I'll see they gets it. What were the names again?'

Magdalen returned to the Theatre to find Louisa waiting for her at the 'tiring house door. 'Did you manage to see your grandmother?' she asked anxiously.

Magdalen shook her head. 'No. An outbreak of plague…'

'Oh heavens, no!' Louisa gasped in horror.

'Did you bring John's list?' Magdalen asked, her throat tight with suppressed emotion.

Louisa's frowned. She was not fooled by Magdalen's swift deflection but, sensing her fragile state of mind, she pulled the folded paper from her purse.

'Yes. I have it here. Where shall we start?'

Magdalen shrugged, disheartened and weary to her bones. How could they track down every name on the list by Friday? It was an impossible task.

'I cannot see how it matters. You pick a name.'

'Very well.' Louisa's eyes narrowed as she read the list. 'Mauritius Griffith, at the sign of the sugarloaf on Aldgate Street. Mauritius is an unusual name, is it not? Shall we start with him?

Magdalen shrugged again. 'As you wish.'

They waited for half an hour or more to pass through Bishopsgate, the road brought to a standstill by a surfeit of carriages and carts, the air rent with the racket of agitated hooves, braying donkeys and men's curses. The girls inched forward, shoulder to shoulder with oyster sellers, apprentices, journeymen, ladies' maids, goodwives and fractious children. Only the oyster seller retained his good humour. Quick to take advantage of a captive audience, he had sold half his wares before he even reached the bottleneck at the gate.

At the crossroads of Cornhill and Grace Church Street, Magdalen and Louisa turned east into Aldgate Street, a paved road of pleasant, well-kept houses, a far cry from the mud and squalor of Shoreditch. Recently re-painted, the sign of the sugarloaf gleamed in the sunlight. The plump round loaf, sprinkled with a thick coating of sugar looked good enough to eat, and Magdalen's empty stomach rumbled. Louisa wasted no time in approaching a passer-by, a soberly dressed, middle-aged man with a receding hairline and a neatly trimmed, pointed beard. He was carrying a young boy on his broad shoulders, the child's chubby legs bouncing against the man's doublet.

'Excuse me, sir,' Louisa began, and Magdalen smiled to herself. Her friend was becoming more confident with every passing day, no longer a timid mouse. How proud John would have been of his sister.

'Good day to you, mistress,' the man replied. 'You're wondering about the Sugarloaf sign, aren't you?' Without waiting for Louisa to confirm or deny, he explained, 'It goes back to good King Henry's time. When he drove out the sinful monks from the priory over yonder, he gave the place to a lady by the name of Mistress Cornwallis, in reward for the very fine puddings she had presented to him over the years.'

'How interesting, thank you, sir,' Louisa replied politely.

'It has been my pleasure.' The man gave a small bow. 'Fare you well.'

'Sir!' Louisa added hastily. 'I must ask, do you know where Master Mauritius Griffith lives?'

The little boy pointed to a group of gentlemen on the opposite side of the street.

'Mishus Griffs is over there!'

'Aye,' his father laughed. 'Well spotted. Master Griffith is the young fellow with the garters and the splendid hat.' He glanced up at his son. 'And now Abraham, let us away before your mother begins to fret over our absence.'

With that, the small boy kicked his father's chest, digging in his heels; a rider urging his mount to canter. Letting out a loud 'neigh', the man trotted off accompanied by the sound of his son's squealing laughter. Magdalen laughed, warmed by their good humour, but Louisa was frowning. She looked Mauritius

Griffith up and down and began to wring her hands nervously, her new-found confidence faltering in the face of such blatant wealth and status.

Griffith wore a tall, wide-brimmed black hat atop a mass of tightly curling hair that fell upon an exquisite lace collar. Narrow, vertical rows of embroidery adorned his doublet which flared to a scalloped skirt over his thighs. A rapier hung from his belt, marking him as a gentleman and, above his knees, his black satin breeches were gartered with the finest lace.

'Shall I speak to him?' Magdalen asked, and Louisa nodded gratefully.

On closer inspection, Mauritius Griffith was not a handsome man. His left eye was disconcertingly larger than his right, and his vast bulbous nose left little room for his small, thin-lipped mouth.

'Sir? Might I talk to you about Master John Wood?'

Griffith looked hard at Magdalen, and she knew he was trying to decide whether to ignore her or doff his hat, for her status was hard to define. Eventually his curiosity won the day and he turned to his fellows. 'Would you leave us?'

They took their cue, and wandered away.

'Are you Wood's widow?' Griffith asked curtly.

'No, sir. I am accompanying his sister.' Magdalen gestured towards her friend.

Griffith's small lips curled with distaste at Louisa's humble, workaday gown and blistered hands. 'My condolences,' he said carelessly. 'I heard the poor wretch drank himself to death.' His gaze slid back to Magdalen. 'What did you want to talk to me about? Make haste. I haven't got all day.'

Magdalen gritted her teeth. The soul of such a man as Mauritius Griffith surely resided in his attire alone. 'How were you acquainted with John Wood, sir?' she asked tightly.

'What business is that of yours?'

'Forgive me, sir, but we have the sad task of disposing of John's possessions. We came across a list of names. Your name was on that list. Was John in debt to you?'

'Aye, he was, to the sum of twenty-three pounds and four shillings. He was in debt to half of London. John and the dice were inseparable, but I presume you already know that. I never expected to see my money again, but he came to me, maybe a month before he died, and he repaid part of the debt. He gave me five pounds, and swore there would be more to follow.'

Magdalen and Louisa glanced at one another in surprise.

'Do you know if he paid any further debts, sir?' Magdalen asked.

'I cannot speak for all his creditors, Mistress...?'

'Mistress Morris,' Magdalen lied. 'Did John happen to say how he came by the money?'

'No, he did not, but I doubt it was earned by honest means. I would not wish to speak ill of the dead, but John Wood was a rogue and a scoundrel.'

Magdalen watched hurt bloom in Louisa's eyes and was sorely tempted to point out that Griffith had in fact spoken very ill of the dead. Instead, she asked, 'When you saw him last, did he seem in good humour, or out of sorts?'

Mauritius Griffith laughed, revealing two rows of sharp, tiny teeth, like those of a small rodent. 'John Wood was a player. He played a role on stage and also in life. It was impossible to determine what his true feelings were. But I believe he enjoyed gaming. Why else would he risk so much for it? I have often wondered why he was not festering in debtors' prison. Why did his creditors never come knocking?'

Why, indeed? thought Magdalen.

'Do you know any of these people sir?' She nodded at Louisa, who stepped forward and gave him the list. He read it with cursory haste.

'Aye, I've thrown the dice with Walter Belingham and Symon Smith on occasion.'

'Was John Wood acquainted with them?'

'Aye, acquainted with them, and heavily in debt to them I'd say.' Ignoring Louisa, he returned the list to Magdalen.

'Do you know where they met?' she asked.

'I'd hazard it was in the gaming room at The Oliphant on Grope Lane, out by Whitechapel. It's no place for a respectable young lady.' He eyed Magdalen speculatively. 'Are you a respectable young lady, Mistress Morris?'

'I am indeed,' Magdalen replied coolly. 'We thank you for your time, sir.' Dropping a small curtsey to Griffiths, she took Louisa's arm and hurried away. Somewhere close by a church bell was tolling eleven. She was already very late for the Theatre.

'That man is a toad,' Louisa whispered as they crossed the street.

'Very true, and if you kissed him, I strongly doubt he would turn into a handsome prince,' Magdalen replied.

Louisa's smile quickly faded to a concerned expression.

'Tomorrow we should go to the Oliphant and look for Walter Belingham and Symon Smith.'

Magdalen nodded her agreement but, in truth, she felt disheartened and afraid. There were fifteen names on John's list. They had questioned just one of them, and time was rapidly running out.

'Where did John get five pounds, and the promise of more?' Louisa asked. 'It's a large sum of money.'

'Perhaps he found fortune at the gaming tables,' Magdalen suggested as they walked back to Bishopsgate.

Or perhaps John had been blackmailing Rizzley after all, and the earl had paid him for his silence. Until he had grown tired of it, and tired of John, and silenced him forever?

The following morning Magdalen waited for Louisa outside the Theatre. She had slept poorly beneath the workbench, tormented by nightmares where she was pursued through the streets of London but no matter which way she turned, the gallows loomed ever closer. She had awoken repeatedly, gasping for air, as if a noose was tightening about her neck, and now her eyes prickled with tiredness.

Louisa was late. Magdalen walked to the main gate and looked up and down Curtain Road, but there was no sign of her. Had Marie Mountjoy taken exception to Louisa's protracted 'shopping expeditions' and called a halt? Magdalen hoped not, for she had no desire to venture into Whitechapel alone. With that in mind, she decided she would wait a little longer. Leaning against the high wall that separated Giles Allen's house and gardens from the bustling streets of Shoreditch, she watched goodwives hurry by, some with children in tow, others with friends, baskets on their arms, heads together, exchanging gossip and laughter, perfectly in step like marching soldiers.

Sometimes she envied them. They had husbands, children, a household to manage; they had status and respect. She had none of those things. But, if by some miracle the inquest declared her innocent, would she choose to marry? Would she want to give up her work at the Theatre? Would she want to stay at home, bake bread, brew ale, roast meat, grow vegetables, scrub laundry and endure the mortal dangers of childbirth?

Perhaps her answer would be 'yes', if she was to wed Matthew Hilliard. The endless drudgery would be a small price to pay for a life at his side. Every day would be an adventure, filled with the unexpected, with laughter…

You silly girl. He is far beyond your reach. Put him from your mind.

Wistfully, Magdalen looked up at the clear, forget-me-not blue sky. On the farm in Hampshire, such a sky would be filled with the sound of trilling skylarks. But there were no skylarks in London, only pigeons, their coos lost amidst the cries of street vendors, the hammering of carpenters, the shouts of carters and the rumble of a thousand wheels.

A figure turned the corner from Hog Lane, and Magdalen's spirits briefly lifted before she realised it wasn't Louisa, but Will Shakespeare. He exuded an air of blissful contentment, his manner unhurried, his limbs moving in serene harmony. He raised a hand in greeting and she waved back. She wondered why he was in such good humour until she remembered the banqueting chamber; how he and Rizzley had stood inches apart with eyes only for each other. And then she remembered Will's empty bed in Silver Street, not slept in for days.

'How goes it, Magdalen?' he asked breezily. 'Have you found new lodgings?'

'No, not yet.'

'Well, you can't sleep in the 'tiring house forever,' he said, stating the obvious.

'I doubt I will need to. The inquest is on Friday.'

Two more days of liberty. Two more days before she was accused of murder, and cast into a fever-infected prison to await trial. And then to the hangman's noose. The end was in sight. And a small, secret part of her; the dark, shameful part that was weary of all the pain and guilt, welcomed it.

'I intend to speak as a witness to your good character. You must have faith that justice will prevail,' Will said gently.

How could he believe that? Everyone knew constables and coroners and judges were open to bribes. Everyone knew the poor went to the gallows, and the rich walked free.

And then there was Edmund Stow. How could justice prevail when even now he was sharpening his arsenal against her? With considerable effort, she pushed him from her mind.

'I am waiting for Louisa, but she is very late. Have you seen her? Or are you residing elsewhere…' her voice trailed away awkwardly.

Will did not falter but she sensed he had understood her meaning. 'I have returned to Silver Street. Burbage wants a new play, and there's nowhere better to write than the Mountjoys' attic room. Marie and Christopher's constant bickering pricks my characters into life. So yes, I have seen Louisa. She is quite well, but young Mary is not. Marie is distraught, and has ordered Louisa to stay at home today.'

'What ails Mary?'

'A fever.'

Magdalen's face fell. 'The pestilence?'

'Marie swears not.'

Magdalen's heart was racing. Young Mary had made her life a relentless misery but she would never wish her ill in return. Pray God her fever would soon abate. And what of Louisa? She had taken her friend to Silver Street to keep her safe, but everyone knew how quickly contagion spread through a household. What if she sickened too? What if she died?

'Marie is frantic with worry,' Will went on, 'but Christopher has retreated to the workshop. I strongly suspect he will not show his face again until the danger has passed.'

Magdalen grimaced. 'Does he have *any* sensibilities at all?'

'Suffering and loss can change a man, and rarely for the better,' Will replied dourly.

Magdalen couldn't understand why he was making excuses for Christopher. Surely he was aware of the man's predilections?

'We are like the trees in the forest,' Will said, gazing into the middle distance. 'As the years pass, fierce tempests shake and bend our boughs, and even the strongest amongst us will break in time. Before you came to London, Marie lost seven babies. Some were stillborn, some survived but a few months. I watched the grief eat away at Christopher. As I say, suffering and loss can change a man.'

'I didn't know about the babies.' Magdalen's voice was a whisper.

Her grandmother had mentioned one lost child, not seven. Would she have viewed Marie differently if she *had* known? Would she have pitied her, rather than despised her? She doubted Marie would have welcomed her pity. She was far too proud for that. Marie had risen above life's tempests, but they had broken her husband. Or was he broken long before those dead babies? Would he have raped his serving girls and beaten his apprentices regardless of his own misfortunes?

'Are you coming inside?' Will asked.

'I have an errand to run first, but I won't be late.'

And so they parted; Will to oversee a rehearsal of *Titus Andronicus*, and Magdalen to the liberty of Whitechapel beyond Aldgate, where the roads were no longer paved, and the street signs did not gleam with freshly painted sugarloaves, where windows were draped with frayed sacking, and where stick-thin, barefoot children played listlessly and watched her with starved and envious eyes.

Grope Lane was dark and narrow; lines of laundry strung between crumbling tenements, poignantly personal items exposed to prying eyes and the foul, fetid air. From somewhere close by came the plaintive wail of a sickly baby. Lifting her skirt out of the noxious mud, Magdalen noticed three doors whitewashed with large crosses, and her heart quickened with fear. The pestilence had come to Grope Lane and entire families were dying behind those dank walls. Taking out her handkerchief, she held it over her nose and mouth. She knew it was foolhardy to linger here but if she turned back now, how could she face Louisa, or her grandmother, or John's spirit, trapped in the shadows of this world until his murder was avenged? And, in brutal truth, what did she have to lose when she would most likely hang before the month was out?

The Oliphant tavern had seen better days. The paintwork was peeling and several window panes were missing, rags stuffed in the gaps like a mouth of rotting teeth. Magdalen opened the door, and her senses were instantly assaulted by the reek of rancid ale, mouldy plaster, boiled cabbage, dirty floor rushes, and stale piss.

It took a moment for her eyes to become accustomed to the gloom, for the candles and the fire were unlit. A tall, young man was leaning against the board. She guessed he might be a scribe who saw little daylight, for his eyes looked red-rimmed and his complexion pallid. In the far corner, a screen had fallen over, revealing a man sitting in a carver chair, his breeches around his ankles. His hands were gripping the chair arms, his eyes were closed, his mouth hanging open. A woman knelt before him, her head between his legs. Magdalen quickly looked away. The Mermaid's whores plied their trade in the upstairs rooms, not in full view of the customers. May God forgive her, but she always felt safe in the Mermaid, amidst the players and playwrights and doxies of Shoreditch; men and women she had known since childhood.

But no-one knew her here.

She glanced nervously at the landlord. He was a big man, running to fat, and strands of greasy hair stuck to his huge, sweaty forehead. She realised he was eyeing her appraisingly and she wished she had borrowed Malvolio's costume again, for it rendered her inconspicuous far more effectively than the mysterious invisibility cloak in Burbage's prop box.

'Looking for work?' the landlord enquired. 'I'll not take you if you're pox'd. I run a clean house.'

I doubt that, Magdalen thought.

She looked him firmly in the eye. 'I am a respectable woman, sir, and I am not looking for work. I am here on behalf of John Wood's sister. You may have heard John passed away? He left a list of his creditors and his sister wishes to repay his debts.' She pulled the list from her pocket, and made a show of reading it. 'I believe John owed money to Walter Belingham and Symon Smith. Do you know where I might find them?'

The young man at the board turned around. 'I am Walter Belingham. You can tell John's sister he owes me three pounds and six shillings. Was it the pestilence that took him?'

'No, sir, he was murdered.'

'Aye.' Belingham didn't sound surprised. 'God rest his soul,' he added perfunctorily.

'Sir, do you know if John had any enemies, anyone who might want him dead?'

'How should I know?'

'I presumed you were his friend?'

Belingham snorted humourlessly. 'John Wood didn't have friends. He sucked people dry and then he moved on.'

Magdalen flinched at his cruel choice of words. Approaching the board, she offered him the list. 'Do you recognise any of these names?'

The young man took the paper, squinting to read the handwriting.

'Aye, I know them all,' he said, handing it back. 'I'd wager John was in debt to every one of them, apart from old Nicholas Alwine. He was parson of Saint Clement's on Lime Street. A

317

truly godly man, not like some of the clergy these days. Until he took sick, you'd often see him outside the gaming houses, waving his Bible in people's faces, urging the likes of John Wood to repent of their sins. Not that anyone took any notice of him.'

'Do you know where he lives?' Magdalen asked, intrigued.

Why had John included a priest on the list? Surely a man of God would not lend money to the lost souls he was trying to save?

'Last I heard, he had lodgings on Billiter Street, by the sign of the Black Boy. Come to think of it, I haven't seen him recently. He might be bed-ridden, or he might be dead.'

Magdalen returned the list to her pocket. 'Thank you. You have been most helpful. Good day to you.'

The landlord gave her a perfunctory nod, but Belingham's gaze was now fixed on the whore and her customer in the carver chair. Magdalen had reached the door before he called after her.

'Don't forget now. I am owed three pounds and six shillings. You know where to find me.'

Magdalen had hoped to go straight to Billiter Street in search of Nicholas Alwine, but the city's bells were already chiming ten o'clock. The old parson would have to wait. Heading north towards Shoreditch, she bought a hot codling pie on Bishopsgate, where merchants met in their guildhalls to discuss ways to grow richer still, and stone masons transformed ancient priories into gracious town houses, and where Marlowe had been thrown out of the Bull tavern for standing on the board and declaiming, loudly and repeatedly, 'they who do not love boys and tobacco are fools'.

Where was Marlowe? Was he in the Low Countries as Thomas Kyd supposed? A fine carriage hurtled past, missing her by inches and she flung herself against a wall, her heart pounding.

She rarely considered life's injustices, but today it struck her as odd that the houses of rich and poor Londoners were often little more than a street apart, and yet they may as well have been in different countries for they lived such starkly different lives.

Pushing herself away from the wall, she ate the last few mouthfuls of pie. Had the guard delivered the chicken pie to Mary Ward? As soon as the performance was over this afternoon, she would return to Bridewell. She knew she would be turned away, but she would keep trying because she owed Agnes so much. In truth, she owed her everything. In her mind's eye, Magdalen could see her grandmother perched on the edge of Belle's mattress; so lost, so vulnerable. She wanted to take her away from that terrible place. She wanted to hold her tight and tell her she was loved and safe. It hurt to think of her alone and disorientated and afraid; a raw, clawing pain that twisted her heart.

Turning into Curtain Road, she forced herself to think about the upcoming performance of *Titus Andronicus*. She mustn't forget to collect the sheep's blood and entrails she had ordered from William Herne, the butcher in Hog Lane. She was so lost in her thoughts she barely noticed the small boy. He was one of the city's countless street children; thin, barefoot, ragged attire, so pitiful it was easier to look the other way. As he raced past, he thrust a small piece of paper into her hand.

'What's this?' she called after him, but he didn't stop. Fast as a greyhound, he turned down a side street and disappeared from sight.

Magdalen unfolded the paper. The message was written in a neat hand she did not recognise:

'Tonight, Henslowe's bear pit, Reverend Cooper will be waiting for you.'

319

NINETEEN

'Love sought is good, but given unsought is better'

As always, and for reasons Magdalen never quite understood, the performance of *Titus Andronicus* was a blood-soaked triumph. Alex Cooke gave a harrowing performance as tragic Lavinia. Raped and mutilated, he writhed in agony upon the boards, his tongue cut out, his hands hacked off. Magdalen had sewn up the sleeves of his gown, and splashed his bloodied 'stumps' with sheep's blood. He didn't flinch even as she poured the gore down his face and it ran into his mouth. He was already far away in ancient Rome preparing to endure Lavinia's terrible fate.

Afterwards, as Magdalen bundled blood-soaked costumes into the laundry basket, Henry Condell patted her on the shoulder. 'We'll be there for you on Friday, Maggie. And we won't leave until we've vouched for you, each and every one of us. Edmund Stow will not silence us, no matter how hard he tries. We can make our voices heard above a yard of rowdy groundlings, so we are more than capable of drowning out that surfeit-swelled dolt.'

Magdalen was moved by his kindness. 'Thank you, Henry.'

She had begun to think the players had forgotten about John's death, and Stow's madness, and the inquest creeping ever closer, like Death itself. But it seemed she had been mistaken. She glanced fondly about the 'tiring house. William Kempe, Alex

Cooke and Christopher Beeston were gathered around William Sly, all eyes upon a small leather pouch in his hand.

'Wherever did you get it? It's worth a king's ransom is it not?' Christopher Beeston asked enviously.

'An ounce in weight. A sovereign's worth at least,' Sly agreed.

Alex Cooke, who had evidently arrived late to the discussion, could contain his curiosity no longer. 'What's in there, Sly?'

'Snuff,' Sly explained proudly.

Henry Condell joined them. 'Why the fanfare? It's just tobacco by another name.'

Sly shook his head. 'Not at all. It's far superior. Only the finest tobacco leaves are used in a lengthy process of curing and fermenting. Each workshop produces snuff with its own unique characteristics. This is from the atelier of a Parisian master craftsman, and it is subtly imbued with cinnamon, cloves and rose.'

Kempe rolled his eyes. 'Seems rather a waste to shove it up your nose then. Might as well be imbued with the subtle flavour of snot.'

Sly looked put out. 'I'll have you know it is the medicine of royalty. Catherine de Medici swore it cured her headaches.'

'How ever did you afford it, Sly?' Alex Cooke sounded impressed.

Sly grinned. 'It was a gift from an appreciative young lady, in thanks for a pleasant evening, if you understand my meaning.'

'And will you be seeing this grateful young lady again?' Beeston enquired.

'Sadly not, unless I wish to lose my manhood to a sharp, steel blade. She is the wife of a gentleman of some renown.' Sly opened the pouch with a flourish. 'But I shall enjoy her gift none-the-less.' Pinching a miniscule amount of snuff, he placed it on the back of his hand, and snorted it into his left nostril.

Alex Cooke watched the ritual in rapt admiration. A heartbeat later, Sly sneezed, and a mix of snuff and green snot exploded from his nose. Beeston and Kempe sidestepped to avoid its trajectory, but Alex Cooke's reactions were much slower and the noxious spray hit in squarely in the face.

'Damn your eyes, Sly!' he cried, hurriedly wiping his face with his sleeve.

Kempe slapped him on the back, hard. 'I fear it's *your* eyes that are damned, Cooke! That was a putrid shower, and no mistake.'

'A costly sneeze in more ways than one,' Beeston agreed.

Soon afterwards, the players departed for the Mermaid, leaving in their wake a tempest of abandoned swords, blood-spattered togas and severed limbs. Burbage ordered Magdalen to stay behind and clean the stage. She knew it was her punishment for placing the Theatre in the watchers' sights and so she filled her bucket from the horse pond without complaint. There were many atrocities in *Titus Andronicus*, and each one was marked by a fresh, dark stain on the boards. On her hands and knees, with a bucket at her side and a brush in her hand, she mopped and scrubbed, all the while musing on Adam Cooper's message.

In the Stocks Market he had shouted and railed and called her a whore. So why did he want to meet her now, and in such a clandestine manner? It didn't make sense. According to Louisa, Adam Cooper and John had been close, until something had happened to end their acquaintance, something John had refused to talk about. Something dangerous? Something that had led to his death?

Magdalen dunked the brush into the bucket again. Henslowe's bear pit was on the south bank, in the liberties, a lawless land of taverns, gaming rooms and brothels. It would be dangerous to venture there after dark, but what choice did she have? She had been searching in vain for Adam Cooper, and now *he* had approached *her*. Or was it a trap? In truth, anyone could have written the note. And what of Nicholas Alwine? The priest who had tried to save the souls of Aldgate's chancers and cheats. Did he know the secrets of John's soul? Did he have the answers she so desperately sought?

'Magdalen!'

Startled, she dropped the brush, for she had thought herself alone. Matthew Hilliard was gesturing frantically from the stage door.

'You have to come with me. Now! Edmund Stow has a warrant to take you into custody. To Newgate.'

'What? I don't understand… Are you certain? How do you know?' Magdalen's mind was reeling.

'He's in the Mermaid. He's looking for you.'

Why now? It's Wednesday. It's too soon.

'But I haven't spoken to all the people on the list yet,' she said distractedly.

'What list?' Matthew looked momentarily perplexed. 'Never mind. You must come with me. You must get out of the city.'

'I can't leave the city! I have to talk to Nicholas Alwine.'

'Who?' Matthew asked, and then he shook his head irritably. 'No time! Come! I have a coach waiting!'

'You have a coach?' Magdalen asked incredulously.

Matthew shot a quick glance over his shoulder, perhaps expecting Stow to burst in at any moment. 'It belongs to the Askew family, but that's not important -'

'I've never heard of the Askews. Who are they?' Magdalen was vaguely aware she was focussing on matters of no consequence because the larger ones were too terrible to contemplate.

'There's no time to explain! We have to go!'

But Magdalen held her ground. 'I know you are trying to help me and I am grateful, but I can't run away. It would be as damning as admitting my guilt.'

Matthew ran a hand through his hair, clearly exasperated.

'Very well. We won't leave the city. But at least allow me take you to the Askews' house at Whitefriars. You'll be safe there. Surely you agree it is better you arrive at the inquest as a free woman, rather than as a prisoner who has spent two nights in Newgate's cells.'

Magdalen could see his point. Nothing said 'guilty' more clearly to a jury than a dishevelled woman in a soiled gown. But it was worse than that. Newgate prison was a notoriously corrupt and brutal establishment. She knew what the guards would do to her, just as she also knew Edmund Stow would do nothing to stop them. She would be broken before the inquest began and that, no doubt, was Stow's intention.

'I will come with you,' she conceded, 'but first, I must talk to an old priest called Nicholas Alwine. He knew John -'

'Give me strength!' Matthew raised his eyes heavenwards, but Magdalen held her ground. Finally, he sighed resignedly.

'Where does this old priest live?'

'By the sign of the Black Boy, on Billiter Street, off Aldgate.'

'So be it,' he said begrudgingly. 'Now, come with me. We must make haste.'

Magdalen got to her feet and wiped her hands on her apron, but a tremor of doubt held her fast. She knew so little about Matthew Hilliard, and what little she did know was either contradictory or shrouded in mystery.

'Magdalen,' he pleaded.

She searched his eyes. For what? A sign? A window onto his soul? But her mind was too frayed to sense anything but her own fear. Grabbing her cloak from the 'tiring house, she followed him outside. The noise hit her first, a cacophony of clashing rapiers, shouts and cries of agony. The courtyard was over-run with fighting men, a tight knit melee of close combat. She came to a stunned halt. What in God's name was happening here? Had the Spaniards sailed up the Thames and invaded the city? Had the country-folk marched from the shires in revolt against Her Majesty?

She felt Matthew take her hand, pulling her alongside him until their backs were against the Theatre's wall. 'Stay close,' he shouted. 'We're going to make a run for the gate.'

'We can't!' she gasped in horror. 'They're blocking the gate. There's no way through!'

'Do you trust me?'

Without waiting for her reply, he dragged her into the affray. Instantly, they were surrounded by grunting, lunging, parrying men. The sounds of battle rang in her ears and the earth vibrated beneath her feet. To her left, a man lost his balance and crashed into her shoulder, knocking her sideways. Matthew hauled her upright and then they were moving forward again, pushing on towards the gate.

Magdalen glanced from side to side. Strangely, her vision seemed more vivid than usual, every rapier thrust, every grimacing face defined as clearly as if they were illuminated by the brightest of lanterns. Perhaps this was the battle fever she had heard the soldiers in the tavern speak of; the over-riding, powerful instinct for survival.

'Stay close!' Matthew yelled.

Disorientated, her heart began to beat frantically. She could see nothing but the crush and shove of men all around her; hear nothing but the sounds of their grunts and screams. A blade whispered past her ear, terrifyingly close. How much further to the gate? What were the odds of reaching it without succumbing to a mortal wound? Matthew stopped in his tracks, his route momentarily blocked, and Magdalen stumbled into him. She righted herself, looking about wildly. Something was nagging at the back of her mind, but she couldn't put her finger on it.

It came to her in a blinding flash. She had recognised the man who had knocked her sideways. She had seen the look of concern in his eyes. It was William Sly. The valiant swordsmiths were Burbage's players, giving a magnificent performance, as convincing as any battle the Theatre had ever staged. Evidently, there had been no time for bladders of pigs' blood, but the war cries that rent the air more than made up for the lack of gore.

In that same revelatory moment, she spotted Edmund Stow on the periphery of the melee. She could not hear him above the din, but it was obvious from his wild gesticulations that he was demanding the players lay down their weapons. The players, however, were ignoring him, their skilfully executed feints and lunges effectively blocking his path.

Matthew was on the move again, pulling her along behind him. As they reached the gate, William Kempe and Richard Burbage swiftly raised their swords, a makeshift guard of honour to let them pass. From the corner of her eye, Magdalen saw Kempe's cheery wink. She felt Matthew's hand tighten its grip about hers, and suddenly they were running; hurtling down Curtain Road, muddy water spraying in their wake.

'Whose idea was that?' Magdalen gasped breathlessly.

'It was a fine diversion, was it not?' Matthew replied evasively.

The coach was waiting on the corner of Hog Lane. It was a fine vehicle, with a liveried coachman on the box seat and two harnessed horses, both strong and sturdy bays. Magdalen extricated her hand from Matthew's grasp, and eyed the vehicle suspiciously. She had never ridden in a coach, but she had seen them careering wildly through the city's streets, as dangerous and unpredictable as a runaway bull.

'I swear on my mother's life, I am not going to kidnap you,' Matthew said, misunderstanding her apprehension. 'We must make haste! The players will not hold Stow at bay for long.'

Magdalen pursed her lips, reluctant to climb into a death-trap.

'For God's sake! Get in!' Matthew snapped. When she didn't move, he tried a different tack. 'You'll be less conspicuous in a coach.'

Magdalen raised an eyebrow. There was nothing inconspicuous about the gleaming black vehicle; it spoke of money and status and it cried out to be noticed and admired.

'What I mean is, they won't think of looking for -' Matthew broke off, suddenly shame-faced.

Magdalen knew what he had been about to say. She was a lowly wardrobe mistress, and travelling by coach was far above her station. Edmund Stow would expect her to be on foot. She decided it would be quicker and easier to pretend she hadn't understood his meaning. Grasping the ornately gilded handle, she turned it and opened the door. Matthew offered his hand to help her climb in and she took it, disconcerted by the lightness of his touch, in sharp contrast to his vice-like grip as they had raced along Curtain Road.

Sitting down on the front-facing seat, she looked about curiously. The interior was lined with velvet silk, the deep russet of an autumn forest, the padded bench seats upholstered in the same fabric. There was a pervasive scent of polished wood, leather and expensive perfume.

'Billiter Street in Aldgate. And make haste,' Matthew instructed the coachman, and then he climbed in and sat down opposite Magdalen.

Moments later, the coach lurched forward and she grabbed the edge of the seat in alarm.

'Christ Almighty!' she cried as the coach gathered speed.

'Forgive me,' she added, mortified she had called the Lord's name in vain.

Matthew hid his amusement. 'Don't worry. Finkell is an excellent coachman. You're quite safe.'

Magdalen didn't feel safe at all. The coach was swaying from side to side, flinging her about like a rag doll. And then it hit one of the many pot holes on Hog Lane, shooting her several inches into the air. She felt briefly weightless, as a bird must feel in flight, before she landed heavily. From the corner of her eye, she saw Matthew reach out to steady her, but then he seemed to think better of it, and sat back again.

Magdalen tried not to appear afraid, but she couldn't understand why anyone would choose to travel in such a disagreeable, reckless manner. She looked out of the window, hoping the familiar sights of the city might soothe her tattered nerves, but everyday landmarks were flying past at such dizzying speed that she barely had time to recognise one before it was replaced with another.

'You grow accustomed to it,' Matthew said quietly.

It seemed her nonchalant act had not fooled him. She glanced sheepishly at him, and found she could not look away. She realised he looked less haunted, less anguished than of late, and she felt glad of it, for it had pained her to see him so unwell.

'Your family?' she asked. 'Has there been good news regarding your father's fortunes?'

Matthew looked suddenly ill at ease, and she instantly regretted her inquisitiveness. 'Forgive me. I have a bad habit of prying into matters that do not concern me.'

The coach clattered through yet another pot hole and she tightened her grip on the edge of the seat. She wondered if this was how it felt to be aboard a ship on a raging, stormy sea.

'I have reason to hope that my family's fortunes will be

restored,' Matthew replied, unwilling to look her in the eye.

Magdalen's face lit up. 'That is the most wonderful news. I am truly happy for you.'

Matthew was incredulous. How could she take delight in his good fortune when her own life was in such disarray?

'Why are you helping me?' she asked suddenly.

Her guileless question took him by surprise, and he found he had no answer. He could say it was because he felt guilty. It was his fault her grandmother was in Bridewell, and it was his fault Magdalen had lost her home, and her employment in the Mountjoys' workshop. He could tell her he desperately wanted to atone for his sins, even though he knew that nothing he did could ever truly make amends.

Or he could say it was because he had fallen hopelessly in love with her. He had fallen in love with a girl he had hurt and betrayed, and the tragic futility of the situation was tearing his heart in two. But he couldn't say any of those things, so instead he replied, 'because I am in your debt. You gave me an introduction to Burbage.'

'And yet I suspect you neither wanted nor needed to become a player?' Magdalen glanced pointedly at their luxurious surroundings.

Matthew did not know how to respond to that either. And then the coach came to a lurching halt and propelled her into his arms. All too briefly, Magdalen revelled in the warmth of him, the distinctive smell of him, before she felt his hands on her shoulders, helping her back to her seat.

'Are you hurt?' he asked solicitously.

'No, not at all,' she replied, hoping he would not notice her discomposure.

Matthew alighted first and held out his hand. She took it, conscious once again of his warm fingers encasing hers. It felt strange to be treated with such respect, as if she were a high-born lady.

'Wait here,' Matthew told the coachman as he led Magdalen to the side of the road.

She noticed they were attracting curious glances from passers-by, and she guessed they were wondering why two people wearing work-a-day wool rather than silk were travelling in a gleaming coach.

'Ignore them,' Matthew said under his breath. 'Come, we must not linger. Gossip travels faster than fire in this city. The constables will hear of us soon enough.'

Gallantly, he walked on Magdalen's right, shielding her from danger, but in truth Billiter Street was a land of merchants living above their workshops in orderly, law-abiding respectability. Window boards displayed the handiwork of basket-makers, leather-dressers, felt-makers, drapers and glovers; the air filled with the sappy sweetness of green wood, the earthy scent of animal hide, the oiliness of unspun wool.

Young apprentices loitered at a display of brightly coloured felted hats, goading each other to try them on. Goodwives ran envious fingers over exquisitely pinked kid gloves, as soft as a new-born babe's skin.

Magdalen, however, paid no attention to the wares of Billiter Street. She was looking for the sign of the Black Boy. Why couldn't she see it? If Walter Bellingham had been mistaken, how would she ever find Nicholas Alwine?

'Here! Over here!'

She jumped at the sound of Matthew's voice.

The sign was very old, and countless years of wind and rain had taken their toll. Hanging from the wall of a glover's workshop, its paint was faded and flaking but Magdalen could just make out the image of a small boy clad in a jester's costume.

'Would you like me -' Matthew began but Magdalen was already at the door. She knocked loudly and waited barely a heartbeat before her impatience got the better of her. Peering through the open window, she called out, 'Hello? Is anyone there?'

There was the sound of footfall within, and the door opened. The old woman was small and round, and lightly dusted with flour from top to toe. Magdalen thought she bore a remarkable resemblance to a hedgehog; tiny black eyes, and spiky tufts of grey hair escaping her coif. She looked Magdalen up and down and her nose wrinkled with distaste.

'Be gone with you! I'll buy nothing from gypsies!'

Magdalen grabbed the door before it was shut in her face.

'Wait! I am not a gypsy! My name is Magdalen Bisset, wardrobe mistress at Burbage's Theatre in Shoreditch. Does Father Alwine live here? I need to speak to him, on behalf of John Wood's sister.' Was there a glimmer of recognition in the woman's eyes at the mention of John's name? 'You know John Wood, the player?' Magdalen asked eagerly.

The servant shrugged cagily.

'Might we come in and speak to Father Alwine? It is regarding a matter of great importance,' Magdalen pressed.

The old woman shook her head vehemently. 'Father Alwine is not in good health. He doesn't want to be disturbed. Now, I must get on.' She moved to close the door.

In an instant, Matthew was at Magdalen's side, smiling warmly at the old woman. 'We would be forever in Father Alwine's debt if he would permit us a few moments of his time, mistress,' he said, flattering the servant with a title she did not merit. 'I pray you will trust me when I say it is a matter of life and death.'

Faced with Matthew's fine looks and impeccable manners, the old woman's resolve melted like ice in springtime. Muting her disapproval to a brief huffing sound, she stepped aside.

'Well then, I suppose you had best come in.'

A wide corridor ran the breadth of the house. Magdalen glimpsed a busy leather workshop to their left. From the back kitchen, drifted the mouth-watering aroma of roasting beef.

'I should warn you,' the servant wheezed as they followed her ample backside up the stairs, 'Father Alwine has reached a great age, and he is easily confused.'

A fire was burning in the grate of the bedchamber, wood-smoke only partly masking the reek of old age and infirmity.

'You have visitors, Father,' the servant said loudly, gesturing that they should approach his bed side. 'I'll wait here, in case he needs me,' she added, positioning her bulky frame in the doorway.

It was obvious Father Alwine did not have long for this world. Propped up on pillows, wisps of white hair framing a skeletal face, he was a diminished figure in the huge, sagging bed. He barely looked at Matthew but he stared hard at Magdalen and then he smiled, revealing a mouth almost totally devoid of teeth.

'Ann? Is that you?' His voice was a gummy hiss.

Magdalen cast a startled glance at the servant, who shrugged as if to say, '*I did warn you*'.

'It is you, isn't it?' The old man attempted to sit up, grimaced, and sank back again. 'You have your mother's eyes, and mouth. All these years, you haven't been far from my thoughts. Let me look at you. Come, sit here, my child.' He patted his coverlet with a skeletal hand.

Magdalen hesitated. Should she tell him she wasn't '*Ann*', or should she humour him? She chose the latter, remembering how it always upset her grandmother when her confusions were corrected. She sat down gingerly on the edge of the bed.

There were tears in the old man's faded eyes. 'I have prayed for you, every night. Prayed you were safe. Has life been good to you? Did I make the right choice?'

'Yes, you did,' Magdalen replied.

Nicholas Alwine turned to Matthew. 'Is this your husband?' A look of surprise slid across his face and then, just as quickly, his expression faded to blankness. He seemed to have lost his train of thought.

Magdalen glanced across at Matthew. His eyes were full of respect and compassion for a life slipping away.

Without warning, the old priest reached out and grasped her hand. His grip was surprisingly strong, his bony fingers digging into her skin. 'I swore an oath to carry out her command but, God forgive me, I couldn't do what they asked of me.' The old man was suddenly animated, fervent. 'It wasn't right. I would have been damned for all eternity. You were such a beautiful baby, too precious, far, far too precious. Did they look after you, Ann?'

'Yes, they did,' Magdalen said reassuringly but her heart was sinking. The old servant was right. Nicholas Alwine had lost his wits, poor fellow. This was a waste of time. Proof, if proof were needed, that tracking down the names on John's list was a wild goose chase.

Perhaps Matthew sensed her despair, for he moved closer to the bed and asked, 'Father Alwine, do you know a player called John Wood?'

'Aye, I do. The poor boy has lost his way. Turned to all manner of vices…' the old man's voice trailed away and he gazed into the middle distance.

'Father Alwine?' Magdalen prompted. 'You were telling us about John Wood.'

He turned to Magdalen. 'Who?'

'John Wood, the player?'

'I do not get many visitors these days, so I was glad of his company.'

'He came to visit you?' Magdalen asked, astonished.

'Aye, we read the Bible together. Sins, so many sins…'

Obviously distressed, the old man raised his trembling hands to his face. Magdalen glanced apologetically at the old servant.

'It's all right, Father Alwine,' the woman said loudly. 'No need to be upset. You're quite safe. I'll put another log on the fire for you.'

Father Alwine lowered his hands. He seemed uncertain where he was. 'Ann? Is that you?' He sounded like Agnes; a lost, frightened child.

'Why did John Wood visit you?' Magdalen asked gently.

'John Wood?' He looked blank for a moment and then his eyes focussed on Matthew, and he visibly brightened. 'God bless you, Ann, you have brought a priest. It is a long time since I took the sacrament.'

Not surprisingly, a look of alarm darted across Matthew's face. Impersonating a member of the priesthood was punishable by death.

'He's not a priest,' Magdalen said firmly.

'Then why is he here? Why is he in my bedchamber? Mary? Where are you?' The old man looked suddenly terrified. Magdalen had seen her grandmother so, when her fragile grasp on reality cracked and revealed the dark confusion beneath.

'I'm here, sir.' The servant waddled towards the bed, and nodded meaningfully at Magdalen and Matthew. 'I think you should leave now. Father Alwine needs to rest.'

Magdalen stood up. 'Thank you for talking to us, Father. We will not detain you any longer. We will see ourselves out. Good day to you both.'

Outside on Billiter Street it had begun to rain. Matthew walked

334

fast, scanning the road ahead for any sign of Stow and his men but Magdalen's thoughts were focussed solely on the old priest. His wits were undoubtedly failing, but was it possible there were fragments of truth in his ramblings, if only she could make sense of them?

Finkell looked cold and dejected, his shoulders hunched against the rain. Spying Matthew, he sat up straight.

'Take Watling Street to Ludgate, the traffic will be lighter. And make haste,' Matthew instructed as he helped Magdalen into the coach.

Finkell set off at a fast pace, the coach rolling and pitching along the uneven pavers of Billiter Street. Magdalen's head hit the frame overhead and she winced with pain. Once again, Matthew made a move to steady her then seemed to change his mind. He sat back and folded his arms. 'Hold tight,' he advised, unsmiling.

'Nicholas Alwine knew John Wood,' Magdalen said thoughtfully as the coach hurtled along Aldgate.

'Did he?' Matthew replied. 'He called you Ann, and he mistook me for a priest. Infirmity has rendered him moon-mad. It was a waste of time. I pray it hasn't cost you dear.'

Magdalen didn't reply. The coach was rolling from side to side and she had a worrying feeling she was about to be sick.

Matthew must have noticed her pallor. 'Look out of the window and focus on the horizon. It should help.'

She took his advice but it didn't help at all, perhaps because there was no horizon to focus on, just rows of shops and houses, all blurring into one. Her thoughts drifted to Adam Cooper. She realised she hadn't told Matthew about the Puritan's mysterious message. Was that because she didn't trust him? The more she thought about it, the more she realised she didn't know who to trust. Apart from Louisa du Bois. And today, unexpectedly, the players had finally redeemed themselves, coming to her rescue like knights in shining armour or, more accurately, knights in mis-matched, rusty armour grabbed in haste from the 'tiring house. She glanced at Matthew. He had never walked away from her. He had always walked towards her. He had picked up the playbills from the mud. He had consoled her in the Golden Lion after Edmund Stow's assault. He had offered her a purse of money when Burbage and Will had refused.

Profoundly conflicted, she asked, 'Surely I cannot arrive at the Askews' home uninvited?'

Matthew stifled a sigh. He was sick and tired of secrets and subterfuge. It would be far simpler to lie to her again but every lie tasted like bile on his tongue now. Until his father had made the fateful decision to help Francis Stewart, Matthew had lived a life of ease, untaxed by troubles. And then his comfortable existence had vanished overnight. He could never have imagined, in his cloistered student days, that there would come a time when he hated himself, when he could no longer bear to glance at a looking glass, for fear of seeing his shame reflected there. And there was no way of making amends. No end to the Purgatory. He owed Magdalen everything, and yet he could give her nothing in return. Apart from the truth.

'The Askews are not at home. They are at their country estate in Dorsetshire. Lord Askew is my uncle, on my mother's side. They have supported me during my father's ordeal and they offered me their London house for as long as I needed it.'

His confession did not greatly surprise Magdalen. She had known he was of noble birth from the moment she had first laid eyes on him. There was the rapier, and the fine attire, and the effortless self-confidence that only those of great wealth possess.

'Why did a man of your position wish to become a lowly player?' she asked coolly.

It was one of the many questions Magdalen had wanted to ask him since that day in the Stocks Market when he had helped her pick up the handbills. And it was one of the many questions Matthew had dreaded, because he truly didn't want to lie any longer.

'I can't answer that,' he replied wearily, remembering the Earl of Essex's words: '*I will call on you again when I have need of you. I presume I can rely on your service when the time comes?*'

In truth, it was not a question, but a command from Her Majesty the Queen, a woman who prided herself on being the eyes and ears of her kingdom. A command shackling him to Essex's growing spy network without any hope of reprieve.

A shiver ran down Magdalen's spine. Matthew *had* answered the question, as clearly as if he had shouted it from the rooftops. She had always suspected he was a dissembler, an intelligencer. There had been too many lies, too many evasions. He had used her to gain access to the Theatre. He had played her like a lute, plucked her heart strings and watched her dance. And his betrayal hurt, more than she had ever imagined it would. She looked out of the window, grief building inside her chest, forcing the air from her lungs.

Finkell slowed down as they passed through the Stocks Market. Beneath leaking awnings, the stallholders were as wet and bedraggled as the caged chickens they were hoping to sell. The coach picked up speed again along Watling Street, for the road was wide and well paved. Nearing Ludgate, the coach slowed once more and came to a halt in the long queue waiting to squeeze through the gate.

Magdalen turned to Matthew, her voice flat. 'You were sent to spy on Burbage's men.'

His eyes slid from hers and he didn't reply. He looked wretched, and she suspected he wished to be anywhere but trapped inside this coach with her. Without warning, Magdalen's heart-ache erupted into a torrential outpouring of rage.

'You were wasting your time! If Burbage's players are Papists, then I am the Queen of bloody Sheba!' She was too angry to apologise for her profanity. 'You didn't have to do it! You didn't have to betray their kindness, their generosity! You could have refused!'

'No, I couldn't.'

'Yes, you could! There is always a choice!' she snapped back.

'Not always, Magdalen. Not always.'

The wind vanished from her sails. For a brief moment she had believed she could finally dismiss him as a treacherous dissembler. But his eyes were immeasurably sad and full of suffering, and suddenly she felt further away from the truth than ever. She suspected that no matter how many layers she unwrapped, there would be a hundred more beneath. Layer after layer of secrets.

She turned back to the window. The coach was crawling at a swaying snail's pace towards Ludgate. Dusk was falling and the rain was heavier, running down the window, the street beyond dissolving to a watery blur. She dug her finger nails into the soft velvet of the bench seat, trying to anchor herself to something solid, but she was adrift in a world without substance where nothing was real.

Matthew watched Magdalen's misery and thought his heart might break into pieces. He didn't want to leave her. He wanted to protect her, to keep her safe. He wanted to marry her, and wake up beside her every day for the rest of his life, but instead he was going to abandon her, because it was the only way to break free from the Earl of Essex. The only way to save her from a life of hurt, deceit and betrayal.

'I am sailing to the New World.'

She turned to look at him, stunned. 'What did you say?'

'I have been fortunate to secure a place on John White's voyage to Roanoke Island. He is keen to discover if his colony is thriving.'

'When do you sail?' Magdalen's thoughts were a maelstrom of confusion. Despite his terrible betrayal, she realised she didn't want him to go. She knew it was madness to feel that way, but perhaps that was all love was - a form of blind, agonising insanity?

'I will speak on your behalf at the inquest on Friday and I pray I will clear your name, and then I will leave for Plymouth at the end of the month. The Governor plans to make sail in early May,' Matthew said quietly.

Magdalen shook her head despairingly. He could speak at the inquest until he was blue in the face, but she knew neither Edmund Stow nor the coroner would be swayed by his rhetoric. She was a woman therefore she had poisoned John, and she would hang for it. But the inquest seemed like a dream, an irrelevance, in comparison to the nameless beast that was clawing at her heart and ripping it into bloodied shreds.

The coach reached Ludgate. It trundled slowly beneath the arch and, once free of the bottleneck, began to pick up speed again.

'But you said you have reason to hope your father has been spared. Why would you risk your life on such a dangerous voyage now?' Magdalen asked, clutching at straws blowing in the wind.

'Because the opportunity has arisen, and I cannot turn it down.' He looked away again, his face a grey mask of pain, and she knew he was holding something back.

'What is it?' she asked, filled with foreboding. 'What is it you're not telling me?'

He slumped in the seat, closed his eyes and put his hands to his face. How could he tell her? If she knew what he had done, she would see him for what he truly was: a man without honour; a treacherous, despicable wretch.

And yet, how could he set sail for the New World, on a long, perilous voyage that would most likely claim his life, *without* telling her? He could not in all conscience take such a heavy burden of sin to a watery grave. He lowered his hands and looked into her eyes.

'My father stands falsely accused of treason by King James of Scotland. The Earl of Essex agreed to secure a pardon for him, but on one condition. He asked me to gather intelligence for the Queen. It was me... I...' he could not go on.

Magdalen stared at him, her mind whirring frantically. And suddenly it all made terrible sense. 'You sent innocent men, women and children to the Tower...' she ran out of words, shock skewering her to the seat like a pinned butterfly.

'It was an impossible choice.' There were tears in Matthew's eyes now. 'My family was facing the death penalty. My mother, my younger brother and sister... Christ in Heaven, what was I to do? Let my family die? But I swear on my life, I did not know your grandmother would be at the butcher's house.' He reached out to her beseechingly but she shrank away from him.

'You are sorry?' she raged. 'Sorry?' she repeated, her voice laden with disgust. 'There is plague in Bridewell. For all I know, my grandmother is already dead!'

Anger and hatred welled up inside her. This man, this dissembling monster, had as good as killed the one person she truly loved. She was suffocating under the weight of his betrayal. She needed some air. She had to be away from this coach. She had to be away from this man. She stood up and thumped the ceiling with her fist. The coach pitched to a stop, propelling her forward. Instinctively, she put her hands out, wincing as her palms slammed into the framework above Matthew's head. Righting herself, she fumbled frantically with the unfamiliar latch.

'What are you doing?'

'Isn't it obvious? she snapped, opening the door at last.

'Magdalen, wait! I beg you!'

She stepped down into the rain and turned to face him.

'Don't you dare follow me! As God is my witness, I never want to lay eyes on you again!'

She slammed the door behind her, and then she ran, weaving her way past solitary lawyers heading home for their supper, huddled beneath their black cloaks like pensive rooks. Blinded by tears it took her a moment to realise she was in Whitefriars. Magdalen knew the area well, for Burbage's troupe had often performed for the pale-faced lawyers at their Inns of Court.

She glanced over her shoulder, half expecting to see Matthew coming after her. She had fallen in love with him. If he had offered her marriage, she would have given up everything for him. Instead, he had used her for his own ends, as carelessly as a man might use a doxy. Without warning her emotions caught up with her. She bent double, clasping her hands about herself, trying to hold in all the pain and heartache, but they would not be contained. An eruption of juddering sobs racked her body, wave after wave of all-consuming anguish, until at last she was exhausted, hollowed out, numb.

Taking a deep, ragged breath, she righted herself, tugged the edges of her cloak together and turned south towards the river. Her legs felt wobbly, barely able to support her weight, and she stumbled in her haste. The light was fading quickly. Wherries were forbidden by law to cross the river in darkness, and she could not miss the last boat.

TWENTY

'Out of the jaws of death...'

Magdalen broke into a run down the narrow alley leading to Temple stairs. Hurtling out onto the landing place, she skidded to an ungainly halt on the wet cobbles, and looked about anxiously. The wherries were all moored up, their hulls slapping against the quay on an incoming tide. She was too late. Frustration flooded through her. She couldn't fail now, not when she was so close to finding Adam Cooper. She had to cross the river, but it would take an hour or more to walk to the bridge; along streets where Upright Men watched and waited in the shadows.

A wherryman was leaning against the old customs bench. He had a pipe between his lips, smoke coiling into the cold air. Like all river-men, his upper body was as muscular as an ox, his deeply lined face weather-beaten from a life-time upon the water.

She ran to him. 'I have to cross. It is a matter of some urgency.'

He took the pipe from his mouth. His smile revealed a narrow groove in his bottom teeth, worn away over the years by the pipe stem. 'You might be in luck, mistress. I'm waiting on one last passenger. He paid me in advance, so 'appen I'll wait a while longer.'

Magdalen thanked him, but her impatience was fermenting and threatening to explode. What if the passenger didn't come?

What if the wherryman grew tired of waiting and went home? She paced back and forth along the quay, keeping half an eye on the river; at the lantern-lights appearing in the growing darkness on the south bank. It was a place of theatres and taverns, brothels and bear pits, and all manner of immoral pursuits. So why had Adam Cooper, a Puritan, asked to meet her there?

'He's here,' the wherryman announced, banging his pipe against the customs bench and stuffing it into the leather bag at his belt.

A finely dressed young gentleman was walking leisurely across the jetty, appearing confident that lesser mortals existed to suit his own pace. He was fey of features and unusually tall and willowy; a wood sprite in doublet and hose. The wherryman offered to help him into the boat, but the gentleman refused his assistance, taking the stern seat with a supercilious, graceful air. Gathering her skirts, Magdalen sat down at the bow. Without further ado, the wherryman untied the rope and used an oar to push his boat away from the quay.

It was quiet on the river, the only noise the rhythmic plashing of oars through water. The gentleman stared pensively at his gartered knees, whilst Magdalen looked up at the sky. It had stopped raining. The clouds were clearing and a full moon was rising over the city. She wondered if, somewhere deep inside, she had always known Matthew had sent the watchers to Noble Street. Had she tried to bury something too painful for the light of day? But it was out in the open now, and it felt ugly and raw.

The boat nudged the quay at the Paris Garden stairs and the wherryman stepped out and tied up. The young gentleman alighted, and was soon floating away into the gloom. Magdalen gave the wherryman a penny from Louisa's purse.

'Thanking you, duck. Now, you hurry home. Not a good time of day for a young lass to be out on her own.'

The wherryman pushed off, and began to row back the way he had come. Magdalen looked about nervously. She often visited the south bank on a Sunday, when it was crowded and noisy with families and street entertainers and food stalls, but tonight it was eerily quiet. The trees along the river bank were pretty enough by day, but by moonlight their bare branches were long, witches' fingers reaching down to rake through her hair. An easterly wind was picking up; it smelled of salt and fish and muddy estuaries. It rustled through the branches above her head, and she imagined unseen creatures gathering there, whispering, watching.

Pushing all such fantastical notions from her head, she turned east along the water's edge, past the caged bears and the mastiffs' kennels. The dogs began to bark fiercely but the bears just watched her with infinitely sad eyes.

Up ahead, Henslowe's bear pit loomed out of the darkness, its shadowy bulk resembling a giant whale stranded on the pebble-strewn river bank. Magdalen crossed the cobbled courtyard, and stopped outside a pair of large double doors. A large sign creaked in the wind. It bore an image of a chained, dancing bear above the words, *'Philip Henslowe's Bear-Garden'*. Magdalen thought 'garden' was a poor description for a place of torture and torment, but Henslowe had no time for sensitivities. His eye was always on the money, on outward appearances, on scrambling over the backs of other men in his relentless climb to the top. Was he responsible for Adam Cooper's message drawing her to this place? Had he written the warning she had found in John's hand? *Leave it be…*

It was said half the city's Upright Men were in Henslowe's pay. It was said he was not averse to murder, even if he hired other men to dirty their hands with the actual deed. What if he had killed John? What if he was about to kill her too? Her blood began to pound in her ears, drowning out the sounds of the river, the waves scraping across the shore, a tumble of pebbles as the tide turned.

Ignoring the voice inside her head screaming at her to turn around and run away, she took a deep breath, opened the doors and went inside. The bear-pit's seating galleries looked much like the Theatre, but in place of a stage and a yard for the penny groundlings, there was a circular arena, strewn with sand. The arena was bathed in bright moonlight whilst, in sharp contrast, the galleries were shrouded in shadows.

All was still and silent. Eerily, unnaturally silent.

Shivering with fear, Magdalen walked into the middle of the arena and slowly turned full circle. There were no pigeons cooing on the roof, no rats scurrying beneath the galleries. It was so quiet she could have heard a pin drop, but she was certain someone was here. Someone was watching her. But who?

'Reverend Cooper?' Her voice echoed about the galleries.

She turned full circle again, peering into the darkly shadowed galleries. She couldn't see anyone, but the hairs on the back of her neck were standing on end.

'Who's there?' Her voice was a whisper now, strangled by terror.

A noise. A muffled creak. Something or someone was moving in the lowest gallery.

'Show yourself,' she demanded, her heart hammering.

A figure walked slowly down the stairs and stepped out into the arena. It was Adam Cooper, dressed all in grey save for a white ruff. In the moonlight, he appeared ghostly, ephemeral.

'Thank you for coming, Mistress Bisset.'

Relief coursed through Magdalen. This was no ghost, but living flesh and blood.

'A curious meeting place, Reverend Cooper. I thought

Puritans did not care for bear-baiting, or play-going for that matter.'

'I am not here to discuss my religious convictions,' he replied calmly. He was even thinner than before, his long face skeletal, his doublet hanging loosely about his hips.

'Then why did you ask me here?'

'I know who killed John Wood.'

Magdalen's heart faltered.

'Who?' she asked urgently. 'Who killed him?'

'All in good time. First, I need to explain -'

'No!' she interrupted, exasperated by his phlegmatic tone. 'If you know who killed him, you have to tell me!'

'There is something you need to know first,' he persisted, 'before it is too late.'

Unnerved by the haunted look in his eyes, Magdalen bit back her impatience and gave a small, tight nod.

Cooper inhaled deeply. 'This must seem unlikely to you, but I wept when I heard John was dead. I greatly enjoyed his company. At times, when I suffer a surfeit of bile, I act like a tyrant. But when my humours are in balance, I am sanguine, the very essence of reason. John was intelligent and witty. We discussed philosophy, and I endeavoured to enlighten him regarding the true faith, although sadly with little success. And then I learnt he had a darker side. His drinking, his gambling, his debts.'

Magdalen nodded impatiently. She knew all this.

'John was desperate for money,' Cooper went on. 'He told me he had discovered a secret, something so inflammatory he was certain the Privy Council would pay handsomely to suppress it. I begged him to reconsider. I told him it was too dangerous. The Privy Council does not take kindly to blackmail. We argued about it, but he would not be deterred.'

'And did he go to the Privy Council?'

'I cannot be certain but yes, I think he did.'

'And what was this secret? Do you know?'

Cooper hesitated and she saw strong emotions flash behind his eyes: doubt and fear, and perhaps regret.

'Yes,' he said at last. 'I know his secret. John frequented the gaming houses on Billiter Street. It's where he met Father Alwine. The old priest would stand in the street and beseech the sinners to mend their ways. And then Father Alwine fell ill and kept to his bed, and there was a rumour he had a large sum of money hidden away. It grieves me to say that John started to visit the old man, under the pretence of seeking spiritual guidance, but in truth hoping to benefit from Father Alwine's estate.'

'That can't be…' Magdalen was appalled. Surely John would not sink so low as to prey on a frail old man? But the sincerity in Cooper's eyes was unmistakeable. 'Even if, God forbid, what you say is true, what has it to do with John's death?'

'Let me finish,' Cooper insisted. 'Father Alwine was often not in his right mind, and on one occasion he believed John was a priest who had come to hear his confession. Father Alwine told John a secret he had been keeping for many years, but now he was approaching the end of his life, he wanted to go to God with a clear conscience.' Cooper scowled. 'It would have been far better for all concerned if the old man had taken the secret to his grave, but instead he chose to reveal that eighteen years ago, he had been a chaplain serving the bishop of London at Her Majesty's palace at Richmond.'

'I don't understand what this has -' Magdalen began but Cooper silenced her:

'Let me finish! One November night he was called to the inner sanctum. Lord Burghley, the Queen's closest advisor, handed him a new-born babe. The child was the Queen's illegitimate daughter. Her Majesty greatly respected Father Alwine, and he was entrusted to take the child far away from London to be fostered. Her Majesty did not want to know the name of the family, and she insisted they must never know the child's true identity –'

'No, that's impossible! Even to speak of such matters is treason!'

'Mistress Bisset, I beg you, let me finish! Unbeknownst to Her Majesty, Lord Burghley had commanded Father Alwine to smother the babe and bury it in an unmarked grave. Burghley knew the child of the Virgin Queen of England was far too great a risk to the stability of the kingdom to be allowed to live. But Father Alwine could not bring himself to murder an innocent babe. And so, he rode to Hampshire, to his distant cousin Katherine and her husband. He said the babe was an orphan and needed a home. For Katherine, the babe felt like a gift from God because, after ten years of marriage, the couple remained childless.'

Magdalen shook her head. 'The story is fanciful! Absurd! Much of what Father Alwine says is nonsensical. John was so desperate, he heard what he wanted to hear.'

'John said the old man was particularly lucid that day, and recounted the events in striking detail,' Cooper replied quietly.

Magdalen sighed. She felt both irritated and bitterly disappointed in equal measure. She had dared to hope she might learn something about John's death tonight, but instead she was listening to the second-hand ramblings of an old priest.

But Cooper hadn't finished. 'I knew that if John approached the Privy Council, they would believe they had no choice but to kill him. Elizabeth is our Virgin Queen, married only to her people. Her image would be tarnished forever if it became known she had acted no better than a common whore.'

Magdalen stared at him incredulously. Was it possible the

Queen's counsellors had killed John to keep a secret not only from the Queen, but from her entire kingdom? It seemed too fantastical, but it would explain why Cooper had vanished on the day of John's death. He was afraid he would be next to die.

'I have to warn you, Mistress Bisset. Your own life is in grave danger.'

'I don't understand,' Magdalen said slowly. 'This has nothing to do with me. Why would you say I am in danger?'

'Because you were the babe Nicholas Alwine carried into Hampshire. Katherine and Andrew cared for you, and loved you as their own.'

'Katherine and Andrew? My parents? That's not possible…'

'It is the truth.'

Magdalen searched his gaunt face, searching for something, anything, to prove this was all a cruel jest. He gazed back at her unflinchingly, his pale blue eyes devastatingly sincere. He believed it to be true. She couldn't take it in. She didn't want to take it in. It was all nonsense. And yet… and yet… There was a loud buzzing in her ears, and her vision was fading to white. Without warning her legs gave way and she crashed to her knees. She was vaguely aware the sand smelled of blood.

The sound began in the middle gallery, an ear-piercing crack followed by an explosion of noise, reverberating around the bear-pit like thunder trapped in a valley. Adam Cooper jolted violently and fell backwards into the sand, his limbs splayed like a starfish. There was a hole in his doublet and even as Magdalen watched, a dark stain of blood started to spread across his chest. Numb with shock, she crawled to his side. He was staring up at the night sky and for a moment she feared he was already dead. She grabbed his hand and held it tightly.

'I'm here, Adam. I'm here.'

He tried to speak but made a gurgling sound instead. She could hear the blood filling his lungs. His lips were moving and she leant closer, straining to hear.

He uttered just one word: 'Run.'

She looked up at the dark galleries, but some instinct told her there was no need to run. Whoever had fired the musket was no longer there. She knew there was nothing she could do to save Adam Cooper but she held his hand and spoke soft words of reassurance, watching as he choked on his own blood, watching as life finally left his eyes, to be replaced by the chilling vacancy of death. Only then did she let go of his hand and stumble to her feet. She was light-headed and shaking so violently she could barely stand, her teeth chattering in a rapid, noisy staccato.

Casting a final glance at the lifeless body of Adam Cooper, she walked unsteadily across the arena and out of Henslowe's beargarden. Her limbs felt heavy, her brain sluggish. Cooper was dead, murdered before her eyes. If she hadn't fallen to her knees, the musket ball would have ripped through her instead. She had come so close to death.

She came to a faltering stop. Father Alwine's tale couldn't be true. It was too outlandish, too preposterous. He was old and confused, and John, desperate for a way out of his misfortunes, had grasped at straws and wilfully misunderstood. The story was incomprehensible, beyond belief. It wasn't true. It couldn't be true. But the story had taken hold within her, steadily worming its way to her core. She drew her cloak tightly about herself, a makeshift shield against a world that suddenly appeared more terrifying than ever before.

The south bank was bathed in moonlight. The wind had dropped, the only sound the incoming tide lapping against the pebbly strand. A man was walking away, heading east, towards the bridge. Even with his back to her, she knew who it was.

'Marlowe?' She ran to catch him up. 'What are you doing here?'

He turned around, and she saw he was carrying a musket at his side, the long, slender barrel pointing downwards.

'I'm keeping you safe, Magdalen. God knows, that's all I've ever wanted to do.'

His words froze the blood in her veins.

'It was you in the seating gallery. You shot Adam Cooper...' Her voice was a whisper of desolation. Suddenly, it all made sense. 'John didn't go to the Privy Council, did he?'

'No,' he replied bluntly. 'He died before he had the chance.'

Magdalen stared at him, desperately seeking a glimmer of reassurance as her world crumbled to dust. But his doe-like eyes were no longer sparkling with wit and his lips were no longer curling into that wry, familiar smile. She had known him forever, but suddenly she was looking into the face of a stranger. 'You killed John...' the words tasted as bitter as rue on her tongue.

'Yes, I killed him, to keep you safe. After a night on the Mad Dog, John told me he was going to write a letter to Robert Cecil, and I knew he was signing your death warrant.'

'And Richard Cowley?'

Marlowe nodded. 'John really gave me no choice. I overheard him telling Cowley his plans. Cowley was so drunk it's doubtful he would have remembered a word of it the next day but let's be honest, his passing was no great loss to the world.'

Magdalen had imagined Marlowe to be many things, but she had never imagined he was a cold-blooded murderer. She no longer felt as if she was on solid ground. She felt as if she was being swept downstream, past the mudflats and the oyster catchers and the haunting cries of curlews, and on towards the treacherous, shifting sands of the English Channel.

'You sent those men after me... they chased me... I was in fear for my life, and they hurt me -'

'It was only a scratch. They were under strict instruction to warn you, not harm you. If only you had listened to them.'

The coldness in his eyes shook her to the core.

'Am I really her daughter?' she breathed.

'Maybe. Maybe not. Once a story has been told, it begins to gather momentum and it ceases to matter whether it's true or false. Robert Cecil would have killed you with his bare hands rather than see the Queen's virtue dishonoured. You must understand, Magdalen, there are some secrets that are far too dangerous to sell. Some secrets that must be kept hidden, no matter what the cost.' He smiled wistfully. 'Have I ever told you how much you remind me of my sister? You have the same look, the same smile. She was feisty, just like you. She was forced into marrying a man more than twenty years her age. She died in childbirth at thirteen years old. There was nothing anyone could do. I couldn't save her. But I've saved *you*.'

Magdalen couldn't speak. She had not asked Marlowe to take the lives of three innocent men to spare her own. Did he really expect her to be grateful?

'Nicholas Alwine died an hour ago,' he said carelessly.

'No, Marlowe…no…' This was too much. The final straw.

'Natural causes,' he added but she knew he was lying and it felt like the worst betrayal of all.

'With Alwine's passing, only two people remain who know the baby survived, and they are both standing right here.'
He looked into her eyes. 'You are safe, Magdalen.'

Her hands clenched into fists. Didn't he understand? Didn't he understand that she would rather have died than live with blood on her hands?

'You're wrong, I'm not safe!' she hissed. 'Edmund Stow is looking for me. You killed them all for nothing.'

'The warrant for your arrest has been withdrawn.'

'What?'

'Adam Cooper's signed confession for the murders of John Wood and Richard Cowley has been delivered to the coroner. It seems Cooper believed all players to be sinners and sodomites and, as such, they deserved to die.' Marlowe shrugged. 'It's what you would expect a Puritan to say, isn't it?'

Magdalen watched him saunter to the river's edge and casually toss the musket into the fast-flowing water where it sank without a trace. He strolled back to her.

'Cooper's body will be heading out to sea shortly, thanks to some particularly malodorous Upright Men who will do anything if you pay them enough.'

'I did not ask you to kill for me,' Magdalen's voice was strained with emotion, 'but because of you, I will have the deaths of four innocent men on my conscience for the rest of my life.'

Marlowe shrugged again. 'At least now you will have a life. Go and live it. Your secret is safe. *You* are safe.'

He stepped closer and she could see compassion in his eyes, and a deep well of sadness. Very gently, he took her face in his hands and lightly kissed her forehead. His lips lingered for no more than a heartbeat and then he released her, turned and walked away. He did not look back. She watched him until he was no more than a speck in the distance, and then her legs gave way and she sank into the wet grass. The sound that escaped her lips came from deep inside; an unearthly howl of despair.

Hours passed, the tide turned, and still Magdalen didn't move. She watched dawn break across London, the night sky paling to a wash of soft pinks and yellows. She had sworn to avenge John's death, but she had let his murderer walk away scot-free. Why? Perhaps because, despite it all, she could not begin to imagine the world without Marlowe.

He had told her to go and live her life, but how could she? He had killed for her: John Wood. Richard Cowley. Adam Cooper.

Father Alwine. Their blood was as much on her hands as his.

She thought of Adam Cooper's fantastical tale. If, by some outlandish twist of fate, it was true then it turned to ashes everything she had thought she knew about herself. She was utterly changed, and yet she remained exactly the same. How was that possible? Even if the story wasn't true, no-one must ever hear a whisper of it. What had Marlowe said?

'Once a story has been told, it begins to gather momentum and it ceases to matter whether it's true or false.'

How in God's name was she supposed to go about her life, as if nothing was amiss? As if a deadly secret was not slowly burning through her soul?

On the opposite bank, the sun's first rays were glinting off a skyline of a thousand church spires. London was waking up, a thrum of noise drifting across the river. Matthew Hilliard was somewhere in Whitefriars, making preparations to sail to the New World, but it hurt too much to think about him; a red-raw gash across her heart. In the house on Silver Street, the Mountjoys would be stirring. If God was merciful, young Mary would be recovering from her fever. Louisa would be laying the kitchen fire, whilst in the bedchamber on the top floor, Will Shakespeare would sleep on for hours. And in Bridewell, her grandmother, and Belle and Tommy, would be waking up in the hellish confines of Mary Ward, to face another day of hard labour.

Marlowe had told her to go and live her life. But she would have no life worth living until her grandmother was free. There was much to be done. Magdalen stood up, stretched her aching limbs and brushed the dew from her cloak. She noticed her hands were caked with Adam Cooper's blood. Kneeling down again, she wiped them on the wet grass, and then she took the first wherry back across the river. The wind was cold and fierce, blowing in from the far northern lands of ice and snow. It raked across her skin and made her eyes water. The boatman was keen for conversation but she lowered her gaze and answered him in monosyllables. Not to be defeated, he tried again:

'No wedding band? Does your father keep you?'

Her head snapped up. 'No-one keeps me. I am wardrobe mistress at Burbage's Theatre in Shoreditch.'

The wherryman's cheeks were red with exertion. 'Ah, yes. I like Burbage's plays. Prefer the comedies, myself.'

Magdalen frowned. As proprietor of the Theatre, Burbage legally owned the plays but, considering Will penned them, it didn't seem fair.

It came to her suddenly. She knew how she would keep her secret safe. As always, Will had struck to the heart of the matter. He understood the masks we all must wear to survive. He had given the line to Viola, in *Twelfth Night*:

'I am not that I play…'

A great while ago the world begun,
With hey, ho, the wind and the rain.
But that's all one, our play is done,
And we'll strive to please you every day.

Author's note

I wrote Twelve Nights because I have always been captivated by the glamour and extraordinary creativity of Elizabethan theatre in general, and by William Shakespeare in particular. I wanted to explore his world, and I have loved every minute of my time there.

The rather unimaginatively named Theatre in Shoreditch was built in 1576 by James Burbage, father of Richard Burbage. It was the first permanent, dedicated theatre in England since the Roman era. A section of its long-lost foundations was uncovered in 2008 during excavations by MOLA (Museum of London Archaeology). They revealed that the playhouse was in fact polygonal in shape; so not quite the famous 'wooden O' mentioned in Shakespeare's *Henry V*. The remains of the Theatre will be preserved in situ as part of a new development called The Box Office, on New Inn Broadway.

Finds from the excavation included broken beer bottles, nutshells, seed and fruit pips – compelling evidence that the Elizabethans liked to snack while being entertained, much as we do today. MOLA also found large, green-glazed jars with a bulbous body, a tapering top and a slit in their side. These boxes were used to collect money from the paying audience, and the idea has survived in today's 'box office'.

In 1596, the Dutch traveller Johannes de Witt decided to make a sketch of the Swan Theatre on the South Bank. And thank goodness he did, because it is our only contemporary image of the inside of an Elizabethan playhouse. His drawing shows that the Swan was a circular structure with a thatched roof bearing a flag. There was a raised stage with a couple of doors at the back; a balcony for musicians, and tiered galleries and an open yard for the audience.

After a dispute with their landlord in 1599, Richard Burbage and his players famously dismantled the Theatre and rebuilt it across the river on South Bank. Christened the Globe, it now lies beneath a car park behind Anchor Terrace off Park Street, where a small section of its foundations is marked out. The modern Globe theatre is approximately 225 yards away.

In 2016, MOLA also found the remains of the Curtain theatre, where Matthew Hilliard claimed to be taking part in fencing bouts. (Its name refers to the city's walls - Elizabethan theatres did not have stage curtains.) The excavation revealed the Curtain was not polygonal, but rectangular in shape. Fourteen metres from stage left to stage right, it had the same dimensions as a modern Olympic fencing piste. The Curtain will also be preserved in situ as part of a new development called The Stage, on Hewett Street.

Although few buildings survived the Great Fire of London in 1666, the street layout of the City of London has not changed a great deal since Tudor times. You can still follow in Magdalen's footsteps as she posts the handbills for *Twelfth Night* along Cornhill, Poultry and Cheapside. The Royal Exchange, where she window-shops, was twice destroyed by fire and rebuilt. The third Royal Exchange now sits on the same spot and adheres to the original design of four wings around a central courtyard. It is a haven for retail therapy to this day, housing luxury shops and a branch of Fortnum & Mason.

Far less savoury was the foully-polluted River Fleet which ran alongside Bridewell prison. It was just one of 23 rivers that flowed through London before the majority were built over, beginning in the Victorian era. Many now flow through underground culverts, and some are integral parts of London's sewerage system. Vestiges of the River Fleet can be traced above ground as a small stream that flows from Hampstead and Highgate Ponds in North London.

The players in Twelve Nights are all based on real people, with the exception of John Wood and Matthew Hilliard. Many of them went on to acquire wealth and respectability, including Richard Burbage, Henry Condell and William Shakespeare. Despite being one of the most famous playwrights of all time, Shakespeare remains an enigma. We know his death date, but not his birth date. We assume he attended the grammar school in Stratford on Avon, but we don't know for certain. Where was he for the ten years between leaving Stratford and reappearing as a player on the London stage? Who was the dark lady of his sonnets? And what can we say about his relationship with the Earl of Southampton in light of the frankly toe-curling dedication to the earl on the frontispiece of *Venus and Adonis*? One thing we do know for certain is that Shakespeare lodged with the Mountjoys on Silver Street (although for the sake of my story, I have shifted the timeline). Court records survive of a dispute between Christopher Mountjoy and his apprentice Stephen Belott. Shakespeare was called to give evidence but his testimony is wonderfully vague – it seems he was reluctant to take sides. The court documents contain one of only six known instances of Shakespeare's handwriting. The Mountjoys' house, and Saint Olave's church were both destroyed in the Great Fire of 1666, and were not rebuilt. Silver Street itself survived until the early 1960s when it was swept away for the new road, 'London Wall', so called because it follows the line of the now demolished northern section of the city walls.

Christopher Marlowe did not live long enough to become a wealthy man; his life and genius brutally cut short at just 28 years of age. I am inclined to think he *was* a spy. When he was about to fail his degree for frequently taking leave from lessons, the Privy Council wrote to Corpus Christi College, Cambridge and intervened on his behalf, commending him for his 'good service'.

Magdalen Bisset, her grandmother Agnes, and Louisa du Bois are fictitious characters, but their struggles to survive in the male dominated world of the sixteenth-century are based on fact. Women were expected to marry, run a house and raise children. They could not become apprentices to learn a lucrative skill or join a guild (although there are a few examples of women inheriting their late husband's business). On the whole, women were limited to poorly paid work such as household servant, wool spinner, or laundress. With no meaningful social care system in place, women often turned to prostitution to feed their starving children. Tragically, conditions in Bridewell prison were as bleak as they appear in Twelve Nights.

The Puritans were vocal in their condemnation of playhouses as dens of vice, culminating in their closure during Oliver Cromwell's tenure as Lord Protector in the 1650s. There is no doubt Magdalen would have been seen by many as a 'whore' for working in such an establishment. Incredibly, these prejudices lingered well into the nineteenth century.

We can catch glimpses of Magdalen's life as a wardrobe mistress from a variety of original sources. Thomas Platter, a Swiss visitor to London, wrote enthusiastically about his trip to the Globe theatre in 1599. It is from him we learn of the custom where men or women of rank bequeathed their clothes to their servants who, not being permitted to wear them due to the Sumptuary Laws, sold them on to the theatres. Platter also mentions his admiration for the jigs which brought a play to a close – the same jigs which Shakespeare so despises in Twelve Nights.

Frustratingly, no written records survive from Richard Burbage's Theatre, but Philip Henslowe's detailed papers show us that he spent a huge amount on costumes for the Rose theatre on the south bank. In 1598 he lent £7 to buy 'a doublet and a pair of hose laid thick with gold laces'. (This is a vast sum considering a teacher would be lucky to earn £20 a year.)

Spectacle seems to have trumped historical accuracy as far as stage costumes were concerned. Another contemporary sketch by the English poet Henry Peacham shows a scene from Shakespeare's *Titus Andronicus*. Titus, the Roman General, is holding a spear and is dressed in a Roman toga but Tamora, queen of the Goths, wears a sumptuously decorated Elizabethan gown. The soldiers behind Titus are dressed in Elizabethan military costume.

With no backdrop to the stage, props were an important tool to set the scene. Arguably, Shakespeare's most famous stage direction is, 'exit, pursued by a bear' in *A Winter's Tale*. Intriguingly, Philip Henslowe's 'property inventory' includes such gems as, '1 bear's skin; 1 lion's skin…'

Sadly, no original hand-written scripts of Shakespeare's plays survive, but *A Midsummer Night's Dream* strongly hints that the players were only given their cues and lines rather than an entire script. When the 'rude mechanicals' rehearse *Piramus and Thisbe*, Bottom complains to Flute, 'you speak all your part at once, cues and all'.

Amelia Bassano was a real person. It is a shame she is chiefly remembered today as the mistress of the Lord Chamberlain (and also a possible contender for the Dark Lady of Shakespeare's sonnets), because after her marriage to Alfonso Lanier, she found fame as a poet through her single volume of poetry, *Salve Deus Rex Judaeorum*. It tells the story of Christ's Passion almost entirely from the perspective of the women who surrounded Him, and is arguably the first feminist work published in England.

In 1592, the Spanish Armada was still fresh in people's minds and many believed another invasion was imminent. Consequently, xenophobia was rife, and foreigners like Louisa du Bois and the Mountjoys were treated with suspicion and hostility. Even Queen Elizabeth was persuaded to execute her faithful doctor, Roderigo Lopes. Of Jewish ancestry, he was found guilty of plotting to poison her. He was almost certainly innocent; his conviction politically motivated.

After the massacre of Protestants in Catholic France on Saint Bartholomew's Day in 1572, many Protestants (Huguenots) fled to England. Queen Elizabeth offered sanctuary to the aliens or strangers as they were known, but her English subjects were not so welcoming, blaming the foreigners for taking their jobs and housing and spreading the plague. William Shakespeare writes of the asylum seekers' cruel plight in his co-authored play *Sir Thomas More*:

'Would you be pleased to find a nation of such barbarous temper that, breaking out in hideous violence, would not afford you an abode on earth … What would you think to be thus used? This is the strangers' case, and this your mountainish inhumanity.'

It seems apt, therefore, to finish by quoting his great friend Ben Jonson, who proclaimed Shakespeare was 'not for an age but for all time'.

Printed in Great Britain
by Amazon

80917426R00212